THE SWALLOW

AND THE NIGHTINGALE

A FABLE

BY

THEA IBERALL

Goddess Rising Poem by Rod Boyer (page 277)
Used with permission

(in progress) CREDITS:
Cover art: Spring fresco, Santorini, Greece. Sleeping Woman by Linda
Lundell. Design by Rena Konheim. Photograph on back cover: Penni
Rubin. Interior design by Connie Shaw.

THE SWALLOW SONG, Words and Music by RICHARD
FARIÑA, © 1966 (Renewed) WARNER BROS. INC. All Rights
Reserved

Parts of commitment ceremony from Rabbi Steve Greenberg. Used by
permission.

ISBN-13: 978-0-615-87236-0
Strong Voices Publishing
For inquiries, contact info@swallownightingale.com
www.swallownightingale.com
3.8.14

In English, the word for the swallow is from the prehistoric Germanic *swalwōn* which is akin to the Russian word *solovej* meaning nightingale
-Dictionary of Word Origins

Among the blades of grass stands a lone dandelion, her presence made known by her bright yellow bloom
- Judy Saxon

ACKNOWLEDGEMENTS

A book like this takes a long time to write. I had the idea for it long before I was capable of it. Needless to say, it's been a journey for me as well as for the characters. Plus—the world had to catch up. I also want you the reader to stay with me, so I have included a glossary to help with the scientific and foreign terms. I also want to make clear what is fact and what is fiction. The background is real. That's what's so scary. Check out the endnotes. Any stated facts are there.

The people to thank. My sister Dr. Norrie Robbins who helped me work out the story in Santorini while she patched up her scuba gear to visit the underwater volcano. My sister Penni Rubin who encouraged me to go to Greece. My sister Val O'Connor who has been so supportive. My friend Linda Lundell who helped me stitch together the first 20 page version.

When I took a Creativity Workshop on Samos, Greece, instructors Shelley Berc and Alejandro Fogel told us to take 8 feet of butcher block paper and do something with it. I mapped out the whole plot.

I'd like to thank my first reader Phoebe Larmore who saw where I was going and the potential for where I could take it. And Lucy V. Parker who helped me see where I had taken it. I'd like to thank my writing teachers at USC: Sid Siebel and Shelly Lowenkopf. And my neuroscience professor Dr. Michael Arbib. I could not have written this without the help of scientists–Dr. Vic Leipzig, Dr. Gene Yates, Dr. Robert Gifford, Dr. Charles R. Brown, Dan Knudsen, Dr. Theo Colborn, Geetha P.N., Norm Singer, Dr. John M. Goodman; environmentalists—Sada Anand Kaur, Patricia Burke, Mark Tabbert; Jewish scholars—Rabbi Steven Greenberg, Rabbi Simcha Green, Rabbi Elliot Dorff, Rabbi Tal Perez, Rabbi Neal Linson, Dr. Rhona Stein Singer, Shirley Behar, Rivka Elbaze, Joan Kaye, Chani Getter; feminists—Glory Vernon, Onoosh Gahagan, Jennifer Sharp, Lori Vandermeir; and language specialists—Lupi Miron, Jacqueline Grossman, Dr. Zoe Vlamaki.

Judaism has struggled with change vs. tradition throughout the millennia. Rabbi Steven Greenberg points out that religious values live in action. I want to thank him for his help and to acknowledge the work he does in finding a balance in that struggle for Orthodox women and gays.

I promised my beta readers a home-cooked meal of *shaakshuka*: Tom McCranie, Sue Snyder, Richard Snyder, Charlie Redner, Sharon Saxton, Suellen Zima, Sandy Blair, Brenda Barrie, Robbi Nester, Candace Warzecha, Joan Ross, Dr. Aileen Goodson, Dr. Pauli Merry, Barbara Benom, Bob Hoeffelder, Angela Moore, and Ric Ottaino.

There are others to thank: Lucy Blake-Elahi, Rod Miller-Boyer, Carolyn Coleman, Clara Baker, Patricia Fry, Judy Saxon, Victory Crayne, Paula Michelson, Peggy Edwards, Rena Konheim, Connie Shaw, Tim at the copy center, and to the unknown birders in Spain who answered my questions.

My mother was always drawn to birds. I look around our house and see objects collected from visits around the world: an amethyst parrot, a stone mockingbird, a papier-mâché parrot from Mexico. I realize I bought them for her. She has been my most ardent supporter, reading an untold number of manuscript versions year after year. At 100 years young, she is still helping me.

I'd like to thank my partner Shirley Riga. Her unflagging support and love has helped me to keep going and to finish this. I am forever grateful she is in my life.

And finally, to all the fans of Richard Fariña—we know who we are and how incredibly talented he was. Let's keep his flame alive: his life ended too soon but his music and words live on.

Thea Iberall
Orange County, CA

Dear Dad,

I'm writing a novel about morality. I don't know much about morality so sometimes I feel I'm not the best person to be writing this story. But you taught me to think globally. You taught me to be Aristotelian even though I didn't understand it. You taught me to be a scientist, to question, and yes, to see the big picture. Everyone is caught in their little view of the world—what they'll eat for dinner, what price to pay for gas, what TV show to watch, what to believe. We get mesmerized by these choices while huge corporations stretch to satisfy our insatiable need for more while they and we destroy our environment. You are the only person I know who figured out the big picture, who understood how the planet operates, and who talked about Aristotle's sense of morality as being happy in the sense of perfect wisdom. You said he defined this as the unity of intuitive reason, scientific knowledge, and acting for the good of humanity. You've been dead ten years and yet, it is your courage and your insights I am using to write this book. I'm relying on you to help me bring this story to the forefront—that as long as we disrespect the Earth, its components, and its inhabitants, we are immoral as a species and no amount of finger pointing at society's so-called misfits will make any of us moral.

Love, Thea

TABLE OF CONTENTS

Prologue

They flew more as lovers than sisters. Free, high above the land, they sang their beautiful song in exquisite harmony with crystal clear voices. Slowly flapping their wings, their graceful bodies soared through the clouds. They circled each other in joy over goat herds and burnt fields. Below them, rounded gray outcroppings peeked out from under the dark green forests.

Philomela, the nightingale, happy to have regained her voice, called to her sister, "Let us fly across the sea to the mountains of the North."

"I became one of them!" Chelidona, the swallow, replied, guilt twisting her heart. "I must go away. I must fly over the seas."

"And I must stay near," Philomela sang, looking over the countryside. She did not want to think of their heinous immorality. "We cannot fight this evil. Someday, we'll be together again. When the evil is gone."

"But it won't go away! It will grow upon itself destroying all that is good!" The swift powerful swallow flew out toward the sea, searching for a way to find peace and forgiveness from the Goddess.

Philomela sang out. "Then fight it we must! If we do survive, we'll know each other by our songs." And the graceful gentle nightingale turned to the northeast. Finally able to speak once again, she vowed to never stop singing as melodious and sweet a song as was ever possible. She would find someone to tell her story to so all she knew would not be lost. There had to be a way to stop the great evil so that balance would once again fill the Earth—and she could reunite with Chelidona, her sister, the beautiful swallow.

THE SWALLOW AND THE NIGHTINGALE

CHAPTER 1
THE SWALLOW'S ANSWER
PART I

WORLD NEWS – MARCH 27
New Jersey Shocked by 5.3 Quake
7.2 Quake Hits Tijuana
Guadalajara Feels 7.0 Trembler

DR. DEBORAH WRIGHT'S TENSE face glowed in the blue light of her magic machine. The fragrance of sage mixed with the lingering smell of death. She felt like she was listening in on the conversation of gods at the end of all flesh.

Touched by the rising sun, pink bougainvillea crept down San Juan Capistrano Mission's thick adobe walls as water sparkled under lily pads floating in the fountain. The small bodies of cliff swallows lay all around. She stared at the one living bird she had just recorded. The buff band cutting across its blue crown made it look angry.

"That's really odd," she said. A slight smile started at the edge of her lips as her hazel eyes widened.

"What?" Dr. George Brady slumped in one of the white stone benches surrounded by cacti and white sea lavender. His dark reddish beard made him look like a Pacific Northwest logger. Holding a half-filled Starbucks cup in one hand, he had his other hand jammed into his jeans jacket pocket.

"Listen to this." Deborah's voice rose a notch at the thought of exoneration from the Santorini fiasco. Flipping on the external speakers, she took off her headphones and placed them carefully next to the RAX-1000 machine. She picked up her dark roast coffee. "Do you hear it?" Deborah's eyes eagerly searched for confirmation like homing pigeons.

"I'm not sure." Brady sat up. "It sounds like the speed is off. But I'm a geologist, I don't have your trained ornithologist's ear."

Putting her coffee cup on the bench, Deborah neatly tore off the paper roll spewing out of the machine. "That's because of the processing. Here, look at this." She quickly leaned forward.

He stared at the jagged lines. "You're going to have to interpret."

Deborah took a red pen from the case in her jacket pocket. In her giddiness, she almost dropped it. "See, this is the bird's standard chattering." She marked the beginning high-pitched *churr-churrs* and *zarp-zarps* and then highlighted the next two seconds. "Something here doesn't belong. It seems more melodic, more—" she paused, "—musical."

"And that isn't normal?" Brady scratched his beard.

"No," Deborah said, shaking and nodding her head at the same time. "It's almost as if it has a distinct pattern. As if the bird is singing—" she searched for words, "—a tune."

"A tune? Don't all birds sing a tune?"

"If you can call a cliff swallow's song a tune. That's not what I mean. It's almost as if a song is inserted in it. But that's impossible." She sat back.

"What? Another bird's song?"

"The bird's not just making a normal bird vocalization." Deborah stared at the printout. A smile lit up her face. "It's singing a human song."

Brady squinted. "That's crazy." He took a swig of his java.

She carefully sipped her coffee. "My sentiments exactly." Replacing her cup on the bench, Deborah searched for the swallow's orange-colored rump. She saw its white underbelly next to a microphone. A cold chill cut through her jacket. Laying dead, the bird had taken its secret with it.

Suddenly, the earth jolted. Frightened, Deborah tried to get up but then dug her feet into the ground. She yelled, "Hold on."

"It's okay. That's the P-wave." Brady squeezed his Starbucks cup. "And here's the S-wave."

Her coffee tipped. Deborah plopped back into her chair. "What do you mean, it's okay? Damn." Drops of liquid had splattered over her field boots.

"We're getting these small ones daily. This is Southern California." Brady pulled a Starbucks napkin from his pocket. "But don't worry, a hole isn't going to open under us."

"You call that small?" She grabbed the proffered napkin and carefully wiped her boots.

"It's not just New Jersey getting quakes." He laughed. "Of course, two weeks ago, I would've said that sentence in reverse. Let's just say, so far, they haven't been big here." He took the wet napkin and shoved it back in his pocket.

A tall California fan palm swayed above them. "It's like a war zone."

"Because of the tremors?"

"That, plus the dead birds." She pointed to the swallow's body. Aware of the feathered community constantly circling above the planet's surface, she felt it gave her a sense of the environment—like reading a newspaper to find out the latest calamity or who was cheating on their wives.

"We take the bodies over to the lab for necropsies."

"Any results?"

"The veterinarian hasn't found anything yet."

Deborah turned toward the RAX-1000, putting the headphones back on over her short graying hair. Without living swallows, the mission's central courtyard seemed sterile. Deborah remembered the first time she had visited San Juan Capistrano. Seven years old and tall for her age, she had been exhilarated by the train ride with Aunt Bertha. She limped next to her aunt the short distance to the mission, only slightly hindered by the brace on her polio leg. Loving the smell of the roses, she recalled how the clouded light had turned the tile roof intense red. An old monk stood by the rose bushes. She'd never seen a man dressed in a robe before and asked her aunt why he had on a brown dress. "Shh! Don't make fun of the man. He's religious," Aunt Bertha said. But Deborah didn't understand. She thought 'religious' meant going to *shul* on the High Holidays, a Rabbi wearing a suit, *yarmulke*, and white *tallis*. But a swallow climbed onto the monk's outstretched arm. As he lifted it up into the air, he whispered and the bird answered him with a small song. Mesmerized by the gentleness and astonished by their communication, she knew what she wanted to do with her life.

THE SWALLOW AND THE NIGHTINGALE

"Are you sure we aren't picking up some environmental sounds?" Brady stood up. "Maybe someone's been singing while we've been recording."

Deborah laughed and removed her headphones. "These mics' sensitivity and range are limited on purpose. The internal one less so. Besides, the only other people awake right now are Starbucks baristas. Do you hear anyone singing?"

"I guess not, but there must be a simple explanation." Brady looked toward the other courtyard.

Still giddy, she leaned over to retrieve the empty coffee cup among the pineapple guava plants. Staring at the delicate red and white blossoms, she wondered where the roses were. "I know, I know, everything has to be checked. But even if someone was singing while we recorded this, he couldn't have sung that quickly."

"Can these data be repeated?" Brady took another gulp of coffee.

There it was. Her head drooped as if she had taken a punch to her gut. It sounded like he was worried about the misconduct charges against her. In no way was she going to repeat that mess. She'd get lots of data this time. Compensating for her weaker leg, she stood up and established her balance. At almost six feet tall, she stood a few inches taller than him. "The first subject already did repeat it," she growled. "I'm going to play it really safe this time."

He took the empty cup from her and placed his inside it. "Stephen's got to see this."

"Don't—," she started then stopped. "Let's wait." She nervously reached up and hugged her right shoulder. Stephen was only one of the reasons she didn't want to be in Capistrano. It wasn't the time or place to bring up their marital problems. After all, their separation wasn't common knowledge. "Maybe the road jostled the machine on the trip down from Berkeley. It's still really a prototype." She glanced toward the other courtyard.

Brady studied the device. "You call this a prototype? It's packaged pretty slick, so compact, a ton of controls. Even has the printer."

"What? Oh, right." Tearing off the rest of the printouts, she started rolling them up. "Yes, it's the new shiny bell and whistle in the field. Dan keeps goading me to test the semantic processor. Careful, don't spill your coffee on it. He says it's water-tight but let's not test that feature just yet."

"Sorry," Brady stepped back.

Putting the rolled up printouts into a tube, she knew the machine was the reason Brady had invited her down from Berkeley. Many scientists shunned her after the Santorini mess, but this team was stuck. Even with Stephen on it. *Who I haven't seen in a year.*

He looked at his watch. "I'm going to go find out when Stephen's arriving this morning."

"Don't say anything to him yet. It may be a collection artifact," Deborah said to Brady's retreating form, feeling her neck get hot.

Sitting down, her hand almost shaking, she pulled her field journal from her worn leather travel bag and a black pen from her pen case. Trying not to think about Stephen, she jotted observations from the complicated assortment of controls and readouts on the RAX-1000. To be safe, she replaced the memory cards and put the discarded ones in the wide drawer on the left side of the machine. Seeing the pineapple guava plants next to her, she leaned down, pinched one off, and put it in her jacket pocket for her daughter Rachel.

Deborah's Notes for *Petrochelidon pyrrhonota* Study

The study of *P. pyrrhonota* (cliff swallow) at the Mission of San Juan Capistrano was initiated at the invitation of Dr. George Brady, Chair, Department of Earth System Science, University of California, Irvine. The question is why the bird population that normally returns to the mission on or about March 19 (St. Joseph's Day) is dying. The focus of the research is to determine if the RAX-1000 can detect variations in the swallows' song that might relate to the population's decimation. Sampling was initiated at 5 a.m. on March 27.

Ten minutes later, Brady strode back into the courtyard.

Deborah quickly checked to see if anyone was with him. "Finishing my notes here. What can I add regarding what you've found so far?"

He elaborated, "Whatever it is, it's not affecting the insects or reptiles. We haven't yet correlated this to any other physical or biological phenomena, like the recent Mexican earthquakes or the small tremors we're experiencing."

Closing her journal, she stood up. "Earthquakes? Wouldn't that be a stretch?" Not her area of specialty, she certainly knew enough about them.

"Got to look at *everything*." He shrugged.

Deborah made note of the emphasis. Was Brady still speaking about earthquakes or was he referring to the accusations against her? She tried to keep her focus. "That Tijuana quake was pretty big, what, 7.2?"

A deep voice behind her answered, "Big, but not close enough to be felt here."

Deborah whirled around as if she were falling on ice skates. "Stephen. I wondered when you'd show up."

"Hello, Deborah." Hands on hips, his wide-set eyes pierced right through her. Equal to her height, he had a slight grin on his full lips that made his cheekbones stand out on his dark brown face. She was surprised how much grayer his short-cropped Afro was. His eyes were open wide.

Deborah's insides felt like glue and she quickly crossed her arms. Looking away, she thought better of saying anything personal in front of Brady. Flattening her voice, she turned back toward Stephen. "So, you're working on this project as well?"

"I'm running it. Or thought I was."

Brady jumped in. "Stephen, you know we need a behavioral ornithologist. And she's got that instrument."

Stephen wiped his hands on his blue jeans. "We've got to finish the chemical studies of the air, soil, plants, bugs. Then the temperature component, and the human population density…"

Brady interrupted, "I know, I know, the list goes on."

"I told you, there's a lot to check before we even start with the so-called behavior of dying birds, with or without her fancy machine." He dismissed it with a wave of his arm, taking a step closer to her.

Brady grabbed the tube and pulled out the paper rolls. "But look at what she's found. See? She's marked where the tune starts."

"That's what you've got?" Stephen didn't bother to look. His eyes were on her.

She tried to look away. "We've got something. We just yet don't know what." Deborah could feel sweat pooling between her breasts. Her breathing erratic, she said, "Brady, help me reset the microphones.

I want to make sure we're not getting an echo from the north wall." She pointed at the scattered equipment. "Maybe the mics were affected by that quake."

Putting down the paper rolls, Brady jumped to help her, cognizant of her limp. "I'm glad to cooperate."

"Has it ever failed before?" Stephen kept staring at her.

Deborah spun away and awkwardly stomped past the bench into the cacti garden. "We don't know if it's a failure, Stephen." She emphasized his name like a dirty sneeze to counteract the jolt of his words. "I'm not going to rush to any conclusions until I can verify everything. I'm systematically removing variables."

"Of course," Brady said, "everything has to be verified. But maybe these are actual data points. We've logged a lot of hours here with nothing." His eyebrows rose up with excitement. He moved three of the microphones further away from the walls. Each one was housed in a black circular tube stuck into the ground by a long silvery pole.

Stephen didn't offer to help but just watched Deborah reset the next microphone. His eyes bored into her.

Brady continued, "This machine is so cool. I mean, the results it generated in your European starling study were impressive. How did you figure out how to build it?" He carefully avoided stepping in the yellow Icelandic poppies.

Trying to breathe steadily, Deborah moved away to reset another mic, feeling Stephen's stare. "I stood in the engineer's office and wrote one word on his whiteboard. Semantics."

"Did he know what that meant?" Brady reached toward a mic.

Making sure her green slacks stayed spotless, she leaned down to another mic. "Really. What do engineers know about semantics? He couldn't believe capturing meaning was possible."

"Aha, instead of just capturing the signal itself like our seismographs do."

"Right." Deborah wrenched the last mic into place. "Dan had to choose between competing algorithms like the Milhouse Effect or fractal processing. He says that during the analysis phase, over fourteen thousand different pattern analyses are performed. All I care about is getting results." She shot a glance at Stephen to see if he reacted to what she said. Pain seared through her index finger. "Ouch."

"What happened?" Stephen jumped toward her.

THE SWALLOW AND THE NIGHTINGALE

She had grabbed the leafy blade of a desert spoon cactus bush and blood pooled on the tip of her right index finger. "It's stupid," she said, embarrassed. "At least it's not my left hand. I've got a first aid kit in my bag." She walked back to the table and felt for her small kit. Before she got too entangled, Stephen took the bandage tape from her.

"Well?" Brady asked.

Stephen pulled a piece of tape from the dispenser and tore it with his fingers. He didn't know what to do with the dispenser. He gave it back to Deborah and grabbed her finger.

Deborah complied as she looked up. "Where are the swallows? It only works if birds are singing." She held the open disinfectant packet for Stephen. She could feel his breath on the side of her neck and smell sandalwood soap, his favorite since their honeymoon thirty-two years ago. She almost lost her balance.

Attaching the piece of tape temporarily to the palm of his own hand, he took the moist pad from the packet and dabbed the blood away.

Brady scoured the pink-tinged sky. "What do you mean?"

"No birds have landed since the one we recorded." Trying to not look at Stephen, she took the bloodied pad from him and stuffed it into the paper packet.

"So," Stephen wrapped her finger in the tape. "You brought me over here for one data point?"

"I thought there would be more by now," Brady squirmed.

Eyes blazing, Deborah yanked her bandaged hand away and stepped away from Stephen. "I told you, you've got a war zone here." She started breathing hard.

Brady persisted. "Stephen, at least look at the recording." He spread the printouts length-wise on the bench.

When Brady botched the explanation, Deborah stomped over and knelt down, careful not to lose her balance or dirty her slacks. She swiped red marks down at various intervals, identifying the three separate samples. "Look. Here, and here, and here." She punched at the highlighted intervals. "The tune repeats twice more. It's in the repetitions of this bird's vocalization.

Stephen pointed at the more melodic part. "Why's that there?"

"Exactly. I don't know. 'Why' is always the wrong first question." Deborah tried to stand up. She didn't want him towering over her.

"Maybe it's just there." Stephen took her arm.

Leaning on his arm brought back memories she wanted to shut out. Back on her feet, she jerked away. "Easy for you to say. Forces acting in geological time are different than those acting on an individual life form. Every movement is expensive for animals. Think of the effort it takes to find fuel for those movements."

He countered, "You don't have to teach me about time and space scales. I study the big picture all the time."

"You'll never understand the big picture," she cut back, raising her voice.

Brady jumped in. "We've been testing the food, the water, the air, the birds' nesting materials. So far, we haven't found anything unusual beside the tremors and they don't correlate to anything either. We've got a veterinarian doing necropsies with negative results. It's not like there's been a cold snap or that methane levels are off the charts. So far, there's no measurable reason why the swallows are dying. Stephen, this is a first clue of something."

He had moved to the edge of the walkway.

Ignoring him, Deborah turned toward Brady. "I know it's shaky evidence. But it's really, really odd. It's like the 'tune' is...how can I describe it?" She started pacing. "It's almost like something memorized. You know how you can sing a song in a foreign language and not know what you are saying?"

"Yeah," Brady said, "like an Irish folksong."

"Right." Stephen shook his head. "The bird died after communing with St. Pat."

Brady laughed.

A smile cracked across Deborah's tight face. She stopped pacing and rolled up the paper recordings.

Stephen took a step toward her. "There are lots of reasons for this die off. We haven't pinpointed them yet or identified all the energy flowing through this system. We have to break it down by the scaling, the connections. Fit it into the global picture." He started pacing like she had. "For example, the human population in this area is steadily increasing. There are more trees, fewer wetlands. Available nutrients are different than in the past. The seasons are off. We need to look at past data points."

THE SWALLOW AND THE NIGHTINGALE

Her smile disappeared as she looked at the dead bird. "Past data points?" She exploded, stepping toward Stephen. "Try a billion birds dying every year thanks to humans. But really, this seems different. Maybe the swallows are an early-warning for something."

Brady answered, "You mean like canaries in coal mines? If they are, we'd find it in the toxicity reports."

"The song doesn't belong there. It's something learned."

"But how is that possible?" Brady asked.

Stephen looked at her.

They stood too close and stared at each other for a moment too long. His brown eyes narrowed into thin slits. Turning away, flustered, she almost stepped in the cacti. "I don't know."

Stephen jumped at the statement. "Maybe it's always been there and it hasn't been detectable until now."

Deborah smiled to herself, wondering whether he realized he just complimented her technology. She packed the paper rolls. "I could test for that. Compare it to baseline data." Not that any existed for cliff swallows. But she wasn't going to admit that to him. "What about San Onofre?"

Stephen moved behind the bench, ignoring the cacti. "The nuclear power plant that morally or otherwise shouldn't have been built in a fault zone? They shut it down." He ran his hand along the back of the bench.

"San Onofre's been in use on and off for years," Brady countered. "This finding could indicate something. It's the first identified anomaly. A positive result. Shouldn't we all cooperate?" He sounded almost like a puppy wanting a treat.

Stephen turned, about to walk away. "Yeah, if it's a result and not a bad battery. Listen, we'll have more substantial results when the environmental and geochemical studies are complete. Anyway, I've got bigger fish to fry. I don't care what they're saying in the news, there's been too much seismic activity lately. I mean, an earthquake in New Jersey? There hasn't been one like this since the 1780s. A swarm of quakes in Mexico? And what we're getting hit with daily? They downplay these things so people don't get scared. But I'm studying the USGS databases, doing some comparisons to previous years. That's more important than an incomplete bird study."

Deborah dropped the tube and glared at him. "You don't even care about this project."

Stephen ignored the sprawling jumble of printouts and stared at her. "You'll thank me when half of Berkeley doesn't drown in a tsunami while the other half blames a scapegoat." He started walking away. "Make sure you keep that finger clean and then decide what you're going to do. And wait until you hear Rachel's news."

Deborah froze. Her left hand involuntarily touched her jacket pocket. She stared as he headed to the outer courtyard where scientists and graduate students were gathering.

Helping to pick up the paper rolls, Brady looked as tired as the mission's walls. "What did he mean, decide what you're going to do?" The group had been working around the clock for a week, invading the centuries-old religious peace like an army of ants.

"Huh? Well, he's right." Deborah stormed toward the mics. "It's not like birds are flocking here."

"But this one result might be something. Careful of the cacti."

"Science is science. It's not wishful thinking." She knew all too well what happens when a study isn't complete. She grabbed at the mic, worried by what Stephen had said about Rachel.

"But if it's something…"

Deborah shook her head forcefully. "How can a bird be singing a human song? It's probably nothing, a bad battery." She started putting the mics into long plastic wrappers.

"We both know what we heard. You even more so."

"Yeah, well, more likely it's that barista at Starbucks."

"What are you going to do?"

She closed the RAX-1000's cover. "There's so little chance of my collecting more data here. You're gathering plenty of your own. And you heard your fearless leader, even if I'd love to prove him wrong."

He looked at her. "It's not professional suicide for you to be here."

Deborah closed the folding table a little too quickly, realizing he knew her history. "Easy for you to say, Brady. That damn Santorini paper completely humiliated me. I'm on a suspect list now. If I can figure this project out, just maybe I'll pull my scientific reputation out of the toilet. I may be determined, but I'm not stupid. If I can't validate the data, it will be professional suicide. So let's chalk it up to a very interesting morning and call it a wash." She looked at her watch. "I'm going to my daughter's for breakfast and to spend the weekend with her. Then I'm heading back to Berkeley." She gestured. "Could you carry that box and that one?"

Brady grabbed the equipment plus the table. "What about the bird you recorded?"

She shot a look at him. "I told you, if I work on this project and it goes nowhere, my career is over. I'll wind up a host at the Golden Gate Audubon Society escorting five-year olds." She picked up the RAX-1000 and started walking toward the exit. In her state, her limp almost tripped her up. She stopped and turned back to Brady. "One subject does not a theory make. It could be a malfunction."

He shook his head. "Maybe it's not. Maybe you've got something."

CHAPTER 2

Deborah's Notes for *Petrochelidon pyrrhonota* Study
Sampling was performed on March 27 on one individual of *P. pyrrhonota*, adult male, unhealthy for an unknown reason. Three samples were taken for approximately 5 seconds each. Results: samples contained a sequence of notes resembling a humanly conceived tune at too high a frequency to be detectable by the human ear. Testing has been performed by G. Brady's team on the food supply, water sources, air quality, and nesting materials. William Alfred, University Laboratory Animal Resources, University of California, Irvine, has performed 45 necropsies with negative results. Brady reports that the increased amount of trash, traffic, and infrastructure caused by the growing human population in the area have had a deleterious impact on the environment. San Onofre, a non-functioning nuclear power plant, is 18.2 kilometers away. Dr. Stephen Wright, Department of Geology, University of California, Berkeley, and Senior Scientist, U.S. Geological Survey (currently on sabbatical at University of California, Irvine) is closely monitoring faults in the region including 2 recent Mexican earthquakes and small daily tremors.

RACHEL WRIGHT LIVED IN the Mission Flats section of San Juan Capistrano. Deborah sat in front of her daughter's three-bedroom house in her Toyota SUV, finishing her notes. If Rachel's news was about moving from California, that would be unbearable. They hadn't had a chance to speak in the evening when she had arrived. Deborah had been glad, but now she regretted it.

The short trill of a song sparrow caught her attention. Slowly walking through the white gate, she breathed in the scent of dark green gardenias and wished she was on the road home to Berkeley.

THE SWALLOW AND THE NIGHTINGALE

Sometimes the distance between mother and daughter could span an abyss so large it was hard to find the sides of it.

Rich smells from ground coffee and Middle Eastern spices filled the kitchen. Deborah stood staring at six crayon drawings and photos plastered to the refrigerator door. She could feel tiredness creeping down her neck and shoulders. "Is that Guatemalan coffee? My Starbucks French roast spilled in the tremor."

"From a cooperative on Lake Atitlan. Thought you might like it." Rachel pushed the filled mug to the end of the counter. Left-handed, Deborah reached over and took it.

Rachel rattled. "Can you believe this weather for the end of March?" The product of Deborah and Stephen's interracial marriage, Rachel had skin that shone almost golden. She went back to stirring diced tomatoes with green peppers, swinging her long black hair away from the stove. "And that earthquake in New Jersey, the quakes in Mexico. Do you believe how close the last one was?"

"Did you feel it?" Deborah dissected each drawing. They were a clear reminder that she wasn't going to have biological grandchildren. Feeling a heaviness in her chest, she squeezed her coffee mug.

"Tijuana's close, but not that close." Rachel broke two eggs into the pan over the tomato mixture. "Moroccan eggs okay with you? The dish is called *shaakshuka.*"

"I mean the one this morning." The drawing on the far left showed a stick-figure family, the father and mother holding the hands of a little girl. Her arms were stretched way above her round head. They all had big red smiles and blue shoes. Deborah frowned and looked away. "I like the darker roast from Antigua."

Rachel stiffened. "Guess I was still asleep. They're happening all the time. They can drive you crazy. Dad says not to worry."

"I saw Dad this morning. He said you had news." Deborah looked over at Rachel who focused on cooking. When Rachel didn't respond, Deborah nodded at the refrigerator front. "Who did these drawings?"

Rachel glanced quickly. "Shelley brings them home from the classes she teaches at the library. She's really proud of the kids."

Deborah's gaze shifted to the photos above the drawings. In one, Rachel's deep-set eyes smiled with an adult peace she had never seen before. Recognizing Shelley Abenacar but none of the others, Deborah abruptly turned away. Her eyes ran up the yellow adobe walls while she limped over to the kitchen counter. Putting down her mug, she nudged three spice bottles back into place along the backsplash. Above the sink were a Jewish seven-pointed candelabra and a Kabbalah Tree of Life. Frowning at the Jewish symbols, she folded her arms. "How did the library event go last night? You came in so late."

"Yeah, plates are on the counter." Rachel gestured with her thin arm and long fingers. "It's the one thing about Shelley's job that she doesn't like. But fundraising is necessary to keep her programs at the library going." She reached toward the toaster oven. "Mom, I'm sorry you can't stay here this weekend. We didn't know and, like I said, these friends are coming to stay for the next two weeks."

Deborah grabbed the plates and took them to the table in the small breakfast nook. She sighed. "It's fine." She noticed how each plate displayed a different southwestern color, peach, turquoise, sandy brown—none the same but all blending. "And really, spring break ends today. I hate missing lectures because it disrupts the semester for both me and the students." The side of the breakfast nook opened to a greenhouse window filled with plants in decorative Mexican pots. She turned back to get the utensils from a drawer. "We all know when the swallows return to Capistrano from Goya."

Rachel stopped her. "Whoops, that's the *basari* drawer. Use those." She pointed to the drawer with utensils for milk-based products. "That way we can butter our bread."

Deborah slammed the drawer. She had grown up with the separation of milk and meat. The Sephardic terminology sounded different, but the concept the same. "Why make it so hard on yourself?"

"Mom, we've been through this before."

"Sorry." Deborah slid onto the bench of the breakfast nook and stared at her daughter's long magenta gypsy skirt. It had some sort of embroidery on it. "Is that all we do, apologize to each other?" The chasm between Rachel and her pulsated with each word, its origin lost under layers of expectations.

Rachel reached up into the cupboard to get a serving plate. "You haven't been exactly welcoming to Shelley."

"Sure I have." Deborah shifted in her seat, the conversation getting sucked into what had happened two years earlier.

Rachel put the plate on the counter. "You're never around when we come to Berkeley."

"I'm a scientist. I give papers at conferences. You've watched me do this since you were born."

Rachel shot a look at her mother and then moved back to the stove. "Dad's a scientist too and he's managed to get to know Shelley."

Deborah cleared her throat and looked out the window. "I'm comfortable with your lifestyle."

"It's not a lifestyle, it's a life." Rachel's dark eyes flashed. She transferred the eggs to the turquoise serving plate and placed it on the table. "This is the 21st century, Mom."

She looked down at the exotic-looking dish. "It just seems like you never gave men a chance."

Rachel grabbed the basket of sourdough bread and sat down. "Try the *shaakshuka*."

The aroma of spiced tomatoes and eggs filled Deborah's nostrils. "I'm sorry, I didn't mean to say that. It looks great." She spooned out some of the egg concoction.

"They eat it in Israel." Rachel reached for the butter dish from the counter. "Kind of like *huevos rancheros* without the beans. You poach the eggs on top of the tomato mixture. I've added a spice mix called za'atar."

Deborah took a piece of bread. "Rachel, I know I promised I'd stop asking you about men. You're right."

"I'm 26 years old. Old enough to understand the direction of my life. And you're right, we apologize too much." Rachel began eating.

Deborah slowly slathered the bread as if she wanted layers of butter. "How's work been? Any strange cases?"

"You mean like that guy last year with the fourteen personalities? No, just the regular clients searching for their sanity and their keys."

Deborah laughed, despite herself, and started eating. Rachel became a hypnotherapist because she genuinely liked helping people. She remembered a time in college when Rachel drove a homeless girl back to Denver. Deborah had thought it excessive, even if it showed Rachel's caring had no bounds. *Except when it comes to me.* "This is delicious." She dabbed her mouth with her napkin. "Do you see your father much?"

"We have dinner when we can. It's great, his being here in Southern California." Rachel didn't look up from her plate.

Deborah adjusted her fork and knife, finding it easier to eat European style instead of transferring her fork to her left hand. She stared at the bandage on her index finger. Stephen had always been closer to Rachel and now that he was on sabbatical at UC Irvine, he was physically closer as well. A wave of loneliness gripped her heart. She tried to sound casual. "He said you have some news."

Rachel put down her fork and studied her *shaakshuka* creation as if she were reading clouds. "There's something I want to tell you."

Deborah jerked against the back of the bench. Now she wasn't sure she was ready to hear whatever Rachel was going to say. Rachel's coming out to them had started with those words.

Rachel said, "Okay, I'll tell you what's happening. Shelley and I have asked Rabbi Stern to marry us."

"What?" Deborah almost dropped her fork.

"We want to be married." Rachel pushed her hair behind her ear. "Is that a crime? Rabbi Stern should have said yes."

"What did he say?" Deborah's brain took off in new directions. This was absurd. Yes, it's a crime, she thought but didn't say.

"He said he believes we can find husbands and raise children..." She paused.

Deborah stared at her daughter. "This is crazy."

Rachel looked unhappy. "...'the way your mothers did,' he said, 'the way millions of other women do every year.' He said that he warned us about that from the time we became a couple. Something about Jews having a moral obligation to strive for the right path."

"What did you expect?" Deborah frowned, her eyes gravitating toward the Jewish candelabra.

"It seems hypocritical to me. I argued with him that many in the congregation have accepted us into its midst. We've been going to services regularly for two years, Shelley for most of her life. But he's so much like—like a raging bull, so sure of his place in the order of nature." Rachel picked at her eggs, pushing them around on her plate.

"Where's my coffee?" Deborah got up, seeing her mug on the counter. If only Rachel hadn't started going to that synagogue.

Rachel never quite fit in, from birth on. Deborah thought back to the hospital, the very first time she held Rachel—this little bundle of yawning squirminess. Stephen leaned over them. A new nurse walked in, took one look at the interracial family and the shock on her face said it all. Deborah had been used to the discrimination directed toward her and Stephen, but in an instant, she now had to deal with it being directed at her beautiful daughter. She had tried to protect Rachel, a task easier to do when she was a child. Deborah's heart started to pound. *Stephen should be here.*

"Did you let the Rabbi see you get mad?" Deborah asked, standing at the counter.

Rachel turned to look at her. "What? Probably. I felt really pissed off. I'm not immoral. I'm trying to live my life, you know, be happy. I love Shelley. You say you accept us, but I don't really believe you."

One thing Deborah had learned by being a woman in a scientific community was never to show her feelings. Men discount emotion-based arguments as PMS-related. *Stephen would know what to do.* She held her mug and looked out the window. Morality had swirled around her all her life. She could remember her father admonishing her and the congregation with sermons about *halakhah,* Jewish law. The 613 commandments in the Bible contained more restrictions about marriage, family, and sexual relations than anything else other than sacrifices and offerings. Deborah shook her head thinking about the lack of animal sacrifices and offerings in modern Judaism.

Marriage between two people of the same sex was impossible in Orthodox Judaism. Deborah flashed back to her own wedding to Stephen, her parents' strong feelings against her marriage. She had been 28 years old and had turned away from Orthodoxy by then. Even though her parents had lived another twenty years, the schism was set in concrete. She barely spoke to them again.

Still, she could remember the joy she experienced under the *chuppah* when the Reform Rabbi and the UCC minister both pronounced Stephen and her united in God's eyes. It wasn't the God part she cared about—it was the experience of standing next to someone she loved so deeply, knowing they were building a life together. She felt the exhilaration of becoming an adult by making this public commitment. At the beginning of the ceremony, Stephen had squeezed her hand and whispered, "I love you." A peaceful smile on his face, his eyes were wide-open as if his love were too great to be contained. That moment had taken her breath away. He was like an angel coming into her life—

a rock she could count on. It almost counteracted the pain of her parents' boycotting their wedding.

Tears welled up in Deborah's eyes. She took her mug back to the table. "Rachel, these two years haven't been easy for me. When you started going to the synagogue, I felt shocked that you had embraced Orthodox Judaism, the religion I walked away from. And you met Shelley and suddenly you were gay, like she recruited you."

"But, Mom…"

"I know, just let me finish. I tried to keep track of your boyfriends, what's his name in college…"

"Frank?"

"Yes, the one with the unicycle. I didn't think him right for you." Deborah smiled under her tears.

"He was one of them. You were traveling too much to know any of the others."

"I didn't travel a lot. I—I carried a heavy teaching load." Deborah blinked hard to take control. "I felt glad when you broke up with him. But when you stopped dating in junior year, I worried because I thought nobody could match you. Which is why I thought you just gave up on men." Deborah stared at her coffee mug. "I understand now that Shelley didn't recruit you. Why not get married by a Justice of the Peace? Isn't same-sex marriage legal in California?"

"You're right, we could do that. But that's not the point. We aren't a lifestyle, we aren't immoral. We live an Orthodox way of life."

Deborah played with her mug. She could hear how much Rachel wanted this. How to reach over the chasm between them? How to find a way to erase the years of distance? If only it was as easy as drawing with crayons or reaching over the table. Even that wasn't easy.

Releasing the mug, she stood up. "Then let's go talk to him."

"Who?" Rachel looked at her.

"To that Rabbi of yours." She walked out of the kitchen to find her travel bag.

Rachel followed her. "I can handle this, Mom. Really. What's there to say?"

"We'll figure it out. Where are my keys?" She lifted her jacket off the wooden peg by the front door. Her bag hung below it.

Rachel stood in front of the door. "Mom, Shelley and I can talk to him. You haven't been in a synagogue in years and never in a Sephardic onc. It's different from the Ashkenazi tradition. What are you going to say to him? Besides, we should call and make an appointment." Knowing her mother, she grabbed a barrette and put her hair up. "Remember, he won't shake your hand."

Deborah rummaged in her bag and heard the sound of her keys. "Are you coming?"

By the time they got to the Synagogue Sepharad of San Juan Capistrano, a misting rain had started. Deborah awkwardly hopped up the three stone stairs hunched under her jacket. Rachel followed in apprehension using her windbreaker for protection. They crossed the expansive flagstone entrance to the Moroccan-style synagogue. Two large Jewish stars were carved into the wooden doors.

In the offices, an elderly woman with silver hair shook her head and said the Rabbi was not available. She sat at a desk behind the counter. On the wall, a poster quoted the Talmud—*Deeds of kindness are superior to charity.'*

Deborah stood to her full height. "I'm Dr. Deborah Wright from UC Berkeley. It's rather urgent I speak to Rabbi Stern."

Rachel's feet were half out the door. "Mom, I told you. You don't just barge in on a Rabbi."

"He'll know what it's about." Deborah stared at the woman until she picked up the phone. On the counter, Deborah could see a volunteer signup sheet for *bikur cholim,* visiting patients in hospitals. There were flyers about the Sisterhood's food drive for the needy.

The woman hung up the phone. "His office is down the hall."

The gray hair above Rabbi Stern's ears fluffed up like little wings below his silk *yarmulke.* He stood to greet them, taking off his silver-rimmed glasses. Behind him were floor to ceiling bookcases filled with a wide range of texts including multiple copies of the *Tanach* or Jewish Bible, the *Talmud,* the *Mishnah,* books on philosophy, the *Kabbalah,* and the *Zohar.*

The sheer weight of the books made Deborah take a deep breath. But she plowed forward. "Rabbi Stern, you know my daughter Rachel. I am Deborah Wright." She reached out to shake hands, but Rachel pushed her arm down.

His eyes were steady under straight brown eyebrows that met above his strong nose. "I assume this is not a social call, Dr. Wright," he said, formally. "Please, have a seat."

Sitting down, Deborah said, "You're right, it's not. Rachel informed me of your conversation with her, how you disapprove of her relationship with Shelley."

"I didn't quite—" the Rabbi's bushy gray beard jerked quickly.

Deborah didn't let him finish. "Rachel and Shelley have been together for two years. Their relationship is different, I admit it. But then I realized that they probably know more about love than most heterosexuals. I think you should reassess the situation." She could smell peppermint on his breath.

The Rabbi squinted at them and put his glasses back on. "Dr. Wright, it is not only my assessment. There are very large historical issues at work here." He swiveled his chair gesturing toward the books behind him.

Deborah felt sweat at the back of her neck. His gestures reminded her of her father. "You may have your *halakhah* and books with their proscriptions and answers, but what do you know about this? You must have children, but do you know them?" She couldn't stop. "Do you think all these books have the definitive moral answers? It's moral to be loving. It's moral to respect. What's not moral is to pass judgment on something one knows nothing about."

Deborah could see him trying not to react. He carefully rearranged the books on the right side of his desk. "Dr. Wright, we must have respect for the Jewish faith. You are a Jewish woman. How can you question something over fifty-seven hundred years old? Or the definition of *kiddushin*, of Jewish marriage? How can you question the morals of a people older than you can comprehend?"

Rachel shifted in her seat. "Rabbi, my mother has been invited to Capistrano to work with the scientists."

Rabbi Stern nodded and sat back, glancing at his desk. "And she should stick to problems she can understand. Not all problems have the same weight in God's eyes. Nor do they have the same simple solution." He picked up a silver pen.

Deborah's eyes blazed. "Science is not as straight-forward as people think. Scientific problems don't have easy answers."

THE SWALLOW AND THE NIGHTINGALE

He signed a paper and then looked up at her. "I didn't mean to imply what you do is easy, Dr. Wright. It has a definitive outcome. Either one proves a hypothesis or one doesn't. You may find the reason the swallows are dying, even if it has baffled all the scientists around here. But no one can know the ways of God, and no one can change the laws laid down in the Torah. These laws are older than our modern science. They are the traditions on which our lives are based. The *halakhah*—these laws and traditions—require respect. *Kiddushin* sanctifies a bride to a groom. Period."

Deborah knew he was right, but if she didn't support Rachel, she'd lose her daughter as she danced off into adulthood. She stood up behind her chair. "What is love, Rabbi Stern? According to this lawful religion, what is love? Why does God say some love is all right, other love is not?" She walked over to his bookcases and then started to pace. "Where in this great book of yours does it say to be careful with whom you fall in love?"

He tried to interrupt. "You know where it is said. Rachel has told me that your father was a Rabbi..."

Deborah jerked at his mention of her father. She turned to the books. "Where are the concrete rules, the laws? Where is the good? I would think this God would be more concerned about moral problems like genocide and grand theft than about loving the 'wrong' person."

The Rabbi's eyebrows narrowed, moving even closer to each other. Just then, the building shook. "Another tremor." He stood up.

Deborah grabbed a chair as Rachel rose. "Here we go again."

Glancing around to see if everything was okay, Rabbi Stern moved toward the door. "Besides these on-going earthquakes, we have plenty of problems facing our synagogue—anti-Semites attacking Jews for many reasons." He walked out of the office. "Bernice, are you okay?"

Deborah and Rachel followed him, saw the woman nod her head.

"Start the call tree to check up on the elderly," he told her and then continued toward the sanctuary. "Dr. Wright, people make choices in their lives. The girls can choose their actions. They can go to other Jewish synagogues. They can marry in a Reform or Reconstructionist Synagogue. Even a Conservative one. They don't need me."

Rachel caught up to him. "But this is our congregation, Rabbi Stern. We are Orthodox. Shelley spent her whole life here in this Sephardic synagogue."

The Rabbi entered the sanctuary and walked toward the *bimah*, the dais in the center of the room. In front of him stood a large stained-glass window and the cabinet with the Torah. He checked to see if everything was in order and looked at Rachel. "Then you can choose to be moral according to Orthodox *halakhah* and marry men. This is the natural way, the bringing together of opposites. Man and woman are meant to unite, have children. Living any other way is an abomination in the eyes of God."

Rachel stepped back in tears and said to her mother, "I told you."

Deborah stared up at the stained glass window. Tiny leaves were falling from heaven, their colors muted in the glass. Rays extended from the left upper corner toward the ground—God's approval shining down on His chosen people. Deborah cringed at Rachel's pain, her father's voice echoing through her head berating her for wanting to marry Stephen. Breathing hard, she knew she had to say something to save her relationship with her daughter. She took a few steps toward the Rabbi. "It is about choice, Rabbi Stern. People can be trained against doing all sorts of natural things. That doesn't make them moral. Jews avoid eating pork because of dietary issues left from a nomadic lifestyle thousands of years ago. They don't have slaves or worry about Nazarites, even though these too are *halakhah* laws. People are afraid of differences. And deviance is defined by whoever is in power."

Rabbi Stern steadied himself by holding onto the back of a congregational bench. "Are you giving me a lecture on morality, Dr. Wright?"

"No. Or yes, maybe I am. Can you tell me what morality is? What is Jewish morality, or any morality?"

He squinted his eyes even with his glasses on. "Now you are playing with me. For thousands of years and at great cost, Jews have lived by the commandments written in the Torah." He looked down at a copy of the *Tanach* on the bench. He picked it up, cradling it in his hands. "The commandments cover every aspect of Jewish life. To us, it is a gift. There is a reason *most of us* stay with their powerful truths."

Deborah ignored the veiled judgment. "And so you own the standard of rightness? You can't ignore the fact that Orthodox rulings have changed over time."

Rabbi Stern stared at Deborah. He looked like a pot about to boil over. "All right, you are such a good scientist, Dr. Wright. Can you prove to me that this quote, gay love, is moral? This has never been done. Let us start there."

Deborah stared back at him. She had left the Orthodox community after college, knowing how entrenched its ancient practices were. Over these last forty years, the orthodoxy had never wavered even as science uncovered more and more about the brain and human behavior. Down to her core, she understood his arguments.

"And if you can't prove it, they can leave our community. We have enough problems as it is." He put the book away in the shelves along the back wall.

Deborah grabbed the back of the bench. "If that's what it will take, all right, I will prove their love is moral." She stormed out, Rachel rushing to keep up with her on the wet pavement.

Deborah struggled to start the car. With only the windshield wipers making a sound, they drove toward the San Juan Capistrano Library.

Rachel sent a text message to Shelley that they were on their way.

Pulling in front of the library, Deborah took a deep breath. The building was white and rectangular, fronted by eight adobe columns topped with an overflowing rounded lattice planter. A façade looking like back-to-back musical notes dominated the left side. Shelley waited out front, her curly red hair quickly getting matted. Jumping out of the car, Rachel ran to her.

Deborah rolled down the window. They looked forlorn like helpless children in long skirts. Rachel held open her windbreaker to protect Shelley from the mist.

"Hey, you two." Deborah half-smiled at her daughter. "You okay?" She put her hands in her jacket pockets. Something felt silky and soft.

Rachel didn't lie. "No."

Deborah looked down. "Maybe it's a start."

"What did you expect? You could just waltz in there and fix it?" Rachel blinked hard. "I didn't ask you to do that."

Deborah had forgotten about the red and white pineapple guava blossom. "Here," she extended it to Rachel, "I brought this for you from the mission."

Shelley nudged Rachel. "Yes, it's a start. Deborah, thank you."

Rachel looked at the flower for a second and then took it.

"And I loved the *shaakshuka* eggs." Deborah smiled through her tears. "Go inside, you're getting wet." She watched them scramble up the steps and pass through the dark double doors.

As Interstate 5 slugged through the Central Valley on toward northern California, Deborah stared at the flat scenery without really seeing it. Satellite radio provided damage reports for the New Jersey earthquake—three collapsed office buildings in Newark, thousands had broken windows. Then about the earthquakes in Mexico and one in Ecuador. Commercials touted the latest drug for men's impotence, followed by an oil conglomerate describing newly found reserves.

She turned off the radio and thought about the morning. *Why did Rachel have to embrace the rigidity of the religion I can't stand? Can I prove to Rabbi Stern that Rachel's lifestyle is moral? If I don't, I lose all semblance of a family. Add that to my screwed up career.*

Why does life have to be so hard? It feels like everything is speeding up. Too many strange things happening. Geology and zoology don't mix, Stephen said. Was he talking about science or our marriage? We're like two barn swallows sitting on a telephone line. Close, but separated by a wing span. Will the distance between us ever be bridged? There's his blustering. I'm used to that. But I can't forgive him for what he did. Never.

Damn it, Stephen. Why did you have to ruin everything?

Chapter 3
What The Nightingale Said
Part I

"Companions! Let me tell you a story.
I will keep repeating it so that you take it
upon yourself to begin a quest for the Truth."
- Farid ud-Din Attar (1142-1220)
The Conference of the Birds

MY NAME IS FARID UD-Din Hamid Muhammad bin Ibrahim, but everyone calls me Attar. My father wants me to study the *Quran*, the book given to the people by Mohammad, but I follow the prayers without interest. "If you don't pray to Allah, you will die," my father warns me. All boys at my age of seventeen study the *Quran*.

"But, father, you know what I love. You are a perfumer!" We are on a winding road looking for the exotic flowers that grow high in the mountains above Shadyakh, my small village in northern Persia. A road forks to the left twisting down the pass toward Nishapur, the trading center of the area. "Look, I think there are some white roses in that rock crevice." I scramble up the boulders to a small place that catches bits of sand and dirt in the changing winds from which bloom flowers of enormous beauty.

"Attar! Attar!" My father reaches out and extracts the petals from my hand. "You must think of other things, there is more to life than perfume."

"Father, teach me everything you know. I promise I'll study the *Quran*, but I must be the greatest perfumer that ever lived. I am Attar!"

"That," my father sighs, "or the biggest fool."

One day, he tells me to look in on Muhammad bin Marwan. I like to visit the wealthier customers who won't come to us.

The richness of the aristocrat's household pleases my sensibilities. I am ushered into the courtyard, where an elaborate chessboard is prepared. Muhammad bin Marwan sits on a rug with a pattern of elaborate blackberry bushes intertwined with olive trees in rich greens and reds. A fountain in the garden sprays water rhythmically into the air to refresh us. My father taught me to play chess as part of the elaborate negotiating procedure.

Soon, the game is over. "You win again, Attar," ibn Marwan says, shaking his head.

I smile, feeling the fountain's light mist in the afternoon heat. "I only follow the direction of the game. The pieces know their way."

The older man laughs. "And you had nothing to do with it! Well, you played as a man."

"Now let me show you my latest mixture." I open a small vial, wave my hand over the top to release the bouquet and hand it to ibn Marwan. "It's taken me six weeks to prepare it."

Ibn Marwan takes full whiffs. "Heavenly, heavenly! I must have four jars of it. It is too wonderful. You have a special sense that understands the roses."

We finish the exchange and I begin the trip back to the shop.

It is the heat of the day, so most people are inside. Around me grow numerous thickets of chokeberry. Beyond them is a grove of tall trees. The wind comes down the pass catching the thickets in a whirlwind. In front of me, the mountains loom large. I look at a small gnarled tree on the side of the road and see a nightingale perched on one of the branches. With its head bent sideways, the bird seems to be watching me. I stop.

"Attar! Attar!" the nightingale sings out from her branch.

"What? Who is there?" I look around in amazement.

"Attar! Attar! Listen to me," the bird sings out and flies from its perch, settling down in front of me on a small branch. The bird is so light the bush doesn't bend. A beautiful rose bush suddenly appears amid the thickets of chokeberries. A red rose flower, full and delicate, sways next to the nightingale.

"How is it you can talk to me, little bird?" I walk around the rosebush and stare at the golden brown bird.

THE SWALLOW AND THE NIGHTINGALE

"Attar! You make perfumes as sweet as this rose. How will you ever leave?"

"Why do I have to leave my perfumes?" I look around to see if anyone is watching or playing a trick on me.

"To contemplate death," the nightingale says, "and forsake these worldly possessions."

I kneel down and look at it very carefully. "You mock me. You are only a bird. What do you know?"

"I am very old. I have seen and learned much," the nightingale sighs. She jumps to another branch.

"You do not know anything," I speak with scorn. How can a bird talk to me? Is this some sort of omen? These things happen in fables, but not out on the road to Shadyakh.

"Then listen, I will sing you a story. My name is Philomela…"

At first, I don't want to listen. But the bird's song is mesmerizing. I sit down. The story is so sad and desperate, filled with betrayal and revenge. I've never contemplated evil before. The tune is beautiful, haunting and melancholic. At the end, the bird asks me, "Are you ready for the good?"

I know nothing of love or death. I don't know if I am ready for the good, whatever that means. Is this knowledge in the parts of the *Quran* I am supposed to have studied? Does Allah know of such mysteries? Is the bird telling other people this story? Or am I the only one?

I am greatly moved. "And what have you learned, my little nightingale?"

"The shadow is lost in the sun."

Chapter 4

"As soon as you enter the Valley of the Quest,
a hundred painful questions will endlessly assail you.
At every moment you will meet a hundred challenges;
the parrot of the sky is merely a fly in such realm."

-- *Attar, The Conference of the Birds*

"BUT, FATHER, A BIRD spoke to me."

"Attar, I need you to make perfume. Don't speak of a talking bird." My father sits in the back of the shop, mixing oils.

"But father," I cry out, "it was the most amazing thing. The story! The melody! Why did this nightingale speak to me?"

My father looks hopeful. "Only Allah knows. Go see the shaikh for the answer. He can teach you. Maybe this will help you reach Allah."

I run to the shaikh's tent at the edge of the village. Shaikh Bukn-ud-din, a great Sufi master, knows things beyond the understanding of most men.

We sit on the floor. The flame of a glass oil lamp casts deep shadows on the old shaikh's lined face. I breathlessly describe what happened. Bukn-ud-din tells me, "It is easy to answer the question, but not as easy for you to hear it."

"But how do I find the answer? Why did this nightingale speak to me?"

"Many years ago, as I walked outside of town, I saw a man searching for gold in a great mound of dirt. The longer he looked, the more he piled up dust. A rich man rode by and threw his gold bracelet onto the piles before riding off. The man picked it up and continued to search. In my surprise, I called out, 'Old man, why do you continue to look? That rich man threw you a golden bracelet. You now have all your needs met for the rest of your life, yet you still continue to search.'

The man looked up at me. 'Yes, I found the bracelet. But it is because I have found these riches that I must continue to search.' "

I am perplexed. "What more did the man need? He was given a great gift but didn't appreciate it. The nightingale didn't give me gold." When I feel a bag of coins in my hand, I know that I have done well. While I live for the exquisite smells of the perfume, I know my existence depends on that gold.

"Be like that man!" the shaikh replies. "It is time to search for the answer. Search until the door opens. Your eyes will not always be closed. Go find the door."

"What must I do?" I am confused. My eyes aren't shut. I see the water in the fountains, the chess pieces on the board, even the veiled girls who cast down their eyes. My senses are more opened than most people.

"You must take a journey, Attar," Bukn-ud-din responds, gesturing toward the tent flaps. "There you will find the answer."

"You mean a pilgrimage? To Mecca?" A *hajj* is a great obligation that every Muslim man takes once in his lifetime. According to the village customs, I am still young but could go. I am fearful and confused. I have never left my village.

"You will journey." Bukn-ud-din's long beard bobs up and down. "The direction you go is for you to decide. However, when you seek the door, all directions are the same."

"How will I know when I have found the answer?"

"Open your eyes. Tell what you know. Listen for the answer." The shaikh turns to his cup of tea.

I feel the enormous weight placed on my shoulders. I must take to this path no matter how ill prepared I am. I start to tremble.

"Father, the shaikh said I must journey." Pleading with my eyes for my father to disagree, I want him to tell me the talking nightingale was a joke, all to make fun of me. Even being made fun of is something I would prefer.

But my father respects the word of the shaikh as if it came from Allah Himself. "If this is what the shaikh says, then you must do it. It is Allah's will. Besides, you can sell perfume. Our perfume will become famous. Traders will come to demand more from us. You will return in six months with new customers."

"But where will I go?" I ask.

"You'll have time to reach Mecca by the month of *Dhu'l-Hijja* for a *hajj*. This pilgrimage you must do in your lifetime."

"But we have heard of infidels on the land causing great troubles!" I say, still trying to find a way out. I've never seen an infidel. I've heard they have four eyes and make clanking noises when they walk. They breathe out smoke and fire and eat little boys.

"Allah chooses the time for a *hajj*, Attar. You don't."

The thought of leaving Shadyakh begins to outweigh my fear. It could be an adventure, and it won't be forever. Only six months. Think of all I will see in that time. Maybe I won't be near the fighting with the infidels. Or maybe I will.

My father makes a plan. I will travel to Baghdad and sell perfumes. I will stay there until the month of *Dhu'l-Hijja* when I will join other pilgrims traveling to Mecca.

He borrows an old donkey and we ride in silence. As we approach Nishapur, I become more excited. It is the largest market I have ever seen. Merchants bring porcelain and paper from China and spices and dyes from India on their way across the Empire to the bazaars of Baghdad. I feel like I am at the center of the world.

My father buys a camel with a scratchy brown coat and long eyelashes. It stands a full two heads taller than me.

"All right, boy." The caravan leader looks me over. "You do what you are told and help get supplies when we reach a town."

I nod, too afraid to speak. My perfumes, prayer rug, and extra clothes are packed into baskets hanging from the camel's seat. Standing by the kneeling animal, I turn to my father. Pushing an extra blanket into my hands, he hugs me. "Do well, Attar. Honor your name and family."

"Yes, father." I look at the ground to hide my tears.

Rising before dawn every day, I place my prayer rug on the ground. Facing Mecca to the southwest, I follow the others as we purify our bodies, washing our faces, arms, feet, and hair with the dry sand of the desert. We stand, raise our hands with our palms forward and say, "Allah is most great!" Prostrating ourselves, we recite passages from the *Quran*. At the end of our prayers, we sit, turning our faces right then left, saying, "Peace be with you and the Mercy of God."

After our prayers and a small breakfast of dates and figs, we mount the camels and fall into a steady pace. Some days, we journey for as long as twelve hours through the mountainous terrain. We skirt the desert, seeing long-rooted acacia plants, thorny shrubs, and other vegetation that dots the landscape.

Most nights we sleep under the stars. I wrap myself in the frayed woven blanket my father gave me. Reassured by the warmth of home, I ponder what the nightingale told me and what the shaikh Bukn-ud-din said. Am I ready for the good? I don't know. Nor do I understand what shadow the nightingale spoke of. When I look on the ground and the sun is in the sky, I can see my shadow. It isn't lost at all. And if a treasure is found, why look for more? And why did the nightingale choose me, Attar, a humble perfumer? The nightingale said I have to turn my mind toward death, but only old men think of death. I have my whole life in front of me. And the song! When I try to sing it, it is never as beautiful as the nightingale's song—haunting as it was. I can't get it out of my head.

CHAPTER 5
THE SWALLOW'S ANSWER
PART II

WORLD NEWS – APRIL 6
Mauna Loa Volcano Erupts on Hawaii
Plumes From Alaskan Volcano
Beached Whales Associated with Naval Sonar Activity

DEBORAH TRIED TO REGAIN control of her Introduction to Biology class, but Michael Bridgeman wouldn't let go. "It seemed to me there were fewer birds in Hawaii than here in Berkeley." During spring break, he had been surfing in Maui. His rich tan made his teeth shine and spiky hair blonder. His longs legs stretched into the aisle between the rows of chairs.

Jeff Hodgdon snickered, brushing a lock of black hair off his open face. "Duh, dude. Maybe the volcano had something to do with it." Wire-framed glasses couldn't hide the amusement in his big eyes as he ran a hand down his long braid of hair.

The whole class broke out in laughter. Michael retorted, "Better there than going to Penn-syl-van-i-a." He dragged out the name of the state, swaying his head to make it funnier.

With strong hands, Jeff wagged his protruding ears at his friend.

Deborah smiled. "All right, folks, I know the end of the semester is in sight, but we do have to review for the final."

"But, Dr. Wright," Michael said, "this is more interesting than cells. What do you think about two volcanoes blowing almost simultaneously while earthquakes are escalating?"

"The Alaskan one was smaller. The amount of particulates released into the atmosphere will affect avian populations. Speaking of avians, their organs are composed of tissue made up of eukaryotic cells…"

"They were giving helicopter rides over the flowing lava from the volcano for like only $400," interrupted an Asian girl sitting in the front, filing her long nails.

A kid in the back snickered, "Anything to make a buck."

Deborah explained, "Well, it's a good thing it wasn't a Plinian eruption, shooting skyward like the Alaskan ... what's that noise?"

Everyone turned their heads toward the open windows where loud voices assaulted them. Deborah walked to the side of the second floor classroom and looked out.

"It's the Earth Day Awareness Fair," Jeff said. "It started getting rowdy yesterday when those black suits showed up to demonstrate."

"Demonstrators? Against saving whales and discarding batteries?"

Someone else said, "Oh, it's gone way beyond that."

Deborah looked outside but could only see a crowd of students and rows of white tents. "Could someone shut the windows? Thanks." She walked back to the front of the classroom to command control. "Now, getting back to the review. Cells are like little factories synthesizing proteins and producing ATP for energy, keeping the organism alive ..."

Michael interrupted. "What about the study you're doing in San Juan Capistrano? Are the eruptions affecting the swallows?"

"How did you know about that?"

"They printed the story in the *Daily Californian*, saying you were invited there because of the machine you built."

The article in the school newspaper had slipped Deborah's mind. "Oh, right. I had been working on it," she answered vaguely, turning toward the whiteboard behind her. She could see a previous professor's notes about whale beaching in the Mediterranean. She rubbed the bandage around her right index finger, remembering the mission.

Half-slouching in his chair, Jeff sat up. "I heard there might have been a problem with the RAX-1000."

Deborah saw it hopeless to stay with her prepared lecture. She sat down on the instructor's desk at the front of the seminar room and sighed. "Okay, okay. My visit to San Juan Capistrano. No, the machine is fine. Dan, the systems engineer, went over the instrument component by component."

"Did he check it for aliasing?"

"I think that's the term he used, Jeff. He listened to the recordings, traced the wiring and tested all the boards, internal and external mics. He said it's working fine."

Michael asked, "Can you tell us what you found?"

"I didn't find much and have since dropped the project." She had decided to look for some other way to rescue her scientific reputation.

Michael persisted. "But you did find something."

"Okay." It was a teachable moment. She stood up. "There's something unusual about the recordings." Deborah erased the whales and started drawing a generalized model of a bird song. She briefly explained how it's analyzed in terms of pitch, rhythm, pattern, and repose. "I did an analysis of this section where it makes a transition from the swallow's regular pattern to what sounds to me like a human tune. As far as I can tell, it's a smooth shift, with no obvious break."

Michael said, "That means the Raz is working as you designed it."

"Exactly." Smiling at his nickname for the machine, she stared at her drawing. "There would be a detectable break if there was a malfunction."

"That's so cool." Jeff raised his hand and tilted his head. "How did you figure out how to build this?"

Deborah sat down remembering that evening in her living room. "I had been listening to James Galway playing a Mozart concerto on the flute. The piece is very elaborate and fast. I remember wondering what's inside those notes. And then I realized I couldn't hear him taking any breaths. That astounded me. When I found out that engineers had constructed the piece, editing out his breaths, I wondered whether one can look at how a bird's song is constructed."

"Constructed?" Michael asked. "That's an interesting word to use for a biological entity. Like it's a robot?" The class laughed as Michael stood up and made mechanical robot movements.

Deborah smiled. "I agree, it's a funny word. Dan said what we built has the same feel as the machine the British built in World War II for cracking the Enigma Code. The RAX-1000 analyzes signals as many ways as humanly possible."

"Or machinely possible," added Jeff

"Like it's a big puzzle," Michael interjected.

"Exactly. That's what science is. Figuring out how the world is put together. It consists of so many variables. Doing science well eliminates

the unknowingness from each unknown." She thought to herself—
*which is the problem with Capistrano. I don't have enough data to eliminate enough
unknowns. And it could've been the end of my career if I had tried to get more.*

"Engineering, too?"

Deborah nodded. "Scientists need you engineers to apply the
theories and make the machines, Jeff."

Michael said, "Dr. Wright, do you think the bird knew it was
singing a human song?"

"That's a really interesting question, Michael. Off hand, I would say
no because their brains are relatively small. You know, bird-brain," she
emphasized the typical putdown to get their attention. It worked.
"But," she continued, "there's some bird behavior that's very
sophisticated. And there are even examples of interspecies
communication. I teach a whole course on that. Meanwhile, we should
get back to the intro course material. Now, about cells—"

Michael persisted. "You said cells are like little factories. Maybe the
birds don't know what they're doing, but do you think cells know
they're keeping an organism alive?"

She looked at him. "I've got five books you should read in order to
begin thinking about the depth of that question." Deborah smiled to
herself. *Michael will make a brilliant scientist.* He reminded her of Stephen
who approached geology from a systems perspective, exploring the
space and time scales up and down looking for connections. *Could a
systems analysis help figure out how to approach swallows singing a human tune?
Wouldn't it be a real coup to figure it out?* She made a decision and stood up.
"Okay. Here's a start on it."

She erased the whiteboard and picked up a black marker. "It's
about the local versus the global view. Does a stomach neuron *know*
about pizza shops? Do our individual neurons *know* what a house is?
The answer is no—each neuron in the nervous system has only a local
view of its part of the incoming data. And they work in cooperation
with and also compete against each other to perform their tasks.

"One. Competition." She wrote the word in capital letters. "They
compete against each other for resources. Or else, two, cooperation."
She wrote that as well. "They help each other to succeed."

She looked at what she had drawn. "You can think of people as
cells. They are contained entities—like biological cells, only bigger.
Biological cells have a membrane, a nucleus, and mitochondria. The

cells form collectives of biological cells that cooperate and compete. People are cells that have a containing membrane called skin, and they have organs, bones and blood. They form collectives as well—clans, tribes, nations. Now," she changed markers and started drawing again, "each of us as an individual is happily living our life with our own local view, studying for final exams, surfing in Hawaii, whatever."

The class laughed as she proceeded to draw a surfer with spiky hair. She noticed Jeff intently scribbling notes.

She laughed as well. "So, here's our Michael cell on a surfboard. The task at hand is to maintain his balance in an unstable environment. That task becomes the global problem that the biological nerve cells in his body are trying to solve. But do the cells in Michael's feet know about surfboards and riding the tube? Do the cells in his muscles know what gravity is? Do they know Newton's law of universal gravitation? Have they even heard of Isaac Newton?"

Deborah looked around for comprehension. She saw smiles as they struggled. "No to all these questions. But his vestibular system evolved to help him maintain his balance." She picked another color and drew arrows. "It reacts to rotations of his head. When his head turns right, the vestibulo-ocular reflex turns his eyes left so that they stay focused on the same spot on the horizon. But what if a pretty bikini-clad girl starts surfing next to him?"

The class all snickered. Michael puffed out his chest.

Deborah drew another stick figure with breasts. "Areas in the prefrontal cortex begin competing for control of his eyes so that he can take a quick look. Which is going to win? There's only one resource—his eyes—and two neurological areas vying to control them."

The students were rapt as they grasped her words.

She felt energized. "Forces push, pull, and twist his head. His vestibular system senses the resulting movements and accelerations. It sends signals down to his spinal cord for quick reflexive compensation by his muscles. They in turn all work together so he doesn't lose his balance—which will happen if his muscles are set one way and the forces acting on his body push him another. And if his attention pulls his eyes away from their reference point for too long," Deborah pointed to the other stick figure, "he'll lose his balance. And probably any chance of a date."

Everyone laughed.

THE SWALLOW AND THE NIGHTINGALE

Deborah smiled. "So while the individual cells don't understand the global problem, they interact in a balanced way to perform the task. Success," she concluded, "is found in the dynamic balance of the competing and cooperating actions performed by the cells in order to solve the global problem. Even if the individual cells don't understand it."

She picked up two more markers. "We, too, are like cells. We humans are all interconnected in a collective. Insurance companies even predict behaviors of our collectives. Our interactions create economic and political systems, and we are part of this whole, more global, living system that makes up a planet called Earth. But do we think about it? Other than on an approaching Earth Day?" She nodded toward the window. "Are we like those neurons living in Michael's brain which are unaware of surfboards? Are those opportunistic price-gougers at the Hawaiian volcano aware of their effect on other cell-like people in our economic system? Are they aware of the global problem like the great Carnac would be?"

The students were right with her and some even smiled at the reference to the old Johnny Carson routine on The Tonight Show.

"Those so-called businessmen don't realize it, but they, too, are like biological cells. They're competing for resources—in their case trying to gather as much money as they can for themselves. When there are limited resources, there's a lot of competition among the players, all of whom have local views of the global problem. They can't see our whole economic system and all the forces acting on it. I'm not saying all competition is bad, just as not all cooperation is good. But remember, success is achieved by the dynamic balance of the competing and cooperating actions working to solve the global problem."

She started pacing. "How does one balance competition and cooperation? Economists make up a reference point, or metric, to define the global state, such as the gross national product or rate of inflation. They set goals and track monthly or quarterly progress of the collective. But what really is the global economic problem? We don't know. We're inside it, we can't see it. Like fish who can't see water. Like ancients not knowing there's oxygen in the invisible air around us. We're inside it, we can't see it. What's the global political problem? We don't know—"

Page 40

Michael shouted, "We're inside it, we can't see it."

"Right!" She quickly limped back to the whiteboard, gesturing. "We are only little cells with our own local views. Think of helium balloons rising. Our leaders are like helium molecules in that balloon trying to direct it sideways. They can't do it. Maybe they think they can when an outside wind pushes the balloon sideways. But we're all embedded deep in the system with local views and can't see the big picture.

"And what's the global *global* problem, if you will, the metric that defines the problems the planet is solving? Is it to keep itself alive? At all costs or within certain limits? Will Earth Day Awareness keep our planet alive? We see situations and infer the causes. We determine our metrics but they're based on how things relate to us—how many people killed or the cost to restore damaged structures. What's the effect of all these natural disasters on the global global problem? We don't know. What's the effect of a large human population on the global global problem? We don't know."

Every student joined in this time. "We're inside it, we can't see it."

Deborah laughed and stepped away from the board, contemplating her artistry. She hadn't anticipated where she went with the lecture, but it was true and the students all got it. She thought, *no matter what I feel about Stephen, he's right. There's too much seismic activity. Wild weather from the changing climate is one thing but a 5.3 earthquake in New Jersey is another. Not to mention the dead birds.*

Her eyes were dancing as she concluded her lecture. "As for the swallows, I don't know the answer. They may be like cells in that they only have a local view and they don't know they're singing a human song. Or they may be like the great Carnac and are harmonizing along with who knows what."

As the class laughed again, Michael asked, "Can we help you with your research?"

Deborah looked at him. Returning the markers to the tray, she shook her head. "I've checked out the machine. I'm finishing my report. I'm ending my involvement there."

"You said the machine didn't malfunction," Jeff said.

"You're right. But as of yet, there aren't enough data."

Michael persisted. "Isn't there something we can do?"

She stared at the tape wrapped around her finger. Then she ripped it off and threw it in the wastepaper basket. "Actually, nothing wrong with doing a data search. There may be other useful discoveries in the literature. I can't justify asking my graduate students if I'm not going to continue on the project. But I guess it's worth looking. Who's interested?"

Michael's and Jeff's hands shot up into the air, something Deborah would have predicted. They were her smartest students.

"Meet me after class," Deborah glanced at her watch, "which seems to be right now. I guess that's it for today. See you next Monday. Office hours on Thursday."

As the others filed out, Michael and Jeff came to the front of the classroom and stood by her desk. They seemed so opposite from each other—Michael being taller, Jeff more intense. But after almost a semester of knowing them, she could understand their friendship. "Okay. There are 5,000 passerine species but we'll focus on the oscines which reduces the number to about 4,000."

"Oscines?" Jeff played with the end of his hair braid.

"Sorry. Oscines are songbirds. Search PubMed and other journal indices for any similar findings. Check BIRDNET, the Cornell lab."

Michael understood immediately. "Using what search terms?"

"I don't know. Use your judgment."

Jeff jumped in. "How about human tunes in bird songs?"

Michael added, "Or human music? Or compositions?"

"Try anything you can think of. There are also results too new to be published. I'll ask people about their field data. Sam Dadich at Cornell has followed the research of the *Alaudidae* and *Thraupidae* closer than I have. Anything I miss with larks and tanagers, he might know." She didn't realize she was thinking about the problem again.

"What about Dellon at Stanford and Antonos at Tulsa?"

Deborah nodded. He already thought like a researcher. "Good point, Michael. They've all done extensive field recording of bird songs. I'll contact them as well."

"Dr. Wright, one last thing?"

"Yes, Michael?"

"Can I borrow those five books you mentioned?"

Deborah laughed. "Remind me when I'm in my office."

🕊 🕊

Deborah's Notes for *Petrochelidon pyrrhonota* Study
A statistical analysis of the Capistrano recordings has been completed. A *P*-value of 0.02 suggests that the unknown pattern is repeated in all samples. As of yet, no similar sequence has been found in the literature. Samples have been shared with Sam Dadich (Cornell), Tobias Dellon (Stanford) and Phil Antonos (Tulsa). Possible explanations: 1) the one subject is a unique aberration, 2) the unknown sequence is across the species but previous recording devices lacked the capability to sample it, or 3) the unknown sequence is across the species and recently introduced into the birds' song. Recordings from other subjects would provide answers.

Sitting in her living room, Deborah willed relaxation into her shoulders by listening to Gregorian chants. She held a mug of Jamaican Blue Mountain coffee. The loveseat looked over a low deck where birdfeeders attracted hummingbirds, chickadees, and finches. Along the edge of the deck grew manzanita bushes and hummingbird sage.

Wanting to call Rachel, she remembered they had their friends visiting. Deborah thought about her daughter's coming out. Rachel had driven up to Berkeley for the weekend. After dinner, she said she had met someone, a woman. Deborah had been speechless but Stephen found a way to be supportive. It was a gift he had. When Rachel had been a teenager and they were living in Japan, he took her on field trips to study geological formations with his students.

Her eyes filling up, Deborah reached for a tissue on the coffee table. She studied the empty birdfeeders. If she didn't prove this same-sex love moral to the Rabbi, she would lose Rachel for good. She hadn't even tried to figure out a solution. Where was the answer? Feeling a heaviness, she understood prejudice on so many levels. The looks she and Stephen used to get—still get. Used to get, she remembered. She could feel the heat pooling between her breasts. *At least we are heterosexual, well-educated, living a normal life. If being separated is normal.*

Smelling the intense coffee, she was brought back to her living room by the aroma. The warm glow of the outdoor wrought-iron lamps played over the garden. Making a mental note to refill the sunflower seeds before going to campus in the morning, she thought of her friend Thomas. An anthropologist, he dealt with soft human issues all the time. She'd call him during his office hours.

🕊 🕊

WORLD NEWS – APRIL 9
VOC Toxins From Paint and Cleansers Worse Indoors
Widely Used Herbicide Implicated in Diseases
Engineered Corn Classified as Pesticide

Deborah's phone rang as she unlocked her office door in the Valley Life Sciences Building. Maneuvering around her conference table, she placed her travel bag, field journal, and course notebook on her desk and picked up the receiver. It was the Dean of the College of Letters and Science.

"Milhouse, you caught me as my office hours are starting." Deborah checked her large calendar. Gracing the credenza were neat piles of papers organized in color-coded folders. Bookshelves dominated the wall next to the door. It looked like the janitor crew camped out there to maintain the office's perfection.

"Good." Dean Harvey Milhouse's voice rasped like an emery board. "My secretary looked up your schedule. How was your trip to Capistrano? Heard a few things."

She sat down, reminded that a university was like a little universe churning on its inhabitants. "It went all right." She wanted to end this conversation quickly.

"And how's Stephen? Enjoying his sabbatical? He's not going to New Jersey, is he? He's always in the thick of things."

Deborah saw right through him. "Listen, Milhouse, as you've probably already heard, I didn't get enough data."

"Well, good. I mean, it's too bad you didn't get the data. But we know what a tenuous situation you're already in. I don't want to have to remind you of that…"

Deborah cursed under her breath. *You already have, you wing nut.*

His voice slid into a grandfatherly tone. "But, Deborah, another paper like the Santorini one could easily be a cause for review. Tenure or no tenure, contract or no contract."

Deborah rubbed her neck. "You wouldn't—"

"I'm not saying anything you don't already know," he rasped, "but science is science. There are rules we scientists live by. Data supports hypotheses, not the other way around."

Harvey Milhouse had a career as a biomedical engineer before getting his MBA and politicking into the Dean's position. Having developed the Milhouse Effect in signal processing, he wouldn't shut her down because of his curiosity about the RAX-1000. Besides, she had tenure and he wasn't her boss.

Still, Deborah knew she shouldn't take the threat lightly. "Harvey, Harvey. I'm off the project. I finished my report and sent it. I'm going to look for other studies where the RAX-1000 will be more suited. I'm already in contact with Dadich at Cornell." She didn't say why she contacted him.

"What? That's good, very good. The Capistrano study has disaster written all over it. Go visit Stephen, sure, but stay away from the project. Make sure he returns to campus when his sabbatical is over. We like him here." He hung up.

Deborah glared at the receiver wondering whether for spite she should reevaluate her decision to walk away from the Capistrano project. That's not a reason to do science, she argued silently with the phone.

Michael popped his head into the office. "Dr. Wright, have you heard anything?" Jeff stood right behind him.

Deborah looked up. "Hi, Michael. Hi Jeff. Nothing yet. I've completed my analysis and sent it to the Capistrano group."

Jeff leaned on the door. Michael walked in close to the bookshelf. "Now we have to wait for answers from your queries."

Deborah frowned, the Dean's voice still in her head. She shook her head realizing how wholeheartedly these two were jumping into this project. And they were still undergraduates.

Her plan for the RAX-1000 had been big and the mimicry study of the European starling was a start. But the machine didn't demonstrate an inkling of its abilities there. That result could have been found using standard sampling techniques. From the moment she had heard the swallow singing at Capistrano, she knew she had found something brand new. Where it could go, she had no idea. *Is the timing of the swallow die off with all the other natural disasters a coincidence? Is Stephen right?* Feeling her back tense up, she wanted him to be wrong. Or at least, to apologize for what he did.

Michael stared at her.

"Oh, sorry. What did you say?" Deborah rubbed her neck.

"I wonder if I can borrow those books you mentioned."

Deborah smiled. "Oh, sure. Let me find them." Picking up her travel bag, she stood and hung the bag on a peg by the bookcases.

Jeff stepped forward. "Dr. Wright, do you have any books on how they genetically engineer food? I heard the herbicide they spray on crops could be damaging when we eat the food."

"That's a new one on me." She limped toward the wall of bookshelves. The books were carefully organized by topic—biology, ornithology, botany, and systems science. She pulled out two and handed them to Michael. "They wouldn't market food that wasn't safe."

Jeff frowned. "My fiancée wants to study what's happening with our food supply."

"Fiancée?" Deborah jerked around. His broad forehead and smiling eyes turned everyone into his friend. Long hair and high cheekbones highlighted his Native American heritage. "Aren't you a little young to get married?"

He pushed a lock of his black hair off his face. "It's natural to want to marry the one you love. We'll tie the knot when we graduate, before she starts medical school at Penn and I start grad school."

Deborah winced internally. *Why can't Rachel's plans be so easy? Marriage is such a magnet.* Deborah slowly handed the last of the books to Michael. "This one's my husband's book on systems. It might be tough going, but you'll like it."

Deborah stared out the window. She had dropped the project but the project hadn't left her. *The machine hadn't malfunctioned.* She had three hypotheses with too many unknowns. She had students willing to do research. *Any kind of research is a good thing for a wannabe scientist. There's no harm in encouraging them.* Surely Milhouse will appreciate her mentoring them. It's not like she would keep working on it.

Chapter 6

What The Nightingale Said
Part II

"Following the first valley is the Valley of Love.
To enter it one must dive totally into the fire;
What say I? We must ourselves be fire,
Otherwise we could not survive."

-- *Attar, The Conference of the Birds*

IT HAS TAKEN OVER a month for our caravan to reach Rai near Mazandaran Sea at the base of the Alborz Mountains. After we set up camp near the edge of the city, I go into town. I feel like a world traveler seeing the wide streets and tall buildings. Not so long ago I had never been outside of Shadyakh. Now I am walking into another city as if I have seen all the great cities of the world.

I move through the bazaar buying rice and lentils, carrying them in large corded bags. The smells of rich spices, dung, and foodstuff fill my senses. Porters shout above the cries of beggars. A man dressed in a brown cloth robe resting on a long wooden staff calls out to me. He asks me where I am going.

"My father put me on a caravan to Mecca." Not many people talk to me. Shaikh Bukn-ud-din told me to keep my eyes open and to listen for the answer. Maybe this man has something for me. I add, "I travel to learn."

"And what have you learned?" The stranger shifts his weight on the pole.

"I have learned a story from a nightingale." I didn't realize someone might ask me for an answer, not that I have any. The nightingale didn't tell me to not repeat her song. The shaikh didn't say I shouldn't talk either.

The man throws his head back so that his bushy black beard reaches for the sky and laughs. "So, tell me, what can a nightingale say that is so wise?"

My chest shrinks. Gathering my courage, I say, "This is what I learned." And in the gentlest voice I can muster, I sing the song of the nightingale.

The stranger raises his eyebrows. "She was in love with the rose."

"Why would a nightingale be in love with a rose bush?"

"Come with me. I'll show you." The man walks through the crowded bazaar with its colorful textiles, traders, beggars, and animals. I follow him past the Mosque, its tall minaret and wide dome. Below the pointed top of the minaret is the balcony for the *muezzin*, the crier who calls the believers to prayer.

We reach a great palace with walls that rise high into the air. The stone walls are built of large marble blocks. A large crowd gathers. I jostle my way through them to keep up with the stranger.

We stop. "What are we waiting for?" I ask.

"You will see."

The palace doors fly open. A panoply of horses and riders comes streaming out. A princess emerges, escorted by thirty young men riding horses with golden bridles and elaborate white saddles. Her skin is exquisite, her long black hair flowing. The aroma of her perfume is a bouquet of fragrance. The stranger dashes in front of the princess, his face flushed, eyes shining. He bows. The princess ignores him. Dropping his staff, the stranger stumbles and falls.

The royal hurricane passes, leaving the stranger on the ground. I help him to his feet. "What would you have with her?" I ask. "She is a princess, you are a beggar."

"I am in love with the princess. I have no possessions, I am not a prince. Whenever she rides through the streets, so perfumed and so beautiful, I run out to see her. It is painful to see her and not be able to be near her."

"That is absurd." I sit down next to the man. "You can never satisfy this love."

"You think of me as a common beggar, but I am not inferior to nobility when it comes to love. You think you are better than me because you look like a rich merchant?" He spits on the ground. "You could be the king for all I care, but have you ever been in love?"

"Yes, of course, I have been in love," I lie.

"Bah! You think you have been in love. For love, for real love, one needs a heart on fire." The man turns to me and grabs my robe and shakes me. "Compared to mine, your love for anyone or anything is ordinary."

"It is? Why?" I try to pull away.

"My beloved is absent from my life. I suffer." He releases me and I help him up. "For love—for real love—you must sacrifice your life. Until then, don't speak of love." The stranger turns and walks away.

I run after him. "You think the nightingale loved the rose so much, she sacrificed herself for it?"

"She learned love was the answer. Love can mend pain. She could purge her bad deed through true love. In the end, she had no awareness of herself, so great was her love."

I stand stunned. Why didn't I see that? Is that really what the nightingale meant? What about the shadow? *The shadow is lost in the sun.* Am I ready for the good? Are bad deeds overcome by love? What bad deeds have I done that need to be resolved before my death? I haven't studied the *Quran* as much as my father demanded, but I am a hard worker. I love my father but I am traveling when I should be helping him as he grows old. Does my love compensate for my meanderings around the world? But I am on a religious quest, so I can't be that bad a person. I know the love of the smells of the perfumes. Is that love? That is pleasure. Are they the same?

I think my head will burst from the confusion. I remember the song, how soothing it sounded when I sang it out loud. I make my way back to the caravan, carrying my supplies. Maybe I can try again and sing the song better.

CHAPTER 7
THE SWALLOW'S ANSWER
PART III

WORLD NEWS – APRIL 10
Smart Grid Causes Adverse Health Effects
Cancer Higher Near Cell Phone Transmitter Stations
Toxic Waste Dumping Rampant
Nuclear Power Spent Fuel Causing Cancer
Plastic Islands Swirling in Pacific Oceans
Greenhouse Gases Causing Earth's Temperature to Rise

THE KOSHLAND BIOSCIENCE Library was quiet. Walking past the 65-million-year-old *Triceratops'* skull on display which she secretly called Gramps, Deborah turned toward the reference area. The question, she realized, related to what she had concluded in her lecture on Monday. Did the swallow know what it was singing? Young birds learn their songs from adults of their species, who learned from the adults that were around when they were juveniles. Open-ended learners like European starlings and nightingales learn new song material every breeding season.

But what about mimicry, she wondered. She knew some birds mimic other birds, varying the order, sequence or repetition of phrases. She found a report regarding a pet starling bought by Mozart. He purchased it when he heard the bird singing phrases from his new piano concerto. It must have learned them from Mozart himself as he whistled the musical composition. The bird lived for three more years.

This was evidence of a bird learning a tune from a human. Even though it didn't kill the bird, at least it was something. But the literature didn't mention any anomalies in cliff swallow songs. She checked for the *Hirundinidae* family—the martins and swallows. No reports.

THEA IBERALL

Next, she tried the Museum of Vertebrate Zoology on the third floor. They had one of the largest bird collections in the US. Their Laboratory of Natural Sounds had an extensive collection of avian recordings. Choosing recordings of various species of swallows, she looked around to see if the Dean was anywhere in the area. *I'm not doing anything bad. This isn't for the Capistrano project.* She made the copies, telling herself she'll show the students how to compare them to the RAX-1000 recordings. She closed her journal and placed it back into her travel bag.

Deborah liked to have lunch near the eucalyptus grove by Strawberry Creek where it ran adjacent to the building past West Circle. It reminded her of why she became a biological scientist. Normally quiet, the lawn area between the Valley Life Sciences Building and Haviland Hall was a mass of agitated activity.

Students were everywhere. The on-going fair for the upcoming Earth Day attracted attention. Booths and tables lined Wickson Road and the walkways. Posters plastered lampposts. The campus band rehearsed at Goldman Field, adding to the general hubbub.

She could see booths about earthquakes and energy. A sign stuck in the lawn said, "Agribusiness cares only about its profits, not about our health." It competed with other signs from large corporations and non-profits. A downy woodpecker drummed in the eucalyptus trees to her left. Looking up, she saw the white underbellies of a flock of chestnut-backed chickadees above the trees, their quick whistling chirps filling the air above the students' voices.

"And here in this corner is the infamous Dr. Wright," a deep baritone announced from a bench a short way away.

Whirling to her right, she smiled. "Hey, Thomas, I've been trying to find time to call you. Do you believe all this?" Deborah sat down next to him and pulled out a tuna sandwich wrapped in plastic.

Tall and muscular, Dr. Thomas Bonheur had been a quarterback in the National Football League before becoming an anthropologist. He had square ears that stuck out under his shoulder-length dreadlocks. A thin chinstrap beard graced his jaw. His eyes took in everything around him. He and Deborah were long-time friends, both having been at the university for almost thirty years.

"It's crazy," Thomas said, finishing a vegetarian burrito. The afternoon sun played across his light brown skin. "What's Stephen say about the likelihood of the 'big one' hitting Berkeley soon?"

"He's at UCI studying the USGS databases." She shifted uneasily. "What's the word? Think we're going to survive lunch?"

"Lunch, yes," he nodded, "dinner more problematic. How's your sandwich?"

She cleared her throat. "I love my tuna. Added a new spice mix." Taking a bite, she looked at the booths. "I've never seen anything like this."

"I've always said you travel in limited circles, my dear."

"Well, I'm sorry, Mr. Hall of Famer, we don't usually hobnob with the governor." Deborah rolled her eyes.

"Only when you come to visit us," he retorted. Thomas's wife was Susan Bonheur, the Senator from California. Deborah had known her since elementary school. Thomas continued, "So, you were going to call. Committee stuff?" For the last year, they worked together on the Committee on Classroom Policy and Management.

She kept eating. "My limited circles are expanding. I need your help."

He stopped in mid-bite. "Stephen?"

"No, it's something even deeper. It's Rachel."

He looked at her. "Well, it's about time."

"Maybe for you it's about time." She related what Rachel had told her and what happened at the synagogue.

A biology student on a skateboard handed them a flyer. "Genetically-engineered corn and soybeans are linked to cancer."

She looked at the yellow piece of paper. "I heard about this."

"Hello, Dr. Wright. Read it and you'll never eat corn again." He skated on handing out more flyers.

"Everybody's got flyers." Thomas leaned over to pick up two that were blowing on the ground. "Rachel knows how you feel."

"What do you mean? I accept her homosexuality."

He wiped his stubbled beard and sat up. "Right. They're called gay and lesbian."

Deborah shrugged. "I just don't understand this homo—gayness thing. She used to date men."

"Look around you. Look at all these kids."

There were students everywhere, standing at the booths, talking with the ones passing out flyers. They had on jeans and shorts of every color, shirts and blouses with textures of silk, cotton, suede. Some had their hair in ponytails or short cuts. Some had glasses, some didn't. Thomas said, "They're all different. Some are straight, some are gay, some want to be engineers or psychologists. They're all over the place racially—white, Asian, black, Latino, Native American. They came to Berkeley to prepare for their lives. They all want jobs in order to participate and to contribute to society. What right do you have to judge them for who they are?"

Deborah stared at the students. A girl wearing blue shoes reminded her of the crayon drawing on Rachel's refrigerator. She frowned. "But none of them is my daughter. There's such a taboo against it."

"A taboo from the Bible—something you've told me you don't believe in."

"I'm not religious." She stiffened.

His white teeth flashed as he broke out in a belly laugh. "Your whole body is infected by religion. What you resist persists."

"What's that supposed to mean?" She shot him a look, folding the plastic wrapper from her sandwich.

"Just because you've turned your back on religion, doesn't mean it's gone out of your life. You know," he said, shaking his head, "there used to be laws about interracial couples marrying."

Deborah sucked in her breath. "Are you seriously equating racism with thinking being gay is wrong?"

He crumbled up his lunch bag. "It's called homophobia, and aren't they both prejudice? It's bullshit that religion has decided to co-opt feelings." Thomas took the flyers and the remnants of their lunches, stood up, and threw them away into trash receptacles, separating the recyclables. He wiped his face again.

Deborah called after him, "That's your learned scientific opinion?"

He turned and faced her. "You've got a choice. Kiss your daughter goodbye like you have your marriage or try to salvage your relationship with her. This is who she is, my dear. Do you really think anyone has control over who they're attracted to? If people would stop for one second and just think about it, they'd see it. When you're attracted to someone, don't you just feel it? You don't consciously decide it. Come on, you think birds have control over their biology?"

She stood up and gathered her travel bag. "We aren't birds."

He walked toward her. "No, from what I've learned from your lectures, birds are a lot smarter than we are. They don't get caught up in judgment. They feed their young, protect their homes, call out to their mates."

"Sing out. Calls are different." Deborah frowned.

"You know what I mean. Let's walk. I've got to prep for class."

She pulled a small bottle of hand sanitizer from her bag and cleaned her hands. His words felt stark and breathed into her ache of loneliness.

A white student with brown curly hair in a pink tank top stepped in front of them. "It's going to happen! A shift in the magnetic poles. These natural disasters are revving up the planet!" She handed Deborah a little compass. "Take this."

Thomas leaned over. "Speaking of intelligence, nut cases are always predicting a shift in the magnetic poles."

"Really." Shrugging, Deborah looked at the toy compass. She put it in her travel bag along with the sanitizer. "They say somehow it will happen—they never explain how—and that it will destroy humanity. I want to know why it will destroy us. Wreak havoc, yes—like mess up birds' compasses—but destroy us?"

"Let's go through here." Thomas cut between two booths, holding onto her arm to make sure she was safe. "A lot of other things will destroy us first." He let go.

They passed by an earthquake safety consortium. Deborah nodded. "This threat's more likely here near the Bay." Students and faculty jostled them trying to get information about tsunamis. She remembered driving to Lincoln Park the morning the tsunami hit the California coast from the Tohoku 9.0 earthquake. After traveling 9,000 kilometers from Japan, the ripples came into the bay steady like a long washboard. The persistence of it astounded Deborah. The day was only marred by the fight she had with Stephen.

The drumming of the downy woodpecker brought Deborah to the present. She had never seen so many organizations. The sign in front of her pointed out that genetically-engineered food does away with the need for pesticides. "It's disease-resistant and reduces the cost to market," the company rep said. He had black hair and a square jaw.

Deborah cocked her head. "Someone just told us it was bad."

"Perfectly safe to eat," he smiled broadly. "There's no unmanipulated evidence to the contrary. We're world-wide."

Thomas walked ahead and Deborah limped quickly to catch up to him. "So what do you suggest I do about Rachel?" They passed a non-profit booth about the adverse health effects of electromagnetic waves from cell phone towers and smart meters. It made no sense to her. Cell phones were everywhere.

Thomas shook his head. "Look at homosexuality through the eyes of an anthropologist, not with the hammer of religion. Can you?"

She stopped in mid-step and stared at him. The excited hoarse call of the downy woodpecker punctuated the air.

A short middle-aged white man in beige slacks and a polo shirt thrust another flyer into her hands. "Don't listen to them. We need a smart energy grid. Don't you want reduced costs and independence from imported energy?" He did a double take when he saw Thomas. "Aren't you Thomas Bonheur?"

Thomas nodded.

"I used to watch you play football all the time. You were great."

"Thanks, man." Thomas kept walking.

Deborah tried to keep up and called after him, "What does that mean?"

An Indian student with black-rimmed glasses came by wearing a T-shirt with a picture of a car belching smoke that had a big X through it. "We can't survive with non-sustainable behavior." He tried to hand Deborah a flyer. "Dr. Wright? Dr. Wright? Here read this. Coal-fired power plants generate sulfur dioxide and CO_2 into our atmosphere."

"What?" Deborah stared at his T-shirt. *Religion is a hammer,* she thought. *Don't I know it.* She caught up with Thomas. "This is all crazy. Maybe we should use coal-fired automobiles instead. Get away from oil then. Tell me how you would--"

"It's not a laughing matter," Thomas burst out at her. "Talk about destruction, you think all these things aren't catching up with us?"

Deborah tried to wave it all away. "But really, after Earth Day, all this will fold up as something else takes over, like graduation."

He shot her a look. "You're lucky to be right in the middle of it with the Capistrano project."

"I've dropped the cliff swallows problem."

He stopped and spun around. "Are you serious?"

"I can't afford to—"

"You're afraid for your scientific reputation? Come on, Deborah. Things are screwed up on this planet and you've got an opportunity to help figure it out." He gestured forcefully. "Look around you, this isn't going away."

Bewildered, she glanced toward the eucalyptus trees. The woodpecker's mate responded with a whiny call. "What, you think all the birds are going to start dying now?"

"Let's name it for what it is. Greed."

"Greed?" she raised an eyebrow. "Sure, people are greedy. We want the best for our daughters—our children. Besides, with a large population, you have to protect yourself more."

They stood in front of a non-profit consortium on human rights. "Altruistic greed, that's okay. Even making sure you have enough is okay." He grabbed a flyer from a young *latina* with long hair wearing a striped sweater, and he thrust it at Deborah. "It's this type of thinking that's symptomatic of everything." The flyer had a news report about toxic waste being dumped in a city in Africa. "The company didn't want to pay the extra charges to dispose of it correctly in Europe, so they dumped 500 metric tons of poison on unsuspecting people in Africa. And then claimed it would only cause flu-like symptoms." He spat out the words.

"Why would a company do that?"

"Exactly. Because they can. Companies are doing whatever they want. The company's board swore it wasn't their fault." The flyer listed the dangers of toxic waste in ash and sludge. "Who gives permission to any corporation to create such pollution?" He pulled the flyer out of her hands and flipped it around to the other side. "And look at this. Our oceans are not vast toilets. Just because you can do something, doesn't mean you should. What type of thinking believes dumping 180 million tons of mercury, arsenic, and lead into the ocean each year won't cause harm to us? 180 million tons of mine waste each year!"

"It's why I drink bottled water." She started walking. "Speaking of, the Vice Provost wants the committee's next report to recommend earthquake kits in every classroom. Did you see his note?"

"Come on, you're a biologist." He ignored her question.

"I know the effect it's had on water birds, sure. Mercury turns toxic in water. The fish eat the zooplankton and the birds eat the fish. Lots of dead birds. A billion birds--"

"And poisonous fish in our lunches and dinners, leading to sick people and dead kids. Didn't you just eat a tuna fish sandwich? Deborah, you can't stay naïve anymore. They are raping the land and water with their pollution."

Deborah stopped as if she had hit a wall. The band started a drumline beat that reverberated against the trees and buildings. She thought about the dead bird she had recorded, the beauty of its song. She also thought of the risks staying on the project. "But Brady said it wasn't pollution killing off the swallows."

Thomas came up next to her. "Have they checked all the pollutants?"

"I don't know. Thomas, they'll figure it out. The project doesn't need me."

He glared at her. "You chicken. What about the carbon accumulating in our atmosphere?"

Deborah looked puzzled. "Carbon isn't affecting swallows. They breathe in oxygen, breathe out carbon dioxide like we all do."

Thomas snorted. "You know my research area is the ancient Pueblo Indians—the Anasazi—in New Mexico. They had to abandon their settlements because of a change in the climate. Drought and lost resources."

The band drumline got louder. She stared at Thomas and shouted, "Are you saying climate change is affecting the swallows?"

He started walking again, raising his voice, "I'm saying you're nuts if you walk away from this problem just because some people think you screwed up. Come on, you've got to go for this. Start right here. You've got a great opportunity to talk to companies and to the non-profits. They'll help you find out what's going on." The drumline hit a crescendo with a big roar.

"What do you mean?"

Thomas pointed to the right. "Gotta go. Remember, civilizations collapse. It's happened before. It'll happen again." He turned, taking Campanile Way on toward Kroeber Hall where the Department of Anthropology was located.

Deborah watched his retreating form, her forehead furrowed in confusion. *Who's going to tell me what's going on?* She started walking back toward her office.

"It may be clean energy, but the 51,000 tons of spent nuclear fuel isn't." A short multiracial blonde with red glasses pushed a flyer toward her. "The waste is a ticking time-bomb."

"Even San Onofre? Isn't it closed?"

"So what? Their 4,000 tons are going to sit right there on a fault for decades. What's going to happen to people nearby when there's an earthquake?"

A cold sensation gripped Deborah's heart. *Rachel lives there.*

Next to her stood another non-profit booth. The sign in front of it said, "Our 10,000-year picnic is over." A white man with a flat nose, neatly clipped mustache, and goatee smiled at Deborah. "It's not like we have another planet in our back pockets, is it?"

Deborah smiled slightly. "You make it sound serious. I'm not sure I believe in climate change."

"We're even. I don't believe in gravity."

"Huh? Of course there's gravity." Deborah was taken aback.

"I stack papers on my desk and they don't fall. So much for gravity."

She stared at him, trying to figure out if he was for real.

"But you know, science isn't religion. When it comes to climate change, it doesn't matter what you believe, only how you act." He handed her a flyer. "It's been known since 1896 that increased carbon dioxide in the atmosphere raises the surface temperature of the planet."

"It has?" Her eyes went wide.

He nodded. "That's verifiable science. Whether you believe it or not. So, tell me, how do you feel when your temperature rises a few degrees?"

She stared at the colorful graphs on the flyer. "Not well."

He pointed to one of them which showed redder and redder temperatures. "A 3.6 degree Fahrenheit rise will seriously affect our lives. And we're about forty percent there—already starting to lose resources like coast land, snow packs, and forests."

Her neck started to tingle as she backed away. *It's like what Thomas had said about the ancient Pueblo Indians.*

The man called after her. "There are consequences to our behavior. Hope you don't float off the Earth."

She waved at him, putting the flyer in her bag as she walked on.

Another booth talked about a giant whirlpool in the North Pacific. Deborah grabbed a flyer that described how sea birds fed on the millions of tons of plastic decomposing in the ocean. Walking while reading about the dying albatrosses, she bumped into an older woman standing in front of her. "Oh, sorry."

The woman looked like a flower child from the Sixties with beads and a long paisley skirt. Feathers and purple and yellow flowers graced her long gray hair. Mint green dominated her peasant blouse. Her eyes danced into a smile. "Here." She handed Deborah a pendant.

Dangling from a thin braided cord, a small round, wooden case was covered with strange markings and symbols interspersed with flowers and birds. She had never seen anything like it.

The woman took one of the yellow flowers from her hair and twirled it. "What am I?"

"You mean the flower? Isn't it a dandelion?"

Putting the flower inside the wooden case, she closed it. "Wear this." Then she placed the pendant's sisal cord over Deborah's head. "And think about it."

Deborah glanced down at the pendant hanging from her neck. It wasn't a toy like the compass. "I can't take this…" She raised her eyes, but the woman was gone. Scanning the area, Deborah couldn't see her. She stared at the pendant. There were strange words written on the back of it.

Shrugging, Deborah found herself in front of a booth from a multinational corporation with signs saying, "Clean, affordable energy." Men wearing sky blue shirts with corporate ties and carrying clipboards were talking to students. Deborah heard one say, "Our program to transform ethane into plastics is creating high paying jobs." Students were signing up and looking at flyers with interest.

One of the company reps came up to Deborah. He had a high white forehead and a big smile. "We're developing hydrocarbon fuels that maximize energy content, designing lithium-ion battery packs for the next-generation of electric vehicles, and converting municipal solid waste into renewable energy."

His words assuaged her growing fear. "That sounds great. But aren't some of these non-profits upset by what your company does?"

He laughed and handed her a green and white brochure. It explained how a smart grid infrastructure will maximize energy efficiency and how the company is extracting natural gas and oil from shale formations. "Look, we're even building photovoltaic cells for powering houses and buildings. Two-thirds of houses in the US predate modern energy codes. Wouldn't you like a net-zero energy home?" He pointed to a picture of a house with special shingles on it. "No more utility bills."

It seemed too good to be true. She tried to remember what Thomas had said. "What about the carbon problem? Does it affect birds?"

"It affects everyone. But our insulation materials reduce emissions of greenhouse gases like CO_2. We've got a CO_2 capture technology for coal-fired boilers and electric power plants. And we're helping to build high temperature, gas-cooled nuclear reactors which is a CO_2 emission-free energy supply." He opened the tri-fold brochure to show her graphical images.

This sounded plausible, all ways to get rid of the belching smoke. "What's the government think of your products and services?"

He nodded. "Good question. We work closely with the Department of Energy doing joint programs and pilot studies." He thrust the clipboard in front of her. "Would you care to sign up to learn more?"

"Not at the moment." Deborah put the brochure in her travel bag.

"Well, you know how to find us. Don't you worry—free enterprise capitalism will solve these global problems. We're right in the thick of coming up with solutions." He turned to talk to others.

She smiled staring at the utopian vision created at his booth. It felt like solutions to what everyone else was worrying about. But striding on, she realized there were too many contradictions.

She walked past a booth describing large-scale reengineering of the weather. That sounded incomprehensible. How could anyone control the weather? The person at the booth had to be another nut case, like the woman talking about the shift in the magnetic poles.

Deborah looked out at the sea of white booths, hearing voices blur into a hollow echo. The band played Berkeley's "Big C" fight song. She felt she had just walked through a funhouse in an amusement park where everything distorts. The non-profits said one thing, the corporations another. It felt like a game show where you have a choice—what's behind door number 1, 2 or 3. *That's what Thomas meant.* There was no way to know who was helping and who was being greedy. She stood stunned. All the colors of clothes and skin and trees vibrated as she saw that the problem of the environment was more extensive than she had believed. She rubbed her temples. *No wonder the swallows are dying. It could be from any and all the activities that people are doing as civilization tries to compete and cooperate into survival.* The swallow's song gave her a clue to something going on. What it was, though, she had no idea.

As Deborah reached West Circle, she heard another voice, louder than the gauntlet she had just escaped from.

"God has said 'enough is enough!' " A large man wearing a black jacket and white shirt on a platform spoke into a microphone. "Yes, our environment is under siege. When will it stop? Who can say? But these things just don't happen. There is a reason for everything. God is sending us a message—loud and clear. Our Creator knows what's right, and evil thinking has taken over our society."

At first, Deborah thought he was expanding on what Thomas had said about corporate greed. Students were standing and sitting on the grass listening.

"Marriage rates are at an all-time low. Our children need stable families. Marriage is a faithful, exclusive life-long union between one man and one woman. Anything else is an abomination to God, and He is making His views known loud and clear. We must stamp out this scourge or else we all will die!"

Deborah sucked in her breath, realizing this was the group that had caused the ruckus in her classroom. What had the students called them? *The black suits.*

A student near Deborah yelled out. "What about Masters and Johnson? What about Kinsey?" Deborah gave him a thumbs-up, pegging him as a psychology student. She stared at her own thumb.

The speaker countered, "What did they know! Scientists manipulate data. How do you think the scientific method works? Form a hypothesis and look for supporting evidence. If you believe homosexuality is normal, you'll find people to support your claim. Of course, you won't find children which is God's purpose for marriage."

The psychology student responded. "It's part of human experience. People don't wake up one day and decide to be gay."

Someone else chimed in, "Yeah, like a cool accessory lifestyle app."

A big male student in shorts standing next to Deborah pulled at his glasses. "I'm putting on a new pair of sunglasses. I think I'll like men today." Everyone around laughed.

Deborah stared at his glasses, remembering her own attraction to Stephen. It had felt as natural as putting on a pair of glasses.

Out of the crowd, someone yelled, "Hey, let the guy speak."

Mr. Black Suit continued, "Just because something is part of human experience, it doesn't make it right or moral. Scientists say bonobo chimpanzees are bisexual and therefore that makes it all right for humans. What morality does a chimpanzee know? We aren't chimpanzees. Sure, we have natural instincts but we have so much more. That's what separates us from the animals. We have codes to live by—the Ten Commandments. People not living by God's laws are making God angry indeed! 'And God said unto Noah, the end of all flesh is come before me; I will destroy them with the Earth.' What is happening today is a repeat of the past! God is retaliating for our keeping these sinners in our midst!"

Deborah wrenched her head around in disbelief. *He's blaming Rachel for these natural disasters. And using the Bible to do so.* Knowing as much about the Ten Commandments as anyone else, Deborah yelled, "Oh, good, lay down the requirements for obeying a monotheistic code, and then claim it as the law."

"It is the Law!"

Her eyes blazed. "The commandment says 'Thou shalt not kill' but Christians and Jews go off to war. Religious leaders condone it because the commandment makes a distinction between murder and killing. That's not morality, that's hypocrisy."

"I'll tell you what's not moral. Choosing to be homosexual isn't moral."

Deborah could feel sweat on the back of her neck. Students around her motioned to her to continue. She raised her voice. "Religion and psychology have tried to stamp it out but failed. Gay people aren't going away and you have no proof that they're the cause of the natural disasters!"

People started cheering. The speaker made a quick motion to the other black suits. "The Bible is quite clear. In Leviticus, homosexuality is an abomination. In 1 Corinthians, homosexuals will not inherit the kingdom of God. Our country's laws are made by God-fearing lawmakers. We live in a Christian state and if you don't abide by the laws, God will take revenge as He has done in the past!"

Deborah saw four men walking toward her, anger scrawled across their faces. She blew out her breath, looking around to see if campus police were nearby. Two white male students jumped up to stand in front of her.

"What the hell is going on," she mumbled. The two students turned to face the angry suits. Suddenly, someone grabbed her from behind. "Hey!" She felt herself being pulled away by two strong hands. As she tried to fight off her abductor, the two students pounced on him. They yelled, their voices mixing with everyone else. Her travel bag went flying. The students punched whoever it was, trying to make him release Deborah.

"Let go of me," a deep voice boomed.

Deborah fought for balance but was pushed to the ground. Falling back, she saw the man scrambling to extract himself from the students. One was on top of him, the other pulling him back at his waist. "Stop," she screamed. "He's a professor at this university."

The students stopped, letting go of the black man. One of them said, "Dr. Bonheur! We thought you were hurting this professor."

Thomas raised himself to his full height, brushing his pants off. "I'm all right." He reached toward Deborah. "Let's get out of here."

One of the students retrieved her bag and journal. The other student helped Deborah up. "Are you both okay? We're really sorry."

Thomas straightened his tie and jacket. "You protected her from those nutcases. Just get to class." He steered Deborah away as the two students took off down Wickson Road.

"You okay?" Deborah brushed her slacks and green blouse off, looking for campus security. "We should find someone…"

"Forget it," he said too quickly. "You know what it's like."

"But everyone even knows who you are. It isn't right to just…"

"I said forget it," Thomas snapped. He ran his hands over his dreadlocks. "You've lived with Stephen over thirty years. You don't protect him, do you? Racism defines this country, you know that. Besides, those students had a good lesson. Lots of ways to teach other than in the classroom." He started walking. "They can tell everyone they tackled a Hall-of-Fame quarterback. Don't you try to protect me."

She followed him. "But it's okay for you to try to protect me?"

He smiled. "That's different. I don't want you to add an arrest record to your growing infractions against our esteemed university."

"Me, arrested? I'm too in control."

He continued walking. "If that turned uglier, it could have been in the cards," Thomas said, avoiding bumping into people.

As best she could, Deborah quickened her pace to keep up with him. "I thought you were prepping for a class. Why did you come back?"

"You didn't answer my last question about Rachel."

She grabbed his arm. "Maybe you're right. I think I'm ready to learn, oh doctor anthropologist."

He stopped. "Good. I'll have to figure out where we can go for a lesson."

"What, like a bar on Castro Street?" She let go of him.

He smiled. "Nope, we're way beyond Gay 101." He jogged off to his office, looking around as he did.

Chapter 8

*"Come wander quietly and listen to the wind,
Come near and listen to the sky,
Come walking high above the rolling of the sea
And watch the swallows as they fly."*
                    - Richard Fariña

WORLD NEWS – APRIL 16
*Oil Pipeline Bursts in Suburban Area
Cancer Alley Produces a Quarter of U.S. Petrochemicals
Tropical Diseases Spread North*

"BRING THE RAX-1000 over here." Deborah pointed to where it sat in her office. "Or what did you call it?"

Michael walked to the bookshelf. "The Raz!"

"Oh, right." She smiled, charged up.

Jeff moved the pile of books from the conference table to make space. Trying to place them on the credenza, he dropped them. "Sorry, Dr. Wright. What can I say," he grinned, "I'm a klutz."

"Dude, no, you're not." Michael put the machine on the table and helped him pick up the books.

"It's all right, Jeff, I'm a klutz, too." Deborah unlocked the cover. "This experiment will get rid of an unknown."

"Will it work?" Michael sat down to take notes.

"We have to rule out the possibility. That's the process of science." Deborah explained the setup, almost giddy. "Be sure to open the cover. I talked to Sam Dadich and he's as surprised as I am about the recording. He hasn't heard anything like it."

Jeff helped with the cover. Then he reached into his jeans pocket and placed some sort of medium-sized seashell next to his notebook.

Deborah continued, "Sam wanted to know if I'm going to test other birds. I told him the project's on hold. But we'll at least test the library recordings."

"And we're helping?" Michael's eyes widened. "Cool."

A knock sounded on the door frame. "Am I interrupting?" Dean Harvey Milhouse stood looking at them. A balding white man with a thin Roman nose, he had a way of compensating for his short height by entering a room like a dog checking out scents.

"Hello, Dean Milhouse." Deborah smiled, quickly slamming close her notebook. "Office hours, semester almost over, you know."

The Dean planted himself in the middle of the room. "Dr. Wright, did you get into some sort of altercation at West Circle yesterday?"

Her face froze and she cursed under her breath as the two students looked at her. "That's an exaggeration."

"Is this the RAX-1000?" He peered at the machine's controls.

She closed her eyes for a second. "Are you aware—" she hesitated and rubbed her forehead, weighing what to say. Thomas's words echoed in her head about not protecting him. "It was just a short shouting match with that group at the Fair."

He shook his head. "My algorithms would have worked just as well as fractal processing." He reached to touch the controls.

She snapped at him. "I've told you, Dan made the final decision. I'm working with my students here…"

"But it's your machine." He straightened, walking toward the door. "We don't appreciate any biases in our scientific community."

Jeff interrupted, "Dr. Milhouse, I'd be glad to do an analysis to compare the algorithms."

Milhouse turned. "Who are you?"

"Jeff Hodgdon, first-year undergraduate engineering student."

"Where are you from?" Milhouse stared at his braid.

"Oneida, New York. I'm here on a scholarship. I could do a complete Fourier analysis."

Milhouse turned away. "We're role models, Dr. Wright. That's why I'm very glad you dropped that Capistrano project. In your tenuous situation, it would be professional suicide to continue on it. Especially if you started doing field work. We don't want any controversy in our academic setting. Just excellent science."

She glared at him. "Then why's that black suit group on campus?"

The Dean jammed his hands into his pockets. "What? Well, because, uh, students have to learn all sides of the issues." He walked out.

Deborah stared at her notebook. "Where were we?"

Michael looked at her. "We were about to review some recordings for the project the Dean thinks you dropped."

Furrows stretched across her forehead. "Right. It's just a small test. Barry will finish this as part of his doctoral research."

Michael looked disappointed.

"Okay, okay. Better shut the door. I'm sure I can convince him to take on a helper. Graduate students need to sleep once in a while." Michael closed the office door.

Holding his head, Jeff peered at the machine. "What's the procedure for recording?"

Deborah asked, "Are you okay?"

"It's just a headache. It'll go away. I took some meds."

"Good." She opened the drawer in the RAX-1000. "You have to make sure the memory cards are prepared, like this." Pulling out the cards, she inserted them into the slot. "Let's play one of the recordings." She nodded to Michael to touch the ANALYZE button. She set the volume to low. The sound of birds singing filled the room. Like in Capistrano, the semantic processor added its slower, more elongated voice. After a few minutes, Deborah stopped the recording. She touched another button and the printer spewed out the results.

"What did you hear?" Jeff asked.

"What did *you* hear?" She shot back at him.

He played with the seashell. "Sounded like a bird, then it sounded really slowed down."

"Let's look." Deborah pulled off the printout and pointed. "Here's the normal vocalization."

Michael's eyes were alive with excitement. "Is the tune there?"

"Let's see if we can find the waveform of a tune."

They poured over the printout. Michael shook his head. "No, I don't see anything like that."

"Right. Let's try the others. You both run them." She smiled, watching the two students follow the procedures. Michael did most of the work while Jeff tried to help. She glanced at the door a few times, worried the Dean might return.

When done, Jeff said, "We didn't find anything. No results."

Deborah shook her head. "Let's reword that. Negative results are just as valid as positive results. We're eliminating unknowns. And it supports my hypothesis—the library recordings do not contain the tune. Fractal modulation won't help them."

Michael made some notes. "Our results don't rule out other species or individuals carrying the song."

Deborah's neck tensed up. "Right. But we do know that only the RAX-1000 will provide us with the measurements. So, I guess that's that."

Jeff turned the seashell around and held his head tilted. "Can we hear the Capistrano recording?"

Deborah hadn't listened to it since she recorded it. "Huh? Sure." She sorted through the memory cards, inserted one, and hit PLAY. When she touched ANALYZE, the swallow's voice slowed down. And then the song filled the office. Closing her eyes, she was brought back to Capistrano—the smell of the sage, the dying birds, and the feel of standing close to Stephen.

Michael swallowed hard. "That's amazing. It's not like the others."

Jeff sat up. "And it doesn't sound like a malfunction."

"I know." Deborah stared at the machine. There was something about the song but she couldn't put her finger on it.

🕊 🕊

WORLD NEWS – APRIL 21
Massive Gulf Oil Spill
Shrimp and Crabs Deformed from Oil
Sink Holes Caused by Injection Mining
Fire Season Starting Earlier Than in Past

The Iron Horse Used Bookstore and Café squeezed between two colorful Victorian houses on Ashbury Street in San Francisco. On the street, a homeless man in a frayed raincoat looked like he was still drugged out from the Sixties. Posters were taped to the large front window. A schedule for the upcoming months showed the performances of unknown-local artists, but also a few nationally-known singers. Rich coffee smells enticed Deborah as she followed Thomas into the store. She was excited to be solving Rachel's problem.

High bookcases displayed rows of books, almost too many to comprehend. At the rear, chairs crammed around a makeshift stage. On thick barnboard walls, yellowed newspaper clippings flaunted youthful faces of folksingers like Bob Dylan, Phil Ochs, and Joan Baez. The ambiance felt like a sponge—if a giant hand compressed it, out would tumble years of folk music history.

It reminded Deborah of the Green Parrot Café in New York in the Sixties. When she attended Stern College of Yeshiva University, she'd nurse virgin tequila sunrises in a dark corner and listen to bearded poets rant protest songs, grateful to be away from her father's orthodoxy. He believed girls were put on this Earth to have babies and cook dinner for their husbands, and he spent her childhood trying to convince her of that. Her neck felt hot at the memory.

Thomas had picked wisely. The Iron Horse had all the ingredients for an answer—a large gay section mixed in with religion, poetry, and philosophy. Front counters displayed books about earthquake preparedness. The next day being actual Earth Day heightened awarenesses and the store was doing a brisk business.

They waited in line for coffee. People were talking about the ongoing saga of yet another huge oil spill in the Gulf of Mexico. Conversations could be heard about the ill-effects of the oil on marine life and huge sinkholes growing in Louisiana—the result of drilling. There was mention of major earthquakes occurring on every continent and the wildfires already burning across Southern California a month ahead of schedule.

After settling on a Kenyan coffee made with AA graded beans, Deborah and Thomas moved away from the bustle. He had said there was a particular book he wanted to find and they headed for the philosophical sciences.

Animated like a helium balloon, Deborah looked at the rows of books and the small green cardboard plaques labeling different sections. She smiled and turned to Thomas. "Where does one start in order to prove same-sex love is moral?"

"You can't."

She walked ahead of him and stopped, almost spilling her coffee. "What? Ha, ha, very funny." She began walking again. "Let's find that book. It'll show the Rabbi he's wrong." She took a sip of the dark liquid, liking the medium dark roast. It tasted almost chocolaty, with a hint of some nut.

Thomas stayed still. "We can't change the Rabbi's mind."

"You're not serious." She turned back to him.

"Look, my dear," Thomas rested his cup on one of the shelves, "the Rabbi stacked the deck against you. You can't prove homosexuality is moral against divine command. To be God-like, you follow God's law by adhering to a set of rules which are all laid out in the Bible, written by God."

Deborah sucked in her breath and leaned against another bookcase. Her ears pounded. She heard the conversations about earthquakes and oil spills merging with Thomas's stacked deck. In the inner recesses of her brain, she could hear her father yelling at her in Hebrew and Yiddish that she must learn the duties of a woman.

A man in his late 40s came around the corner and did a double take. "Aren't you Thomas Bonheur, the football player?"

Thomas nodded. "Ex-football player."

The man smiled broadly. "Wow. Ex? You're not just an ex. You were great. Do you still wear your gold jacket?"

"Just when I go visit my bust at the Hall of Fame." Thomas laughed. He autographed a flyer for the man and then picked up his coffee and started walking.

Deborah unfroze her body and caught up with him. Her voice raised a notch. "Thomas, two weeks ago you were telling me homosexuality is okay because birds don't have control over their biology. Now you're telling me it's not okay?"

He scanned book titles. "By the Rabbi's standards, you can't prove being gay is moral. Rabbis have gone over the Bible's admonishments for thousands of years, slicing and dicing them all which way to Jupiter. By definition, it's pretty clear—it's an abomination." Thomas stopped and faced her. "And you know it. I heard what you said to those black suits on campus. 'Lay down the requirements for obeying a monotheistic code, and then claim it as the law.'"

Deborah swallowed hard. *That's how it had felt growing up.* All those commandments the religion required her to follow—what to eat, when to eat, what to wear, how to believe. It was the law, firm and real. *But someone had invented it for their own reasons.* She glared at her cup and took another sip of coffee. "Then what are we doing here?"

"Before you can have a real conversation with the Rabbi, you're the one whose mind had to change. I had to first convince you Rachel is moral and that prejudice is insidious."

Deborah's eyes went wide and blazed at him. "I'm not prejudiced."

Thomas laughed, walking. "Sure you are. I am too. It's too ingrained into our culture for anyone not to be. It's everywhere. Look, there's even prejudice against lefties like you." He turned back. "And too many ways to justify prejudice. You know this. You're white, you're married to a black man. And you have an interracial lesbian daughter."

She stomped after him into the Christianity section. "It's not the same thing."

"What you resist persists." He laughed harder and then took a big gulp of his coffee. "This is good stuff."

Deborah felt like she was being slammed up against a brick wall. How could Thomas do this to her? She wasn't going to be able to prove anything to the Rabbi. Cursing under her breath, she remembered his ridiculous eyebrows. *He'll make the girls leave the synagogue and they'll lose their community.* She thought back to Rachel's high school graduation. An ornithology conference was scheduled that same week in Boston. When Deborah had returned from the conference, Rachel tried to act as if everything was fine but she couldn't hide her anger.

Was that where the chasm began? Deborah almost choked on her coffee. She looked around for Thomas. Finding him in the gay section, she frowned. "So there's no hope?"

He drank the last of his coffee. "There's a small possibility. Religions based on a book follow morals based on a set of rules. They've fought and argued over the interpretation of these rules for thousands of years. Protestant churches broke with Catholicism because its rules were too strict. Same with the Reform and Conservative movements of Judaism. Which means there are other moral ethics and also a historical development of secular moral codes—like virtue ethics based on character. Aristotle defined that as the unity of intuitive reason, scientific knowledge, and acting for the good of humanity."

Small lights turned on along the bookshelves. Deborah jumped on what he said. "So let's tell the Rabbi that. That sounds moral." She took his empty cup and put hers inside it.

THE SWALLOW AND THE NIGHTINGALE

Thomas paced in the narrow aisle. "You think he isn't aware of it? Some Orthodox rabbis are already into virtue ethics, seeing the purpose of Jewish ethics as creating a holy person, someone imitating God. What are you going to do? Study Kant, Mills, St. Augustine? Come on, you'll need a Ph.D. in philosophy to figure it out. You think it hasn't been tried? And this stuff is evolving. People used to just worry about how to be in large groups, but then they had to figure out conduct between individuals. Hence things like the Hammurabi Code and the Bible. Someday we'll be legally responsible for modifying the characteristics of others for the preservation of the species, but we're still too immature to handle that concept."

Deborah could barely breathe as he dashed her hopes. She felt like she was in The Twilight Zone. "Thomas, you're making no sense."

He stepped close to her. "Exactly. Morality and ethics are not something you want to mess with. You're a scientist. You don't even understand that science separated itself from ethics and let religion take it over. We need to find a way for you to argue from your strengths, like find some weakness in his argument."

The lights dimmed. "What's going on?" Deborah looked around, annoyed.

Thomas pointed to a sign. 'Elizabeth Rafferty, Folksinger.' They were standing in a section not far from the stage area. About twenty white plastic chairs were set up around it. "Wonder what Sixties history Ms. Rafferty will retro up." He smirked, still searching the shelves.

Deborah felt for the pendant around her neck. She had decided to keep it because it had the look and feel of the flower power of the Sixties. "Find a weakness? How do I do that?" Her eyebrows raised.

"Here's a lesson on culture. Did you know Socrates was bisexual? All the elite males in classical Greece practiced bisexuality. It was an acceptable aspect of society. Part of the male bonding ritual. Initiate younger males while still being married to a woman. But then," he stopped for a second, "Greek women were second-class citizens without the right to vote. And they called that democracy."

An older woman with long hair flowing down her back walked up to the microphone and started strumming her guitar. She looked vaguely familiar to Deborah.

Deborah took another sip from her coffee and then whispered to him, "What's that have to do with science?"

Using the glow from the small lights along the shelves, Thomas searched along the top row. He whispered loudly, "Across cultures and throughout time, human kinship relationships have been all over the place. There's never been an exclusively heterosexual institution."

"There hasn't?" Her eyes went wide. "They make it sound like homosexuality is some modern curse." She tried to stay close to him so as to keep her voice down.

"They like to argue that sexuality exists to propagate a species. But does it? If so, then pair bonds would have dozens of kids. Sexuality has to exist for a reason beyond propagation."

Deborah's eyes narrowed, connecting the dots to Rachel.

Thomas continued, "Sexual love strengthens pair bonding."

"Wait, not so fast, let me write this down." She put down her cup and pulled out her journal and a pen.

"Have you read *The Naked Ape*? Desmond Morris placed human behavior into the context of evolution. Even if his conclusions are suspect, it's worth reading."

Deborah stared at the words she had just written down. It made perfect sense. Sexuality had to evolve along with everything else. Evolution moves in mysterious paths. She had read that sparrows in the Galapagos Islands began making softer shells in response to climate change. So sparrows with softer shells proliferated. Why not homosexuality being nature's way to ensure that childless adults will be around to help human parents in their enormous eighteen year burden of nurturing a child into survival competency? Wouldn't every parent love to have an extra single adult around to help in their children's upbringing? Especially one with a car. She drank the last of her coffee and threw away both cups. After cleaning her hands with her sanitizer, she put her journal back in her bag.

Thomas called out, "Hey, we're in luck! I found it."

She excitedly limped to where he was while nearby bookstore patrons glared at him.

Thomas shot them a look and whispered loudly, "They won't dare shush me. The perks of being big and black, even if I am dressed correctly." He tossed his dreadlocks like a crown.

It's so true, she thought. She remembered being impressed by how sharp a dresser Stephen was when they first met. He stayed up with the styles. It wasn't until five years into their marriage she began to understand why he did it. He even used to scrunch down, in order to appear less threatening. She was glad he stopped doing that.

Someone else came by for an autograph.

Thomas turned back toward Deborah. "I should have remembered. The author's name is Boswell. It's called *Same-Sex Unions in the Early Christian Church*." He flipped it open. "Earlier cultures used to condone same-sex unions. Now they don't. Ergo, so much for rigid rules. Everyone used to marry, even priests."

"Really?" Deborah blinked. "I thought celibacy was an ancient sacrament in the Church."

"It was enforced only from the 12th century onward. As for same-sex unions, this book shows that biblical interpretations are cultural and not set in concrete. And if you consider the fact that women used to be priests in the early Church, you begin to understand the prejudicial cultural view of gender." Thomas handed her the volume. "Buy it. It's a good source for an argument. Maybe I can find that Morris book. Not that your Rabbi will give a hoot about sociobiology." He looked around for the science section.

Deborah glanced down with mixed feelings, knowing a book about Christianity wouldn't open the Rabbi's mind. The audience applauded the end of the first song. The singer started in on the next song. Deborah caught up with Thomas and whispered, "Doesn't respect count for anything in religion?"

"Oh, that's a whole topic. If Christianity respects anything, it's faith. Having faith in Jesus, in the Trinity."

"What about Judaism? What do you think it respects?"

"You should ask that rabbi of yours. It really all boils down to the same problem—the patriarchy. Write that down. It's why males can bond, play a lot of football and make wars. Gives us our hierarchical view of the world. Men will occasionally talk about women needing more protection, but never ever talk about lessening men's advantages through their unearned and conferred dominance. Notice I don't say 'our' because racism is tied up in it."

Deborah's shoulders slumped as she grappled with his words. *There's no balance.* It's all about competition, very little about cooperation. Her mind raced through history—women persecuted as witches, whites enslaving black Africans, sex-trafficking. She thought of patriarchal institutions—male-only schools, the big business of male sports, guns and wars—everything based on domination and competition. *No one talks about a patriarchy, yet it's another thing we live in. We're inside it, we can't see it. My white privilege—I can't see my own racism. I'm inside this hierarchy. And now I'm competing with the Rabbi, trying to figure out a weakness in his argument, like we're in a sports game.* She felt hot on her neck.

The singer started on her third song. The echoes of a familiar chord progression stopped Deborah mid breath. She turned toward the performance area. "Thomas, I need to listen to this." Like a homing pigeon, she walked toward the singer and sank into one of the chairs.

She knew this song. *The Swallow Song* was written by Richard Fariña, a folksinger from the Sixties who used to perform with his wife Mimi. Deborah was surprised she still remembered. It had been so long since she had last heard it. She glanced around to take in the faces around her. A couple in their twenties were holding hands and giggling to each other, too young to have known that era. Next to them sat a balding man, transfixed, with leathery wrinkled skin, his black eyes sharp and piercing like a Mayan Indian. Beyond him was an older woman with watery eyes.

It was Fariña's song, a plea to his new-found lover to join him on a peaceful moonlit ocean-side cliff, sometime long ago, when the world was going crazy. He was asking her to join him, away and above the nonsense of the world. *Join him and listen. Join him and watch, seeking peace.*

And Mimi did. But then he died.

Deborah remembered the first time she heard it in high school. Her best friend Betsy Ellen Kasselhorn took her to a poetry reading. She had nodded her head with each recitation, although the poems made no sense. A scrawny senior stood near a green chair reading about the Vietnam war. Deborah stood half in the living room, leaning against an alcove, watching the moon catch the kids' profiles on the floor. She became aware of a song playing on a turntable behind her. At first, the elegant guitar beat drew her attention. She got caught by the simple beauty of the words and by the blending of the two voices. They expanded in such perfect harmony she found herself turning around to stare at the bobbing arm as it floated over the record.

"Who's that singing?" she asked.

"It's Richard and Mimi Fariña." Betsy turned the album cover over.

"Can I see that?" Deborah wanted to wrestle it out of her hands.

"I'm not finished reading it," Betsy said.

"Let me see it." Deborah extended her hand.

"Oh, here." Two idyllic faces stared up at Deborah. Mimi, on the left, had long shiny black hair, deep set blue eyes, and a nose like her sister Joan Baez. On the right stood Richard, his hair wild and curly, his mouth held in a puckered, vulnerable grin. Their shy faces peeked through a picture frame. They seemed connected in an almost mystical way. The song's words dragged her into fantasies; the melody was haunting, old, and pure. She could feel a tingling, an acute awareness like when your world perception is suddenly changed.

"I was just trying to see how he died." Betsy turned away.

The words hit teenage Deborah like a brick wall. "What? He's dead? That voice is dead?" She tried to steady herself.

"You okay? Yeah, a motorcycle accident or something."

A wave of loneliness spread over Deborah. She had found him and lost him all in the same moment. Hugging the album cover, Deborah wanted to go with Richard, hear what he heard, see what he saw. She wanted to sing with him, feel the wind with him, high above the sea. But he was gone. She didn't care what anyone thought, she started to cry.

Playing with the pendant, Deborah refocused on the long-haired singer as she finished the song. She hadn't heard the song in at least thirty-five years. Had it been an adolescent crush that had caused her to have such a reaction that day? Or the sensory overload of hearing the song, looking at the album cover and feeling alone?

Something else nagged at her. Something sounded so damned familiar. She knew the song. Her high school memory. But it felt like something more. She couldn't put her finger on it.

She was focused on Rachel's problem, the search for an answer to satisfy the Rabbi as Thomas babbled incomprehensively. In a way, this quest with Thomas was similar to the problem Deborah faced in doing scientific research. A search for something no one has ever figured out before. Like the swallows singing a human tune. How do you define what that thing is if you don't know what it is?

"Oh, my God!" Deborah realized what was nagging her. The cliff swallow in Capistrano had been singing Richard Fariña's song.

CHAPTER 9

"There is no sorrow like the murmur of their wings,
There is no choir like their song.
There is no power like the freedom of their flight
While the swallows roam along."
- Richard Fariña

DEBORAH JOLTED UP IN her chair, dazed, wanting to demand answers from Elizabeth Rafferty even before she finished performing. This song of all songs.

When the concert ended, Deborah hurried over to the singer and complimented her. "I love that song, *The Swallow Song.*"

Elizabeth beamed with puffy cheeks, swinging her hair out of the way. She had a calm detachment. "Oh, yeah, Richard Fariña. He achieved poetry in his songwriting."

"I remember his incredible talent. Do you—"

"Did you know him?" Elizabeth reached for the water bottle sitting on a wooden stool.

"No, I only discovered his music after he died. But I was—"

"Same here." She took a swig. "Boy, I needed that. Yeah, our paths didn't cross. And I wasn't a relative of Joan Baez's."

"I can't understand why Richard became obscure. He and Mimi made such a splash." Deborah shook her head. "Do I know you?"

Elizabeth sat down on the stool, waving away the question. "I get that all the time. Yeah, they were starting to make it at Newport and their Carnegie Hall performance. Great songs, *Pack Up Your Sorrows, Children of Darkness, Bold Marauder*—now there's a percipient song."

From the echoes of her brain, Deborah could hear snippets of music and lyrics as if in a time warp. She had bought their albums after high school and listened to them over and over so that she could sing along. But it was so long ago. *Bold Marauder* only sounded vaguely familiar.

Elizabeth leaned down to pack up her equipment. "Joan Baez helped them but he lost the competition fame game to Dylan." She put her guitar into a taped up case. "Dylan simply outshone him, but then, hey, Dylan had more time to grow as a songwriter."

"Would you know when he wrote it?"

Elizabeth turned back to her. "*The Swallow Song*? I'm not sure. Mimi died in 2001 so you can't ask her. But it's on their second album, which came out around I think like '65. So maybe around 1964." She picked up her case. "Check the Internet. Isn't that what the kids do?"

Deborah watched her walk away, remembering those two twenty-something faces staring up from the cardboard album cover. Both gone, neither able to provide answers to the song's mystery. Somehow Richard had communicated with another species. Deborah's mind lurched in circles. Who was left who knew anything about it?

Thomas joined her. "Ready to go?"

She had a big smile on her face. "Thomas, I need to know more about Richard Fariña."

"Was he gay?"

"No, no. Different research topic. You know, the bird thing. I don't know where to begin looking."

He squinted, searching his memory. "Fariña wrote a novel, if I recall. Come here." They went to the fiction section on the back wall of the bookstore. "Here it is. *Been Down So Long, It Looks Like Up To Me.* It's a strange, funky book to say the least. He was ahead of his time when it came to writing style and brilliance of range. I think he was riding home from its publication party when he died." Thomas handed her the book and then reached for a slimmer one. "Here's another one, a collection of his writings Mimi compiled after his death called *A Long Time Coming and A Long Time Gone.*"

Deborah bought them both along with John Boswell's book on same-sex unions. It was something. If she could figure out the connection between swallows and Fariña, maybe she could figure out why the birds were dying.

WORLD NEWS – APRIL 23
Deforestation Affecting Species and Land
Bird Concentrations Moving North
Treelines Shifting Poleward and Northward

Deborah's office was almost too small to contain all the students now interested in the project. Besides Michael and Jeff, Barry and two other graduate students gathered around the small round table.

"Let's keep a focus, people," Deborah kept her voice low. She especially didn't want the Dean to catch drift of this meeting, even if she could justify it as helping the graduate students in their research. And though far from promoting swallow fieldwork, she made sure the door was closed.

"If this tune is in the swallow's song, how did it get there?" Jeff asked. He looked like he had lost weight.

Deborah nodded, her eyes sparkling. "We have one bird and one man who did not live in the same time frame."

Michael was doodling on his pad.

"But the coincidence is too impossible for it to be a...coincidence," Jeff said.

Everyone laughed. Jeff was confused. "What's so funny?" He fingered his seashell.

Deborah stopped mid-smile. "Don't you hear what you just said?"

He looked dizzy. "I mean, for Dr. Wright to have happened to record the only bird singing it? I mean, the bird died like all the other ones, it's not like it was so special that it survived."

Her eyes went wide. "Scientists think in probabilities. Jeff, you're right, the coincidence is too impossible for it to be a coincidence."

He smiled weakly, rubbing his arms as if they were numb.

Barry started writing the first letters of the words. "Okay. We now have a new study group mantra. A 'coincidence is too impossible for it to be a coincidence'. And a name—the CITIFITBAC study."

"CITIFITBAC? Oh, it's an acronym, I like it." Michael copied it down. "We should get T-shirts made. It'll go with this one I got at the Earth Day Fair." He pointed to the words 'Tree Hugger' across his chest and then started writing it in different ways. *CitiFitBac. Citi Fit Bac. City fit back into your space.*

"Okay, okay," Deborah laughed, "good name, but let's not go overboard. Science is science, not wishful thinking." Having a code name for the study was good, she thought. "Let's start with what we know."

Michael looked at his notebook where he had drawn a surfer with a bird above him. "It happened in Southern California not far from a decommissioned nuclear power plant."

Jeff added, "At the Mission of San Juan Capistrano. That whole area is pretty sacred to the Acjachemen Indian Nation."

Deborah nodded. "Good context for us. What else? How about avian behavior?"

Michael stared at his drawing. "Why do they sing?"

"Excellent question. Barry?"

A graduate student had to be up to any challenge. "Male birds sing to communicate in order to establish territorial ownership, attract mates, and maintain pair bonds."

"How do they do it?"

Barry sounded like he was practicing for his oral defense. "They vocalize using their syrinx, a box-shaped organ that lies at the bottom of their windpipes." He drew a picture for the undergraduates. "It's like the human larynx, but instead of vibrating vocal cords, pitch and sound quality are varied by changing the tension on the muscular walls of the syrinx that vibrate as air passes through them. Communications are generally carried out with species' members."

"Thanks, Barry." Deborah smiled. "Great job. And there's a precedent for interspecies communication between birds and human."

"You mean the honeyguide?"

"Right. The greater honeyguide in Africa can direct the ratel to the location of wild bees' nests..."

"What's that?" Jeff sat up and almost fell off his chair. "All I know is from the intro class."

Deborah helped steady him. "Are you okay?"

"Oh, sure. I'm taking stronger meds. I'll be fine."

She looked at him as she continued. "The ratel. It's a badger-like mammal. The honeyguides make a special call which the ratel follow. When the ratel gets close, the bird will perch and flutter its tail, making another call to indicate the nest is nearby. The ratel excavates the nest and claws out the combs, leaving bee grubs and beeswax for the bird."

Michael had drawn a little animal on the surfboard. "That's cooperation between a bird and a badger—not a human."

Deborah nodded. "Good point. The honeyguide will also attract members of the Boran tribe in northern Kenya, getting the people to follow them to their nests using the same calls."

"So birds can sing to humans."

She corrected him. "No, Michael, a bird call is different from a bird song. Calls are innate. Some songs are also, but the complicated songs are learned. A call is more of a sound used for various situations." She smiled at Barry. "In fact, Barry is writing his dissertation on the calls of killdeer."

Barry listed them. "Alarm calls are for warning each other about predators in the area. Birds' maintenance behaviors include calls for staying in contact, territorial aggression, finding food, and adolescent begging."

Deborah added, "Plus, calls are made by both males and females, while songs are usually just made by the males."

"I've heard those alarm calls," Michael said, pointing to his notebook. "I was in Hawaii surfing and almost got dive bombed by a low-flying bird."

"Nice drawing," Deborah joked. "Pet ratel?"

He laughed. "Never can tell when I might need some wild bees."

Barry ignored them. "Birds survive by sensing danger. Immediate danger, I mean. We humans can threaten them big time with everything from our presence all the way up to destroying their forests. When danger is nearby, they signal it."

Deborah tried to get serious. "Species even respond to each others' flee alarms."

"The alarm call of the black-capped chickadee contains information about the degree of threat the predator poses. I'm looking at the same thing in killdeer."

Deborah sat forward and rapped on the table. "See, avian semantics."

Barry scrunched up his face. "But there's no evidence of birds in the wild understanding human behavior or languages like dogs do. Or pet birds."

Jeff said, "Yeah, parrots can repeat all sorts of words, can't they?"

Deborah nodded, wondering if Jeff was really okay. He didn't look well, his cheeks were flushed. "That's mimicry. Some birds do copy. Mozart had a pet starling that sang one of his piano concertos. But there's no evidence of mimicry by a swallow species. If this is mimicry, then a mimicking individual has passed on the mimicked piece."

"That would mean adaptation," Barry said.

"Yes, in a relatively short amount of time, right before our eyes, so to speak. It's not unheard of. A lyrebird in the 1930s in Australia not only learned fragments of two songs played on a flute, the phrases were detectable in generations over seventy years later."

Barry persisted. "Doesn't an adaptation have to contribute to reproductive success?"

"Sure. Adaptation is necessary for survival. I've been doing some checking. The range boundaries of birds on average are moving north as the climate gets warmer."

Michael said, "But how could singing this song contribute to reproductive success?"

Deborah shook her head, feeling stumped. "Yes, that is the question."

"If only we had more data." Barry doodled in his notebook.

Deborah looked at the phone, Milhouse's words echoing in her head. She knew that if she did this, it could cost her her job, not to mention hammer the final nail into her crumbling scientific reputation. She squeezed the pendant around her neck, looked at the students and took a deep breath. "Okay, CITIFITBAC club, who wants to do some fieldwork?"

As Jeff raised his hand, he fell off his chair and passed out.

Deborah curled up in front of the fireplace with the Fariña novel. A cup of Costa Rican coffee sat on the coffee table in front of her. The semester was ending with quite a jolt. Jeff's collapse in her office was hard. In thirty years of teaching, it had only happened once before when a pregnant student fainted from low blood sugar. But Jeff's problem wasn't as obvious and the nearby Alta Bates emergency room admitted him into the hospital. She looked to the coffee table and picked up his seashell. Realizing it was a fossilized brachiopod, she sighed deeply, wondering where he got it.

The book was unusual. She understood Thomas's statement about Fariña's brilliance. His riffs were like musical progressions, all done with historical and literary references. He was well-read, not the drugged up ne'er-do-well of his protagonist Gnossos Pappadopoulis. She wondered if that was a Greek name.

Fariña had traveled pretty extensively. One of his more interesting moments was working as a blind street musician in Paris. She read how he had met Mimi Baez at Chartres Cathedral and they romantically sang and danced down the Champs-Elysées. The only problem was he was married to someone else at the time.

Deborah felt heat on the back of her neck and she sucked in her breath. *Why do men have affairs? What was so wrong with our marriage that Stephen had to have an affair?* Listening to the crackle of burning wood in the fireplace, she thought about the times they used to read to each other. The smell reminded her of his sandalwood soap. She remembered the time he said her voice was his favorite sound in the world. Tears moistened her eyes.

She thought about what Thomas had said about morality and philosophy. If she could find a weakness in the Rabbi's argument...

Deborah looked blankly at the book. *Just think about Richard Fariña.* He always carried an Indian leather box that contained one hair and a piece of paper with two words written in a strange language. Was this hyperbole or was it real? What was the language? Where had he been? Had he heard the song from a swallow while in Paris? Most species of *Hirundo* stay in the New World in their seasonal migrations but *H. rustica* travel to Southern Europe. Fariña had been in the Mediterranean and southern France. Also, his father's family came from Cuba and his mother's from North Ireland. When young, he had traveled to Matanzas Province in Cuba to visit his cousins. Fariña had also traveled to County Tyrone in North Ireland to visit his mother's family after he left Cornell. Swallows are common there in the summer.

Where else had he been? California. The Carmel Highlands. It's where he was living in 1964 and where he died. Deborah picked up Jeff's seashell again and stared at it. Carmel was not far from Berkeley.

🕊 🕊

WORLD NEWS – APRIL 28
Antibiotics Losing Effectiveness
Coal-burning Power Plants Emit Mercury
Mercury Levels in Lakes and Oceans Rising

THE SWALLOW AND THE NIGHTINGALE

Deborah's Notes for CITIFITBAC Study

It has been determined that the tune found in the *P. pyrrhonota* samples from San Juan Capistrano statistically matches ($P <$ 0.001) a tune entitled *The Swallow Song* by R. Fariña (1937-66).

On April 25, a field test was conducted in Eastshore State Park in Alameda County, California. The test was to determine if the human song has been inserted into avian songs. Sampling was performed on six adult male *H. rustica* (barn swallow) and on five adult male *P. pyrrhonota* (cliff swallow). Three samples from each were taken, approximately five seconds each varying the length of time and sampling rate. In all cases, results were negative. There is no indication that the normal song pattern for these species in this area is affected.

Tubes snaked into Jeff's mouth and arms. His unbraided hair was gathered at the back of his neck and down his right side. He was in a coma and weak from the ordeal. Deborah stared at his fragile frame. His vibrant playfulness had disappeared under a sickly ashen hue. Without his glasses, he looked younger. A woman with long black hair sat next to his bed. She introduced herself as his mother, Katherine. The pale charcoal walls of the Alta Bates Medical Center room made the room feel peaceful.

Katherine's eyes held an ancient sadness. "Dr. Wright, Jeff has talked about helping you with your important problem."

Deborah lowered herself heavily into a chair. "Jeff is a valuable member of our team. He's still an undergraduate, but he has unique insights. You should be very proud of him."

Katherine nodded, her strong hands sitting in her lap.

"Even as he got sicker, he stayed at it. He's our budding engineer."

"He said something about one of your lectures giving him a new perspective on his life as a Native American."

"Jeff said you're from New York, one of the tribes." Deborah remembered the Dean's discomfort and glanced down, thinking about the field test she did three days earlier.

"We're Oneida, from upstate New York. Part of the Six Nation Confederacy of the Haudenosaunee, what you call the Iroquois. He's switching his major from engineering to biology because of you."

Deborah looked at Jeff's still body. She pulled the fossilized seashell from her travel bag. "He carried this with him all the time. I didn't want it to get lost." She held it out for Katherine.

"He has a shell collection. You hold on to it. That way, he'll still be at the University."

Deborah stared at the shell. She could remember how he played with it, as if he was tuning into an ancient knowledge. Tears welled up in her eyes. "What's his prognosis?"

Katherine shook her head. "The coma is good for his recovery, the doctor said. He's been exposed to benzene and he has an acute form of leukemia. There are also complications from mercury poisoning."

"My god. What was he doing?"

"Don't know. When I talked to him after his trip to visit his friend in Pennsylvania, he complained of headaches."

Pennsylvania. He had talked about Penn. "His fiancée?" Deborah asked, putting it together.

A monitor beeped. Katherine sighed. She filled in the silence. "He hadn't told me."

Deborah's face flushed with embarrassment.

A nurse came in and changed an IV. A large man, he leaned over to check Jeff's blood pressure and oxygen rate. The two women watched and then the nurse left.

Katherine shifted in her chair. "He'll tell me when he's ready."

"I'm sorry." Deborah cleared her throat.

Katherine nodded. "We birth them. Then we have to let them go."

"It's what mothers do." Deborah closed her eyes. She felt that they were being witnesses for Jeff's ordeal. In Judaism, people guarding a dead body are called the *shomrim*. Don't go there, Deborah told herself. *He's not dead. He's not going to die. We won't be sitting shiva.*

🕊 🕊

WORLD NEWS – APRIL 29
CO2 At All Time High– 400 PPM in Alaska
Sea Level Rising
Droughts and Flooding on Low-lying Islands
Alaskan Villages Opt for 'Climigration'

THE SWALLOW AND THE NIGHTINGALE

The Cabrillo Highway to Carmel wound out of the Santa Cruz Mountains along Monterey Bay. Thomas steered his hybrid car, focusing on the road.

Thinking about the field test, Deborah watched the forested hills give way to the slow, rolling expanse of the ocean. "Any plans for the summer?"

He nodded. "The usual. Summer in Washington D.C., teaching at that non-profit camp."

"Really. So you can be with your beloved." Deborah winced as she reached into her bag and pulled out sunscreen.

"Otherwise, we barely see each other. Maybe Memorial Day weekend. She'll be in session with the Senate until August." Thomas paused. "What's happening with Stephen? When's he returning?"

She rubbed the sunscreen on her arms, looking out over the waves as they slowly broke over one other. Having grown up on the East Coast, she still felt disoriented by the ocean being to the west. "UCI is on a quarter system; they don't end until sometime in June. Then he'll be back and we'll decide what we're going to do."

"You can't get a divorce. You two belong together."

Deborah stared at the wildflowers on the side of the road. "Yes, well." Her voice petered out. She closed her eyes and put her head back. "It's good to get away."

Thomas glanced sideways at her. "You mean because it's the last week of classes or because you need to chill?"

She took a deep breath. "Let's just say it's been a long semester."

"Tell me about it. We should go hide on some Polynesian island."

She laughed and pulled out her hand sanitizer. "You're so famous they would know you even there."

"Got you to smile. Did you read the Boswell book? What did he say about marriage?"

"Still processing it."

"Look into the sociobiology thing. How's your student?"

Cleaning her hands, she looked at the ocean. "I was at the hospital yesterday. He looked pretty bad. They put him into a medically-induced coma." She repeated what Jeff's mother had told her.

"So it's coming to that." Thomas hit the steering wheel at the list.

"He's not going to die from this, is he? Chemotherapy gets results, especially for someone young and otherwise healthy." She put away the sanitizer and sunscreen.

"The mercury is probably from eating fish. As for the leukemia, depends on whether it's fast-acting or slow-acting. And what he was exposed to—hard to say. That oil spill back east isn't an isolated event you know."

"What's Susan have to say about what's happening?"

"The President has called out the National Guard, declaring New Jersey a national disaster area. Then he did the same thing for Louisiana. Pennsylvania isn't on their radar screen because it's business as usual." He glanced down at his side-view mirror and passed a slower car. "Internally, they run scenarios to predict the first massive failure and then pretend it's not going to happen. But we're all vulnerable."

Scanning the sky, she saw the deep steady beat of a great egret. She always associated its white crest with hippies from the Sixties with their outrageous hairdos. "What's that mean?"

Thomas got back into their lane. "You heard my Staley Prize lecture, about the ancient Puebloans."

"I thought their climate change was a natural drought."

"But that's the thing. The early group into Chaco Canyon could have survived that drought. But they grew too large and complex during the good times, all the while cutting down the woodlands and digging irrigation ditches. They wound up using up their resources and the ditches became arroyos too deep to use."

"So when the drought hit..."

"They couldn't survive at their population density with a compromised environment. It's a lesson for us. Look at the size of the world population, how we are overusing resources. There's a real limit to the amount of greenhouse gases we can pump into the atmosphere before we lose our garden of Eden."

"Why the Bible reference?" She asked, annoyed.

He smirked. "Because it's a good metaphor. What's happening is like Genesis in reverse. We're going to hit some tipping point, like a frog in a pot slowly being exposed to boiling water not noticing it's dying."

Her eyes followed the egret as it glided into a descent. Its long white body was like a soft pillow stuck between its yellow bill pointing forward and its black legs streaming out behind. "I talked to some of those company reps at the Earth Day Fair. They said technology will fix things—bring down the CO2. They have lots of ideas."

"Right. Counterbalance climate change plus make a profit." He looked over at her. "Anything to avoid taking a loss on an enormous investment in fossil fuels."

She looked back at the ocean. Sandpipers ran along the water's edge. "Look at how beautiful that is." She cracked her window and breathed in the fresh smell of the sea. "We'll all be okay."

"You obviously don't live on the Oka River in Russia or the Marshall Islands."

She laid her head back on the seat again and closed her eyes, smelling the tinge of a forest fire. "Neither do you. Okay, some companies are doing bad things. We just don't know the effect that ten or a hundred companies are having on the planet. I do believe in technology. Modern medicine and science know how to fix things. What can be done anyway?"

"Come on, are you serious? Deborah, you can't just go to a store to buy ice fields or plunk down $1.98 to purchase a new environment. We need to learn from history. Those ancient Puebloans had to relocate and leave their houses. We will too. It's already happening. Even in the United States—entire communities in Alaska are moving. So are low-lying island nations because of extreme weather."

A chill went down her back and it wasn't from the open window. "Relocate? Like leave Berkeley?"

Thomas glanced over. "We're at sea level. And the sea is rising."

She stared out at the ocean again. The small lapping waves seemed so gentle. "It's like a funhouse. When is this going to happen?"

He shook his head. "It's hard to say. Half of the US population lives within fifty miles of a coast."

She stared at the waves, trying to see the future in their benign movements. It reminded her how she had watched the Japanese tsunami waves washboard their way past Lincoln Park after traveling so far. *Nature responds to its own laws. It doesn't care that I love Berkeley. What did that guy who didn't believe in gravity say at the Earth Day Fair? It's not about beliefs.*

He continued, "There's no more time for naivety. To really know what's happening, we must integrate the data. And I mean all of it—the pollution, the climate change data, and the bad technology."

Deborah rubbed the space between her eyebrows and ran her fingers to her temples. "How's anybody going to integrate it all? Are they going to include every little shock felt around the world?" The car bumped like it hit something. She sat up. "Speaking of, was that a tremor?"

Thomas fought the wheel. "You tell me. You're the geologist's wife."

She gripped the inside door handle. "It could've been. Is it starting to happen here?" The waves looked a little more choppy. *Nature responds to its own laws.*

"I don't know." Thomas let out his breath, scanning the landscape for any evidence of an earthquake.

They drove into the outskirts of Carmel. She closed her eyes again. "How can anyone deal with all this?"

Thomas shot her a look. "Did Harvey call you again?"

"He thinks I've stopped working on the swallow project, but I haven't. I took some students into the field." On the right side of them, a stone wall separated the road from tall evergreen forests.

"Good. It's called teaching. And the best happens outside the classroom. What's he going to do, fire you? Even if he finds out, he can't. You've got tenure. Ignore his threats."

"He can do things. I wouldn't put it past him. He gets weasely. Our results were negative." Deborah stared at the low wall. Her eyes searched for a small stone marker to indicate where Fariña had crashed on the motorcycle.

"Where to now, my dear?"

"Don't know, really. I thought there would be some roadside post or something, but now what's the point."

"C'mon, we aren't giving up yet."

"Well, maybe he's buried here."

"Good idea! Let's go find the cemetery." Thomas looked around for a visitor's center.

They stopped at the village's Tourist Information kiosk. Probably built in the 1890s, the wooden cottage had a fresh coat of white paint with lime green trim. Deborah got out of the car.

THE SWALLOW AND THE NIGHTINGALE

An older woman sat at the counter, wearing a blue floral dress and a string of pearls. "We don't have cemeteries in Carmel. Would you like directions to the Highlands Sculpture Garden? There are some excellent bronzes and ceramics there on display."

Dead end, Deborah sighed deeply. Her mind flashed to vases floating in a rising sea. She got back into Thomas's car. "No luck. They don't have cemeteries."

"Where do they bury people?" Thomas gazed out the open window, smelling the ocean breeze. "Maybe they don't die here."

"We could wait for pearl lady to kick the bucket and then we'd know for sure." Deborah watched the foot traffic along the street. Tourists strolled carrying gift bags on the sidewalks. A teenager on a skateboard ignored the signs. She saw no black faces, except for Thomas's. She wanted to cover her own white skin. "It's a wild goose chase and what's the point anyway?" She rubbed her temples.

"There's a music store. I bet they'll know something."

Deborah looked up to where he was pointing. Music. Was it worth it? She got out of the car.

With a big laugh, he called out after her, "Don't get arrested."

Posters on floor stands advertised the latest rock stars. Deborah didn't recognize any of them. Shelves were piled high everywhere with cases. Small white signs gave some order for the wary visitor. There were a few patrons in the aisles. Sitting behind the counter, a clerk read his email. His brown hair was short and he wore Mr. Peabody glasses.

Deborah let the door close. "Do you have any records by Richard Fariña?"

He stared at her and laughed. "Records? Hey, nobody sells records any more. Gotta get 'em from Ebay or like that, if you're serious."

Deborah stared back at him. He was the same age as her students but with questionable intelligence. She hadn't come this far to be insulted. "What about Richard Fariña? Do you have any of his music?"

"Never heard of him."

Deborah looked around. There were thousands of titles, lining the walls up to the ceiling. Shelves and bins were filled. This was Carmel. Fariña had to be here. "How could you not? He was a folksinger from the 1960s. Richard Fariña. Richard and Mimi Fariña?"

"Hey, don't take my word for it. I just work here. Go check out the bins. Folksinger? Try the far wall, three quarters the way down, in the F Section."

Deborah sidled past people through the narrow aisles to where he had pointed. She looked through the plastic racks, all neatly filled with music cases of recordings. Everything was crowded but orderly. And there were no Fariñas.

Deborah stared at the titles even more depressed than before. After reading his two books, she was expecting Carmel to be holy ground. The store would have his picture encased in an ornate silver frame with the epithet, "Richard Fariña, The Black Irish Mad-hatted Rose." Maybe an incense holder lightly exhaling musk into the air above a purple-clothed oak table, faded snapshots, and his dulcimer sitting next to his books with a sign, "Please do not touch." His voice would fill the store accompanied by the rich tones of intricate guitar virtuosity and Mimi's bell-like voice.

Dealing with people felt frustrating. Science presented challenges, but it was straightforward. With each question, one could find a solution, which in turn would lead to another question. Her conversation with Thomas swirled in her head, disheartening her as she mulled over the idea of relocation.

A gray-haired woman was standing near her and as she moved away, Deborah saw the Fariña name. She pulled the box off the shelf, a retrospective of his songs. On the back was a song list, and there it was, *The Swallow Song*.

Deborah dropped the case on the counter and smirked at the clerk. He looked at it. "Whoops. Well, what do you know? Can't know everything."

"No, I guess you can't, especially if you're distracted. Do you go to school?"

"Yeah," he rang it up, "Monterey Bay State. That's $15.34."

Deborah extracted the bills from her wallet. "What are you studying?"

"Business administration. Here's your change."

"Thank you. Learning the ins and outs of your product line is good for business." Deborah grabbed her package.

"Yeah, that's what one of my professors said."

THE SWALLOW AND THE NIGHTINGALE

Deborah walked to the car realizing that with her package and walking shoes she looked like the other tourists. Getting into the car, she said, "Let's drive."

"You found his music?"

"I think it's the fourth track." She opened up the package and handed the recording to him.

He inserted it into the player and started driving.

The soft guitar chords filled the car and then the two voices gently intertwined in subtle harmonies. Deborah leaned back, closed her eyes, and listened. Caught between the present and the past, she floated on the simplicity of the tune. Could Fariña have learned the words from the birds? *That's absurd. Birds don't speak. They'd weigh too much if they could talk. What about the tune? They can make the tune with their syrinx, obviously, because one swallow did it. But it's not audible to the human ear.*

Deborah started to feel clammy. "Can we get out of the car?"

"You okay?" Thomas glanced over to her.

She rolled her window down more. "I don't do well in closed spaces."

"A little claustrophobia?"

"Yes." She leaned her head out of the window. "Stopping soon?"

"I know a great place, a state reserve. You'll see why they call this the Carmel Highlands."

The song ended and the next song began. It was the *Bold Marauder*, the one the folksinger at the Iron Horse had mentioned. The hard driving beat brought the words out of her memory. Fariña sang about a white destroyer using fear and religion to destroy the rivers, the winds, the food.

Thomas stared at the player. "My God, when was this written? He's predicting our world."

She could feel another chill go down her back.

Thomas drove into Point Lobos State Park. They got out of the car and Thomas helped her as they walked down a trail above the ocean through sagebrush and short evergreens. She found a large rock.

Thomas took in a deep breath. "I'm going to hike along the cliff."

"Go ahead." She sat down on the rock.

He stood with his arms to his sides. "For what it's worth, I don't know if you realize how much the change in Rachel's life affected you and Stephen."

Turning around, she stared hard at him. "Do you think Stephen messed up sleeping with a graduate student?"

"Yes."

"Even if she was African-American?"

He held her gaze. "Yes."

"Thank you. You're a true friend, Thomas."

He smiled, shrugged and took off.

She called after him, "Don't get arrested."

"I can see the headlines now," he yelled into the wind.

Deborah tightened her jacket. Scraggy shrubs and thin bent grasses shook from the force of the ocean breeze. The sage stirred in the wind and a minty fragrance filled the air. White clouds floated in long stringy puffs. Below her, sea waves formed white swells, broke and sprayed the air. The force of the water on the cliffs had carved caves and arches. Slow-flying brown pelicans and Western gulls clipped the waves. Small sandpipers skipped into the shallow water, darting away as the surf covered their long legs. A lone gull soared overhead to her level, sometimes flapping its powerful wings, sometimes floating on the air currents.

Deborah couldn't stop hearing *The Swallow Song*. The gull descended toward the tide pools, flying through one of the arches, then out and upwards toward her. It started its long spiraling descent again, just like the birds in the song.

She couldn't understand why Fariña's music was lost. The song was timeless. Folksingers don't achieve a great deal of fame, but many have stayed around for generations. What if the song contains a message?

Deborah looked around. Could Fariña have written the song in this park? Here, she thought, even sitting right here. It's a good habitat for cliff swallows. Deborah could imagine flocks of swallows flying by, Fariña staring out from this spot, strumming chords on his dulcimer and letting the birds teach him the tune.

Deborah looked up for cliff swallows. She didn't see any square tails and white foreheads, but then, their migration range was changing.

THE SWALLOW AND THE NIGHTINGALE

She stared at the breaking waves. Their constant rhythm held a hollow laughter. The ocean's power was like a mute god whose oracular message could be interpreted as benign or vengeful. Which was it? The thought of moving from Berkeley stung at her eyes.

Suddenly dizzy, she began sensing an image. It was as if she could feel—or see—two women running, along the trail in front of her. *Heather and Queen Anne's lace clung to their heels. They looked frantic and scared, their breathing hard with each step, terrified they wouldn't get away. As they ran, their feet became very light, lighter than air. They were floating. Suddenly they were transformed into two birds—a swallow and—was it a nightingale? Both were flying toward the clouds first in distinct spirals around each other and then in parallel. A graceful and powerful swallow with long tail streamers, quick wings, and a dark-colored throat. A nimble and sure nightingale with red brown wings stroking powerfully through the air. They circled each other in joyous grace.*

The image quickly disappeared. Deborah felt even more chilled. She took hold of her pendant. Looking down at the strange words on it, she remembered what the woman had said—*what am I*. It's a dandelion, Deborah remembered. Why did that woman give it to her?

Deborah thought, *if only I can find out what's happening with the swallows, beat Stephen to the punch.* As soon as she felt her competitive urge, she kicked herself. There it is, patriarchal competition. *What am I going to do about Stephen? Even Thomas agrees Stephen screwed up. Most women won't forgive their husbands for having an affair. They get on with their lives.* She clawed away the ache she was used to by now.

She realized something. There was another test she hadn't tried yet. She would have to go back down to Capistrano. *I've already done one failed experience.*

Screw what the Dean says.

Chapter 10
What The Nightingale Said
Part III

"After the valley of which I just spoke,
one other presents itself. The Valley of Knowledge
has neither beginning nor end. None disagree
on how long the road is across this valley."

-- *Attar, The Conference of the Birds*

OUR CAMEL CARAVAN continues south, slowing as we travel through the Zagros Mountains. In the distance, I can see great shimmering salt lakes. We meet traders returning from Baghdad, carrying paper and silk from Arabia and gold from Africa. We hear stories of infidels massacring towns and villages. There are also robbers and thieves attacking caravans. Our leader has been careful to pick a route to avoid trouble.

In the small villages, I gather a crowd and sing the song of the nightingale. Some people give me dates and other treats. Others scoff at the idea of a talking nightingale but the song is so beautiful, most stay to listen.

Wending our way through the mountain passes along rich fields of wheat and barley, I wonder how I will find the answer. Perhaps on the pilgrimage to Mecca when I stand before Allah at the Plain of Arafat, the mystery will be solved.

We cross through desert scrub, through low hills and then climb to Kermanshah where we stop for a rest. I walk among the colorful stalls at the bazaar, admiring rich leathers and glass-like pearls. I stop at a bird seller's booth. A stooped man greets me and asks me why I am traveling through their small town.

"Traveling is how I learn," I reply.

"I could never travel like that," the bird-seller says. "I stay stuck here in my village."

"Let me tell you a story about a nightingale. In her previous life, the bird did a horrible deed, and she traveled looking for a cure for her aching heart. By searching, she fell in love with the rosebush as it bloomed in the spring." I sing the love song of the nightingale. People are drawn by my voice and the melodious tune.

When I finish, the bird-seller says, "So what? I'm more like this parrot here, enclosed so long in a cage that I don't have the strength for a trip."

I smile at the man. I too had been timid before the Shaikh sent me out of Shadyakh. "To get anywhere is only to struggle with yourself. The journey begins with the first step."

The bird-seller's son calls out from inside the booth where he reclines on large cotton pillows. "But how do you take that first step?"

"Look at me. Why am I here? I was confused and my teacher told me to seek the door. It takes the willingness to seek the answer. I joined a caravan and began the search."

"I'm willing," the son says, "but how do I do it?"

I stop. I can't talk of my own fear upon leaving my father. Where did my willingness start? Maybe that beggar at Rai was right. "Beyond willingness, it takes passion." I tell them the story of the beggar and the princess, how the beggar's passion to see the princess everyday was enough. His burning heart was greater than any human drive.

When I finish the story, the group argues about whether the beggar was wise or crazy. A guard breaks up the argument and everyone disperses. I leave the bazaar and walk to the inn when I am stopped by the guard.

"Oh, teller of tales, let me tell you my story. I am in love also. But I am a soldier, not a beggar. My story doesn't have the same outcome."

I turn and smile. "What is wrong with that? Passion is good. Sacrifice everything for it."

The soldier continues. "Because of my love, I cannot sleep. I am restless, all I can think of is my love. She is so beautiful."

"Aren't you a guardsman? Mustn't you stay up night after night on duty, guarding the city? I see your love is your friend. Your love helps you in your duty."

"Is that good?" He knit his eyebrows. "Or am I insane to live like this?"

I put down my bundles. "You are always on the watch. This is as I must be today as well. The shaikh Bukn-ud-din sent me on this journey to learn. He told me to open my eyes. He told me to tell what I know and to listen for the answer. I don't even know what I am looking for, and yet you have taught me something very important."

"I have?" The guard tilts his head.

"To learn, to seek, I must always be on watch." I thank the man. I begin to understand. The Shaikh told me to open my eyes. But I realize that he meant my eyes and ears. All the answers are there, to be picked off trees like dates. But only if you are aware of the trees.

After months winding through the mountains, our caravan reaches the low-lying hills above Baghdad. Great streams of water gush out of the mountains and flow into the Tigris River. Surrounding the river are rolling plains which were carved by the power of this great waterway.

We see the walls of the great city looming in the distance. I have heard stories of its magnificence but to see the enormous walls and the green-domed palace is a dream come true. The white marble walls shimmer in their radiance.

We reach the markets sprawled along the eastern bank of the river outside the protection of the concentric walls. An imposing gate gives us glimpses of buildings.

In the bazaar, I gather an audience. "Let me tell you a story of two birds. Let me sing you their song." I sing of the nightingale, of her love for the rose as it bloomed in the spring. Her love was so great she could not fly anywhere. I sing of the parrot who also could not travel. He had no strength being so used to the cage.

"What are birds to us?" A man in the crowd calls out. His black beard waggles when he speaks. "We do not care about the worries of birds."

"Yes." Another man agrees. "We need food for our families. That is more important than a poem about some birds."

"Oh, no, you are wrong." I search for another metaphor. "The anxious owl wanted to remain among the ruins, searching for treasures. His eyes could only focus on those earthly treasures, never seeing anything else."

"But, poet, what else is there? How else would we survive if we didn't live for these earthly needs?"

"There is so much more." I smile.

"How do we find it?" The first man asks.

"You take a journey," I explain. "There was a soldier who was in love and because of his state, he could never rest. As a sentinel, he had to be on duty and stay awake. Being in love was good for him and his wakefulness became a part of him. He who reaches this state will ever be on watch. True knowledge will come to him who can stay awake. He who keeps watch will be aware."

Someone calls out, "How do we take this journey?"

"Seek the door," I reply. "Your eyes won't always be shut."

Thunderous poundings coming from the north cause people in the bazaar to run outside. Others begin packing up their wares. I find myself jostled and I run outside to see what is happening.

A great army is descending upon us from the north.

CHAPTER 11
THE SWALLOW'S ANSWER
PART IV

WORLD NEWS – MAY 1
Fracking Contaminates Drinking Water
Injection Wells Cause Earthquakes
Fracking Adds to Greenhouse Gases
Scientists Alarmed—International Conference June 4-10

DEBORAH DROVE BACK to Southern California. In an unexpected downpour, she hurried across the UCI campus. An onslaught of emotions flooded every recess of her body. Her fists clenched as lines furrowed her face and a smile hid on the corners of her lips. *There's so much to tell him.* She found Croul Hall which housed the Department of Earth System Science.

Brady looked up from his computer screen. "Hey, this is a nice surprise."

Deborah took off her wet jacket, excitedly looking toward the other offices. "I was in the neighborhood, thought I'd drop by."

Brady smiled. "How's your daughter? We got your file." He picked up her report from the edge of his desk. "It looks in order for what you got. We've finished up at the mission. Hope that's not why you came."

They're finished? Slammed simultaneously by the failure of her plan and guilt for not devoting more time to her daughter, Deborah mumbled, "Rachel's fine, but she's not the only reason I drove down." She explained why she returned, skipping the part about not wanting the Dean to get wind of her field work.

"You've pinpointed it to a Sixties folk song?" Brady asked.

"And found a recording of it."

He grabbed his coffee mug. "So do you think this Fariña learned it from the swallows, or what, the birds learned it from him?" Brady stood. "Want some coffee? Let's hang up your jacket out here."

She noted he said birds in the plural. Realizing he wasn't believing it was a coincidence, she thought to herself that he could be a potential member of the CITIFITBAC Club. She quickly followed him into the shared open area outside the faculty offices. Clearing her throat, she tried to sound casual. "I want to try another test. Play a piece of the Fariña song for the swallows, see if the birds respond to it."

He poured her a mug. "It's not gourmet, but it's freshly brewed." The coffee pot was sitting next to a seismograph. Its needle was recording a constant low level activity.

She hung up her jacket and took the mug, straining to look into the other offices. "Any will do."

Brady looked surprised. "This from the world's expert on coffees?"

"Freshly brewed is fine," Deborah said, taking a sip.

Stephen stepped out of his office with his coffee mug in his hand. "I thought you were off the project. We've wrapped up at the mission. Nice pendant."

Deborah spun toward him and sucked in her breath. He wore the tie she had given him seven years ago for his birthday. It had two birds flying, half circling each other. He kept walking past her as if he didn't want to see her.

Brady caught him up on the new development.

Stephen refilled his mug. "Fariña probably heard the song from the birds."

"Right." Her eyes tracked him like a homing pigeon. "Ignore the fact that it's undetectable to the human ear. Ignore the fact that birds don't talk to people. And that he died decades ago."

Stephen turned toward the window. "What about St. Francis Assisi? He talked to birds."

She tried to get his gaze. "No one knows for a fact that St. Francis talked to birds. Christianity claims lots of events, but so much is suspect."

Stephen stared out the window, his chin thrust out. "It's an aspect of faith you'll never understand."

Deborah looked away, taking a gulp of coffee. Religion had been a problem between them. Years ago they had made a truce—Stephen strongly believed in Christianity and went to church. She went to parish parties with him at the Berkeley United Church of Christ and knew his minister Peter Brawster. But she didn't believe in God and never went to *shul.*

Deborah didn't want Rachel to grow up Christian, so she enrolled her in Hebrew classes at a nearby Conservative Temple to be *bas mitzvahed.* Her parents took Rachel to the orthodox *shul* whenever she visited them. But that stopped in Rachel's teen years when they died. Deborah had thought the religion topic over—until Rachel met Shelley. Then she embraced the orthodoxy of Sephardic Judaism.

Brady jumped in to counteract any sparks. "Maybe humans once had the ability to speak to birds but lost it at some point in time."

Stephen ignored Brady. "If St. Francis talked to birds, then Fariña could have learned the tune and words from one."

"I only believe in what instruments can measure. Like that seismograph." She pointed to the machine. "The objective world. That's what exists. There's no scientific evidence of other living forms verbally speaking a human language. And if Fariña heard the tune from a bird, then he had hypersensitive hearing."

"Maybe he did."

She felt moist between her breasts. "That's why I need to do this test." Looking at Brady, she abruptly asked, "Can you get me into the mission on Sunday morning before anyone arrives?"

"Not sure."

She wondered what she would do if Brady couldn't get her into the mission. She'd need to get a permit to set up her equipment in a public park like she had for the Eastshore Park in Berkeley. It would take time. *Break the law and sneak in?* She wasn't that type of person, but what was a scientific answer worth? *It's more than my professional reputation on the line.* Weighed down by worry, she felt it even harder to know what's what. *Especially, now, with truth swimming in a rising sea of funhouse distortions.*

The needle on the seismograph jumped. They all felt a small jolt. If the two men weren't running for the door, Deborah wasn't going to either. Putting her hand against a wall, she took a sip of coffee.

Stephen spun and stared at her. "You believe in instruments—well, that instrument is measuring real data. There are usually about 500 earthquakes a week around the world, only about 4 of them are major. At the moment, the Earth's crust is having about 45 significant earthquakes a week." He turned to look at the seismograph. "That's real data."

She blew out her breath, jolted like being hit by a tsunami. "What's happening?" She limped hurriedly toward the instrument. "We experienced a small earthquake up in Berkeley yesterday."

Stephen ignored her and leaned over the seismograph. "We're recording about twelve of those a day here, not all you can feel. But it's like what used to be magnitude twos are now fours. We're trying to sort out which are natural and which are man-made."

She stiffened. "What's that mean?" The floor felt like it was still shaking. She reached out again for the wall.

"Companies are injecting wastewater from hydraulic fracturing operations back into the ground. Fracking's happening all over the country. Even all over California if you can believe the insanity of that. It lubricates stuck faults, complicating the picture big time. That might be what you felt. But was it real or was it Memorex?"

Most of his words made no sense. But breathing quick, shallow breaths, she related to the idea behind that old commercial. "Why would they do that?"

"Because they can." He hunched over a spiral-bound book and logged some notes. His eyes darted to her. "Some people think they can control earthquakes that way. You know, generate a bunch of magnitude fours instead of waiting for a five."

She fell back into a chair, her head beginning to throb. "Are you serious? Why?"

Brady walked to the coffee pot. "Because it looks like a win-win. Pull billions of gallons of oil and natural gas out of the Earth and control earthquakes in the process."

Stephen started pacing. "Except no one is thinking of consequences and things are getting out of control. Just because you can do something, doesn't mean you should."

Brady refilled his mug. "Yeah, future generations are going to pay. No one knows what chemicals they're using."

Deborah rubbed her temple. "Chemicals? What are they using chemicals for? Don't they just dig a well and the oil or gas comes out?"

Stephen stopped pacing and stared at her. "What have you been doing, watching old movies?"

She searched out his eyes.

He quickly looked away and walked to the window again. "In the modern world, they pump millions of gallons of fluid—water with sand, lubricants, disinfectants, and who knows what else—down to make fractures in the shale, releasing the oil or gas. Problem is, the water they use has to be put somewhere—it doesn't disappear into la-la land. They inject the wastewater back down into Class II underground wells. Millions of gallons, causing earthquakes."

Deborah felt her heart beating quickly. She tried to remember back to the Earth Day Fair. "Where are they doing this fracking?"

"All over," Stephen said. "Oklahoma, Texas, Pennsylvania, Ohio, Arkansas, Louisiana. Wherever there's shale. Did you hear about the latest activity along the New Madrid fault? It's like they're squeezing every drop of oil they can out of the earth so they don't lose their financial investment in the technology."

A shadow crossed her face. "Would benzene be in the chemicals?"

"Sure," he pointed to a chart on the wall, "benzene, ethylbenzene, toluene, xylene, a host of others."

Deborah stood up and walked to it. The poster had been presented at a geological conference. Little oil well symbols dotted major portions of the United States. A legend showed the companies; hatching showed the shale. Depicted by Roman numerals, quakes were everywhere. Graphs indicated the types of chemicals being found in contaminated wells and water aquifers.

Brady agreed. "Luckily, nothing's going to happen in our lifetimes, but I've got five grandchildren. What kind of world are we giving them?"

She stared at the chart. "Aren't there fossils in shale?"

The two geologists looked at her. "Sure," Stephen answered, "mollusks, brachiopods, gastropods, and lots of microfossils. Black shale like the Marcellus in Pennsylvania formed where there was no oxygen so it has great fossils in excellent condition."

Jeff's fossilized seashell was a brachiopod. He must have been drinking water from a contaminated well on his spring break trip. Studying the legend, her eyes glommed onto one of the names. It was the company she had spoken to at the Earth Day Fair.

Stephen moved back to the seismograph. "At least our daughter won't be having kids."

Feeling dizzy, she reached into her travel bag and pulled out the green and white brochure the company rep had given to her. There it was—crisp and clean verbiage about their modern and safe extraction from shale. *A funhouse of distortions.*

Stephen saw the brochure. "Yeah, that's the worst of the companies, doing things no one should be doing. They're only greenwashing, pretending they're green. Can I have that? Are you okay?"

The blood drained from her face and she started to feel nauseous. *Was this who Jeff was up against in Pennsylvania? The ancient Pueblans cut down their trees and dug too many irrigation ditches. We're contaminating our water and heating the planet. What's the difference?*

He came up beside her, waggling his fingers to take the brochure. His eyes were wide. "Nothing's going to happen to Rachel." Taking the piece of paper, he walked back toward his office.

Deborah put down the mug and moved to get her jacket.

Brady called after Stephen. "You know, Stephen, Deborah's data will be useful for the International Anomaly Conference. And it in turn might shed light on the bigger issue."

Deborah stopped in mid-step. "What are you talking about?"

Brady turned to her. "The international conference to discuss the anomalous events happening in the world. Don't you know about it?"

"No. Been a bit busy."

"It's going to be in Seville, Spain next month. Every team is sending someone."

Thomas had been right. She asked, "Are you going?"

"Stephen is."

Deborah looked at Stephen. "Will you present my data?"

"No," Stephen turned at his office door. "I'm going to discuss the nature of this increased seismic activity. We're competing with Tomiko from Japan and Alvarez from Guatemala to come up with better interpretations of the seismic data. If nature is being pushed off balance, maybe we can show how it's pushing back. There's something definitely going on across all the systems."

Deborah felt hot between her breasts and lashed out at Stephen. "Couldn't you at least try to find out whether birds are being affected elsewhere in the world? It's not all in the literature."

"That's the exact reason for the conference," Brady said. "Communication. Everyone's feeling that way. Not enough time to publish everything and make sense of it, even with the Internet. People need to talk."

Stephen scowled. "I'm not going to ask people about birds. We're almost done compiling the data from our studies. I'm trying to find the heart of the problem. Maybe the Yellowstone super volcano is about to blow."

Deborah couldn't believe his pigheadedness. She dropped her jacket.

Brady reached to pick it up. "Part of the conference's goal is to set up a centralized database to track and correlate the problems. Stephen, you'll be adding significant data points. By contributing *all* our data, you could be the one to tie together diverse results."

Stephen stiffened at the word 'all'. Deborah knew he liked the idea of data integration, especially in such a complicated environment. He had the best lecture on systems she'd ever heard.

Stephen grabbed the jacket from Brady and took it to Deborah. He stood right in front of her, his eyes squinting hard. "Why don't you figure out how to get to the conference yourself? You must have travel money in your NSF grant."

She glared into his eyes. "I can't. I'm preparing for finals and I have no compelling reason to go, except to ask some questions. And you know Milhouse. He's on my back big time."

Brady tried to be sympathetic. "Once the database is completed, the answers will be available to everyone. You'll be able to ask your questions then. Get answers."

"Right. Get answers then." She broke Stephen's stare and grabbed her jacket. "Brady, let me know about Sunday."

How long are we going to keep hurting each other?

CHAPTER 12

*"The nightingales sing with sighs of love
my soul and my fate are in your power."*
-*Sephardic folksong*

WORLD NEWS – MAY 2
*War—Pollution From Depleted Uranium, Toxic Dust, Scorched Earth, and
  Land Mines.*
Corporations Cut Corners to Boost Earnings

THE GREEN ROOF OF SYNAGOGUE Sepharad sparkled in the
Saturday morning drizzle. "I told you it wouldn't be a bad walk to the
kehilla." Rachel shook out the hood from her raincoat. Her maroon
dress had a high neckline and covered her knees and elbows.

The dark green of Shelley's dress offset her red hair and dark eyes.
"Even in the rain. It's why we live where we do. To be near our
community and the library. Whoa, careful!"

The earth trembled slightly. "And so close to the ocean," Deborah
said, trying to maintain her balance and ignore her guilt. Shelley
grabbed her jacketed arm to steady her. "Thank you, Shelley."

Shelley nodded and let go. "Wish we were closer."

Remembering the walks to *shul* in New York every Saturday
morning, Deborah thought about the convolution of melding ancient
religious beliefs with the modern world. Not working on the Sabbath
meant not driving a car or turning on a light bulb even though these
things hadn't been invented when the law was written. It also meant no
umbrellas in the rain because opening one would create a structure.

The *Shacharit* service was in progress. Ushers greeted them with big
smiles. On their way to the right-side benches, Shelley and Rachel were
hugged by the women. The Rabbi was at a lectern in the front of the
sanctuary. The cantor, or *Hazzan,* stood in the imposing central dais or

bimah in the middle. Each was wrapped in an enveloping *tallis*, large prayer shawl.

Shelley tapped an older woman on the shoulder in front of them. The woman, in her late 70s, turned around and squealed in delight, hugging Shelley. Small but regal, she also hugged Rachel. Shelley whispered, "*Nonna*, this is Deborah, Rachel's mother. This is my grandmother, Anna Nessim."

Deborah silently nodded.

"Dr. Wright," Anna said, excitedly, "what an honor to meet you. Did you feel the earthquake? We did."

"Call me Deborah."

The women around them ambushed them with looks. On the other side of the *mehitzah*, the wooden barrier between the genders, a few men gave them looks to be quiet. Neither Anna nor the girls seemed to care.

Rachel handed Deborah a prayer book. "Page 348 to follow the Hebrew."

Deborah felt a bit surreal. Her body tensed. It had been thirteen years since she had been to a service and never to a Sephardic one. Perhaps it was the layout of the synagogue with its central *bimah*. The Ashkenazi tradition had the *bimah* in the front. Some of the prayers weren't familiar. And what language were they mixing in with Hebrew?

"You must come to dinner tomorrow night," Anna whispered loudly to Deborah.

Shelley said, "We'll be there, *Nonna*."

The *Hazzan's* rich baritone voice filled the synagogue with the chant of the *Hatzi Kaddish* prayer, indicating the next part of the service was beginning.

Deborah opened the prayer book. Early on, her father had insisted on teaching her Hebrew despite her being a girl. She remembered going to a private Hebrew school at nine years old. When her parents found out that strict teachers were hitting her knuckles with a metal ruler, her mother yanked her out of the school and her father continued the lessons himself even if she was a girl.

The *Hazzan* picked up the *Torah* scroll which was encased in an elaborate silver-plated cylindrical box. Deborah watched the Rabbi, the *Hazzan* and the other men snake between the benches carrying it. Men reached out with the fringes from their *tallism* prayer shawls to touch the Torah. The group stopped at the front of the *mehitzah* barrier. Deborah watched as Rachel and Shelley walked up and touched the Torah with their prayer books.

The parading group brought the Torah to the *bimah*, opened the box, and began the elaborate process of reading the weekly portion. It was Leviticus Chapters 26 and 27, a portion about blessings and curses. Deborah remembered her father talking about how the world was created 'very good' and that adherence to ritual makes God's presence available. For all the ritual she did as a child, not once did she feel God's presence. Her father had said it was because she was a girl, adding that in her marriage she would feel God's presence.

Deborah listened to the *Hazzan* intoning in Hebrew what God promised man if he obeyed Him and what God's curses were if he didn't. God established his covenant with those who have children. She remembered feeling something when Rachel was born, but was it a covenant with God? It was more like being stunned that she and Stephen had created this living human being. Feeling warm, she took off her jacket. As she did so, she fingered something odd in her pocket. It was the toy compass from the Earth Day fair.

When the Torah was finally closed and returned to its place, Rabbi Stern looked at the congregation to give the *D'var Torah,* his sermon. "Gandhi says there are seven social sins—commerce without morality, pleasure without conscience, knowledge without character, science without humanity, wealth without work, politics without principles, and worship without sacrifice. Let us see how this relates to the Jewish concept of morality. In our weekly Torah portion, God says, *im bechukkotai telechu,* 'if you follow My laws and faithfully observe My commandments—My *mitzvot*—I will grant peace in the land.' He is saying I will look with favor upon you. I will be ever present in your midst. He is not saying, if you maybe observe My commandments or if you observe only a few of them. This is a tall order He requires of His faithful.

"And what is the extent of the requirement? Rabbi Akiba says 613 commandments were given to Moses on Mount Sinai. These are the principles of law and ethics of the Jewish faith." The Rabbi gestured emphatically and continued, "They outline a life of sanctity and purity involving prayers, festivals, marriage, civil and criminal law, dietary constraints, and ritual purity.

"God goes on to say *v'im bezot lo tishm'u*. 'If you do not obey Me, if you reject My laws...I will smite you sevenfold for your sins.' In Hebrew, there are three levels of sin. *Pesha*—an intentional sin acting in deliberate defiance of God, *Ovon*—a sin of uncontrollable emotion, knowingly done, and *Cheit*—an unintentional sin. Judaism believes no human is perfect but there is always a road to repentance, or *t'shuvah*, return. Jews used to practice animal sacrifices as a way to atone. But with the destruction of the Temple, sacrifices ceased and many grieved. Midrash says, 'Be not grieved. We can still gain ritual atonement through deeds of loving-kindness.'

"In this week's portion, the Hebrew word being used for sin is the third one, *Cheit*. God is saying that even if you disobey Him and reject His laws, you are doing it unintentionally. Perhaps you were brought up Jewish but no longer practice, or perhaps you aren't even Jewish and the idea of obeying 613 *mitzvot* seems immense."

Light murmuring from the congregation agreed. The Rabbi smiled and glanced at the women's side of the room.

"Like Gandhi's seven social sins, there is a set of seven moral imperatives God gave Noah as a binding set of laws for all mankind. Laws which are incorporated into the *mitzvot* and which are, in essence, the bottom line." He surveyed the men's faces in front of him. "Sort of an executive summary."

People laughed.

Then Rabbi Stern became more serious. "First, a requirement to have just laws, and then six universal prohibitions—a prohibition against murder, theft, sexual immorality, idolatry, blasphemy, and eating live animals.

"This week's *Haftarah* portion says 'cursed is he who trusts in man who makes mere flesh his strength and turns his thoughts from the Lord.' When we turn our thoughts to the Lord, staying in conscious morality and humanity, faithfully follow His *mitzvot*, we are no longer unintentionally sinning. *Refa'eni hashem ve'erafe hoshieni.* 'Heal me, O Lord, and let me be healed; save me, and let me be saved; for You are my glory.' This is the Jewish imperative, our stay against social sins. We are bound by these laws. We live by them."

The congregation nodded with approval when he finished. Deborah felt the Rabbi had been talking to her. It was God's irrefutable word on morality—to follow God's laws in order to be god-like. There was no way to refute it.

But there has to be. What had Boswell said?

After the service, Rachel and Shelley greeted friends saying *Shabbat shalom*. Anna took Deborah's arm and walked into the reception hall where the congregation gathered for lunch. Rabbi Stern greeted congregants. The women brought out dishes prepared before the Sabbath, spreading them out over a long table—tuna fish, potato salad, and some sort of stewed dish.

Deborah nodded a little too quickly to the Rabbi. She remembered this time not to try to shake hands. "I understand now that I can't prove what you asked to your satisfaction. You set me up."

His smile disappeared. "Dr. Wright, that wasn't my intent. It had been a hard day. I had a lot on my mind."

"That's usually my excuse." She shrugged. "But, Rabbi, I have a question. The Jewish Bible is the Jewish Bible, and yet Conservatives, Reform, and the Orthodox interpret it in different ways. If Reform rabbis perform same-gender marriages, are they being immoral?"

He stared at her and then smiled again. "You found a weakness in my position. Your daughter is right—you are a good scientist."

Deborah was thrown off-guard. Having butted heads with him, she hadn't expected this response. She felt a sense of relief invade her body as she read into his words. A smile started forming on her lips. Believing all the disappointment in her relationship with her daughter could be put past them, she glanced around. Rachel was in an animated conversation with a young man in a wheelchair. Deborah pounced in with something she learned from the Boswell book. "Religious practices change over time. After all, marriage wasn't declared a sacrament until the 12th century by the Christian church."

Rabbi Stern puffed up his chest. "Christians do what they do. And reform rabbis follow a moral practice choosing which of the *mitzvot* to follow. Behaving correctly out of choice instead of out of command is a good thing. It fills a person with integrity."

Deborah felt her smile grow. "So you'll marry them?"

"For the orthodoxy, there's no question of which *mitzvot* we follow—we follow them all. A community without standards is not a community—it's a group of private individuals. Just because morality can do a hop, skip, and jump depending on the point of view doesn't mean orthodoxy will jump off its position on the *mitzvot*. No, I won't marry them."

Her eyes blazed as he walked away. Feeling her stomach flip-flopping, she saw everything in slow motion—Rachel laughing along with the man in the wheelchair, people filling their plates with food. Children pleaded with their parents for cakes. Deborah knew she couldn't eat a thing.

Anna pressed Deborah's arm. "Dr. Wright, have you met my grandson Robert?"

"Grandson?" Deborah was directed toward the young man in the wheelchair. He was muscular with short brown hair. "I didn't know you had another grandchild." Anna's words pounded in her ears. "Very nice to meet you."

Robert grinned a male version of Shelley's smile. "I'd stand up but it wouldn't look pretty."

Anna said, "My daughter Sarah and her husband Gerald had two children. I've been raising them for the last 17 years."

"*Nonna*," Robert complained, "you make us sound like babies."

"Nonsense, *mijo*," Anna straightened his hair, "you are my babies." She looked around at the long table of food. "Now where is the *hamin* I brought? Dr. Wright, you must try some. It's a stewed chicken dish, simmered for hours."

"Sounds like what the Ashkenazi call *cholent*." Deborah looked at Anna and Robert. Rachel had known Shelley for two years and Deborah didn't know anything about her family. Her stomach was on the verge of nausea. She saw Rachel bringing plates of food and motioning for them to sit. Walking to where she pointed, Deborah saw Shelley and some other women at one table eating lunch next to a table where men sat.

Shelley shook her curly head, fork in mid-air. "You're a white heterosexual male, Ben, and can't even begin to see your unearned advantages." She stood up to help her grandmother sit down. Rachel put the plates in front of them.

Ben dug into his tuna fish. "Men aren't as emotional as women and can make the tough calls. Do you think women could declare war?"

Deborah took the chair next to Rachel, wondering what the fewest number of bites of the *hamin* would be considered polite. An overcooked hard-boiled egg sat on top of the chicken and rice mixture.

An older woman came by with flyers. "Don't forget the Sisterhood's clothing drive for battered women this month."

Rachel grinned. "Oh, Leah, I'll bring our donation on Monday."

"Thank you, *Shabbat shalom.*" Leah walked away to other tables.

Shelley sat back down. Her eyebrows moved as she spoke. "Ignoring the fact that women have declared wars and that war is a highly destructive patriarchal solution, men haven't always been in control. Women used to be the religious and political leaders. For some reason, the balance of power changed and the patriarchy took over. Nobody knows why. Women became sexual objects and the property of men."

Ben spoke loudly, "That's not true. Lots of women have high status. Isn't Rachel's mother a professor? Don't you know one of our senators?" He turned toward Rachel.

Rachel leaned forward. "Benjamin, I'd like to introduce you to my mother, Dr. Deborah Wright. Mom, this is Benjamin." She continued the introductions, and then said, "My mother is friends with one of our Senators."

Deborah stared back blankly. Her brain kicked in when she realized what they were waiting for. "Yes, I know Senator Susan Bonheur." She looked down at the food. "Don't eat tuna fish."

Ben eyes widened. "The wife of the hall-of-famer Thomas Bonheur? Cool."

Rachel frowned at her mother. "Mom, are you all right? There's nothing wrong with the tuna fish."

Anna turned to Rachel. "You gave her my *hamin*, yes? The other women make it just as well, of course."

"Yes, *nonna,*" Rachel giggled to Anna.

Deborah couldn't eat. She looked around for the restroom in case her stomach got any worse.

Shelley's eyes flashed. "Sure, some women have reached high levels but what happened at your wedding, Ben? Who gave the bride away?"

"Why? Her father of course. What a question." He laughed.

Shelley shook her head. "You don't think that's a symbol of being male property?"

Deborah looked around. "Is there any coffee?"

Rachel glanced at her mother again. "I wouldn't bother. The coffee's not up to your standards."

Shelley sat forward, excitedly. "Men perpetuate their lineage by controlling women's sexuality. Marriage between a man and a woman is a sociosexual necessity for tying down women and their babies. Through its cultural messages and religions, the patriarchy ostracizes anyone not participating." She looked at Rachel.

Robert interjected, "Are you equating patriarchy with all men?"

"No, of course not," Shelley frowned, "men are caught in the system just as women are."

"Good," Robert continued, "because there are lots of men who would like to see women running things."

"I believe that," Shelley's voice rose. "But women's values have been left out of public discourse and we're all blinded by this patriarchal filter affecting how we evaluate things."

Ben said, "I don't think that—"

Leah came running into the reception hall. Her long skirt was flowing and she yelled, "Come quick!"

Rabbi Stern jumped up. "What's wrong? Did the earthquake do damage?" He started running to the door. People quickly stood.

Shelley and Rachel ran to the woman. "Leah, what's going on?"

"There's graffiti all over the outside. It's horrible," she gasped, trying to catch her breath. "Get someone to call the police."

Deborah hurried outside, almost tripping. Rachel and Shelley followed behind her, along with others. Standing on the flagstone entranceway, they stared up on the synagogue wall.

Scrawled in red paint were various religious and Nazi symbols. Below them were the words 'AT-TACKUN OLAM'.

The congregation started gathering around them. Rabbi Stern was livid. "This was what I was afraid would happen. We've had threats, and now this." A siren could be heard in the distance.

People were murmuring about the symbols and commenting on the words. The men stood together gesturing themselves into a frenzy. The women stood near them, in a more quiet rage.

A passerby on the street asked, "What do the words mean?"

Shelley shook her head. "It's a play on the Hebrew phrase *tikkun olam*—healing the world. We're obliged to perform acts of loving kindness to make this world a better place and someone turns it against us. Makes no sense."

Staring at the Rabbi, Deborah retorted, "No form of discrimination makes sense."

He turned to look at her. Seemingly about to say something, he walked off to talk to the police.

🕊 🕊

It had been years since Deborah had done a *Havdallah* service to end the Sabbath. The ritual separated the holy from the ordinary. Not that the day had been ordinary by anyone's standards, Deborah thought. The sun having just set, the three of them stood in the kitchen next to the table by the greenhouse window. Shelley led the blessings over the wine, a spice box, and a braided green wax candle. She brought the spice box to her nostrils and inhaled the fragrant aroma of cloves and cinnamon. Then she held it for Rachel to smell.

Fingering her pendant, Deborah stared at the braided candle. Rachel and Shelley's closeness cut through her like a machete. They reminded her of when she and Stephen were first married. The dances at George Washington University, how they would do the hustle and disco. He would have a champagne spritzer waiting for her when they sat down. The sharpest dresser, he was the best dancer she had ever seen. *Is that how people make the major decisions in their lives, by the way someone moves or fills out a purple shirt?* She used to meet him for coffee and they'd talk for hours. They'd walk along the Potomac, saying hello to a little old man with long ears and a gilded walking cane. Stephen couldn't suppress his passion for geology, and he would explain what happened a million years ago to the rocks and formations right in front of them. It was magical.

She remembered their hike down the Grand Canyon before Rachel was born. Deborah's left foot had bled as her toenail cut into her skin. He doctored it, wrapping tape around the bleeding toe. She had burst into tears. He said, "You are as strong as any man." It was the first time someone had offered support to change her place in the hierarchy. He told her how he had conditioned himself to not get caught up in people's racist attitudes. Rachel became everything Stephen is, Deborah realized. Where am I in this family?

"*Shavuah tov.* A good week." Rachel put the spice box and candle back in a cabinet and motioned toward the living room. "And a *Shabbat* we won't forget."

Deborah knew Rachel was talking about the graffiti attack. Guilt pounded on her heart and all she could think about was her conversation with the Rabbi. Following behind Shelley, Deborah asked, "Has an anti-Semitic attack like that happened before?"

A shadow crossed Shelley's eyes. "I think the worst one was just before my parents died when the Jews were emigrating from the former Soviet Union."

Deborah stumbled on the carpet into Shelley. "Sorry." She turned red. *Why don't I know anything about this?*

Shelley steadied her. "It's okay. I'm used to helping my brother in and out of his wheelchair." She led Deborah to a large yellow armchair with thin blue stripes and then sat down on the couch. "There was a week of smoke bombs. I was pretty young—I just remember the horrible smell. The police have been good about watching over our congregation ever since."

Rachel brought a tray with light snacks and three mugs. "Not all that good if graffiti got written on the building. Mom, here's a cup of Jamaican Blue Mountain. I know you like this one." She opened a food storage container brimming with slices of fruits, next to a plate with little cakes. "Try the strawberries—they're a new variety from Spain. And there are oatmeal date bars and homemade banana bread." She turned on small track lights above the couch and sat down next to Shelley.

"Thanks." Deborah took the mug, looking out the window. Small outdoor spotlights glowed softly on the green gardenias. "Can I ask you a question?"

Shelley nodded.

Deborah cleared her throat. "I guess I knew you had been living with your grandmother when you and Rachel moved in together. But I hardly know anything else about you. What happened to your parents? When did they die?"

Shelley reached for Rachel's hand. "They took Robert to a conference my dad was running. I was at camp that summer or else I would have been with them. They stayed at one of those fancy hotels with a big atrium. The three of them were on a walkway above the atrium when it collapsed."

Deborah sucked in her breath. "Oh, no."

Shelley's voice darkened. "My parents were killed. Robert survived. The doctors said it was because of his age—eight years old." Shelley didn't elaborate on the rest of the story. Deborah could only guess. Shelley shrugged. "And he's been in a wheelchair ever since. Luckily, it's only his lower spinal cord that was affected. He's a very talented musician."

Deborah sipped her coffee. "Things like that shouldn't happen."

"The safety board determined that the subcontractor had doubled the weight on the bolts holding the walkway beams because they didn't want to spend the extra money and time to connect the beams correctly."

Rachel squeezed Shelley's hand and then got up. "Anyone want wine?"

Shelley smiled. "A glass would be lovely." She reached for a strawberry and ate it. "These are delicious. I think they're called *niebla*." She gestured to Deborah to try one.

"I'm fine with the Jamaican Blue." Deborah turned back to Shelley. She remembered Thomas telling her about the company that dumped toxic waste in Africa. *These aren't isolated incidents—the oil spills, the mine waste, shoddy construction. Even what Jeff is trying to recover from.* "Corporate greed."

Shelley rearranged her legs under her. "That's too easy to say. Wording like that makes it mythical, you know, good versus evil. A corporation exists for one thing only and that is to return value to its stockholders, the owners. It's obliged to care about nothing other than money. It has no conscience—only a financial bottom line." Shelley's voice raised up a notch and she leaned forward. "That's the system we live under. The problem is when people treat other people with disrespect and put money first. Like today, that graffiti."

Deborah could hear her passion. She took another sip of coffee. "What happened after the report came out? Was anyone held responsible?"

"There was a huge lawsuit because so many people died. All the families won."

Rachel entered with the glasses and handed one to Shelley. "Not that losing your parents is winning." As she sat down, she picked out an oatmeal date bar.

Shelley took the wine and turned toward Deborah. "I'm using the money to create a non-profit organization to counteract this—this—" she searched for the words, "—this thing that's like a cloudy filter imposed on us by the patriarchy distorting our vision of reality. Learning ethical behavior has to start with the children. I use Gandhi's seven social sins as a place to begin discussions."

Deborah shot a look at her. "That was the Rabbi's topic in his sermon."

Shelley took a sip of wine and quickly put her glass down. "Exactly. Who do you think brought them to his attention? We center our work on the Gandhi philosophy mixed with Jewish teachings. We're developing a curriculum." She sat forward excitedly. "For example, redefining commerce to go beyond money. Judaism believes the intrinsic value of every human being is the same, and that goodness is produced by a sincere commitment to good acts."

She's standing up to Rabbi Stern, Deborah thought. *Did Rachel even need me to go charging into his office? She has Shelley who knows exactly what she wants and how to get it.* Deborah could feel her face flush with humiliation. She closed her eyes, took another sip of coffee, and almost choked.

Shelley looked concerned. "Deborah, are you all right?"

I'm fine." Deborah cleared her throat. "You know, wrong pipe."

Shelley continued. "I've collected a lot of data but I'm not quite there. Something is missing. I've been studying philosophical thinkers. Nothing stands out yet."

"What's missing?" Her head was pounding.

"I don't know enough. At the library, I study what's happening in the world. I want to figure out how I can use the money to do the most good. I can't yet grasp the big picture."

Her words reverberated off the walls and windows. Taking a deep breath, Deborah put her mug down on the coffee table. "That's a thought. A month ago, I gave a lecture about competition and cooperation. I pointed out that businessmen trying to make a fast buck are acting within an economic system that they can't see because they're inside it. They don't know their effect on others down the street or halfway around the world. Think of cells inside an organ. The cells don't know about the organ, but their combined activity creates the organ and its functionality." Deborah picked up her mug again. "Do you know the name Joseph Priestley?"

"He was some type of scientist?"

"Right. 18th century. Before people figured out how to create a vacuum, they viewed the world as filled with stuff, and between all the stuff was nothingness. No one studied the nothingness. When Priestley was a boy, he'd put bugs in jars and watched them die. As an adult, he put a mouse into a vacuum chamber and watched it die. But when he put a mint plant in the vacuum with the mouse, both lived. It was an astounding discovery which changed millennia of scientific thinking. In discovering oxygen, Priestley, in effect, invented air, turning it from nothing into something."

"What are you saying?" Shelley furrowed her forehead.

Deborah's eyes gleamed in the soft light. "The big picture entails a lot of things. Everything's connected in ways we can't begin to comprehend. There are synergies. I agree with you that one can't say it's all corporate greed because corporations are made of people and no one knows how everything is connected. A colleague from Berkeley told me how companies use the oceans as vast toilets for toxic waste and pollution. That's an easy connection because we need water to live." She looked at her mug of coffee and slowly placed it down on the table, thinking of Jeff. "Our environment—we're inside it and can't see the impact we have on it. There will always be scientific discoveries that show our thinking is incomplete. Our economic system—we're inside it, we can't see it. It exists based on the competitive and cooperative actions of all of us. Everything we do affects everything else. And too much competition kills and too much cooperation suffocates. There needs to be a balance. Something our human social and economic world sorely lacks."

Shelley sat up, excited. "And to find that balance, there have to be principles, like Gandhi said, so people can translate goals into lifestyle. There has to be some path, some guiding principle to personally follow that makes sense."

"What's happening in the world now is crazy." She stared at her mug.

Shelley leaned forward. "I'm not going to stop working for the kids, but the more you learn, the more you wonder. I need to find a guiding principle that feels right, one not tied to any religion." She grinned at Rachel. "This is related to the decision we made today."

Rachel nodded.

Deborah caught her breath. "What?"

Rachel smiled at Shelley and glanced at her mother. "We'll tell you tomorrow night at *Nonna* Anna's."

Deborah looked at the both of them. Shelley was indirectly asking for her help. *Can I risk failure again, or is this a way to reach Rachel?* Deborah stood up. "I'll keep my eyes open."

🕊 🕊

WORLD NEWS – MAY 3
Raising Livestock Causes Massive Pollution
Production of Meat Leads to Resource Depletion

Brady said, "You sure you want to do this?" He bundled his jacket around him to ward off the bite in the air.

It was Deborah's favorite time of the day, that time when the morning was about to begin. The world around the mission was thinking of waking while she soaked in the passing seconds, aware a spectacle was about to occur—the rising of the sun. A quiet, majestic event, mystical, yet as common as every day, like taking a slow breath. She tried to blot out the Dean's voice running wild in her head cautioning her against doing field work. Brady didn't even know half the problems she would have if this experiment failed. "It'll work."

"You saw how few birds are left."

"Let's do this." She walked to the inner courtyard as he picked up the other cases. They set up the equipment, adding the music system for playing *The Swallow Song* and a video camcorder.

Deborah cued up the music for normal speed. If the birds responded, it would indicate they were able to hear a human tune and perhaps internalize it. Knowing it was important to have multiple observers, she showed Brady what to look and listen for.

No swallows arrived.

THE SWALLOW AND THE NIGHTINGALE

"I told you," Brady shook his head, doodling on his clipboard, "this place is basically dead now."

Deborah stared at the controls of the RAX-1000 as if that would bring the birds.

"It's no use," he said.

"Let's give them another half hour." The sun had risen. She scanned the sky for any signs of life. There weren't any. "So Stephen is definitely going to the international conference?" She tried to sound casual.

"Yeah, he's been totally focused on that."

"Is anyone else going?" She hesitated for a second. "From the team, I mean."

He looked over at her.

She blushed, bent her head down and studied the console.

Brady stopped drawing mountains. "You don't have to tell me, I've known for a long time things weren't right between you."

Deborah turned to face him. "Oh, you know what I'm asking."

"You want to know if he's taking anyone with him."

"Yes, like that. We've been separated for a year. It hasn't—it hasn't been easy." She stood up. "Okay, forget it." She grabbed the equipment, a coil of cables and the music player.

He stood up. "I could definitely tell something was going on." Brady withdrew a brochure from his pocket. "Look, I brought you the information about the conference. You should think about going, too."

She took the brochure and stuffed it in her pocket. "Well?"

"No, Deborah. He's alone. He's going alone."

🕊 🕊

Deborah stared at the photos sitting on the Steinway piano in Anna's living room. A formal wedding picture from the Eighties, pictures of Robert and Shelley growing up, crazy wide smiles directed at two loving parents. Shelley's mother had high cheek bones and wise eyes. Her father had a mustache and was tilting his head in a way that included everyone. There were more recent photographs as well—one of Robert with a guitar singing on stage, Shelley in a black graduation cap and gown. Deborah's stared at one of Shelley, Rachel, and Robert together, the two women crouching next to him.

The black grand piano dominated the room. Thick white wall-to-wall carpeting was covered by scattered intricate blue rugs. Floor-to-ceiling windows on the far side of the room opened up to distant rising hillsides giving way to scrub-covered Saddleback Mountain. A slight breeze from the trees mixed with the fresh smell of hyacinths, the mustiness of antique furniture, and the sweet odor of roasted chicken and freshly made bread.

Anna came up next to her and smiled at the wedding photograph. "That's my daughter Sarah and her husband Gerald."

"Shelley told me what happened." She felt tired.

"I started raising the children when I was 63 years old." She picked up the framed picture of Shelley and Robert with Rachel.

Robert pointed to the photo of himself. "My first recorded performance. At the Coach House here in Capistrano."

Followed by Rachel, Shelley walked into the room with a plate of hors d'oeuvres. "Our *nonna* loves to cook and insists everyone try everything." She was almost giddy.

Deborah turned away. She thought, families are microcosms of the world, so fragile and yet so resilient. Hers was receding further and further from her.

Anna sat down. "Rachel tells me you have traveled extensively, Dr. Wright. Sit here." She motioned next to her on one of the loveseats. She thrust the photograph with the three smiling faces toward Deborah. "Isn't that a beautiful picture?"

Deborah walked toward her and took the photo as she sat. "Please call me Deborah. Yes, it's beautiful."

Shelley shook her head. "She won't. Too old country." She sat down next to Rachel on the other loveseat. Robert rolled up between the loveseats.

Angling the photo on the coffee table so she didn't have to look at it, Deborah tried an appetizer. "My husband's career took us to many remote locations. This is delicious. What is it called?"

Anna leaned forward. "They're called *bourekas*. I think you call it a knish. And those are *albóndigas*. Meatballs."

"I've never known any Sephardic Jews before."

Anna adjusted the photograph so that they could both look at it. "My beautiful family. Our culture has Spanish and Middle Eastern influence, your Ashkenazi has the German and Russian. You can see the influence in our foods."

Shelley turned to Deborah. "The histories are the same but different. Sephardim had to choose between leaving their homes, converting, fighting, or remaining hidden. Some killed themselves. We learned flexibility, but those that converted, the *conversos,* were suspect, for good reason usually."

"How did your ancestors arrive here?" Deborah stared at the photo. *What's the announcement they're going to make?*

Shelley answered for them. "We believe they left Spain with the edict of 1492. Eventually, they immigrated to Istanbul, keeping their faith hidden until it was safe to be more open. My great-grandparents immigrated to New York in 1942."

"I was twelve years old," Anna added. "And then I came out here to California when I married Joseph Nessim."

Shelley continued, "My father's family, the Abenacars, have a similar story. Our families have all been caught in these fights between peoples. Your family got caught in the Holocaust, my family was caught in earlier bloodbaths. The agonies of people being expelled from their homes, or killed, all in order to stay true to who they are. And what for?"

Deborah drummed nervously on the arm of the couch. "It's usually the same thing, whether they say it or not. Prejudice."

Shelley nodded. "But what's left when people are killed or run off? Their property. Underlying prejudice is greed for power and resources. There are books on this topic."

"Anti-Semitism, racism, sexism, homophobia. Shelley's and my lives are political statements," Rachel said, "without us even opening our mouths."

Deborah added, "Sinistrophobia."

Everyone looked at her.

She chuckled almost too hard. "Fear of left-handedness." She raised her hand. "I read about it in a book."

Anna shook her head. "You all quote books, even the Rabbi does. The answer isn't in any book. I know my granddaughter," she confided to Deborah. "There is nothing in the world bad about her. Surely the Rabbi knows that."

Everyone laughed. Shelley got embarrassed and Robert started in on her. "Oh, yes, she is *soooo* perfect. Never mind the times she stole my comic books and made me promise to wash the dishes on her chore night. You still owe me for those, you know."

Shelley asked for quiet. "We have an announcement." She had a big smile on her face. "We've decided to get married."

Deborah jerked forward. "But the Rabbi? I thought he hadn't agreed." *How had they changed his mind since yesterday?*

Rachel grinned. "Now that same-sex marriage is legal in the State of California, we're going to get married."

Deborah rose from the loveseat. "You mean…"

Anna beamed. "This is exciting news. When and where are you going to do it?"

Rachel jumped up, avoiding looking at her mother. "Call it what you want, a commitment ceremony, a wedding. We're getting married."

"Who's going to officiate?" Her stomach started to flip-flop.

Rachel sat back down next to Shelley. "We want an outdoor ceremony at Doheny Beach, nothing really fancy." She looked at Anna. "We've picked a date of June 7th."

Anna's eyes went wide. "June 7th?"

Shelley ran over to her grandmother. "Yes, *nonna*. Let's turn a sad memory into a happy anniversary."

Surprise, sadness, and delight all crossed through Anna's eyes. She took her Shelley's face in her hands. "Yes, my granddaughter. You are so wise. We need to celebrate life."

Shelley smiled and hugged her. Then she went and sat back down next to Rachel.

Rachel said, "We want to get married because we want to have a baby."

"What? A baby?" Deborah was stunned. Her hand went to her stomach.

Anna beamed. "How wonderful. This is a new world indeed, isn't it, Dr. Wright?"

Deborah began breathing heavily. *The joy of a baby, but to a homosexual couple?* "How are you going to do this?"

Rachel stood up and walked toward Robert. "We've decided Robert will be the sperm donor and I will carry the baby."

Shelley got up to stand next to them. "It's perfect. A true family solution."

Deborah searched out Rachel's eyes, but Rachel wouldn't look at her. Feeling like she was at the wrong end of a telescope on another planet, she fell back into her seat and tears filled her eyes. *The burden of proving same-gender love as being moral is over. Rachel no longer needs me. And they're going to have a baby. A grandchild.* She stared at the photo on the coffee table. Three smiling faces, Rachel in her new family. She looked up at the three young adults mirroring the image in real life. As they all talked about the exciting possibilities, Deborah excused herself to go to the bathroom.

"Shall we?" Anna guided everyone to the dining room where Rachel finished putting out the food. Shelley pushed Robert's chair. Deborah followed, wanting to talk to Rachel.

Gracing the table was a platter of chicken stuffed with rice, almonds and raisins. Next to it was a salad of avocados, oranges, melons. Deborah sat next to Anna. She looked over at Rachel who still wouldn't look at her.

Robert said two short Hebrew prayers, one over each platter. Then he turned to Deborah. "Even though some end a meal with this next prayer, we like to add it at the start." He began singing in a strong tenor voice.

> *"Tzur mishelo, mishelo ohalnu borhu emunai.*
> *Sovanu sovanu sovanu v'hosarnu kidvar Adonoi.*
> *Rock of plenty, life to living, blessings to Him sing.*
> *Life and food all creatures giving, Thou art Lord our King."*

Deborah half-listened to the Hebrew as she monitored Rachel. She knew the words from a prayer her family had sung. *Am I losing Rachel for good? A baby? It's a beautiful tune, so different from the Ashkenazi. But still it sounds familiar.* Deborah thought, why would I know it, theirs is a whole different tradition. *But I know this song. Where have I heard this before?*

Robert's voice vibrated in harmony to his guitar. The tune had a beautiful simplicity. It's rich sound reminded Deborah of—she couldn't believe it. *I know what this reminds me of.* She stiffened in excitement. When Robert finished, Deborah asked, "What was that prayer?"

Shelley passed the chicken. "It's called *Tzur Mishelo*. I hope you like the chicken. It's kosher, of course, but also free range. We don't eat red meat anymore."

With two hands, Anna picked up the salad bowl. "Salad, Dr. Wright? Are you upset we start our meal with that prayer as opposed to a more ordinary one?"

Deborah took the bowl. "Thank you, it looks delicious." She quickly spooned a portion on to her plate and too much onto Anna's. "We used to sing this same prayer at the table." She hurriedly passed the bowl and took some of the chicken. She took a deep breath and tried to calm down. "It's not the tune we sang." Starting in on the meal, she said, "I am wondering where the tune came from."

Shelley shrugged her shoulders, receiving the chicken back and served herself some. "It's the tune we've always sung."

"It was my idea to sing it first instead of last." Robert dug into the chicken. "*Nonna*, you outdid yourself with this meal."

Rachel agreed. "The chicken is superb, as always."

"But where did it come from?" Deborah was insistent.

Anna looked at her. "The chicken? Shelley and Rachel insist on all our food being locally grown without any injected hormones or genetic modifications."

Deborah smiled. "Thank you, Anna. I mean the tune, where did it come from?"

"It's an old tune. Sephardic," Robert answered.

Anna picked up her fork and started eating. "Why are you asking? It's beautiful, isn't it?"

Deborah took another bite and swallowed hard. "It's the tune the swallow sang at the mission."

"What?" Rachel stopped eating and looked at Deborah.

"I recorded a dying swallow at the San Juan Capistrano Mission. This tune was contained in its song."

Rachel looked confused. "I thought you said it was singing something else."

"This is the same tune." Deborah tapped her fingers on the table.

Robert quipped, "Do you mean that the birds are Jewish?" This was followed by jokes about little *yarmulkes* and birds *davening*.

THE SWALLOW AND THE NIGHTINGALE

When they quieted down, Deborah explained the RAX-1000 and how it could detect sounds the human ear couldn't.

Everyone began talking at once. How did the bird know the song? A Hebrew song even. Deborah described the American folk song *The Swallow Song* which had the same tune.

Robert didn't seem too surprised. "In the Jewish culture of Spain, there is a tradition of reusing tunes for both secular and religious songs."

Anna put down her fork. "I grew up speaking *espagnol*, the language some call Ladino."

Robert kept eating. "In fact, there's a secular version of this song in the *espagnol* language called *Los Bilbilicos*."

Almost giddy, Deborah ate some salad and said, "I'd love to hear it."

Robert leaned back. "My guitar."

"I didn't mean a concert in the middle of dinner."

Anna gestured to Shelley. "Never you mind. Music is more important than eating."

Shelley brought Robert his guitar. He began strumming and singing the Ladino song.

"Los bilbilicos cantan con sospiros de amor,
Mi neshama mi ventura estan en tu poder.
La rosa enflorese en el mes de mai
Mi neshama s'escurese sufriendo del amor.
Mas presto ven palomba, mas presto ven con mi
Mas presto ven querida, corre y salvame."

The tune was the same as the prayer's, and the connection to *The Swallow Song* was clear. Deborah's heart was pounding and she didn't know what to ask first. "What is the song about?"

"It's about nightingales. *Los bilbilicos* means 'nightingales' in *espagnol*," Anna explained.

Deborah's head reeled. "What's it mean?"

Robert translated the song.

"The nightingales sing with sighs of love
my soul and my fate are in your power.

The rose blooms in the month of May.
My soul and my fate suffer from love's pain.
Come more quickly dove, more quickly come with me;
more quickly come, beloved, run and save me."

Deborah sat stunned. Had Fariña heard the Ladino song? He did have Spanish connections with his Cuban heritage. He also spent a lot of time travelling in Europe.

"Interesting." Rachel nodded. "Both songs are about birds."

Shelley agreed. "And the same two birds from that ancient myth where the two women turn into a swallow and a nightingale."

"What ancient myth?"

"The women were sisters. Something bad happens and one of them loses her voice. In revenge, they kill the older sister's son and feed him to her evil husband."

"That's horrible." Rachel grimaced.

"I'm sorry, my love," Shelley squeezed Rachel's hand, "but that's the myth. When he chases after them, the two women turn into a swallow and a nightingale."

"Where do these stories come from anyway."

Deborah flashed to an image she had had. *They looked frantic and scared. Their breathing hard with each step, terrified they wouldn't get away. As they ran, their feet became very light, lighter than air. They were floating. Suddenly they were transformed into two birds.*

Robert laughed. "What perfect dinner conversation. Let's write a song about that." He strummed the guitar.

"Better you lose your voice," Shelley joked back, then turned to Deborah. "Do nightingales have the same tune in their song?"

They flew toward the clouds in distinct spirals around each other. Deborah stared at her. "What? I don't know. I haven't tested nightingales. They're not found in the U.S."

"Are you going to?"

"In order to do that, I'd have to go to Europe. It's their prime breeding ground this time of year."

"Isn't Dad going to Europe sometime this summer?" Rachel blurted out.

Deborah sat up in her chair. *Of course. The conference in Seville.* There are plenty of nightingales in Spain. No cliff swallows, but there are barn swallows. And birds communicate.

Deborah looked at Rachel who was whispering with Shelley. There was so much to talk about—marriage and now a baby—but a steel gate was descending between them. *What's the point of trying anymore?* She knew what she had to do. Stephen and the Dean be damned.

Deborah announced she was going to Europe.

Rachel looked up. "When's the conference?"

"I'm not sure." She remembered the brochure Brady gave her. "I have the information in my jacket pocket."

Rachel ran to the foyer to get it. Shelley started clearing the table. When Rachel came back into the dining room, she was staring at the tri-fold brochure. Her open ease from moments before was gone and she glared at Deborah with the same angry look as when Deborah skipped her high school graduation. "It's fine, Mother," Rachel said. "The conference is more important."

Deborah stood up. "Rachel, I'm sorry." Her heart felt like it was going to break. "Look, I won't go." She slowly blinked. "Your wedding is more important."

Shelley reentered the dining room with a platter of small cakes. "Nonsense, you two. Let's just step back. We found one solution, we can find another." She placed the platter down in the middle of the table. "It's simple. We'll move the date up a week." Shelley stared at Rachel trying to make her smile. "That way your parents can attend."

Rachel looked at her. "What about June 7th? That's the date we chose."

Anna reached to serve the cakes. "We'll have two dates of honor in our family. Shelley is right, it's as simple as that."

Rachel looked at them. She inhaled and let her shoulders relax. "I'll call Rabbi Stern and tell him the change of date."

Visible relief washed over Deborah. "Is he coming to your wedding?"

"We've invited him."

CHAPTER 13

WORLD NEWS – MAY 7
Disease-causing Microorganisms Resistant to Drugs
Millions of Tons of Toxins Being Released into Air Yearly

"THERE HAVE BEEN new developments," Deborah said to the students gathering in her office. Michael walked in, his face grim and clenched. He was carrying his notebook and a paper bag. "What..." she involuntarily rose from her desk. "How's Jeff?"

Exhaustion beyond tiredness clung to him. "He died last night."

"Oh, no," she fell back in her chair. "I knew he was in bad shape but I thought the chemo was going to cure the leukemia." Her voice broke.

His eyes moved slowly not able to land anywhere. "There was a lot going on, the leukemia, the mercury poisoning, toxic chemicals."

Deborah ran her hand along the side of the RAX-1000, remembering the day they joined the project. She looked up, her heart going out to him. "How are you, Michael?"

"The rest of his family came in last night from upstate New York." His voice was flat. "They're making all the arrangements to bring him...his body home. I guess there's going to be some sort of Native American ceremony for him while they are here. Saturday or Sunday."

"Do you know where?" She motioned him to sit.

"They want to find a suitable place, like an outdoor, you know, area."

Deborah closed her eyes. "I'd like to go to it."

"Sure."

"Was his fiancée contacted?"

"She was with him when he died."

Tears forming at the back of her eyes, she got up and retrieved Jeff's fossil from off the bookshelf. "I guess that's it then."

THE SWALLOW AND THE NIGHTINGALE

Michael stared at the fossil. "You called us together. You said you had something to show us."

"You sure?"

"There's nothing else to do at the moment. And he was part of this team. He would have wanted us to go on."

She looked at him. His eyes were bright with pain. "All right." She walked over to the conference table and touched the PLAY button on the music player. Robert's voice filled the room. Deborah watched the shock of recognition appear on each face.

Michael spoke first. "It's the same song."

Barry chimed in, "Yes and no."

Deborah tried to stay focused. "It's called *Los Bilbilicos*—The Nightingales—in a language called Ladino."

"It's slower," Barry said.

Deborah nodded. "The differences are intriguing."

Michael started writing some notes. "The first phrase is repeated in *Los Bilbilicos*. The second phrase uses the same chord changes, but it goes up instead of down in one section."

Barry looked puzzled. "Do you think this is the source for *The Swallow Song*?"

"If it is, why is the tune slightly different?" Michael asked.

Deborah shook her head. "I don't know."

Barry mused, "Perhaps Fariña heard the song somewhere and then modified it."

Deborah sat. "But then why did the swallow sing the song? It definitely sang *The Swallow Song* version."

"What if nightingales are singing the song as well?" Michael asked. "Could you test nightingales?"

Barry squinted and shook his head. "Nightingales don't come to North America. They range across Europe."

"Exactly." Deborah sat back. "Which is why I'm going to Europe."

"Wow, that's hot," Michael said. "What if nightingales are also singing a human tune?"

Barry tilted his head. "Which one will they be singing? Is there a real difference to the tunes or are they superficially different?"

Deborah watched them. "I'm going to need help getting ready for this trip. Michael, you don't have to help, I'll understand."

Page 130

"Tell us what you need." Michael drew a line in his notebook. "It'll give me something to do." He absently drew more lines.

"I'll do whatever I can to help you review for finals next week." Deborah looked at the fossil in her hand and started playing with it, the way Jeff used to. "I'm going to coordinate this project with the international conference coming up in Seville next month. First, I need a contact in Seville. Barry, get me some names of birders at the biology departments at Seville universities. Find some of their papers."

"What about airplane tickets, rental car, hotel?" Michael connected some of the lines.

"Right. Get the registration forms for the conference. Maybe the department secretary knows something about it."

Michael tried to make a note. "I'll download it from the conference website."

"I'll take care of it all. You've got a lot on your mind." Barry looked at him.

Michael blinked hard.

Deborah looked at the papers in front of her. She put the fossil down. "Okay. Travel arrangements. There's a travel service on campus."

"I'll check it out." Barry added it to his list.

"As for the tests I'll be conducting, I'm going to need some recordings."

Barry looked up from his notes. "You have all the ones from the previous tests."

"Yes," Deborah slowly pulled the recording out of the player. "I'm going to need the same set, but with this as a source. Make sure all the speeds are there." But then she realized she had an even bigger problem. "There's going to be paperwork getting the RAX-1000 out of the country." She tried to remember the complexity of university rules around prototype equipment. It was funded by her grant, classified as exempt property vested to the University of California, Berkeley. Where were the papers? "I'll work on it."

Barry got up to leave.

"Dr. Wright," Michael cleared his throat and motioned Barry to remain. "This is as good as a time as any. Especially since you're going to Europe now to continue this study. We want you to know that your team is behind you all the way." He handed her the bag. "So we got this for you. It was Jeff's idea."

She opened it and found a black T-shirt with "CITIFITBAC" blazoned in bold red letters across the front. Her eyes welled up. " 'The coincidence is too impossible for it to be a coincidence.' I can't believe you did this."

"Jeff thought you'd really like it." The tears he had been fighting off brimmed over. He wiped his eyes.

"I do, Michael. Thank you."

The students shuffled out the door.

Deborah reached for a tissue and sat back.

She was still staring at the T-shirt when Thomas rapped on the open door. She looked over, his face deadly serious.

Thomas took one look at her. "What happened?"

"Jeff died last night."

"I'm so sorry." He shook his head. "I can't...," he started but stopped. "I'm sorry."

Deborah's eyes went back to the T-shirt, afraid to look anywhere else. She felt sick to her stomach.

He punched the doorjamb. "This is only going to get worse, you know."

"Thomas, we don't know that."

"Don't you read news reports?" Thomas glanced down at his shoes. "Can you handle more bad news?"

She looked up at him.

"I guess this isn't a good time, but here." He handed Deborah a letter. "The Dean's putting you on administrative leave."

"What?" She stiffened, feeling almost punched in the chest. "He can't do that. I just planned the whole trip." She stared at the letter.

"You know he can do this witch hunt, even with your tenure. I was appointed head of the committee by the Vice Chancellor for Research."

"Damn it." She dropped the letter on her desk.

He walked over to the bookshelves. "It stinks."

"I know it looks like I'm repeating my behavior." She swiveled her chair around and leaned forward. "Thomas, I've found something else. I've got to go to Europe. I know the experiment will work this time."

Excited, she squeezed her hands together. "Look at it this way, I'll be another Berkeley scientist at the conference."

He ran his fingers along the spine of a book. "You don't have to justify your behavior to me, Deborah." He stared at the book as he tried to form his thoughts. "If you go to the conference, what will you talk about?"

Her eyes widened and then narrowed. She spoke quickly. "I wasn't going to give a talk, only try to get my data into the database. Don't worry, I'll keep a low profile." Her eyes searched for his. "Don't screw this up for me, Thomas. You're my friend."

"Damn it, Deborah, I know you're a good scientist. What the Dean does isn't in my control. Besides, I think you should give a talk. What an opportunity to put forth a message to get the world's attention."

"What?" She stared at him, stunned.

He sat down at the conference table. "Look, people have to connect their own behavior to what's happening in the world. You know what Tolstoy said over a hundred years ago? 'Everyone thinks of changing the world, but no one thinks of changing himself.' Do you think these anomalies are just happening out there and you aren't a part of it?"

She reeled back. "Jeff just died. You think I'm not affected by his death?"

"I'm sorry," he backed down, "I didn't mean…"

She picked up the fossil. "Stephen said companies are doing things they shouldn't be doing."

He smirked. "I told you that at the Earth Day Fair. And your answer was, 'It's why I only drink bottled water.' "

"That was pretty stupid of me."

Thomas stood up and pointed to her books. "Exactly! Humans aren't thinking of the complexity of the system when they take an action." He looked back at her. "I mean, we jump into cars to go pick up imported bananas but not for one second do we think of all the energy that took. Don't you see? We don't connect it. After all, there's no smoke coming out of our tailpipes. And all we see is a tasty banana, as if we plucked it from our backyard."

She squeezed the fossil. "It's because we don't know the global *global* problem. I gave a lecture about this. I've got my students saying a new mantra, 'We're inside it, we can't see it.' "

THE SWALLOW AND THE NIGHTINGALE

"Good. Now give that lecture to the world's scientific community."

"Seriously?" Still holding the fossil, she stood up and walked over to the credenza.

"Yes." He raised his voice. "Just because humans can squeeze every bit of energy from fossil fuels, dump millions of tons of crap into the ocean and release toxic chemicals into the air, doesn't mean we should. These are common resources that a few are exploiting and soiling at the expense of the rest of us. Business' bottom line shouldn't only be corporate profits, it should include some morality."

"Morality? We're scientists, not philosophers, isn't that what you told me in Carmel?"

"Look, one of Gandhi's seven social sins—have you heard of them—is commerce…"

"I know, I know, commerce without morality." She couldn't believe he was talking about this.

"Yes. And science without humanity. When I said that science separated itself from ethics, I didn't mean to imply it should stay that way. Someone has to take a moral stance. A real moral stance and not this baloney that religions sell in order to control people."

"Can you calm down?" Everything was closing in on her. She sat down on a corner of the credenza and looked at the fossilized brachiopod in her hand. It had small ridges in it from an extinct life form. *Am I going to go to Seville and give a talk about morality? This is too bizarre—I need another opinion.* She wished she could speak to Stephen. "What do you think I should talk about?

He took a deep breath and started pacing. "The interconnections, the synergies."

"That's what my lecture was about. Balancing competition with cooperation."

"That's why I say screw what the Dean thinks." Thomas stopped pacing. "He's just jealous of you. Add the morality issue and elevate the language from undergrad-speak. No, wait, bring it down to an 8th grade level so everyone gets it."

"Jealous of me?" Her eyes widened.

He shook his head and rapped on the bookcase. "Don't you get it? You didn't use his algorithms in your machine. This is payback."

Her eyes went wide. "Will you help me get the paperwork for getting the RAX-1000 out of the country?"

THEA IBERALL

"Consider it done."

🕊 🕊

WORLD NEWS – MAY 10
More Wildfires That Burn Hotter
Greater Health Risks Living Close to Fracking Wells
Forests Less Hardy

Standing looking north below the summit of Mt. Tamalpais, Deborah could hear the crash of the waves behind the chanting voices. She heard a slight syncopation between them that Jeff would have liked. Live oaks scented the already moist afternoon air. A distant forest fire wafted into the mix. Above her, she could hear the *keeer-r-r-r* of a red-tailed hawk soaring on a thermal. Colorful California poppies and purple lupine protruded below the rock outcropping on which the mourners stood. Deborah pulled her green jacket tighter.

The circle consisted of members of the Oneida Nation from New York combined with Coast Miwok Indians from nearby. Berkeley faculty and students joined them. Jeff's mother, Katherine, stood directly across from Deborah looking south. Michael was at the east point of the circle to Deborah's right. A young woman with long black hair stood on Michael's left. Deborah was surprised to see the Dean. At the west was an Oneida man who looked like Katherine. Next to him was an older version of Jeff.

At the center of the circle was an abalone shell with a smoldering bundle of sage. They couldn't build a full fire because of the danger of forest fires. The Miwok men sang, accompanying themselves with clamshell rattles. Their healer took the sage and walked clockwise around the circle, slowly waving the burning bundle in front of and behind each person. The smoke wafted around them.

Unsteady on her feet, Deborah stared at the ocean. She felt as if the endless rolling waves were laughing at her. *It's not like the sea is stoppable.* Glad the world's scientists were getting together next month, she wondered whether all the knowledge gained in thousands of years had really added anything beyond the basics of a smudging ceremony. The hawk seemed to agree with her. *Keeer-r-r-r.*

Taking out a noisemaker, the Miwok healer explained that they used the deer-toes rattle to connect to Mother Earth. The two Oneida men handed clumps of tobacco to each person to scatter on the ground. The Jeff look-alike put a little onto the burning sage bundle resting in the shell.

The Miwok healer then told a story about creation, how Sky Woman fell from the sky and all the animals did what they could to make her landing gentle. From Sky Woman were born good and evil. And humans were created to become the caretakers, but they keep forgetting their role.

When the ceremony ended, Deborah walked over to Jeff's mother to share her condolences. She could sense the Dean standing nearby. Deborah cleared her throat and spoke loud enough for him to hear. Katherine thanked her and shook her hand. "Jeff was so enthusiastic about life, he jumped into our cliff swallow project and helped wherever he could."

Sadness crossed behind Katherine's eyes. "He felt it important to visit his friend in Pennsylvania who said her town was having problems. In order to fix it, he said, you have to know what you're up against. The tribe was giving him the chance."

Deborah put her hands in her pocket as she tilted her head. "What do you mean?" She could feel Jeff's fossilized seashell.

"The Oneida people believe very strongly in education. He was on a full tribal scholarship."

Deborah shook her head and rubbed the seashell. Feeling something next to it, she realized it was the toy compass. "He was up against the whole fracking industry."

One of the Oneida men came over. "Start big, I taught him."

Katherine looked tired. She took the man's arm. "He wanted to know firsthand what was going on."

The man agreed. "And work for the benefit of seven generations into the future."

"That's the great law of the Iroquois." Katherine turned. "This is Jeff's father, Cody, my brother." Cody was a head taller than his sister with piercing brown eyes and small ears.

Deborah was confused. "I don't understand. Your brother?"

"That man packing up his rattle over there is his father, Terry." Deborah looked to where Katherine was pointing to the Jeff look-alike. "We are a matrilineal society. Cody and I raised Jeff in our clan, the

Wolf clan. But genetically, Terry is his father. You're a biologist. I'm sure you understand the reasons."

Deborah's eyes tried to take them all in. She thought everyone lived under the patriarchy. But here was a culture outside of it. The genes came from a non-relative but the cultural values were transmitted through the mother and her family. "How does it change things, between men and women I mean?"

Other people were gathering around them, trying to get Katherine's attention. "Let me put it this way. Long before the United States Constitution's pretense of equality, women in the Six Nation Confederacy were respected by men. The women's rights movement started in upstate New York because our tribes were their role models." She turned toward others.

Deborah watched her greet people. Her words reverberated down the mountainside as they slowly sunk into Deborah's brain. She turned away from the group and was stopped by the Dean.

"Hello, Deborah, tough circumstances." Harvey Milhouse's balding head reflected the bright sky.

Deborah scowled. "I got your letter. Thomas delivered it."

He didn't smile. He kept his hands jammed in his pants pockets. "I warned you of the consequences of staying on the project."

She stared at him, feeling unsteady on the rock outcropping but not wanting to appear weak. The memory of him snubbing Jeff's offer to help flashed through her mind. "What are you doing here?"

He shrugged. "Someone had to represent the University. I got the short straw."

She drew in a sharp breath. "Look, I got it. You put me on administrative leave. But you can't stop me from going to the conference." She started walking to hide the fact she almost fell.

He laughed. "No, you're right, I can't. But I can make it difficult for you and your half-cocked research methods. I know what you've been doing in the field."

She turned back toward him. "I've got tenure. This is my chance to tell people what I've discovered."

He took a step toward her and looked like he was going to elaborate on something. But he stepped back. "You've discovered nothing. You'll see." He walked back down the path toward his car.

Deborah spun toward the ocean and almost tripped on the irregular surface. Michael caught her before she fell.

"Careful, Dr. Wright."

She grabbed onto his arm and steadied herself. "Thank you, Michael." She sighed. "This ceremony would have meant a lot to Jeff."

He let go of her when he saw she was okay. "I think they believe he's here with us."

"He knew what was important in life. Like friendship."

Michael looked down at the outcropping and then at her. Slowly he filled in the silence between them. "Dr. Wright, what's going to happen?"

The red-tailed hawk still circled above them. "I don't know, Michael. People live their lives believing the future is going to be better. It gives us hope, a reason to live." She thought about her grandparents, aunts and uncles, all living in Germany. The generation before the Holocaust—they had no idea what was coming.

He put his hands in his pockets. "I don't feel much hope at the moment."

"Neither do I. My friend said we could be like a frog in a cold pot of water, slowly having the heat turned up on us. The Nazis did it to the Jews in the 1940s. They put them in ghettos and slowly closed in the walls and changed the laws until their lives became an interminable hell of burnings, shootings, starvation, and death camps."

Michael looked as if he had aged ten years in the space of a week. "If we're facing a holocaust, what should we do?"

"That's the question. At least with the Nazis, there was a cadre of generals in Berlin making the decisions. Where's our enemy? Where's our Berlin?"

"Jeff tried to figure it out and look what happened to him."

She reached into her jacket pocket and pulled out Jeff's fossilized seashell. "Jeff's mother gave me this, but I think you should have it."

Michael looked at the shell, fighting tears. "I'm not sure we'll ever know what it meant to him." He took it from her.

They started back to the cars, along the trail as it descended along a creek. The whiff of the distant fire tainted the rich smell of damp earth. Three bushy-tailed squirrels scampered along the brown-needled branches of a stand of Douglas fir trees. The sound of the rushing water combined with the rattles still playing in her head. A pileated woodpecker drilled into a hollow tree. Deborah remembered walking through the Earth Day fair—was it just a month ago? She knew nothing then. Now she saw greed everywhere. Shelley had tried to put a human face on it calling it disrespect. But that sounded too genteel. She thought of the ancient Puebloans. *They had to relocate. At least they could. If the whole planet's affected, where do you go?*

She almost tripped again, and Michael took her arm. "Dr. Wright, do you remember your lecture on competition and cooperation?"

"Yes, I do. Jeff's mother said it really affected him."

"You said people are like cells and they form these teams—nations, states, cities, tribes."

"Yes. Collectives. They cooperate within it for the benefits they receive. They compete with the other 'teams'—"

"—like the Raiders versus the Giants, one religion versus another, country against country."

"Right." She was impressed.

He stopped and let go. "People are real. Even though as a group, we look like a collective, we're not gas molecules. We have birthdays, we have our likes and dislikes. We live a life, we die. I think maybe the people running corporations and governments forget that."

At the parking lot, he said, "Where's it going to end?"

Deborah looked at him. "I don't know, Michael, I don't know."

She got into her car and pulled out onto Panoramic Highway. *We're all contributing to this lifestyle that's killing us. The companies get away with it because we want the stuff they dribble out for a price. They get the benefit, we get the costs. How do you live in a world without a cell phone or where you can't drive 350 miles to visit your daughter, someday grandchild? I'll be getting on a plane soon to jaunt off to Europe. What can I do? Where will this end?* She stared at the road curving along the ocean.

I'll start by giving up one thing. For Jeff. For myself. For the world I live in.

🕊 🕊

WORLD NEWS – MAY 16
Compact Fluorescent Light Bulbs Emit More EMFs

THE SWALLOW AND THE NIGHTINGALE

Peter Brawster, the minister of the United Church of Christ in Berkeley, offered Deborah a chair in his small office. "Coffee? I recall you're a real connoisseur."

She shook her head. "I'm not drinking coffee anymore. Any herbal tea?" She looked at his wall of books, seeing texts on Christian thought, ethics, and philosophy. Biographies of great Christian thinkers. Holy books from every faith. Even the *Quran*.

Peter walked toward the electric kettle. "I've got plenty. You said on the phone you had a problem. I know things between you and Stephen have been rough."

"Thanks, Peter. If that were my only problem."

"What kind of tea would you like? We've got chamomile, honey lemon, green." He pushed a basket of store-bought packets in front of her while he pulled out two mugs from a small cupboard.

Looking through the foil packages, she picked the green tea. "You've heard about the world scientific conference in Seville?"

"Of course. Who hasn't?" He unwrapped the tea bag.

"I'm going next month. I'll be giving a talk."

"Congratulations." He poured the tea with a nod. "Is Stephen going to be there as well?"

She looked away. "Yes. He's always called on whenever anything happens and…" She shrugged and was quiet.

Peter sat down in front of her. "So tell me about your talk."

"I saw the dying swallows at Capistrano. It was unbelievable."

" 'And God said unto Noah, the end of all flesh is come before me.' " He touched the Bible sitting on his desk.

Deborah continued, "…*ki male'ah ha'erets chamas mippeneihem; v'hinni mashchitam et ha'aretz.*"

Peter translated, " 'For the Earth is filled with violence through them; and, behold, I will destroy them with the Earth.' You know your Scripture."

"And you know your Hebrew," she said. "There's so many insane things going on in the world, natural problems, man-made ones—new diseases, pollution, the rising sea levels…" her voice trailed off and she took a sip of tea. It definitely didn't have the richness of coffee.

"And you think the dying swallows are part of all these disasters?"

"I don't know. It's something to consider." She sipped her tea. "My colleague suggested I talk about it at the conference, but more importantly, point out the lack of morality underlying business decisions. And he says science is contributing to these problems because it isn't supplying moral answers."

Peter held his mug to contemplate her words, pursing his lips. He took a sip. "Science isn't known for moral answers. Religion provides people with a moral compass."

"A patriarchal one," she shot back. She could feel heat on the back of her neck.

"That's true. Our monotheistic religions are patriarchal."

Deborah put down her tea mug. "Meaning male-dominant."

Peter shrugged. "The word literally means 'rule of the fathers.' "

Deborah stared at him. "We're so entrenched under the filter of the patriarchy, we don't see it anymore, like fish don't see water. Don't you think it has caused a few problems?"

He looked at her quizzically. "But it's a truth. God is masculine, and Jesus Christ is the only head of the church. It's a good enough system. Besides, women are getting more involved in politics and science. Like you are." He took another sip of tea.

"But, frankly, only with men's permission. It's like a 'father-knows-best' mentality. And look where it's gone to—humans are doing things they shouldn't be doing. We're accepting destructive technologies. Bad things are starting to happen." She grabbed a quick sip of tea. Not wanting to talk about Jeff's death with someone who didn't know him, she remembered the latest news. Her voice rose. "Did you see on TV how these new light bulbs are dangerous to your health? I mean, they even have mercury in them. Science has proved how bad mercury is for people and yet, we're using them."

He looked at his books and then back at her. "And that's how you're getting to the moral question? That's your example? Science doesn't help people distinguish between good and evil, religion does."

Deborah sat forward and rapped hard on his desk. "Are religions weighing in on the depletion of common resources? Peter, we live less than three miles from a rising and acidifying ocean. I'd say that's the real moral problem, how a few people exploit resources at the expense of everyone else to the point of collapse, without regard to any ethics—like even a land ethic. And yet, patriarchal religions care more about things like homosexuality."

THE SWALLOW AND THE NIGHTINGALE

Peter pursed his lips again and put his mug on his desk. "Because that's what the Bible speaks to. In the Old Testaments—Leviticus 18:22 and 20:13. In the New Testaments—I Corinthians 6:9, Romans 1:26. There are others. Some people say that any type of evil condemned in the Scriptures cannot be honoring to God."

Deborah shook her head and leaned toward him. "The Bible says lots of things. It condones slavery, it prescribes dietary laws—things Christians no longer accept."

Peter folded his hands on his stomach. "The Bible is God's gift to the church, but you're right, it can be used to strike down opponents. I like to say that God is not imprisoned in the Bible."

Deborah's eyes flashed. "The reality is that verses get taken out of context."

Peter pressed his thumbs together. "If that's your point, you won't hear me disagree. Verses are translated *sans* culture from ancient languages. In the Old Testament—your Jewish Bible—the first seven verses of Leviticus are laws on animal sacrifices and burnt offerings. Do we still do these? No. The next ten verses contain lots of proscriptions but Christians get riled up around only one of them."

Deborah sat back and nodded. "Jews, too. My point is, here's a place where science can help with morality. Not argue against immorality, but explain the reason. Like incest. As a culture, we don't condone incest because it leads to a degradation of our species' genes. We call it immoral. But biologically, close proximity in early years turns off sexual attraction. So, a mechanism has evolved that helps improve our species." She drained her mug.

Peter stood up to get more tea. "And we know some Christians would say the mechanism didn't evolve but that God put it there."

Deborah held her mug up for a refill. "Not here to argue that, Peter. The point is the moral code and the mechanism go hand-in-hand."

He looked at her, pouring from the kettle into her mug. "You're saying homosexuality follows the same idea? Whoops." He had overfilled it.

She grabbed some paper napkins and gave them to him to wipe up the spilled water. "Right. We have this moral code against it."

He sat down again, giving her the tea. "But there are cases of incest, so it isn't totally turned off which means the mechanism isn't foolproof, and the behavior is then truly deviant, morally and according to science. You aren't making a case for homosexuality. In fact, you're proving it's deviant."

Deborah shook her head hard. "That would be one way to look at it. Another way is to think of left-handedness. It seems useless but over time, it hasn't gone away. It's always there in a small percentage of the population, like me." She held up her left hand. "Why? We don't know. It must be there for some reason. We just don't know what that reason is. Do we make a moral code about it? Some teachers try to get rid of it, but no one today thinks it's morally wrong. Think about homosexuality. We've made a moral code against it like we've done with incest, but in reality, we don't know why it is there, like left-handedness. Most people are not attracted to people of their same sex which is a good thing for the species."

Peter smiled. "Right, we don't want the whole population gay."

Deborah took another fast sip of tea. "But some percentage in every generation is, which could be a good thing for the species. We just don't know why. Our behavior says parents need to have extra adults around during child-rearing years. We hire nannies, teachers and housekeepers, even get grandma and grandpa involved. Wouldn't having non-burdened adults be useful to the species? The mechanism of being attracted to one's own sex would ensure that."

They watched the sunlight play across the wall. A small prism on the window sprayed the colors of the rainbow on his bookshelves.

Peter took a sip of tea. "Most Christian ministers and priests won't care about this argument. Neither would an Orthodox Rabbi."

She put down her mug and looked at him.

"Stephen told me everything. I don't think I'm betraying a trust here."

Deborah stiffened. "How much do you know?"

"I know about your family."

Deborah looked at her tea mug and gripped it. She felt like the balloon she was riding on popped. *He doesn't know what's happening in two weeks.*

"If I can make an observation, Deborah. You have a lot of anger in you."

She let go of the mug and drummed on his desk. "I didn't deserve this treatment by Stephen. Are you condoning what he did?"

THE SWALLOW AND THE NIGHTINGALE

He sat back. "I'm not condoning it. There's this idea of forgiveness. I've heard it's not just a Christian concept."

A small smile edged onto her lips. "No, it's not. I want an apology from him."

"Oh, the chicken or the egg problem," he said, softly. "Forgiveness or apology. Well, suppose God is about to destroy the world for all the immorality He sees in it. Are you going to continue playing chicken with Stephen? See who blinks first? "

Tears welled up in Deborah's eyes.

Peter smiled at her gently. "While you're in Europe, find a quiet place and think about who you're really angry at. Forgiveness can only come from God, Deborah. Stephen will realize what he did was wrong and he'll come clean about it. I mean, even in a worst case scenario, when a Christian knows he's going to die, he confesses his sins. I have faith that deep down, Stephen is a good man and he'll confess them long before that." He leaned forward. "I also believe that if you heal your relationship with Stephen, you'll be healing your relationship with Rachel. You're making her choose between you two and it isn't fair to her."

Deborah slowly blinked, finishing her tea. "I'll think about it."

Peter picked up the two empty mugs and carried them back to the teapot. "So when are you going to Europe?"

"Beginning of the month." Deborah gathered her bag and stood.

"What are you going to do while you're there? Besides give your talk."

She walked toward the door and turned. "I'm going to do some field work. Peter, it's like I'm on a path. With my new scientific instrument, I've discovered something. It's tenuous, but the more I continue following it, the more I learn."

"Stay on your path. It could lead you to wisdom."

"Wisdom?" She reached for the doorknob, smiling at the thought.

Peter continued, "Who knows, it may bring mankind closer to God."

She looked at him. "What if it brings us closer to the end of the world?"

"Then Heaven help us."

THEA IBERALL

WORLD NEWS – MAY 31
Urban Runoff Makes Beaches and Ocean Unsafe
Sea Temperature Rising

Deborah looked out over the ocean while they waited. A white sailboat twisted into the light wind. The sky gathered pinkness from the slowly setting sun as if determined to concentrate all possible shades at Doheny State Beach. The ocean was heading toward low tide, and tide pools sparkled with anemone and abalone. A great blue heron stood on its long legs with its sinuous neck, staring at the small crabs scurrying along the rocks and water. With their bright white heads and gray-blue backs, Western gulls were chasing small snails and limpets. The bird calls and surf mixed with soft music coming from speakers beside her feet.

Robert wheeled in front of the gazebo on the sand-dusted boardwalk. "Let's begin. Rabbi Stern is obviously not coming." He held the *Tanach,* the Jewish Bible, in his lap.

Deborah's head whipped around, looking past Stephen who stood next to her. Anna was across the way. Her eyes searched for Rachel. The gazebo cut the wind from where they stood under a *tallis* which served to create a *chuppah,* the wedding canopy. The prayer shawl was held up by four poles. Three of Rachel and Shelley's friends held corners; Thomas held the fourth. Deborah's face was flushed. *It fits the description of a framework for a Jewish wedding. But without a rabbi, what will this be?*

Senator Susan Bonheur nodded to the DJ. Her piercing blue eyes took in the gathered friends and family. She touched her coifed blonde hair before adjusting her reading glasses.

The DJ started Wagner's Lohengrin processional. Sitting in the white folding chairs set up on the beach were the guests, men on one side, women on the other. They turned to watch Rachel and Shelley walk down the aisle.

Deborah inhaled, caught by their stunning beauty. They were both veiled and wore long white Moroccan dresses with thick piping along their dresses' rounded neck and down the front. Bird and flower motifs were intricately sewn into the soft cotton material. The sleeves extended to their wrists.

Deborah could sense Stephen next to her. She felt hot between her breasts. Her leg almost buckled, and he grabbed her arm and held her.

Page 145

She tried to wriggle out of his grasp, but he was too strong, holding her. Tears formed at the back of her eyes. She could see people smiling watching the two beaming women. Deborah didn't dare turn her head to look at Stephen, but she already knew what was in his eyes. She yanked her arm away.

As Rachel and Shelley arrived under the *chuppah*, Susan opened a thin black leather notebook. "We are gathered here today because Rachel Wright and Shelley Abenacar want to be married, to bring their private love story out into the world. Let us first take a moment to welcome the spirit and memory of those not with us. Shelley's parents Sarah and Gerald Abenacar, her grandfather Joseph Nessim, and grandparents Abraham and Rose Abenacar. Rachel's grandparents Rabbi Hershel and Leah Katz and Martin and Mary Wright. As for anyone else not here, it is their loss to not be experiencing this knitting together of family and friends."

Deborah was glad to hear the veiled reference to the Rabbi.

Susan turned to Robert and nodded.

Robert was wearing a *yarmulke* and a white shirt with ballooning sleeves. "*Od yishama b'arei Yehudah uvechutzot Yerushalim, Kol sasson v'kol simcha.* 'Yet shall there be heard in the cities of Judah and the streets of Jerusalem the sound of gladness and the sound of joy.' Every Jewish wedding involves two movements, one away from the world and toward each other and another toward the world together as a couple.

"Traditionally the *erusin* ceremony turns inward. Through it, a couple excludes all others from their intimate circle. *Erusin* makes paramount the exclusivity of relationship. Rachel and Shelley, you will both take an oath that depends upon receiving a ring from the other. This oath before God binds you exclusively to one another in an intimacy that is yours alone. Shelley, do you understand that by this oath you relinquish your full self-ownership, and that, at the moment you receive a ring from Rachel, in way similar to *kiddushin*, you and your body will belong to Rachel?

"Yes."

He turned to his grandmother. "*Nonna*, do you have the rings?" She nodded and gave one to Shelley and one to Rachel.

Robert continued, "Shelley, put the ring on Rachel's finger. Then before this community and in the presence of God, speaking directly to

Rachel repeat after me. *Harei at mekudeshet li*—behold, you are consecrated to me."

She took Rachel's hand and placed the ring on her index finger, repeating the prayer.

Then he turned to Rachel and repeated everything.

"Now we turn outward, connecting your love for each other to a bigger picture. You two share a love of people, a deep love of the Jewish tradition, its wisdoms, and its vision of a better world. You are an embodiment of *tikkun olam*—healing of the world by your actions.

"Couples who marry offer their love of each other as a divine resource, as a tool in God's hands for greater purposes. Straight weddings are about the garden of Eden and Jerusalem rebuilt. Every woman is Eve and every man Adam. So what is God up to in the love of two women? Until now, the very idea of same-gender marriage was thought to be a violation of the order. There is a story about God diminishing the moon. The mystics of Safed have a mystical prayer to restore the moon. This prayer points to a future time of gender equality, reminding us of a time before the fractures that led to male domination. The ability of two equals to share power and not to default to an embodied gender hierarchy is a profound gift of same-sex love. Tonight we pray that the committed love of these two women will help to pave the way for us all to share power without hierarchy and in a gesture no less redemptive than the rebuilding of Jerusalem, to restore the moon to her former glory.

"Blessed are you Lord, ruler of the universe, who renews the months and makes all things new. May it be your will, Lord, our God and the God of our fathers to fill in the darkness of the moon that she not be diminished. May this joyous love overwhelm all the fears and heal the fractures. Rachel and Shelley—*yehi ratzon shetivnu bayit neeman b'yisrael.*"

He turned back to Susan.

Susan nodded and smiled. "By the power invested in me by the State of California, I now pronounce you married."

Someone in the audience let out a big *mazel tov*. Deborah held her breath.

Robert continued, "Until all broken things are mended, no celebration is totally complete. It is a Jewish aspiration that someday justice will cover the earth as water covers the seas. While this wedding marks great joy, we cannot forget the many people here and abroad whose love is still a dangerous secret. We carry them with us today in singing *im eshkachech* followed by the shattering of a glass."

Stephen put a wrapped glass on the ground, and the two young women stepped on it. Everyone burst out into *mazel tovs* and song and applause. And Deborah burst into tears.

White tents surrounded the picnic tables with small lights shining on the teal blue tablecloths. The DJ was playing music while guests, full from their dinners, danced on the specially set up dance floor. A *mehitzah* barrier separated the men from the women. Waiters in short maroon jackets were still serving wedding guests wine and cake.

Deborah stood under one of the tents next to Susan watching Rachel and Shelley being encircled by dancers, Anna ecstatically with them. Deborah could still feel the ocean just beyond the tents. A waiter came by with wine. She declined. "I don't drink much." She complimented Susan. "Beautiful ceremony."

Susan nodded. "I've run committee meetings and given commencement and nominating speeches, but that was the first time I officiated at a wedding. Even with California State Law allowing it."

Deborah had never seen her daughter smile so widely. "Having a Senator around is pretty handy sometimes."

Susan shot a glance at her. "Sorry this could only be a short trip. Memorial Day Weekend. I have to get right back to Washington in the morning. Meanwhile, how's our machine?"

Deborah saw Stephen dancing in front of the girls. "The RAX-1000 found something." She explained the discovery of the bird song.

"But the semantic aspect of it?" Susan turned to look at her.

Deborah shrugged. "I haven't been able to validate that part of the design."

Susan snorted. "You mean it doesn't work yet. I helped you get all that grant money, a lot of it mind you. Don't let me down now. Presenting semantic data at this international conference would be a big plus. It'll offset all the doomsday news about oceans warming and acidifying." She nodded toward the water.

Deborah felt like a junior high school student being reprimanded. "The first thing I'm doing when I get to Europe is a fieldtest."

"Good. Deborah, don't fail me now. It's my reputation as well as yours."

Without touching her, Stephen escorted Anna toward them. He stared at Deborah and asked Susan to dance.

Deborah hugged her arms and felt stinging at the back of her eyes. Being friends with Susan was like befriending a hawk, she thought as she stared at Stephen laughing while they danced.

Anna giggled. "They made me part of the celebration. Your husband is very gracious, Dr. Wright. A very good addition to our family."

Deborah blinked her eyes. "Can I take you to a seat?" She took Anna's arm. "Robert did a beautiful job as well."

"He could have become a Rabbi." Anna smiled as they walked. "He loves these formal ceremonies. They're so important in validating people's lives, aren't they?"

Deborah shook off memories of her own wedding. She wanted to hang onto the image of Rachel looking so beautiful standing under the *chuppah*. Thinking about formal ceremonies, she remembered the ceremony for Jeff on Mt. Tamalpais. "It's what people need." They reached the picnic table near to where Robert sat finishing his cake.

Taking a seat, Anna picked up an empty glass. "What they need is to accept change. Live long enough and you learn that. Don't you agree, Dr. Wright?"

Deborah sat down. "Change is hard. But changing moral awarenesses shows cultural biases for exactly what they are."

Robert poured water for his grandmother. "Ergo the need for a new approach."

Deborah froze. "What do you mean?"

"The willingness of Shelley and Rachel to take a step outside."

Deborah inhaled sharply. "What? Can't they stay in the synagogue?"

"We all knew the Rabbi wouldn't condone tonight. They'll have problems when people in the synagogue get wind of this." He looked around. "Which they will because congregants are here."

Her breath went shallow. The reality of the moment wrenched into focus. Flooded by feelings, Deborah remembered the first *shaakshuka* conversation with Rachel and going to the synagogue to plead with the Rabbi.

THE SWALLOW AND THE NIGHTINGALE

Rachel and Shelley walked to the microphone and Rachel spoke. "We would like to thank everyone for sharing this blessed event with us tonight. Our brother Robert, our *Nonna*. Susan and Thomas Bonheur who are like an aunt and uncle to us. Thank you to all our friends. I would also like to thank my mother and my father, Deborah and Stephen Wright."

The guests applauded. Rachel motioned to her parents. "Next week, scientists will gather in Europe to study the world's problems. The United States and the University of California at Berkeley are sending these two as representatives."

Deborah slowly rose, swallowing hard as she walked with a smile plastered on her face. Stephen took her hand and raised it. She hadn't told anyone about the Dean's letter putting her on administrative leave. Looking at Thomas, she saw him slightly shake his head.

Rachel continued, "They both will be addressing the gathered scientists. This is a great honor for both of them, for our families. I'm very proud of them and thank them for all they've done for me."

The applause continued. Deborah wrenched her hand away from Stephen. Fighting back tears, Deborah hugged Rachel and Shelley. "You two are so beautiful. You pulled it off, more graciously than I could have ever imagined."

Rachel smiled. "We did it. I can't believe it!"

Rachel and Shelley climbed into a white stretch limousine. People gathered at the parking lot curb and waved good-bye as they rode off into the night. Saddleback Mountain was just visible in the moonlight.

Deborah turned toward the beach. Thomas was standing next to her and took her arm to help her walk. "Where are they going?"

"Two nights at the Ritz Carlton, just down the beach. They feel guilty, but they deserve it."

"One little extravagance won't hurt anyone." He smiled.

In silence, they walked toward the water's edge. Deborah let go of his arm and stared out over the ocean. "You should go dance with your wife."

Thomas looked out over the low tide. "This beach used to be so beautiful. It was a magical place. It had oyster reefs and seaweed, lots more to explore. Now it's the most polluted beach in California."

"That's right, you grew up around here. What happened?"

"We moved to Santa Ana when I was a teenager in 1958. Since then, they've straightened the beach, filled in the parking lots and built beach volleyball courts. I guess that's what people want." He shook his head. "I used to come out here and watch the surfers."

She was surprised. "I didn't know you were a surfer."

He laughed and turned to look for Susan. "I didn't say I surfed. Black people don't surf. Or swim."

"But…"

"We're talking about the late Fifties, my dear. There weren't a thousand African-Americans in the whole of Orange County, thanks to so many sundown towns. Now the beaches are filled with all sorts of creatures, human and otherwise, even starving baby sea lions."

"Starving sea lion babies?"

"Yeah, with the coastal waters warming, the mothers have to go further out to sea to find food, abandoning their babies." He turned. "And I think I see a beautiful woman looking for a dance partner of the male persuasion. Have a great time in Europe. Keep ignoring the Dean's letter. We'll sort it out when you return after you knock 'em dead." He left.

Deborah stared out over the ocean. A ballad played below the pounding of the surf. The ocean had a power of its own. She remembered the remnants of the Japanese tsunami hitting San Francisco Bay, so small but potentially one could be much larger. *How vulnerable we are, like the poor sea lion babies. How could a mother abandon her child?* She stared at the tide pools glinting in the moonlight and thought of her parents' burial plots on Long Island. *What if flooding overruns their cemetery?* She felt a chill through her body. *What's going to happen to Rachel? Are they going to have to leave the synagogue?* She was glad she was over her homophobia. It was such a beautiful wedding. She could no longer remember why she ever thought it was wrong for Rachel to be a lesbian.

But she could remember why she was mad at Stephen.

Chapter 14

What The Nightingale Said

Part IV

*"Next is the valley where neither pretentiousness
can be had nor spiritual sense discovered.
From here a cold wind rises whose violence
instantly creates an immense distance."*

-- Attar, The Conference of the Birds

THE FIGHTING RAGES fiercely. I am caught in a conflict I do not want to be in. A sultan from Persia has attacked the capital of the Caliph, spiritual leader of all of Islam. The Caliph calls the attackers infidels because they are waging war on the successor of the Prophet. But they are not the infidels I feared—these are Persians like me. In quick succession, they have overwhelmed the western part of the city and hundreds are roaming the streets. The Caliph orders all the bridges over the Tigris River to be destroyed. I am offered a sword to help in the defense, but I cannot bring myself to fight. Instead, I hide most of my possessions in a part of the city not yet overrun.

The Caliph's soldiers install catapults on the walls in order to repel the attackers. Thousands are camped outside the walls, preparing to attack. There is hand to hand fighting. Again, I am offered weapons. Too many innocent people are dying. I watch the sultan's soldiers set fire to a house and kill the people coming out screaming. But then these soldiers are killed by the Caliph's troops. Am I to join this? I cannot, so I help women and young innocents.

I find a hiding place, a structure built for animals. I eat food scraps thrown for the pigs and cows. Most of the time, I starve. I am sure I will be slaughtered with the other animals. Only by singing to myself am I able to keep alive. Soon, even my singing stops. How can I sing of love? At night, my dreams fill with piercing and frightful yells. I don't know whether the screams are memories of others or my own.

The bombardment begins. With their own catapults, the enemy throws huge stones at the city's walls. The soldiers protecting us attack them in return. Thousands of arrows fly as ladders raise onto the walls. I see the agony on the enemy's face. I see despair in the people around me. Blood flows everywhere, caked onto everything. All around are the cries of children, the agony of parents.

The enemy is repelled by the army. I spend my days bringing what little water can be found to the injured. With scraps of cloth, clean or otherwise, I bandage up their wounds.

Rumors spread that the enemy has repaired one of the bridges and more troops have crossed into the city from the west. We don't believe it, but suddenly they pour through the streets. I huddle in my hideaway. Many non-soldiers have taken up the sword and help in warding off the enemy. What does one's life matter if it is lived by the sword? What is the difference between friend and foe if both are doing the killing? I want to shout to them. All are human beings. It is how you live your life that matters.

We hear booms in the distance. As soon as the fighting around me subsides, I dash toward the sound, afraid of what it could be. "They are trying to breach the gate," a man says running in the other direction.

I stop in my tracks. The booms are slow and ominous. With each heavy thud, I feel my heart shut down. Stepping back, I press hard against a building. I am near the gate and can see our defenders on top of city walls. There are yells and screams as arrows fly. Besides the battering ram, the enemy throws ladders up against the walls. Bloody bodies reign down on us. I watch the scene in horror. Time seems to slow down as the cries stretch out in eternity. Boom, boom. Arrows screech, swords clang. I have no more tears. I feel dead inside.

The assault is repulsed. The soldiers on the wall manage to fight off the attackers. The booms stop. There are heavy casualties on both sides. While we live amid the agony of death, we wait for the next attack.

But it never comes. The sultan's soldiers are leaving. Is the war too much for them? Did we win? What did we win? Only rumors answer these questions.

THE SWALLOW AND THE NIGHTINGALE

The city returns to normal. Markets reopen and caravans return, filling the bazaar again with foodstuffs, trade goods, and life. I wonder if I will ever be the same. I have not sung the song of the nightingale in months. I have seen too much pain, too much suffering. Will I ever sing again?

It is the month of Ramadan, the time to fast during the daylight hours. Each morning before dawn, hearing the call to prayer from the minaret, I rise, eat a small meal, and pray. My prayers are more serious now, and I use the time more reflectively than in Shadyakh. During the day, I walk the streets, play chess, and talk to other men. I find one of my hidden caches of leather pouches with the perfume and coins that I cached before the war. But I no longer have any interest in selling or even in singing the nightingale song to crowds of merchants and travelers. It is time to be watchful, nothing more. At night, I break my daily fast with dates, rice, and lentils. I sleep on the floor of a gentlemen's community house near the mosque.

At the end of Ramadan, the *Id al-Fitr* festival begins. I am invited by new companions to a dinner near one of the city squares. It is a part of the city that I am unfamiliar with, but I want to see how *Id al-Fitr* is celebrated in the capital city. Even after a war, it is elaborate.

My companions are generous. Spread out before me are plates filled with thin pancakes, chicken cooked with eggplant and onions, stuffed lamb, and rich sugar candies and pastries.

"We never feasted so elaborately in my village," I exclaim, wiping grease from my chin with the back of my hand. It feels good to be eating meals again. War has given me a better appreciation of food.

The men laugh. "Of course not, this is the capital. We have everything. Even in times of war. Try drinking this."

"What is it?" I reach for the thick liquid.

"Qamar-al-deen," one of the men says winking and smiling at the others.

I lift the cup to my lips and drink. "This is very, very good. I have never had anything like it." It is not like me to drink such a rich drink.

"Have as much as you want!"

After my third glass, the ground feels rubbery and I black out.

When I awake, the sun is rising, I can barely open my eyes. My mouth feels parched. A dog is licking my face. Then another one, and another. I try to push them away but am soon surrounded by dogs, everywhere.

The keeper of the dogs comes upon me and shoos the animals away. I try to sit up but the movement brings a deep throbbing pain. "Oh, my head." I reach up to hold my temples. I crack open my eyes to look around. "Where am I?"

"You're in Mosul," the dog keeper says.

"Mosul! That's north of Baghdad." I try to sit up, but the man gently pushes me back.

"So it is. What is the last thing you remember?"

I try to think back, but my head is pounding. "I remember feasting. I was drinking a drink I had never tried, *qamar-al-deen*. Some new friends gave me as much as I could drink."

"So much for your new companions. They probably robbed you and threw you on a barge going up the river."

I reach for my money belt. "Gone! My money is gone. All I managed to keep through the siege. I am supposed to be going on a *hajj*." I lean on my arm and begin to weep. "Now everything I own is gone."

"But you haven't lost all." The man sits down next to me. "You only think you have. Let me tell you what I lost." He has a gentle voice with a timbre that tells me I am not alone in my suffering or in my seeking.

He begins his story. "I was a spiritual man for thirty years and gave up everything because I fell in love with a woman. She was the daughter of a dog keeper. Her father told me that if I loved his daughter, I had to become a dog keeper, too."

I look around and see all the dogs. "But how could you give up a spiritual path to become a lowly dog keeper?"

"It was not a hard decision," the man answers.

How could it not be a hard decision? To seek a spiritual path and to give up his studies after thirty years for the love of a woman? "I am searching for spiritual understanding. How could you walk away from thirty years of spiritual living?"

THE SWALLOW AND THE NIGHTINGALE

The man replies, "How do you know what is a spiritual path? You see a man kneeling and praying in a mosque, and you think, that is a spiritual man. How do you know you see things as they are? You don't really know. You only *think* you see what is true. If you wish to honestly understand, you have to learn that Allah alone knows the secret of a spiritual way. Only He can reveal it. And it is probably not what you think it is."

"But in your spiritual path," I ask, "wasn't Allah revealing His secrets to you? Now you walk around tending dogs. How spiritual is that?"

"I would rather look ridiculous than only appear as if I know the meaning of a spiritual life." The man gets up. "Come with me. Let me show you what I mean."

I groan, holding my head as I gingerly get up. The dogs surround us, jumping and running about. After walking for some time, we arrive at a small farm, and the man opens a gate to let the dogs into a large yard. He hands me a soft brush and towel and shows me what to do. Each dog has to be carefully brushed, cleaned, and clipped. I then follow the man to the back of the house where we find a large feed bin. We fill gourds with food and set them out for the dogs. The dog keeper shows me how to fill other gourds with water from the well at the side of the house.

That night, I stay with the man and his wife in their small farmhouse. They feed me a light dinner of rice and lentils. I sleep in a small room behind the kitchen on a narrow straw bed.

The next day, I get up and we say our prayers. After a light breakfast of figs and bread, I repeat all the chores I did the day before and then walk the dogs. That night, I sleep better than ever before I left Shadyakh for my *hajj*.

For the whole next week, I repeat this daily routine. Brushing the dogs, feeding them. Week after week, month after month. With the simple work and peaceful existence, I let go of the pain of war. I think about what I am gaining as I detach from my search. I am enjoying the simple gift of taking care of innocent creatures.

Early one morning, I rise before sunrise and take a walk. The air is fresh and scented. A light wind rustles the acacia plants. Pink tinges the wisps of clouds. The dawning sky is my audience. At first, I begin to hum softly. Then I lift my voice with the song of the nightingale. A flock of birds fly by as if to show their approval. This is the first group of birds I have seen in a long time. I feel whole again.

I think about the nightingale's message. How does the shadow lose itself in the sun? I still do not know. But I no longer have to push to find the answer. I know I will find it. How I will do this, I do not yet know. It is enough to be living a homesteader's life. And the months turn into years.

CHAPTER 15
THE SWALLOW'S ANSWER
PART V

"Los bilbilicos cantan con sospiros de amor,
Mi neshama mi ventura estan en tu poder."
- Sephardic folksong

WORLD NEWS – JUNE 2
Air Travel Increases Greenhouse Gas Emissions
Airports Spew Tons of Toxic Pollutants
Benzopyrene From Jet Fuel is Carcinogenic

DEBORAH'S RELIEF TO get off the airplane was palpable. She stretched and looked around. The Charles de Gaulle Airport in Paris was going through extensive renovations. At customs, the RAX-1000 checked through smoothly when she presented the ownership papers. Silently thanking Thomas, she collected her bags and tried to figure out how to get her flight to Seville.

An airline representative, a young woman with a close-cropped Afro and big smile, explained that she needed to pick up Air France bus number 3 at Terminal 2F. When Deborah asked why, she explained that she had to switch airports—her flight to Seville was leaving from Orly Airport.

Waiting for the shuttle, Deborah felt a bubble of privacy descending upon her as if she was in a barrel. People nodded but didn't speak. A man silently put her luggage onto the shuttle as she pulled herself up the steps. She watched the terminals flow past her window, each bigger than the previous. There seemed to be endless planes landing and taking off. At Terminal 2F, she got off the shuttle and began a search for the Air France bus.

Turning a corner, she bumped into a woman. "Whoops." They both went tumbling to the ground. *"Pardonne moi, s'il vous plait,"*

Deborah managed to garble out in her limited French. She found herself sitting against a wall, her travel bag and the RAX-1000 clutched under her left arm, her luggage on the floor.

People sidestepped them. A man in a wrinkled blue suit leaned down. "*Etes-vous bien?*" His American accent was obvious.

Relief mixed with helplessness crossed Deborah's face. "I'm American, too." She looked at the other woman as a younger man knelt down next to her.

The woman shooed him. "I'm fine, John. Stop doctoring me." She was older and sported brown hair in a bun.

Deborah felt pain as she put weight on her right wrist but tried to mask it. "I'm so sorry. I hope you're all right."

The woman said, "Like I told my son, the doctor, I'm fine. I may get a small bruise, that's all." She pointed to her bottom as John helped her up.

Deborah reached with her left arm and the man in the wrinkled suit pulled her to her feet. She had to steady herself.

"Are you all right? That was quite a bump you two had. You're limping."

She shrugged him off. "Childhood polio. I'm all right as long as I don't have to explain anything in French."

"I know what you mean. Richard Fisher." He extended his hand. He looked like Marcus Welby with a kindly smile and square glasses. All he needed was a stethoscope.

Deborah winced shaking hands. "I'm Deborah Wright."

The younger man cupped Deborah's arm. "I'm John Fisher, his son. Your wrist is bruised. Don't try to hide it." His blond moustache wiggled when he talked.

"It's nothing." Deborah's face flushed. She looked around and saw the sign for the Air France bus. "I have to be going."

"Let's sit somewhere while I look at it. It's the least I can do." He motioned to help her with the RAX-1000. "You can't carry your luggage like that."

The woman nodded to her son. "Don't argue with the doctor." He took the bags off Deborah's shoulder while she slipped her arm into Deborah's left arm and started walking. "I'm Alexandria Fisher."

Richard picked up her suitcase and followed. They walked to a large waiting area facing the runways where they could see the planes taking off. Everything seemed so different from the States. Even the chairs and partitions had a European-looking quality to them, thinner and in starker colors.

John pulled out a small first-aid kit from a leather backpack. As he encircled her wrist with tape, Deborah asked about his work. He was finishing a cardiology residency. He said his mother was an archeologist at Stanford, specializing in ancient languages. His father, an engineer.

Alexandria had warm brown eyes and seemed like a cross between Shelley's grandmother and an old biology teacher Deborah once had. "All our seven children became doctors."

"That's why there was a doctor so handy." Deborah laughed.

"They aren't all allopathic doctors, you know, *normal* medical doctors. Two are chiropractors, one is holistic, two specialize in acupuncture. They're all working on the two normal ones," she joked, "but they make a point to cooperate with each other."

Deborah looked at John. "I bet you felt pressured into following your sisters and brothers. Or are you the oldest?"

"Youngest." John finished his doctoring. "The family joke was that I should become a lawyer to take care of the rest of them. All patched up. Mom, do you need water?"

Richard stood. "Coffee? Snacks?" Deborah shook her head and the two men left.

Taking out her hand sanitizer, Deborah looked away. She watched a plane land, remembering coming home from Tanzania one year where she had been studying avian influenza viruses. Rachel was about five and she brought her a thumb piano. Stephen devised a Simon game with it that the three of them played for hours. Deborah could still hear the shrieks of laughter when someone made a mistake.

She looked back at Alexandria. "Stanford, huh. Practically right down the street from Berkeley. Are you familiar with Ladino?"

"That's a Spanish-Hebrew mixture." Alexandria gave Deborah her business card. "My research is more ancient. Ugarit, Cypriot, ancient Greek. I've worked in Linear A." She recounted how hieroglyphics had excited her since seeing a visiting Egyptian exhibit when she was eight.

The men returned with bottles of water for Deborah and Alexandria. They also brought Deborah a cart for her luggage. John admonished her. "With that wrist, don't you carry your bags."

She smiled gratefully, glancing at her watch. "Thank you. Are you going to the conference in Seville?"

"We're on vacation." Alexandria took a sip of water. "Going on the *Dawn Princess* through the Aegean Isles."

Richard pulled out a flyer about their cruise. "The trip's been planned for a long time. We figure, if the world is going to collapse, better do what you've always wanted to do."

"Interesting attitude." Deborah was taken aback.

John asked, "What have you always wanted to do?"

"Huh? You mean my bucket list?"

"I'm serious."

Deborah looked at him. "Is this the new question of the year?"

Alexandria sat forward. "It may well be. For myself, what I've always wanted to do is to decode undeciphered ancient documents, like the proto-Elamite tablets of Susa and the Phaistos Disc of Crete."

Deborah raised her eyebrows. "I've never heard of them."

"The Phaistos Disc is from the 17th century BCE. It's an intriguing document. The proto-Elamite tablets are even older."

John took the flyer from his father. "Are we going to see it when we get to Crete?"

"Most definitely," his mother said.

Feeling claustrophobic in the cavernous waiting area, Deborah looked at her watch again and stood up. "I better find that bus."

Alexandria wrinkled her forehead. "Are you sure you are all right?"

"I'm fine. The cart is a big help. Thank you." She smiled. "Let's get together when we all return to California."

"Great idea. Now take care of that wrist."

WORLD NEWS – JUNE 4
Polar Caps Melting at Alarming Rates
Greenhouse Gas Methane Released as Permafrost Thaws
Oceans Becoming More Acidic
Agriculture Depleting Aquifers
Are Storms Manipulated?

"We are heading to the Parque Nacional de Doñana." Mercedes placed a finger on the map about 30 kilometers southwest of Sevilla. Dr. Maria

THE SWALLOW AND THE NIGHTINGALE

Mercedes Asturias was a professor at the Universidad de Sevilla and an expert on thrushes. Her graduate student, Enrique, drove them in the department's Peugeot. The city's streetlights cast pale shadows on the cobblestone streets. Holding an espresso in one hand, she pointed through the open window with her other. "Our city was named Ishbiliya by the Arabs who used to dominate Andalusia. This part of Sevilla was the Barrio Santa Cruz."

"Barrio?"

"It is the old Jewish district. One or two doorways have a *mezuzah* on them, those little prayer scrolls. Though they aren't the originals. No practicing Jew survived the expulsion."

Deborah knew about *mezuzot*. Besides one being on the side of the doorway of their house growing up, she had worn one everyday of her life until she left for college. She remembered the day she took hers off. Standing on the subway platform, she saw it reflected in a Chock Full o'Nuts display and realized she suddenly had options. Feeling grownup, she ordered her first cup of coffee and removed the *mezuzah* from her neck. When she finished the coffee, she put the *mezuzah* in the empty cup and threw them both away.

The rich smell of the espresso brought her back to reality as she felt for her pendant.

Mercedes said, "The place where we are going is thought to be the location of the lost city of Atlantis which was destroyed by a tsunami."

Deborah nodded slowly. "I live a few kilometers from a bay of the Pacific Ocean. We get tsunamis."

They reached the park. Enrique helped Deborah set up the RAX-1000. He was fascinated, taking notes the whole time and asking questions non-stop in broken English. Deborah explained things in their common language of science. Mercedes helped in the setup.

"This is a perfect place and time for nightingales." Deborah cleaned her hands with a hand sanitizer. She saw the tape on her wrist and took it off, even if it still hurt a bit.

"What do we have to do?" Mercedes asked.

"Sit quietly while I'm recording." She turned on the microphones and began the calibration.

A nightingale landed five feet from them. Deborah tapped RECORD as the bird's drawn out crescendo wail began. *Pew-pew-pew-pew.* She monitored the progress of the recording. Another nightingale landed. These were healthy birds, not like in Capistrano. An inspiration to poets for centuries, the nightingale's melodic vocalization made other bird songs sound ordinary. Nightingales can sing 200 different songs, trilling faster than any other bird. Deborah thought about the evening at Anna's house, how Robert sang *Los Bilbilicos*. *Are these nightingales singing the same song?* Feeling her whole career on the line, she plastered a confident smile on her face. *I'm just doing a recording here, like John Audubon used to do, traipsing in and out of forests and swamps.*

Switching to ANALYZE mode, Deborah played back the results. Mercedes looked at her in anticipation. Deborah listened carefully and stared at the printout. "It's not there. The nightingales aren't singing a human song."

"*Qué lástima.*" Enrique was disappointed.

Slowly taking off her small field headphones, Deborah turned on the loudspeaker and adjusted the volume. The nightingale's tune was audible but slowed down to a very eerie sound. She dropped the headphones on the ground.

Mercedes tried to make light of it. "But you heard a human song in the swallow's vocalizations. What do you think it is?"

"I have no scientific explanation for the phenomenon yet. And so far, no evidence of it happening in other species." She could hear Susan's voice berating her. Not to mention the Dean's. The smell of the coffee didn't help.

Enrique stretched. "What if it is like the men under the ground, with the canaries to breathe. If the bird dies, all the men go away."

Deborah remembered wondering that same thing that maybe the swallows were early-warning detectors. *Early-warning detectors for what?*

They tried again, sometimes while playing the recordings. No responses.

Mercedes squinted, her glasses moving on her rounded nose. "What about *H. rustica*, the barn swallow?"

Even in her disappointment Deborah realized she could repeat tests while she was in Europe. "I've tested various species in California. But you're right. We could test the barn swallow and any others we can find. This includes the *H. daurica*..."

Enrique interrupted, "The red-rumped swallow!"

"Exactly." Deborah wondered if Mercedes knew of her reputation.

THE SWALLOW AND THE NIGHTINGALE

Enrique asked, "What about their...how do you say...vocal tracts? Maybe the nightingale vocal tract is too difficult."

Deborah rubbed her temple. "Being oscines, their tracts are similar but not exactly the same. That could potentially be it. Is there any evidence of a nightingale die off?"

Mercedes shook her head. "I am not aware of any reports."

"Maybe we to try some other place," Enrique said.

They packed up the equipment and drove to a spot Mercedes knew. "Barn swallows are seen here." ꞏ

Deborah supervised as Enrique set up the equipment. The open area had lots of low vegetation. Two hours of testing yielded only more evidence that not all bird species were affected. Negative results, Deborah cursed. *What I need are positive results. And a cup of coffee.*

On the drive back to the university, Mercedes said her husband was a bullfighter. She would be gone the rest of the week, watching him fight at a festival. Deborah hadn't realized bullfighting was still practiced.

"It is a very popular sport. My husband travels around Spain for about six months and is in much demand. I want to be with him."

Deborah shot a look at her. "Is it dangerous?"

Mercedes said, "He has many scars but the bullfighter always wins. The bull always dies."

Enrique tilted his head. "What you have wanted do, Dr. Wright?"

Deborah laughed, realizing Enrique had echoed John's question from the Paris airport. *It's what's on everyone's mind. This woman wants to be with her husband.* "Do you have any children, Mercedes?"

"Two daughters and one son," she smiled. "It's another reason for my trip. A new granddaughter."

A grandchild. Deborah remembered Rachel and Shelley's announcement, how it had gotten lost in the wedding ceremony. Memories of the wedding flooded her mind.

Enrique asked, "Do you have children Dr. Wright?"

"I have a daughter about your age."

"Oh, is she *casada?* Married?" He pretended to flirt with an imaginary woman.

"Yes, she is." Deborah smiled.

Enrique acted heart-broken. "To a man too big for me to fight?"

Her smile froze and her face reddened with embarrassment. Deborah changed the subject. "Perhaps you can drop me off at the conference?"

🕊 🕊

Deborah's Notes for *Luscinia megarhynchos* Study
A series of tests was conducted in collaboration with Dr. Maria Mercedes Asturias, Assistant Professor, Department of Zoology, Universidad de Sevilla at the Parque Nacional de Doñana, south of Sevilla, Spain. Sampling was performed on June 4 at 5:00 a.m. on six adult male *L. megarhynchos*. Recordings of *Los Bilbilicos* (Sephardic folksong of Judeo-Spanish tradition; singer: Robert Abenacar) were played at 10 speeds, ranging from 1x to 1000x. Microphones and a video camera recorded observable behaviors. The video camera was synchronized with the RAX-1000 and stimulus source. Three observers classified a response as any vocalization or wing flapping occurring within 10 seconds of stimulus onset. No human song was heard to be inserted into their vocalizations and no behavioral responses to the stimuli were observed. The same experiment was performed on five adult male *H. daurica*. Samples were taken on June 4 at 5:30 a.m. Results negative.

In her welcome packet, Deborah read that the Universidad de Sevilla was founded in 1505 in the capital of Andalusia after the Catholic monarchs Ferdinand and Isabella regained control of the region from the Muslim *taifa* kings.

The conference was in the *Rectorado*, an old royal tobacco factory built during the reign of Fernando VI in the 18th century. She walked through the large wrought-iron gates that stood in front of the main door. The imposing Renaissance entryway featured a balcony and a sculpture of an angel playing a long horn.

Deborah slowly limped into the large conference hall. Recessed lighting glowed onto large flowers silked into the walls. The same motif graced the carpet. A long table stood next to the speaker's dais. Every seat was filled, including a balcony. *These are the people who are trying to understand.* The last few months rushed over her like a storm. She patted her travel bag with her talk in it, confident that her lecture would contribute useful insights to the proceedings. Feeling a burst of exhilaration, she furrowed her forehead. Susan was not someone to mess around with.

At the dais, Pedro Alvarez from the Universidad de San Carlos of Guatemala was mixing English with Spanish, but his data were clear. An image, projected on the right side of the stage, showed sample points indicating two giant quakes in the Indian Ocean, evidence the Indo-Australian tectonic plate had cracked in half. Then he showed massive numbers of quakes along the New Madrid Fault and Reelfoot Rift in Missouri and Tennessee, and an upsurge along other active and previously dead faults. His next image showed more than 1100 earthquakes of magnitude 5.0 or greater over the last six months. *Stephen was right; the media weren't reporting everything.* A murmur went through the audience.

Deborah's eyes became transfixed on the left side of the stage. Dominating the wall was a huge screen filled with graphs and maps. Engineers from Sevilla's *Científico y Tecnológico Cartuja* had created an integrated three-dimensional graphical display. As Alvarez spoke, the data were added in real-time. Over a thousand earthquake data points popped up on the screen. He laid out evidence for plate tectonic activity at every plate boundary and in several intra-plate regions like the crack in the tectonic plate and the New Madrid in Missouri.

Stephen was next. Deborah wondered what he could add that Alvarez hadn't already covered. She watched him walk up to the lectern. There had always been something about the way he walked and held himself that made her weak in the knees. He had a deep solidness to him. She tore her eyes away from him to look back up at the screen.

He began. "Some people have argued that the Earth is currently imbalanced. I've been asked to talk about what a balanced Earth is. I agree with other scientists who say our planet is a living thing." He showed a slide with the four parts of the Earth system—the atmosphere, hydrosphere, geosphere, and biosphere.

Deborah was surprised. Stephen had said he wanted to present the seismic data. Yet, this was his standard systems talk.

"A simple system, like a bicycle or a motor, comes with an instruction manual. Even a car—you turn it on, it runs. The user manual is in the glove compartment. At the other end of the spectrum is a complex system. A complex system consists of many players. In the complex system called life, examples of players are cells, humans, and governments. What's the difference between simple and complex systems? Complex systems don't respond immediately to stimuli, but there is a delay appropriate to their size. Biological cells react at the milliseconds level. Humans react more at the six-second level. Face a government with a problem and it can usually react in 48 hours.

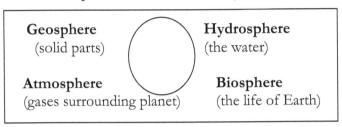

Geosphere
(solid parts)

Hydrosphere
(the water)

Atmosphere
(gases surrounding planet)

Biosphere
(the life of Earth)

"Here's another simple system—a baseball game. It has players, equipment, a field, and rules. If you don't know American baseball, each team has nine players. A pitcher throws the ball to a player of the other team who tries to hit it with a bat. If the batter succeeds, he or she runs to the first base. If he doesn't, he is out. The further the hit, the more bases are reachable. A team scores a run when a batter reaches the last base, or home base. Each team gets nine time periods, or innings, in which they have three or more chances to get a player on base. The goal is to score more runs than the other team in those nine innings."

Deborah looked around. She couldn't figure out why he was giving this talk. Most of the world didn't know baseball, but he talked about it because it was the analogy he always used. He had told her once it's because the rules of baseball are so simple and yet, no game is ever the same. It doesn't take complex rules to make complexity—it just takes a twist in thinking. She knew the twist was next.

"Our planet is like baseball played in myriads of ballparks for an interminable number of innings. The players are the planet's components: atmosphere, hydrosphere, geosphere, and biosphere. The rules are nature's laws captured in fields such as physics, chemistry, biology, biophysics, biochemistry, geophysics, geochemistry, and thermodynamics. The games are played for eons. So, what does it mean that the games don't end? It changes the nature of the game. It doesn't matter how many runs are batted in. The game is about the patterns and their infinite repetitions."

TIME: Sample Multi-Scale Cycles of our Planet

- 1 second heart beats (and other short ultradian rhythms)
- 4 hour nasal cycle (and other breathing rhythms)
- 12 hour tidal rhythm
- 12 hour atmospheric tide
- 1 day Earth spin
- 24 hour circadian rhythms
- 3 day human water balance cycle
- 9 day water cycle (evaporation, condensation, precipitation)
- 28 day human menstrual cycle (and other infradian rhythms)
- 4 month ozone circulation cycle (Brewer-Dobson)
- 28-29 month quasi-biennial oscillation
- 1 year Earth orbit
- 1 year sea ice cycle
- Biogeochemical cycles: nitrogen, oxygen, phosphorus, sulfur
- Fast carbon cycle (plant respiration, dissolution, photosynthesis)
- 8-12 year Quasi-decadal Oscillation
- 11 year Sunspot Cycle
- 15-30 year Interdecadal Pacific Oscillation
- 20-30 year Pacific Decadal Oscillation
- 50-90 year Atlantic multidecadal Oscillation
- 206 year Sun Intensity Cycle
- 1,500 year climate cycle
- 1,600 year ocean conveyor belt (Thermohaline circulation)
- 1,800 year lunar tidal cycle
- 21,000 year Earth's tilt and elliptical orbit
- 23,000 Earth's precession cycle (also weak 19,000 yr cycle)
- 41,000 year Earth's obliquity cycle
- 100,000 year Earth's eccentricity orbit
- 300,000 year Earth magnetic pole reversal
- Millions of years Wilson cycle (ocean basins)
- Millions of years - Sea level cycles
- 100-200 million slow carbon cycle
- Millions of years – Rock cycle

Suddenly, Deborah understood why he was giving this systems talk. In order to understand what's happening, the scientists had to have a definition of the planet. It was brilliant. How could you talk about anomalies if you didn't first talk about the baseline? And Stephen had a better description of how the planet worked than anyone else.

"Think of a complex system as a factory. Factories don't usually create everything from scratch. An airplane factory doesn't make steel and rubber. Instead, suppliers provide components at various times. The suppliers to our complex system factory are subsystems."

This was Deborah's favorite part of his systems lecture. It was like he was still talking baseball yet replacing the idea of a three-out inning with one lasting 365 days or 41,000 years. By extending the idea into innings within innings—cycles within cycles each with their own factory day—the complexity ramps up in a hurry. Stephen's chart of cycles filled the screen on the right.

"We can find subsystems by their cyclic repetitions. Our planet turns on its axis every twenty-four hours; it goes around the sun in 365 days. There are repetitions in how water moves through the system, in how air and storms move around the Earth, and how sun activity affects us. From the nine-day water cycle to the seasonal recharging of aquifers. There are repetitions in how continents form, come together and separate, and how sea levels rise and fall. There is a 1600 year ocean conveyor belt caused by salinity and temperature variations transporting heat and matter around the globe. There's the fast carbon cycle where carbon moves through living things during their life span, and the 100-200 million year slow carbon cycle as carbon moves from the atmosphere to rocks and back again through processes of chemical weathering, cementing, compressing, and volcanism.

"Living on the planet are plants and animals with their own factory days. Humans, for example, have repetitious cycles such as heart beat, sleep patterns, breathing, blinking, and fluid and hormonal cycles. Plants have others including the Calvin Cycle and diurnal leaf movements. Birds have seasonal migrations.

"Why speak of living systems when we're addressing the anomalous situation with the planet? Because everything is connected. Living systems experience circadian cycles of about 24 hours which can adjust to local environments. Our sleep cycle is a circadian rhythm. We have internal clocks in order to predict what's happening out there on the planet in order to respond accordingly.

"We can also see the subsystems of our complex factory by their size. These are the components. The air in the atmosphere is made of various sized gases which suspend solid particles. The air moves in differently sized weather systems. In terms of liquids, there are small and large bodies of water. Small and large living systems exist, from microscopically-sized ones to whales and Sequoia trees. In terms of the lithosphere, mountains are made from rocks that are made of minerals which consist of crystals of different sizes. Sediments are created and are buried to become rocks which get uplifted. As they weather, new sediments are created."

SIZE: Components of our planet
- **Gases**—nitrogen, oxygen, argon, carbon dioxide, methane, ozone, other gases, water vapor
- **Liquids**—rain, surface water, sea water, ground water, water bound on minerals, water droplets in clouds, lava, oil, other liquids
- **Solids**—sea ice, freshwater ice, ice crystals in clouds, aerosols (suspended solid particles in atmosphere), sediments, minerals, rocks, oceanic plates, continents
- **Life**—archaea, bacteria, fungi, algae, plants, protists, animals

---

Deborah thought the next part, on forces, was the hardest part to understand. She once asked him why he had to talk about it and he said the form something takes depends on the forces acting on it. When she asked him what that meant, he had said a wind can blow an insect around but it can't an elephant—unless it's a really big wind. But he agreed that talking about all aspects of form was too complicated.

"There are constraints on these components. Gravity limits the size of volcanoes—Martian volcanoes are larger than ours because gravity is much less on Mars. Size and materials matter. Insects must be small enough for oxygen to diffuse to all parts of their bodies. Flying birds must be light enough to fly. Some soar, some flap depending on aerodynamic forces acting on their body and wings. Different forces act on entities differently. For example, small rivers behave differently than large rivers. Large animals can fight off predators but require more food and water. Centrifugal and Coriolis forces due to the Earth's rotation affect high pressure systems like tornadoes and oceanic circulation."

Stephen looked up from his notes. "The question before us is whether the Earth is out of balance. Let's look at this in baseball terms—the myriads of teams in ballparks playing for eons. There's the game of the Rock Cycle—pretty slow with an inning lasting millions of years. There's the Sunlight game which reminds us our planet is embedded in another system, the solar system, where the Sun's Energy team is locked in a game with the planet's Heat Absorbers.

"And look, there's the game of the Fast Carbon Cycle. It's pretty exciting, actually, because things are changing. Due to the nature of their chemical bonds, certain gases in the atmosphere radiate infrared heat back to the Earth. For the last 10,000 years, the score has been tied as carbon sinks such as plants and the oceans have removed carbon dioxide from the atmosphere. But the Atmospheric Carbon team has added to their roster of players and are overpowering the Carbon Sink team. The fans are going wild. Big hitters named Burnt Fossil Fuel have joined. And because they did, the amplifying bats of Thawed Permafrost joined as well. Will Carbon Sink be able to rally the troops and absorb the extra atmospheric carbon or is this a runaway game for the next 100,000 years?"

Everyone in the audience laughed. Even Deborah smiled. He was adding this to his talk on the fly.

"And look over here at the game of the Sea Ice Cycle. The stadium is warmer than before, and the Arctic Ice team is sweating because their hitters aren't as powerful in the heat. As they shrink, the stadium gets even warmer. The other team, the Oceans, are gaining on them and the crowd is on their feet yelling 'you bums.' The excited sun-absorbing blue Oceans are bringing in the runs.

"But look, the Oceans are also playing against the Coastal Lands. They're currently feeling unbeatable since they've beefed up their roster with more water, and they're hitting home runs out of the park in terms of flooding and erosion of the Coastal Lands."

There was more laughter. Deborah thought, who laughs at losing their home.

Stephen got more serious. "I'm sure other presentations will talk of other games. The one where the more Acidic Oceans are playing against the Marine Animals. The game where the ocean's conveyor belt is slowing. And the one where the timing of the seasons is changing. The games dealing with weather are really getting intense. The Amazon rainforest—a big hitter for Air Circulation because it's basically a huge water pump—is drying up. And then there's the games being rigged by humans trying to modify weather with everything from cloud seeding to Project Stormfury and who knows what else.

"We've been making modifications to this planet ever since the Neolithic revolution and the birth of agriculture. We've cut down forests, added pollutants and toxins to the mix. We've begun focusing on single crops which increases crop vulnerability—the exact opposite of how nature grows plants. We're depleting underground aquifers and poisoning them. All without thought to repercussions, focusing only on our own needs. The system's responding in ways we cannot stop because, after all, it's a dynamic system. The subsystems have their own cycle time that no amount of technology will change. We are not the team managers. As for how life's responding, we'll let the biologists talk about that. Until then," Stephen grinned, "batter up. Thank you." He closed his folder.

Deborah smiled, looking forward to giving her talk. She started to applaud with everyone else, loving the precise way he could get to the point. Only he had the guts to at least try to go after the big picture. His context set the stage for all that would follow, while her paper would expand on the connectivity. She loved his brilliance, but she was still angry at him. Her hands froze in mid-air.

Deborah walked into the hallway. People in groups milled around in heated conversations about their data. Along the walls, hundreds of other scientists and graduate students stood in front of their posters. The excitement palpable, it had all the trappings of a normal conference, she thought. *If only the world were so normal. It's changing before our eyes and we're like ostriches with our heads in the sand. Can everything go back to the way it was someday? How does the world recover from amplifying feedback loops out of control?*

Spotting a conference proceedings sitting on a table, she found a seat and began reading. It had the presenters and days broken down by scientific disciplines. The geologists and geochemists dominated the first day. She found the life sciences on the second day, organized by biochemistry and biophysics, ecology, the zoology disciplines, and marine biology. She flipped to the zoology section to see the time for her talk. She did a double take. Her name was crossed out. *What the...? I can't believe it. Who did this?*

The doors opened and people started walking past Deborah. Dazed, she stood up and scanned faces. With scientists from all over the world, there was an assortment of races and sizes and clothing. She saw him with a group. "Stephen!"

She erratically paced waiting for him to reach her. "Did you see this?"

In mid-discussion, Stephen turned to the men he was with. "I'll catch up with you in a minute." He looked at the proceedings. "Yes, I saw it. I did try to get you included."

She wasn't listening. Her eyes flashed. "I'm a joke now. Couldn't they have at least used whiteout if they want to delete me from the annals of science?"

"I've got to grab lunch." He motioned he was leaving. "A lot's going on."

She planted herself in front of him with her hands on her hips. "You don't think I know that? I want to get back on the program."

He squinted. "Talk to the organizers of the biology section. I'm sure you can straighten it out." He started walking around her.

She grabbed his arm. "Stephen, the Dean put me on administrative leave. I don't have any credentials."

He stopped and looked at her hand. She let go. "Were you able to get the rest of the data?"

So he knew she was doing field work. Her shoulders caved in but she snapped back, "I'll get it, it takes time."

His eyes opened a little. "Time is at a premium these days. You saw from the data, things are heating up fast."

"I heard the talks. Lots of natural calamities. Hardly any are happening in Southern California and yet the swallows are dying off. It's got to be because of humans."

He shook his head and took a step closer to her. "You don't know that. You're jumping to conclusions. Maybe it's a tipping point. You need proof. You need a full story, like the seismic activity has."

"But why is that increasing?" Straightening her shoulders, she started pacing again. When he didn't respond, she whirled around to face him. "See, you don't know what's happening either. My samples could be as significant as anything else. How dare they write me off? You're all scared."

"Deborah…"

"What?" she said a little too forcefully.

They stared at each other. His eyes were wide-open. He seemed to fumble for a second. Then, he broke the stare and narrowed his eyes. "Are you going to the reception at the museum this evening?"

Her jaw jutted out. "Yes, I'm going. I need to see if I can save my reputation." She started walking away, then stopped, "Nice lecture. Batter up."

She turned and left.

🕊 🕊

The *Museo Arqueológico de Sevilla* was a good place to wind down from the intense day of scientific discussions. Soft recessed lights accentuated the exhibited pieces. Collected from cultures around the world, they reminded the scientists that much can be learned from the past. Cases stood filled with prehistoric axes, ancient musical instruments, and household utensils.

Along the walls, tables were piled with platters of fried fish, grilled meats, snails, and spinach and chick peas. An older woman in a green uniform ladled out gazpacho soup from a large tureen. Other waiters kept the food flowing. Scientists were dressed in everything from jeans and T-shirts to cocktail dresses and suits.

Deborah could smell the river nearby but couldn't see it in the dark. She wasn't hungry although she had only had a continental breakfast before her morning's field trip. After ordering a glass of white Andalusian wine from a bartender, she searched for the biologists. She couldn't remember the hierarchy of control, but she thought there must be someone who could help her. Most conversations dealt with the geological processes and when she tried to join in, she felt inarticulate. She drank her wine.

She recognized a face from Cornell. "Hello, Jaspers. Quite a conference."

Benjamin Jaspers turned. "Hello, Deborah. Surprised to see you here. They said you were indisposed or something." He peered over his glasses at her, under a thick shock of black hair.

"What do you mean?" Her eyes widened in shock. "Is it Milhouse? Is that why my name is crossed off the proceedings?"

"I've heard friendly rumors and the not so friendly ones. Only you know the truth." He walked away.

Rubbing her shoulder, she glared at the spot Jaspers had vacated. *Without my university credentials, I'm nothing. They're tying Capistrano to Santorini. Fueled by Milhouse's jealousy.*

She dragged herself to the bar for another white wine wanting to fade into oblivion. Walking along the museum cases sipping the wine, Deborah could feel her exhaustion. She was staring at a sistrum wondering how far away the hotel was when someone said, "It's a musical instrument from the island of Crete. One of our many foreign artifacts."

Deborah looked around. A dark-eyed man in his early fifties stood close to her. Offset by light olive-toned skin, his medium-length black hair looked freshly washed. He filled an extremely well-tailored high-collared suit. Deborah looked back at the sistrum. "How old is it?"

He scratched his broad chin in pretend thought. "Maybe 3,500 years old. They say ancient matrilineal cultures used it in their religious ceremonies when the Goddess was worshipped."

"You said *the*? As if there was only one?"

"You are very sharp. God was once a woman." His mouth turned up into a smile as he spoke accented English.

Deborah laughed. "I don't know how sharp I am at the moment. I'm about to fall asleep on my feet." The wine was having its effect.

Without missing a beat, he bowed. "And if you do, I will scoop you up and carry you off to your room. But I must know your name."

"Deborah Wright," she said, and then added, "ornithologist from somewhere or other, getting a little drunk."

"And I am Giorgio Fuentes, Museum Director and rescuer of tired and drunken damsels." They shook hands. She was vaguely aware that her wrist didn't hurt anymore.

Giorgio had a European graciousness in everything from his body movements to his wording. They talked about the range of the museum's holdings. He studied ancient Mediterranean and Middle East cultures and liked to surround himself with religious artifacts. "I get to practice my hobby of flying."

THE SWALLOW AND THE NIGHTINGALE

As they walked through the exhibits, Deborah told him about tracking the songs. While he had never heard of *The Swallow Song*, he knew *Los Bilbilicos*. He said it was first recorded in North Africa, but it likely started in Spain and then traveled through the Sephardic community.

"Do you know who wrote it?" Deborah asked.

"It's too old. Songs like that are handed down by an oral tradition."

Deborah felt a little tipsy. "I'm tracking some secret message in it."

"A secret?"

As a joke, she whispered, "Yes, maybe something being transmitted from aliens."

He looked left and right with exaggerated caution. "We'll have to search the halls of the museum very carefully."

They both laughed. His white teeth flashed inside his broad smile. "Shall we sit down?"

"Sitting is good."

He put his one hand at her waist and gestured with the other to a table by the windows. She told him what she had been researching, how she discovered something astonishing—a bird singing a human song. At first he acted amused, thinking she was continuing the alien thread. But she managed to explain the scientific details, even if her words came spilling out one on top of the other.

Giorgio's eyes widened. "Is there any relationship between this and what is happening in the rest of the world?"

"That's the magic question."

"When are you presenting these data at the conference?"

She frowned as his question brought it all back. "Stephen says there's no connection."

"Who is Stephen?"

"Dr. Stephen Wright, United States Geological Survey, professor, University of California at Berkeley, et cetera, et cetera."

"I have heard of him." Giorgio raised his eyebrows. "Your husband?"

"My estranged husband. We disagree on many things including the significance of my findings."

The older waiter came by with more wine. Giorgio extracted two glasses from her tray and handed one to Deborah. "You are drinking

Viña Odiel. It tastes much better with our Andalucían seafood. You should really try some of the *soldaditos de Pavia,* a fried fish."

Deborah took the glass. The wine was giving her insides a warm rosy glow. "So if you're Spanish, how come your name is Giorgio and not Jorge?"

He smiled and steadied the glass in her hand before she spilled the wine. "Italian mother."

"Excellent." She put the glass down. "Do you think people could talk to birds in ancient times?"

Giorgio took a sip of the white wine. "Nightingales were popular motifs in Islamic literature. Especially in the writings of the Sufis."

"Sufis?"

"Sufism is an ancient sect, the mystical aspect of Islam."

"Mystical?"

"Many religions have a mystical side to them. The Kabbalah for Judaism, Gnosticism for Christianity…"

"And Sufism for Islam."

"Exactly. Schopenhauer says at their highest point, all religions end in mysticism, the point where all knowledge ceases. Sufi adherents work toward deepening their relationship with God and purging themselves of evil. They believe in a personal religious experience."

"That sounds like an oxymoron." She took a drink as she strained to follow.

"But it's not. Much can be learned from mystics. In fact," he added, "I have a book you might be interested in."

"A book?"

"Yes. It is called *The Conference of the Birds.* It was written by Attar, a famous 12th century Sufi poet from Persia. And there is a nightingale in it."

"Like in the song?" She sobered up. "I'd like to read it. What does the nightingale say?"

"Lots of things. The poem is four thousand lines long." He put his wine glass down. "I have a version in English. Let me go get it. My office is close by."

Deborah could feel exhaustion washing over her. Jet lag was always so hard to deal with. So is being separated, she thought.

Giorgio returned and handed the book to Deborah. "Can I escort you to your room?"

She stood up. "I think I'll be fine."

He took her hand. "I look forward to meeting you again." His card was tucked into the book.

She smiled. Heading out, she bumped into the doorway.

🕊 🕊

Deborah woke up at 4 a.m. with a splitting headache. She looked for aspirin in her travel bag which sat on the bedside table. The little toy compass from the Earth Day Fair fell out. She held the compass trying to remember what had happened at the museum. Unable to find aspirin, she saw the book, picked it up and curled back into her small bed.

Attar's story was fascinating. The hoopoe wanted to find the Bird King. He tried to convince the other birds they must all go together, but each had a reason why it can't. The nightingale couldn't go because he was too in love with the rose: *'When I am totally immersed in love for the rose, I do not think of my own existence. The rose that blooms today is full of desires.'*

Deborah was stunned by the similarity to *Los Bilbilicos*. How did a Sufi poem become a Ladino song? And how did Attar come up with these words? Is it possible it is all connected?

Her headache gone, thoughts tumbled like falling leaves. Was a tune once connected with this poem, perhaps the Ladino tune? Did Attar know it? Did he go around singing this song, and did a flock of nightingales, parrots, and the other birds take it up? Is Attar the actual originator of the tune, not Fariña or the Sephardic Jews? Then did Fariña copy the tune from Attar? Did Fariña get the idea of using another bird species because of all the birds in the poem?

Or did Attar hear the tune from one or more birds? Are other species singing the song? And if Attar heard the tune from the birds, it still didn't explain where the words came from.

More possibly, Attar or someone who composed *Los Bilbilicos* from Attar's poem, was mimicked by a bird who then spread it through that avian species' population. Nightingales? Deborah couldn't remember what the literature said about evidence of mimicry ability in *L. megarhynchos*. From what she recalled, it had never been observed.

She continued reading. Some of the birds agree to go with the hoopoe to find the Bird King. But a series of valleys impede their travels. *This is not just a story. Maybe this is what Shelley is looking for.*

She wondered if it was possible to trace back to when the song was introduced into human awareness. Excited by the thought, she grabbed her phone and scrolled to Stephen's number. Seeing his picture, she remembered. She cupped her face in her hands to stop the tears. Extracting a tissue from her travel bag, she thought of calling Rachel. What was there to say? Besides, she wasn't sure of the time difference. *I have to get on the program tomorrow. I came too far not to participate. Look what Jeff took on. If he could do what he did, I can take on the scientific establishment.*

Tired of the emotional roller coaster, she picked up the book to read more. Her mind wandered to talking with Giorgio. She found it hard to concentrate after that.

CHAPTER 16

"Do you hear the calling of a hundred thousand birds
Hear the trembling in the stone?
Do you hear the angry bells ringing in the night?
Do you hear the swallows when they've flown?"
- Richard Fariña

WORLD NEWS – JUNE 5
Endocrine Disruptors in Water
Widely Used Herbicide Implicated in Diseases
Engineered Corn Classified as Pesticide
Human Population Rising to 9.2 Billion

THE CONFERENCE HALL was packed for the biological sessions. This time, Deborah had a mission. She would find a way to get onto the program. In honor of Jeff's memory, she wore the T-shirt with the word CITIFITBAC blazoned across it in red.

An endocrinologist from the University of Massachusetts was at the dais. A small light at the lecture reflected off his wide forehead. "The endocrine system is an overarching system that regulates the development and function of all the organs and systems in the body. Hormones—their chemical messengers—can be interfered with by drugs, pesticides, plastics, heavy metals, and compounds in many, many consumer products ranging from cleaning products to toys."

Deborah saw people at the long table in the front. Working her way there, she glanced up to the right to see on the display a list of those consumer products—things like food storage containers, furniture, carpets, phones, sunscreens, and cleaners. Deborah was surprised—what could be bad about those? *I use those things.*

"Some of these endocrine disruptors are widely dispersed in the environment and are collecting in fatty tissues of living organisms. They accumulate up the food chain in lakes and rivers, in landfills and harbors. They are in our food. They're in their highest concentrations in our homes. They're so pervasive, they're even in the dust in the Arctic."

Deborah stared at the big graphical display screen on the left. The biological data were being added on top of the geological data. A few endocrine disruptors popped up on the multi-dimensional world map as he spoke. She looked forward to her data being added but was getting confused. *What did he mean that things were accumulating?*

The speaker continued, "Studies show a close correlation between exposure to endocrine disruptors and impaired mental development, learning difficulties, and hyperactivity. Small exposures that might not impact adults can permanently damage a prenatal developing brain or any other organ or system. For example, early exposures to dioxin damages the developing immune system, making a child more prone to infections. And incidences of cancer are increasing for children, as is ADHD and early puberty."

Deborah tore her eyes away from the displays on reaching the front of the hall. At the long table, young men with headphones were peering into computer screens. Pinpointing the moderator by his name tag, she thrust the proceedings at him. "Dr. Majors, there's an error."

Majors looked like an orchestra leader without a baton. Growling, he took the book. "I'd be more surprised if there wasn't an error. What seems to be the problem?"

"I expected to be presenting today, but apparently someone crossed out my name."

He glanced at where she was pointing and turned to a student engrossed in combining data on the computer.

The speaker was continuing with charts detailing hundreds of studies. Deborah looked up and stared in disbelief. "Endocrine disruptors affect adults as well. Diseases induced by exposure include diabetes, obesity, asthma, heart disease, and Parkinson's. Sperm count is lowered and fertility rates are decreasing in many parts of the world. There are increases in testicular cancer, increases in breast cancers, and increasing obesity rates."

Majors turned back. "Dr. Wright?"

She whirled around and glared at him.

"I didn't really have to look it up. There's no error. Let's leave it at that." He turned toward the speaker.

Deborah's eyes blazed into him. "I'm not leaving it at that."

"Shhh," came from several attendees nearby. They were watching the graphical display as it lit up with more endocrine disruptors accumulating all over the world.

The speaker continued, "In aquatic systems, persistent chemicals can biomagnify up the food chain. Harbor seals and dolphins are disappearing because their immune systems are destroyed. Fish and whales are not reproducing. Birds in the Arctic are found with DDT and PCBs."

Deborah wanted to know more about the Arctic birds, but she leaned toward Majors, whispering loudly, "What's going on here? I thought this was a scientific conference, convened to find out the truth about what's happening around the world. I need to let people know what I found."

Majors shifted in his chair and stared at her like she was a worm. "Yes, we're here for that reason. But the data presented is the peer-reviewed kind of the utmost integrity. We can't let suspect data enter our databases. What kind of results will *we* have then?"

She started pacing. *This is insane.* What happened to open-minded science? Many hypotheses have struggled along with a few data points until the truth could emerge.

The endocrinologist went on. "The US government lists 85,000 chemicals in use today—3,000 of which are produced in quantities of 1 million pounds or more every year. It doesn't take much for endocrine disrupting compounds to do damage." He looked up from his notes and took in the whole audience with his eyes as if he wanted to speak to each person individually. "Amphibians are a good indicator of environmental healthiness. Frogs in California's Sierra Nevadas have been found with traces of DDT in their tissues, a substance banned in the United States since 1972. If their populations decrease, it's really not good. For them or for us. And these are the facts—their populations are declining. According to the Red List of the International Union for Conservation of Nature, about one third of the world's amphibian species are threatened. This threat is coming from us. That plastic bottle, that hand sanitizer—do you know what it's doing to you, to the rest of the biosphere? Think about it. Thank you."

The audience applauded as the speaker sat down.

Deborah sucked in her breath. *What? Hand sanitizers cause illness?* Confused, she turned back toward Majors and jut her jaw forward. "Are you suggesting I don't have integrity as a scientist?"

Majors raised his voice over the applause. "Dr. Wright, please. We all know about your Santorini fiasco. You're not welcome here. You have no credentials and you know it."

Sweat began pooling at the back of Deborah's neck. All her hard work and persistence—she had had faith in the process of science. *Why can't things be normal? When did it all go wrong?* She pulled her hand sanitizer out of her bag and stared at it.

A biologist from the University of British Columbia came to the dais. His glasses were thick, as was his Canadian accent. "Genetic modification of food involves a process whereby genes from one organism are inserted into another's to reprogram the latter's DNA. The goal is to engineer plants to have a certain trait, for example, maize that can produce an insecticide called Bt toxin. The end result is unpredictable, and irreversible mutations can occur which can be passed as side-effects to future generations."

Staring blankly at the graphic display, Deborah watched images of small plants appear. *This is sounding as Frankensteinian as the last speaker.*

"Studies on animals have resulted in stomach ulcers, toxic effects on liver and kidneys, and disturbed function of testes, pancreas, and immune system cells. Tests with female rats resulted in death of their offspring within three weeks. Sheep died in India after eating modified cotton."

Images of corn, soybeans, cotton, and papaya began covering more and more locations on the map. A memory jolted her—Jeff had mentioned this. Tears formed at the back of her eyes—he had been so young and alive with a smile that lit up his whole face.

"What about the human response to these new foods? Studies have shown the modified DNA transfers into gut bacteria. They show allergic reactions. People living near a modified cornfield in the Philippines developed skin and respiratory reactions. The modified foods also have less nutritional value, missing isoflavones, and less Vitamin E."

Even more food icons were popping up. Deborah felt her throat close up as tears brimmed her eyes. *Who was I that day I told Jeff nothing was wrong with the food supply? He knew more than I did. How naïve I've been.*

"Most of genetically-modified crops are engineered to tolerate herbicides such as glyphosate. Over 650 tons of glyphosate are being sprayed and this number could double. This spraying has been found to cause serious health hazards in terms of DNA damage, cancer, birth defects, and neurological disorders. The commercialized version adds even more toxicity, causing DNA damage, premature births, birth defects, cancers, and ADD. Glyphosate is currently found in the rain and air across the American Midwest. It's in the rivers and the soils. It's in people."

Deborah gripped the sanitizer bottle. Tears streaked down her cheeks. *We don't think about the food we eat. We just take it out of the refrigerator and hope it hasn't turned green. I was going to talk about the interconnections, how we humans are a collective using the resources of the Earth. Everything we do affects everything else. This is like one of Stephen's baseball games. The Food Suppliers team has added heavy batters—large corporations that now supply most of the world's food and who are rigging the game to do so. But why? Is it because the Food Consumers team is growing so large? The news said the population is going to nine billion. Where is this game going?*

"We are losing plant genetic diversity, both in general as species are lost and specifically through genetic engineering. Without biodiversity in our crops, the human race is terribly susceptible to starvation if crops fail. In the early 1970s, a Southern corn leaf blight epidemic wiped out fifteen percent of the American corn crop due to crop uniformity.

"Is it a coincidence that people eating genetically-modified foods are experiencing infertility, immune problems, accelerated aging, problems with insulin regulation and the gastrointestinal system? Is it a coincidence that even if a person stops eating genetically-modified food, the modified genes stay in their gut? Instead of going toward fewer crops, we should be encouraging biodiversity, for the sake of all of us. Thank you."

The word 'coincidence' caught Deborah's attention. She stared at the graphic display with its enormous amount of data. She could see the geological data from the day before. The meteorological data overlaid that with notations and colors for the changing atmospheric patterns. Markers with different symbols showed the biological and chemical problems across the land masses and the oceans. Sophisticated color schemes on the multi-dimensional screen clearly showed emerging patterns in space and time. Disparate events seemed to be fitting together. Was it just coincidental? This was the basic question on everyone's mind—is it nature or human behavior causing these things?

Suddenly, she got it. She almost tripped, in disbelief.

It was as if two controllers were competing for control of the planet—angry earthquakes responding to places where toxic pollution and drilling threatened most forms of life. Invisible CO_2 was made visible as volcanoes countered to cut off sunlight. Nature's wild and unfettered flora fought against fields of robocrops and poisonous dust. She stared. The rising sea level and increasing surface temperatures were like engines being revved up in a game of chicken against human activity. The number of humans populating the Earth was a rising jet with its engines cut off. She remembered Thomas saying human behavior was bringing the planet to the brink. But Stephen had said this ancient Earth had survived a lot worse than what's currently happening. *But what if we're at a tipping point for human existence?*

Looking at the display, Deborah stood frozen. *This is what we are inside of. I'm looking at it.* The two controllers were tightly wound into a game of stark competition, outweighing any cooperativeness. *The future of our lives is on that display.* In her head, she could hear the swallow singing, the sweetness of the song soaring in the cavernous echoes of the hall. Are the swallows trying to tell us something? Brady said his group tested everything, the food, the water, the air. There wasn't anything. The biological markers on the screen weren't affecting the swallows. *It's not human behavior causing the die off.*

What if it is something occurring naturally?

Deborah left the conference hall, dazed. People were looking at her, but she didn't care. At the wrought-iron gate, she heard Stephen calling her. She turned. "What now? Rub it in?"

He looked almost desperate, as if he wanted to reach out toward her. "Let it go. I'll get the dying birds into the database. They're not the cause of all the problems."

Deborah's eyes bore right through him. "How do you know? Because your earthquakes are so much bigger? Did you see what's in that data?"

He rubbed his forearm as if trying to contain himself. "Yes, I saw it." They stared at each other, both aware of the reality shown on the display.

But she couldn't let go and she turned away. "You think you know everything, and that your research always comes first."

"My research is important." His hands went to his hips.

That was all the sign Deborah needed. She exploded. "I've gone everywhere with you including two years in Japan so you could do your research. Never once have you considered what I wanted or how it affected my career. I always made do."

"Don't start blaming me for what's going wrong. You always did your research. Besides, you had Rachel to bring up."

"Then how did you wind up closer to her than I did?"

"It wasn't always like that and you know it."

Deborah started walking.

He called after her, "You're getting really good at pushing people away."

Deborah stopped and turned. "Don't you start with me, mister-run-off-and-have-an-affair-with-your-student." Deborah felt her eyes begin to burn and she took off.

Stephen followed her. "I'm trying to say something here. The words aren't coming out right. I couldn't keep it all together. You do your damnedest keeping me out of your life."

Deborah couldn't believe it. She kept walking. "You have the affair and now it's my fault?"

"Will you stop for one minute? How many times do we have to go through this?"

"I can't believe it. Your minister was really wrong about you."

Stephen stopped. "Peter Brawster from UCC? You talked to him?"

She turned to look at him. "Yeah, in my crazy thinking I thought maybe he had some insight into how we can work toward some amicable ending. What was I thinking? Really. You know what?" She raised her arms in frustration and gestured him away. "Let's not go through it anymore." She ran as best she could toward the hotel.

He called after her. But she was gone.

Back in her room, Deborah thrust the door shut and locked it. She dropped her travel bag on the floor and paced. Her stomach did flip-flops, tears wet her cheeks. Eyeing the bottle of Spanish Madera that Giorgio had sent up, she rummaged through her bag for a tissue and crumbled to the floor. Not finding one at first, she dumped the contents out. Seeing the hand sanitizer, she angrily threw it away. Then she ripped open the packet of tissues and blew her nose.

Her phone rang. It was Rachel. Of all times.

"Shelley's been studying *The Swallow Song* and comparing the words to *Los Bilbilicos*. She suggested I call you."

Deborah tried to hide her crying. She looked at the clock. "Isn't it like the middle of the night there?"

"I knew you were giving your talk today."

Deborah curled up on the floor. "What's she found?"

Rachel sounded excited. "She saw *The Swallow Song* as a very carefully structured song. Four verses, each one has a different theme."

"Like what?" She wiped her eyes.

"The first verse is a request to follow the singer to a place. It's like a preparatory statement, an invocation."

"An invocation?"

"The second verse is a list of statements that were hard to pinpoint. The third verse is about anger and fear. Something to run away from, like an evil or something bad. The fourth verse is a set of questions, asking whether the good or the evil would prevail. If that's the case, then the statements of the second verse are about the good."

Deborah took a breath. "So the message is about whether good or evil will prevail?"

"Right, but it has no answer."

Deborah shook her head. "Really. There's something--"

"Listen, it goes beyond *Los Bilbilicos* in terms of complexity. But the seeds are there in *Los Bilbilicos*. Fariña must have heard them in the Sephardic song."

Deborah sat up. "Rachel, I've found something that might be what Shelley is looking for as a guiding principle for her curriculum."

"You found time to help her?"

Deborah's head shot back at her tone. "Rachel..."

Rachel's voice was non-committal. "What did you find?"

THE SWALLOW AND THE NIGHTINGALE

Deborah reached for the book on the night table. "It's called *The Conference of the Birds* by a poet named Attar. He lived in the 12th century. It might have what she's looking for." She took another deep breath and held it while she waited for a response.

Rachel's voice smiled. "Thanks, Mom, I'll tell her."

"How is everything there?" She stood and put the book back on the night table. She picked up her travel bag.

"Lots to tell you when you get home." Rachel was trying to sound upbeat.

Deborah could hear her evasiveness. "Tell me. What's going on? Is it the Rabbi? Robert said—"

"It'll wait."

🕊 🕊

Deborah met Giorgio outside the Bodeguita Casa Blanca on the Plaza Contratacion. The Giralda dominated their view. Originally a minaret dating from a 12th century mosque but now a bell tower for the Sevilla Cathedral, the Giralda was tall and square with stone lattice work along the upper third. The tower reminded Deborah of the one at the Embarcadero in San Francisco.

She handed Attar's book to Giorgio. "Tell me more about Sufis."

His soft lips spread into a smile. "Let's order some *tapas*. At this café, we stand at a counter." He gestured toward an open window that allowed a view into the restaurant. "Or don't you eat food while in Spain?"

"Very funny." She followed him to the window. The balmy evening air had a slight touch of orange perfume to it. She thought, how can one eat after hearing the biologists' presentations?

"Sufis are very interesting. I fly to a Tunisian Sufi center in my Diamond Katana."

"Your what?" The smells made her stomach growl and she realized how hungry she was.

"It's a private jet. I'll show it to you sometime." He turned to face her, his dark eyes staring into hers.

"Sounds like an expensive toy." She looked away to see what the cooks were doing. They didn't seem to believe they were poisoning their guests. People in the restaurant were laughing, drinking, enjoying each forkful of food.

Page 188 🕊

"Yes, but the jet is a necessity for my job. I can confer with other museum curators. I've seen some remarkable Sufi manuscripts in Nefta at the Dar Houid Museum." He picked up two menus. "They serve excellent *tapas* here."

"What are *tapas*?" Deborah stared at the menu.

"*Tapas* are small plates of delicacies." He put down his menu and stood closer to her, pointing at the pictures on her menu. "This way you get to sample many dishes." He spoke in Spanish to a waiter, then turned to Deborah. "Wine?"

Deborah shook her head. "Not going to do that again."

After ordering, Giorgio said, "Sufis follow the inner teaching of the *Quran*. They dance to increase consciousness trying to establish a union of their souls with God. Have you heard of whirling dervishes?" He spun around with his hand on his head.

She laughed at how he could be boyish and masculine at the same time. "I've heard the term."

"The Sufis are the whirling dervishes. The word comes from the Persian *derwesh* which means 'pauper.' Same as the Arabic word *faqir*."

"Who exactly was Attar?"

"He was a Sufi master who lived in Persia in the 12th century. He wrote hundreds of thousands of verses and for thirty-nine years traveled in many countries. There is something very non-competitive in Sufi writing, something very balanced."

The waiter came with a tray full of small plates and a glass of *oloroso* wine for Giorgio. Deborah caught a whiff of spicy flavors, each smell richer than the last. She couldn't ignore her hunger. "So these are *tapas*?"

"Yes, try each, see what you think. These are *las albóndigas de marisco*. Those are *las gambas*—prawns wrapped in potato noodles."

She tried the first one. "*Albóndigas*? Is that meatballs?

"Seafood meatballs."

"Delicious." The savory juices engulfed her senses. *I can't worry every time I eat.* "Do you think Attar could talk to birds?"

"It's possible." He took a sip of his wine. "Are you sure you don't want to try this? I think you call it sherry. Much better than that white wine last night."

"No, no, had my fill for the decade." She tried another dish. "These prawns are excellent. I wonder, did Sufi poets sing their poems?"

"This was possible. Would you like coffee? Espresso in Sevilla is excellent."

It smelled so tempting. Deborah hesitated. "How about the tea? Probably not that good?"

"On the contrary, the tea of Sevilla is also excellent. We have tea bars even. I will take you to one. It is said that Earl Grey scented his tea with orange oil because he fell in love with *la Contessa de Sevilla*."

"Some other time." She laughed, aware of how relaxed she felt. "Maybe a nightingale heard Attar singing. In his poem, I loved the idea of traveling through the different valleys. I mean, valley one was about starting the quest, how the man didn't stop at the first piece of gold he found. It's like going on a treasure hunt."

Giorgio nodded, brushing his hair from his face. "And one needs to be passionate on that journey the way the beggar was about the princess. Valley two."

"And watchful like the guardsman—valley three. Attar's saying you have to corral your feet, heart, eyes, and ears. Sort of like gathering up a toolbox. But really, I didn't get the next valley—that thing about detachment and the dog keeper. It doesn't make sense. If you're on a journey, how do you detach from wanting what you're looking for?"

He thought for a moment. "I have a friend, Marwan Abi-atoon, who might have more insights. Abi-atoon is a scholar of Sufi mysticism."

"Could I speak with him?" Deborah liked the way Giorgio was willing to listen to her. It helped her think through the possibilities. Stephen used to listen like that, too. A long time ago.

"I will arrange a meeting."

🕊 🕊

WORLD NEWS – JUNE 6
Pharmaceuticals in Water Causing Anti-Social Behavior

Deborah expected Abi-atoon to be wearing traditional Arabic garments, but instead, he wore a western suit and a short black skullcap on his head. His graying hair was a touch long at his neck, adding dignity to his elegant frame. As they entered his living room, Deborah saw artifacts from the Middle East. Four tall vases were covered with stylized flowers. Two intricately carved screens acted as room dividers. An elaborate chess game sat on a black table. A floor to ceiling bookcase dominated one wall. In front of it, a large, open, illuminated book rested on a stand.

Abi-atoon motioned them to sit on the black leather sofa. He had a square forehead and arching eyebrows above piercing brown eyes. A tall teapot sat on the coffee table in front of them. As their host poured the tea, Deborah asked about Attar.

"Many claim that as a poet, Attar was better than Rumi, another Sufi poet," Abi-atoon said in a clipped English. "Especially for the inventiveness of his stories and surprise endings. Rumi described Attar as 'the soul itself.'"

"I know so little of Sufism." Deborah took a sip, noting the unusual taste. "What kind of tea is this? It's excellent."

Abi-atoon smiled. "I make my own blend, a combination of alfalfa and mint. I thought you might enjoy it. Señor Fuentes said you were interested in Sufis."

"Indeed, Señor Abi-atoon. *La doctora* Wright is on a mission," Giorgio said.

"Then let me teach you about Attar. Sufis believe that everyone is born with possibilities for inner development, but we acquire prejudices and accept what others say without regard to our own experience or reasoning. They believe that human life is a journey, made in stages."

"Like childhood, adulthood, and old age?" Deborah asked.

"Those are a start, but they are the physical stages that define and confine the developmental experience. A human life can also be a journey for seeking—what shall I say—seeking wisdom? Individuals choose what nature their path will take. Some take a religious route, some a hedonistic route, and some like yourself, a scientific path."

"I never would have put the words hedonistic and wisdom in the same sentence." She laughed, returning her teacup to its saucer. She was surprised tea could taste so rich.

"Yes, of course. And some are told they should change the path they are on for another." Abi-atoon directed a pointed glance at Giorgio. Giorgio's smile faded and he turned toward sipping his tea.

Deborah said, "Attar's book is about a journey."

"He is talking about a life's journey toward Allah, God, or more precisely, Divine Reality—*haqiqat*. People's notions of God are all different. However, ultimately life is about seeking. Sufis believe that a seeker after God is a traveler who must make great efforts to overcome his weaknesses and faults to obtain true knowledge and understanding. But no matter how much knowledge people have, unless they have examined themselves and confessed to themselves that they really understand nothing, all that has been acquired will be as 'wind in the hand.'"

"I'm a scientist." Deborah took another sip. "My path to what you call wisdom is not to be searching for God but something else. As is the path of Señor Fuentes." She nodded at Giorgio who smiled back at her. "I do like examining myself and I do believe I don't know very much. I hope I'm not collecting 'wind in the hand' because I'm not on a spiritual path toward God." She added to herself, *besides, I've had enough of religions telling me who they think God is.*

Abi-atoon drank more tea. "There are many paths to wisdom. Attar's seven valleys are a guide for getting there. Believing you don't have all the answers is a start. After all, did the birds in his book make it to their goal?"

Deborah took a breath. "Really. Dr. Abi-atoon, was the story of *The Conference of the Birds* real?"

Abi-atoon set his teacup on the table, pursed his mouth, and put the tips of his fingers together. "When and why he was writing this masterpiece, it is hard to say. The poem itself is a form of literature called a *mathnawi*, which combines story elements with teaching elements."

"You mean how he interjects anecdotes about various people in various situations?"

"Exactly. They are didactical elements to learn from, all the while the main story about the journey moves forward."

"Did Attar actually sing the poem? Was that a Sufi custom?"

"Much of it was passed orally using rhyming as a memory device. The goal of classical Sufi masters was to enlighten their audiences toward the transformational reality of religious law. But, for protection, the presentation was esoteric and elusive."

"Why?" Deborah cocked her head.

"They experienced persecutions. Sufi masters put secrets into their poems and stories in such a way to survive translations."

"How's that possible?"

"It is a method used in mysticism. The Jewish *Kabbalah* also uses hidden knowledge. In Sufi wisdom, the knowledge is secreted various ways, one of which is along the lines of animal stories. Like Aesop's Fables." Abi-atoon stood up and walked to his bookshelves to find a book. "Are you familiar with them?"

"You mean like the fox and the grapes? Or the tortoise and the hare?"

"Exactly." Abi-atoon handed her his copy of *Aesop's Fables*. "The fable may sound like it is about animals, but deep inside there is secret knowledge."

She flipped through the book. Each fable had a bright painting depicting the animals.

"People think only of the superficial story so they tell it and convey the underlying secret without twisting or changing it. The wisdom survives translations."

Studying the page with a nightingale and a rose, she couldn't tell if it was male or female because of their similar appearance. "So there's esoteric knowledge in Attar's poem? Can you tell me what it is?"

Abi-atoon smiled. "When I used the word protection, I meant it in two ways. The Sufis were elusive in order to avoid being charged with heresy. But the second reason is that the student has to be ready for the knowledge." He received the book back from her. "You are on a journey and when you are ready to understand the esoteric knowledge, you will."

Reminded of her journey, Deborah asked, "May I play a song for you? Do you have a music player?" She pulled out the *Los Bilbilicos* recording.

"Yes, right here." Abi-atoon stood up and inserted the recording into the player. Robert's voice filled the room. She was reminded of the dinner at Anna's house—the night Rachel and Shelley had announced their marriage plans. Then she remembered the phone conversation. *What's going on with Rachel and Shelley?*

When the song ended, Abi-atoon was quiet. "The Persian word for nightingale is *bolbol*, which is very close to the Ladino word *bilbilico*."

THE SWALLOW AND THE NIGHTINGALE

Giorgio explained, "Both Persian and Ladino are Indo-European languages which means they come from a common root language. The Ladino is so close to Spanish that I can understand the words."

Abi-atoon translated the Ladino. "*The nightingales sing with sighs of love, my soul and my fate are in your power.*"

"Do you think there's any connection between this song and Attar's poem?"

Abi-atoon thought about it for a long minute. "I can hear aspects of Attar's work in it."

"So how did a story from a Persian poem wind up as a Ladino song?" Deborah sat forward.

Abi-atoon smiled and shook his head. "So little is known about Attar. How does one follow the ins and outs of the last eight hundred years in order to answer such a question? Attar traveled but it is not known to where. Arabs conquered the Iberian peninsula—calling it Al-Andalus—and still controlled this southern part in the 12th century when he was alive. Did you know the name Sevilla is from the Arabic Ishbiliya? But I doubt Attar traveled this far. I am so sorry, I do not know the answer."

"I'd like to play something else for you." Deborah retrieved the *Swallow Song* recording. Abi-atoon put it into the player and the room filled with Richard and Mimi Fariña's smooth melodic harmony. Deborah leaned back, closing her eyes, remembering.

"Quite beautiful," Abi-atoon said. "The tune seems very similar. The lyrics are also about love."

She nodded. "And birds. The author Richard Fariña could have heard the song and changed it for his own use. My daughter's girlfr— we've done an analysis of his lyrics and found a structure." She felt her face redden, embarrassed by the simple language problem of describing Shelley. She gulped down her tea and continued. "At first, an invocation bringing the listener in. Then a list of statements about good and then a list about evil. It ends with questions for the listener to choose good over evil. Wouldn't this be similar to a theme of Attar's poem?"

He nodded, impressed by the careful reading. "All this is not in the Ladino song."

She took a breath. "But what if it's secretly in there? What if the esoteric knowledge in Attar's poem is still in these two songs?"

Abi-atoon didn't speak at first. The fading afternoon sunlight caught a hanging glass bead. A small rainbow played across the bookshelves. "Dr. Wright, what are you searching for? What is it you want?"

There was that question again, she thought. *I want my family back.* She said, "I have a theory that Attar wrote the song and a nightingale began mimicking it. Fariña heard it and used the tune to write another song that was mimicked by the swallows. Since the swallow is not an open-ended learner, I think such species' sensitivity demonstrates the existence of a force we cannot yet sense with our equipment. I want to know if this hypothesis is correct."

Abi-atoon put the tips of his fingers together again. "What if there is no answer?"

Her head shot back. "I've always found answers."

"I am certain you have. But for some things, perhaps there are no answers. Or if there are, you have to let go before you find them. Therefore, I suggest you go home to your family and wait for the answer."

Deborah's eyes widened. He was telling her what half of her wanted. She thought about the things still to do while in Europe—the experiments, the data integration. "Haven't you heard about the accelerating rate of natural and man-made disasters? The rising carbon levels, the pharmaceuticals in the water. I've been at the scientific conference, everything is being affected, none of it good."

"I know there are tremendous imbalances in the world. We could all be close to humanity's demise. In Islam, people pray when they are close to death, they say *La illaha illa Allah Muhammad uv Rasool Allah.* 'There is no God but Allah, Muhammad is his messenger.' They don't go searching for answers. This is my advice to you—go back," he said. "The answer won't come if you are searching for it."

"But that's how science works," she exclaimed. He seemed to be almost sidestepping the questions, as if he knew the secret in Attar's poem and wasn't going to tell her.

"All great findings are observations," he said, handing her a piece of paper. "You can't make it happen. You have to wait."

Giorgio and Deborah walked slowly along the Paseo Cristóbal Colón by the Guadalquiver River. Deborah fingered her pendant. "I have to say this, Giorgio. I liked your friend. I learned a lot. But his advice? Wait? It's not in me."

Giorgio looked at her and then out at the green-tinged river. A tourist boat was passing by. Behind them stood the Torre del Oro, an imposing twelve-sided stone tower. "You can run around and get all caught up in solving a problem, can you not?"

"Exactly. That's what I do. Solve problems." Her voice raised up a notch. "If our world is slowly collapsing and even reaching a tipping point, should we sit around and wait for it to happen, trying to understand?" She mimicked Abi-atoon's mannerisms.

"You are bound by your assumptions and theories."

"Yes, I'm a scientist." He wasn't making her feel any better. She rubbed her shoulder and looked at the river but didn't actually see it.

"What was on the paper he gave you?"

"Just the recipe for the tea we drank."

"Oh. Well, let's think a minute. You are a very smart and beautiful woman. There are a great many things you know. And because you do know so many things, as Attar says, stay in that state and remain silent. The answer will come."

Deborah sighed. She remembered Attar talking about the homesteader taking care of dogs. Taking a deep breath, she became conscious of the river. On the other side was a white structure in front of a colorful row of buildings. On her side, she could see the Torre del Oro and behind it, the Giralda. She imagined brushing a dog's coat, repeating the same motion over and over. *It's like making tea. Consciously, step by step. Grow the herbs. Gather and prepare them. Heat the water. Steep the tea.* Everything seemed to stop for a moment, as if the world's clock had ground to a halt. *What is time anyway? Aren't all rivers connected? Does it matter which one you are on?*

For her, it was a new thought. *I'm running around trying to make the answer happen. Attar is saying gather your toolbox and then let it work for you. I have a data point—a bird singing a human song. I have evidence that not all bird species are doing it. I don't need to check all the other species at the moment. What does it matter if one bird or four thousand oscine species are singing the song? Especially if the world is collapsing. What if we are at a tipping point? What if we're all going to die? I should be with my family, Rachel and Shelley. They sound like they need me.*

Giorgio continued, "There may never be a theory for what is happening right now. Perhaps the nearby solar power plants will solve all our energy problems. Or perhaps it is too late and this is the end of the world. Yes, it seems preposterous, but look at history. On one day, World War II started. On another, it ended. One day communism collapsed. Things never thought possible have a moment when they occur. The collapse of the Roman Empire. Your separation from your husband…"

His words cut through her. She flashed to the smiling photograph of Rachel with Shelley and Robert.

"…the fall of the Berlin Wall." He looked at her.

She nodded. "John Kennedy's assassination. 9/11."

"Exactly. And someday the world as we know it will end. Why not today instead of a billion years from now? Either one is as likely. Are you going to stop it, something with such a huge momentum?"

"But we have to do something…"

"Do we? As things get worse, should we accept it or panic? Which is more productive? Is there anything else you can do at the moment?"

Deborah thought about it. *I can go around telling everyone that one or more birds are singing human songs, but sooner or later they'll know. And if the world ends, what will it matter anyway?* "I guess not." She looked again at the river. The boat was where it had been before. "Maybe I should go home to California. Wait there."

Giorgio smiled. "Or maybe you should enjoy Sevilla for a few days. See the Alcázar, the night life, Christopher Columbus' grave."

"I should be home making tea for my family." Worrying that the Rabbi had kicked them out of the synagogue, she added, "Before California falls off into the ocean."

"Let me know." His eyes brightened with hope.

Deborah's Notes for *Luscinia megarhynchos* Study

A Persian scholar Marwan Abi-atoon has been interviewed regarding the possible origins of the Ladino tune *Los Bilbilocos*. Abi-atoon made reference to methods where esoteric knowledge can be passed along through

> time. A secret meaning is hidden in texts so that it transcends translation between languages.

Deborah ducked under the low stone arch feeling like she was walking through catacombs. In the golden light of the setting sun, the Barrio Santa Cruz exuded an ancient, lost culture. The diagonally-patterned cobblestones grated under her shoes. Streets were so narrow one could practically reach between the balconies. She could see the tall Giralda. While looking up into the distance, she almost bumped into an older woman rushing past her. The woman reminded her of Shelley's grandmother, Anna.

This is the Sephardic Jewish district. Each cobblestone echoed with centuries of the hooves of horses, the boots of soldiers, and the blood of the people. Not just blood, she reminded herself, but bloodbaths as Jews were hunted down, tortured, and expelled. Crypto-Jews hid their religion and lived in constant fear. *Conversos* were baptized into Christianity and still abused anyway.

Deborah wondered, how did any Sephardic Jew survive with their religion intact? Shelley had called them flexible. No wonder Anna's last name is Nessim. It meant miracle in Hebrew. *What is it about prejudice that makes people do these things? We live our lives not being up to someone else's standards because we are the wrong religion or are the wrong gender or the wrong color or love the wrong person. Or even use the wrong hand.*

She stared at a wrought-iron balcony with a vase of red flowers. *I thought I was beyond prejudice. I left a religion because it doesn't treat women as equal to men. I've battled white privilege for 32 years of marriage to a black man. And I thought I finally accepted Rachel being a lesbian. I stood next to them at their wedding. But I couldn't answer Enrique's simple question and couldn't call Shelley Rachel's wife. Just when you think you've gotten all your prejudice out, there's more. If I can't overcome my prejudices, how can Rabbi Stern?*

Deborah turned a corner and came to a small plaza with a large four-sided wrought-iron sculpture. It had a large cross on the top with four light sconces coming out of the base. A choir of children and teenagers was singing at the west end of the plaza. People gathered along the walkways to listen. The young harmonizing voices held a sweetness that permeated the air. Their director was the woman she had almost bumped into.

Deborah thought about her disconnect from Judaism. *What was it that Thomas said? What you resist persists. I've been trying to disconnect from it since college. My father shoved it down my throat. The religion makes girls second-class citizens and calls it their duty and honor. I wanted to use my brain to study the Talmud and to be considered for a minyan in order to pray, not clean out cupboards and think about dinner. The Orthodox rabbis say women are wiser than men and aren't obligated to do most of the prayers because they are already pure. And yet, men keep leadership roles and showy rituals for themselves.*

As the children began singing the next song, Deborah recognized *Tzur mishelo*. Their faces were angelic—innocents giving thanks to God. Such a basic message. Who shouldn't be in gratitude for food?

Is that my anger? At a religion? The religion is the religion. Jews believe in one eternal God, they believe in the Torah and the oral teachings. They fill their lives with rituals because it's a religion of action, not only belief. It's a religion that deeply cares about healing the world, about compassion, and loving kindness. It has beautiful psalms, and prayers, and messages. People have died for this religion. People have died for every religion. *I'm not angry at the religion.*

She remembered standing in her father's library. He stood, a wall of books behind him—his long beard bobbing as he taught her.

"*Aleinu l'shabeach la'Adon hakol.* Say it faster."

Nine-year old Deborah couldn't keep up with him.

"We chant it near the end of the Sabbath services. If you can't do it, you will look bad. Praying is about transforming ourselves."

She squirmed.

"And you are old enough to act like an adult now. Stand up straighter, let me hear."

She struggled to say it. The words wouldn't come out right. There was something she didn't like about it.

His face came down close to hers. "You will learn it so you can say the *Aleinu* in the services."

She could smell his rotten breath. She was in tears.

He started to yell. "Don't you start crying. *Aleinu* means it's our duty. It says it's our duty to praise the Lord. This prayer—let me tell you the significance of this prayer. A long time ago they thought Jews killed Christian children for their blood. In retaliation, they killed Jewish families, children even." He stared hard into her face. "Instead of converting, a group of Jews in France sang this prayer as they were tortured and burned at the stake. They were supposed to sing the *Shema* as they died but they sang this prayer," he repeated. "So, don't ever take this prayer for granted. Sing it proudly. Because you can. It's your duty. It's your moral obligation."

She had no place to hide nor even cry. She repeated, *"Aleinu l'shabeach la'Adon hakol."* All she could think of was the children, their little mouths opened, crying as flames surrounded them. The tears on their faces glowing in the flickering light, their arms outstretched for someone to save them. She stared at her blue shoes, seeing their feet burning in the flames.

"Say it again. Say it faster," her father bellowed. "Stop your crying."

Her feet felt hot. She looked up and gulped. *"Aleinu l'shabeach la'Adon hakol."*

"Again."

She did. But this time she recited it without tears as commanded. She recited it that day over and over, and all the weeks that followed.

It wasn't until the day in the twelfth grade holding the record album that she was able to cry again.

Standing in the plaza, Deborah stared at the children singing the song. Their director—her gray hair flowing down her back—made a movement with her arms and they shifted to *Los Bilbilicos* like transcending converts. Even if they were singing in Ladino, Deborah knew what they were saying. *My soul and my fate suffer from love's pain.* Tears poured down her face.

No wonder I got angry when Rachel started at the synagogue and embraced Jewish orthodoxy. She was siding with my father. And that's when she met Shelley.

Deborah smiled through her tears and began singing along. *"Mas presto ven querida, corre y salvame."* Come more quickly, beloved, run and save me.

Deborah's cell phone rang. Mercedes from the Universidad de Sevilla babbled with excitement. "The nightingales! I just heard it!"

"Mercedes, what are you saying?"

"There are reports of nightingales dying on the Greek island of Samos."

Chapter 17
What The Nightingale Said
Part V

"The next is the Valley of Unity where all who enter
Splinters before becoming whole. The illusion of the many
Is but that, an illusion. All are one."
-- Attar, The Conference of the Birds

I STAY WITH THE DOG keeper for the time it takes to soften a man's face that has been hardened by war. One day, a rich merchant named al-Firaas comes through Mosul looking for someone to help sell cloth in cities along the coast of Africa. Because I have no money, I agree to be his helper. I will be able to buy a camel and get home to Shadyakh and my old father. That is my plan, but I know if it changes, it will be all right.

We cross the mountains. There are always worries of robbers and more infidels on the land. When we hear stories from travelers, we listen for places where dangers lurk. By taking care, the trip is uneventful and we reach the sea of Baḥr al-Rūm.

I have never seen such a vast expanse of water and am stunned by its color and complexity. Small white waves play across the blue surface.

In the port town of Latakia, al-Firaas purchases our passage on the *Ivory Merchant*, an aging four-masted ship of huge proportions. I unburden the camels and load the cloth into al-Firaas' quarters, stacking the bolts high in the corner. I help the merchant sell the camels and then find my small room below in the servants' section. I had expected to be sleeping on the deck, so I am grateful for the private space.

THE SWALLOW AND THE NIGHTINGALE

The *Ivory Merchant* heads along the coast to the west, sailing from port to port. Watchmen on the high masts keep a careful eye out for pirates. On the deck, merchants and their help boys pass the time exchanging information, goods, and foodstuffs.

I learn the rhythm of the ship. During the night, I lie awake, listening to the ship's soft swaying and constant creaking. I reflect on my life. The shaikh Bukn-ud-din sent me on this journey. I thought the journey was to discover what the nightingale said; how a shadow can be lost in the sun.

One morning, I walk along the deck looking over the water as the ship plies the waves. The cold wind feels invigorating. Sea gulls play in the spray. I thought I would find the answer standing before Allah at Arafat. Yet, I no longer travel in that direction. The dog keeper taught me that Allah can be found everywhere. I have learned to be open to what is in front of me. I have to see not with my eyes or even with my ears, and not even with my expectations. What the shaikh meant is to see with my heart.

I want to convey this knowledge to other people. I remember what the shaikh told me—answers to questions are easy to say, but not easy to hear. How can I convey what I've learned? Is it even possible? How can I find the treasure if I don't know what the treasure is? Have I learned the answers? Have I found the golden bracelet, and if I have, why am I still searching?

Maybe if I write a poem, it will make sense to other people.

I sit in my small cabin with ink and quill, and I begin. 'Companions! Let me tell you a story. I will keep repeating it so that you take it upon yourself to begin a quest for the Truth.' I write down the nightingale story—how she was in love with the rose and how the parrot was weak.

Each night by candlelight, I write down verse after verse of my poem. During the day, I help the merchant sell cloth. When we are done, I stand in the middle of the square and sing. My voice gains attention, attracting large crowds around to listen to my stories.

As I write out my poem, it grows in length and depth. I add stories. I let the birds tell the tale.

A hoopoe, the great crowned bird, talks to the other birds. As the water guide for King Solomon, he becomes their leader. *Let us go find the King of the Birds, the hoopoe prods the birds.* But each bird has an excuse why he cannot take the arduous journey to the inaccessible mountains of Kaf. *The green parrot, too long enclosed in a cage, does not have the strength. 'No,' says the nightingale, 'I am too in love with the rose.' The anxious owl wants to remain among the ruins, searching for treasures. The shadow-giving humay explains that even royalty seeks shade beneath his wings, and therefore, he has no need for the friendship of the King. The erect hawk says he already delights in the company of kings. The frail sparrow has no desire to strive for something she can never reach.*

How are my birds going to find the King if I myself don't know the answer? My eyes won't always be this shut. I know the answers will come. The answer might be something as simple as feeding a dog, I laugh to myself.

We continue west. Day after day, night after night, port after port. Tripoli, Al-Mahdiya, Tunis, Binzart. Wherever I go, people cry out to hear my poem. I sing the song the nightingale taught me, I sing my poem. It has grown to hundreds of verses, thousands of verses. A beautiful sung story of the birds. People gather at my feet, and my reputation as a poet grows.

I have no ending for the poem. It is growing, but where is it going? Like myself, it has become directionless. I am standing on the deck of the ship looking out over the sea. Small waves break gently as shore birds come to inspect us. We are nearing al-Jazā'er.

The merchant comes up to me. "There are great lands out there," al-Firaas says. "Places merchants can do well."

"But the fighting with the infidels. What is the point?"

He shakes his head. "Land. They want our land, we want theirs. Our people are spread out from Al-Andalus in the west to Persia in the east. We spread the word of Mohammed and they think their Christ is more important."

I look at the sky. "But Allah is the same everywhere. There is only one King of Heaven. And heaven is big enough for all."

"Yes, but people think only about their lives as they are today— what they can get, what they will eat."

"That is why I started writing down my poem. I cannot sing to everyone, maybe my poem will speak to those I cannot reach. But still it feels empty. I don't know how it will end."

THE SWALLOW AND THE NIGHTINGALE

"In my travels," al-Firaas says, "I've heard of ibn 'Arabī—a famous master of the esoteric thought. He is in Al-Andalus at the great mosque in Ishbiliya. They say his poetry is beautiful and that he is very wise."

"Are we going there?"

"No, I am only going to the next port, al-Jazā'er. I have sold most of my cloth."

I think about this. "Then it is not to be that I meet ibn 'Arabī."

The merchant says, "Your service to me is done, Attar. You have helped make this trip successful." He reaches into his bag and produces a pouch bulging with coins. "Here is the gold as I promised."

I now have my freedom. "Then I will continue on the ship to Al-Andalus."

"Will you accompany me to the palace to give this last cloth to the king?"

I see he saved the most regal bolts for the king.

When we land in al-Jazā'er, al-Firaas and I make our way to the palace. We are received by the king on the royal parade grounds, where the king prepares to review his army. The merchant bows deeply and I follow his lead. The king is quite pleased by the textiles and invites us to stand with him to observe his parading army. A large crowd has gathered to watch the display. I am impressed that the king lets many classes of people get near him.

The army marches in formation, a parade of men and horses. All have elaborate costumes with silver buckles and red and white banners. As the great army marches past, the king turns to a beggar standing next to him. "All these animals and my men, are yours. That is how much I care for you. I see you as the king."

The man doesn't respond.

In bewilderment, I lean over to the beggar. "Why don't you respond to this great honor bestowed upon you by the king? You should show gratitude."

The beggar looks me over. "If I want to show my devotion to my king, I can kneel in humility or else speak out his praises. Between showing too much gratitude or too little, it is better that I do nothing. As a beggar and slave, I am the property of the king. My respect is taken for granted. If I do not demonstrate my fidelity, it is because I am not worthy to do so."

"You are grateful to your king, are you not?" I ask.

"But there is more than mere gratitude," the man adds.

"And what is that?"

"When the king decides to look upon me, he annihilates me. Under the rays of his magnificent sun, I no longer exist. Therefore, what can I do? I am his shadow, lost in the sun of his face."

I am stunned as I stare at the beggar. These are the words of the nightingale. The shadow is lost in the sun.

CHAPTER 18
THE SWALLOW'S ANSWER
PART VI

"La rosa enflorese en el mes de mai
Mi neshama s'escurese, sufriendo del amor."
- *Sephardic folksong*

WORLD NEWS – JUNE 7
Overfishing Decimating Fish and Coral Reefs
Marine Species Wiped Out By Mediterranean Pollution
Sonar Activity By Ships Hurts Whales Off Peloponnese

GIORGIO'S DIAMOND KATANA jet flew through hot air currents as the majestic panoply spread out below them. Deborah could hear the rush of the wind. The Grecian islands dotted the Aegean Sea like little jewels. She watched a ferryboat cut through the clean blue water, leaving behind a turquoise wake, long and curled like the tail of a Central American quetzal.

Giorgio pointed to an island looming large before them. "Samos," he yelled above the cockpit noises. She looked at the guide book he had given her. Two miles off the coast of Turkey, Samos stood protected by the strong presence of the Greek Air Force. Thousands of years ago, the island was known as the birthplace of Hera.

Giorgio pulled back on the controls as they passed Mt. Kerketeus and Mt. Ampelos and banked toward the port town of Karlovassi. Giorgio veered south, flying over the Heraion. He pointed. "The ruins of Hera's great temple. It was larger and older than the Parthenon."

Deborah looked out the window. "There's only one column left."

He nodded. "Temple marble is useful when a religion no longer sways people."

Deborah scanned the island's lush greenery. "Can we see the Valley of the Nightingales from here?"

Giorgio shook his head. "That's on the north side. But it's a small island." He veered south toward the airport.

While Giorgio rented a Jeep, Deborah began unloading the equipment and packs. He returned and helped, grabbing his small kit of maps and tools from the cockpit. They drove up into hills toward the north shore of the island, and then through the capital city of Vathi on the way to the village closest to the valley.

Agios Constantinos had ninety full-time inhabitants. During the tourist season, a small number of foreigners added to the natives. The village consisted mostly of two parallel streets, a lower one along the beach and an upper one for travelers. Not far from the valley entrance, Deborah and Giorgio found a tiny pension with two adjacent rooms.

Deborah looked out her window toward the water. Below her, she saw a watermelon garden and beyond that stood stucco houses and a blue and white Greek Orthodox Church. With her binoculars, she could see small pink terracotta faces on the corners of the roofs. Red-rumped swallows made nests below the eaves. Lowering her binoculars, she ached to go walking along the lower beach route. *Attar talked about how a shadow is lost in the sun. Without my anger, who am I? If this field test fails, it's all over.*

Taverne Paradisos sat at the crossroads of the traveler's route and the road into the Valley of the Nightingales. Their contact, Dimitris, was a bouzouki player at the *taverna* and also an avid bird-watcher.

"Yes, dead birds. I found them, no?" He appeared to be in his twenties and had big hands and a wide smile.

Deborah hoped his English functional. "You'll take us there?"

"No one here knew why it was to happen," said Dimitris. "I contact Professor Vassiolades at Athens University. He to know."

Deborah nodded. Vassiolades must have placed the information on the ornithology server where Mercedes picked it up.

Giorgio asked, "When can you take us there?"

Dimitris nodded enthusiastically. "Tomorrow morning, we go before sunrise. It's the only time you to hear the nightingales."

🕊 🕊

THE SWALLOW AND THE NIGHTINGALE

WORLD NEWS – JUNE 8
Coral Reefs Bleaching From Sea Temperature Rise
Toxins Found in Mediterranean Shellfish

Dimitris pointed the way as Giorgio drove the Jeep toward the valley. They followed a stone wall and then pastureland. The only signs of life that early were an old horse and the crowing of a few roosters. Entering a forest of tall pines, silence descended on them as they slowly drove into the valley. It was still dark but Deborah could make out the imposing height of the trees surrounding them.

Giorgio stopped in front of the Aidonia Restaurant, a stone building nestled among the trees. They sat for a moment, listening. If nightingales were present, the forest would be filled with their bell-like song. Instead—an eerie silence. Not even the sound of cicadas. Her heart sank.

Dimitris motioned to them to follow him. "Aidonia is name of bird. How do you call it?"

"Nightingale." Deborah looked around the courtyard. A site meant for locals and tourists to enjoy the nightingales, the Aidonia looked more like a morgue. Dead birds covered the patio and tables.

"The restaurant is closed," Dimitris said. "No one wants to come anymore. Tourists want good food and pretty birds."

Deborah put the RAX-1000 on a table. Dimitris was fascinated. Giorgio helped her set up the microphones, putting the parabolic mic on a table pointing toward the tall trees.

Through the trees, they saw a deep pink sunlight begin in the sky. And then, from high in the pine trees, Deborah heard a nightingale. The long-drawn out wail and falling cadence reverberated off the mountain walls. Then she heard another. Their vocal output sounded strained, but some nightingales were alive. The incredible beauty of their mournful vocalization felt like an opera of sopranos. It was worth the trip to experience this moment—the nightingale's song, the sunrise, the tall trees.

And then, the birds fell to the ground.

Her eyes moistening, Deborah snapped out of her reverie. Not looking at the bodies, she touched ANALYZE. She held her breath.

Giorgio stared at her face glowing in the blue light of the machine.

Her eyes widened as a big smile spread across her face. Cupped in black headphones, her ears began humming. She nodded excitedly,

Page 208 🐦

"Yes! It's there. *Los Bilbilicos* is in their song." Flipping on the speakers and amping up the volume, she let the majestic elongated sound of the nightingale vocalization fill the valley. The plaintive, unbroken continuity of musical tones giving way to the Ladino song was unmistakable. Almost losing her balance as she stood up, she grabbed Dimitris and then Giorgio. The three of them began dancing, their arms around each other. They were laughing and jumping up and down, although she realized the Greek had no idea what the foreign scientists were so happy about. She turned toward Giorgio, her face close to his. In the dancing excitement, she kissed him. They broke off the kiss and all three hugged with big happy smiles.

Deborah wanted to call the Dean and tell him off. The feelings of self-doubt that had been nibbling away at her lifted. The pain of being ignored at the conference abated. She now had enough data. It made up for the Santorini problems. She could publish these results. As for those doubters of her integrity—well, what was that term the students coined? CITIFITBAC. The coincidence is too impossible for it to be a coincidence. She had proved it wasn't a coincidence because now she had positive results—proof that birds were singing human songs. There was no denying it. *Wait until Susan hears.*

But Deborah noticed something was wrong. There was an interference problem in the recording. She stopped dancing and listened. Yes, there was a steady pulse in the wave pattern. "Is there some sort of radio transmitter on this island?" she asked Giorgio.

He stopped, his face holding a soft smile. "Nothing out of the ordinary, I don't think. Why?"

"Listen. There's some kind of signal. I didn't hear it in Spain."

He cocked his head. "It's a very regular pattern. I think it's coming from some man-made source."

"It's so faint." Deborah ignored his smile. "The RAX-1000 is quite sensitive but this is really a stretch even for it."

"Maybe we can hear it better at a higher elevation."

Dimitris knew the island. "We can to climb to top of mountain. Two hours to walk. Much shorter by drive. And lunch in Manolates. I know excellent restaurant."

Deborah didn't understand. "A restaurant at the top of a mountain? Like a McDonald's for hikers?"

Dimitris explained that the mountains were dotted with dozens of small villages. Greeks have a long history of digging into the mountainsides.

They packed up the equipment. Giorgio drove along a gorge through the pine forest following a small creek splashing down the mountainside. The air wafted sweet with the smells of thyme and wild orchids. Deborah appreciated the steel railing on the side of the windy road. The higher they climbed, the more spectacular the views. The rising sun filled the sky with brilliant yellows and pinks, and the Aegean glittered a pristine turquoise in the morning light. She pulled out her sunscreen and was about to put it on when she remembered what was said at the conference. She put it away.

They arrived at a parking lot below Manolates. Dimitris jumped out of the Jeep. "We walk from here."

Giorgio grabbed his kit while Deborah slung the RAX-1000 over her shoulder. They followed a dirt path and then up about a hundred white stone stairs, entering the village. Deborah walked carefully so that she didn't lose her footing. Giorgio helped by holding her arm.

Manolates seemed like any other Greek village—pottery shops, souvenir stands, and restaurants with blue and white tablecloths. Even an Orthodox Church with Greek flags flapping in the courtyard. Shops were opening up. Women in black dresses swept the cobblestones in front of their shops. Everything seemed normal, except for the fact that it was situated at the top of a mountain.

Dimitris led them to the Taverne Loukos. As they entered the outdoor patio, Deborah stood stunned by the spectacular view of mountains across the Strait of Mykale.

"That's Turkey." Giorgio paused close to her and pointed.

Spread out before them was the intensely blue Aegean Sea. The air felt alive, smelling fresh like a banquet. She understood why people stayed their whole lives here. Why go anywhere else when you could experience such a rich sensory overload?

Dimitris greeted the owner and his family enthusiastically like old time relatives. He introduced Deborah and Giorgio and explained what the two scientists wanted to do.

With a big smile, the owner said, "Fine, fine, no problem, no problem." He looked like Zorba the Greek.

Deborah went to a corner table by a low wall facing the sea and set up the RAX-1000. Only the internal microphone was needed. She handed Giorgio the extra set of headphones and turned on the machine.

Dimitris had been right. The signal was stronger at the top of the mountain. Both Deborah and Giorgio nodded their heads. They clearly could hear a powerful, intense pulsing sound. To be thorough, Deborah touched RECORD.

Giorgio took off the headphones. He pulled out the aviation maps from his kit and computed the signal's origin. "It's definitely not from this island. It's coming from the southwest." He pointed. "Over there."

"What's there?" Deborah slipped off her headphones, stopped recording, and powered down the machine.

"It's hard to tell how far away the source is. There are many islands out there, plus the northern coast of Africa."

"Africa?"

"Or islands. Can't tell without further triangulating the source. We'll need another data point."

"Well, let's go get it." Deborah quickly packed up her equipment and started toward the exit.

Dimitris stopped her. "Dr. Wright, this is Taverne Loukos. It is in small village, not famous New York, but the cooking very excellent."

Deborah stared at him, remembering what Abi-atoon had said about waiting for the solution. The answers won't come if you are searching for them. She shrugged and smiled. "He's right. Let's enjoy ourselves. I could sit here all day in this incredible place. How about a local fish delicacy? I've heard seafood is very good in the Mediterranean."

Dimitris gestured like a waiter offering them a table. "Good! No, even better than fish, the best the *moussaka* and of course, *kolokythoanthoi*. Have a fine Greek lunch." He turned to leave.

"You aren't staying?"

"I have to work. My *taverna* is to open."

Deborah called after him, "Do you at least want a ride?"

Dimitris yelled back, "*Eímai Ellinída*. I am Greek. I walk!"

After they ordered, Deborah gazed out over the seascape. Letting the success of the morning sink in, she played with the tablecloth, darting around the memory of their kiss. "After we met with Abi-atoon, were you serious when you said you thought the world might end soon?"

Giorgio scrunched his face. "I have to remember what I said. I think I was saying it is possible."

Trying not to stare at his lips, she said, "On my way to Europe, I met an interesting family. I remember being surprised people were on vacation during these times. The son asked me what I've always wanted to do, because that's how they're facing the situation."

"Makes sense." He ran a hand through his hair. "Instead of panicking, keep focused on what you want in life. Go on an Attar journey to find it."

"So what is it you've always wanted to do?" She stared at him.

Giorgio closed one eye and thought. "Rob a bank."

Deborah laughed at how cute he could be. "Not sure Attar would approve of that. No, seriously."

"All right. Serious. Let's see. I've always wanted to make a great discovery. What about you?"

She tore her eyes away from his. "It's the same question Abi-atoon asked me." Images from the conference display flooded her mind. "If anything, I want to stop the imbalance in the world. But we know what Abi-atoon said about that."

With a great flourish, the owner and his wife brought their *kolokythoanthoi*. He stood back with mischievous eyes.

"What is this exactly?" Deborah looked at the beautiful display of white petals in front of her. The smell was intoxicating, rich with hints of spices. *Nothing could be wrong with this food.*

His wife served her a portion as he spoke. "It is zucchini flowers fried and stuffed with the feta cheese and special herbs."

"Zucchini flowers? How odd." Deborah picked up her fork and tried it. "That is wonderful. I've never heard of eating flowers before."

"Only here on this Samos, you can get it the best." The owner smiled at his wife. She served Giorgio a portion. "Nowhere else but at Taverna Loukos. Enjoy." They left.

"Dimitris was right. This is excellent." Giorgio breathed in the aroma and started eating. "And what did Abi-atoon say?"

Deborah took another bite. "Abi-atoon said to wait."

"Ah, yes. Attar's fourth valley, detachment."

"I have detached," she said. She fumbled for words. "There's an imbalance in the world fueled by a patriarchy we live in but can't see. Like fish can't see water." She looked down at her plate of zucchini flowers and remembered the woman at the Earth Day Fair with all the flowers in her hair. Deborah touched her pendant, suddenly remembering the dandelion in it. *We're always eating flowers. They're called plants. They give us life.*

Giorgio took a forkful. "What's so wrong with a patriarchy?"

"Gandhi said commerce without morality is a social sin. Have you been following the news regarding toxic waste, genetically-modified food, the overuse of fossil fuels? At the conference, they compiled these man-made environmental problems along with the natural calamities. The model would have been incomplete without it."

Giorgio looked out at the Aegean and then back at Deborah. "You know, it is so easy to judge. But we are part of that patriarchy. Would you do anything immoral? What is morality anyway?"

She thought of Stephen's affair, which she considered immoral. "I don't think so." Was the Santorini fiasco immoral, she wondered. "I guess I don't know if I would."

Giorgio took another bite. "Besides, the patriarchy has produced lots of positive things. Look at what men have built, discovered, created. Picasso, Michelangelo, Mozart. Lots of moral men as well, Jesus, Mohammed, Buddha."

"Women have done a few things, too."

"Of course, I didn't mean to imply anything. You said..."

Deborah kept eating. "It's not that all men are bad. We're caught in this system which clouds our thinking. I just meant the patriarchy..."

"Don't you think it's rather entrenched as a system? It's not like we could throw it out and start all over now, right?" Giorgio smiled at the absurdity. "You know, go back to when God was a woman."

"What?"

"I mentioned that concept at the reception when we were standing by the sistrum."

"I was too drunk or jetlagged to hear much of anything."

"You were pretty funny." He wiped his lips with his napkin.

She took another bite. "I always thought Judaism was the earliest, or at least one of the earliest, monotheistic religions, with God being male or genderless."

"Some people question that and think there was an older monotheistic religion."

Deborah remembered that Shelley had talked about women being political and religious leaders at one time before there was a patriarchy. It made sense that there would be female gods, but a monotheistic goddess? She put down her fork, stunned.

The owner's wife brought a platter of *moussaka*—eggplant and lamb topped with a Bechamel sauce—and a Greek salad of tomatoes, cucumbers, kalamata olives, onions, sliced green peppers, and feta cheese covered in olive oil.

Giorgio thanked her. "*Efxaristo.*"

Deborah looked up. "Your dishes are superb. Imagine, eating flowers."

"*Para kalo,*" she responded and left.

Giorgio served up the *moussaka*. "I've never heard a steady pulse like this signal, not this strong. Have you?"

"Maybe it's a force that dying birds are detecting."

"What do you mean?" Giorgio put salad on her plate.

"That's plenty, *efxaristo,*" she said, testing her Greek.

"*Para kalo.* You are welcome." He smiled. "You are very good with languages."

She stared at his mouth, waving off the compliment. "I've been trying to figure this out. The signal may be making the birds more sensitive to human music." She took a bite of the *moussaka*. "This is wonderful."

He picked up his knife and fork and started eating. "But why didn't we detect it before?"

Trying to not look at him, she ate some salad. "Has anyone else detected it? You're a pilot, did you measure it flying here?"

"No, I monitored my instruments—VHF navigation, global positioning."

"Could the signal interfere with them?"

Giorgio shook his head. "The GPS system is a system of satellites. If it was interfered with, we couldn't have flown here. So it's a different frequency."

Deborah tore her eyes away to look out over the sea. "You said there are islands where it might be coming from."

Giorgio tried to remember what he saw on the map. "Africa's in that direction, plus various Greek islands, like Crete and Thera."

"Thera?"

"It's a funny little island, shaped like a reversed letter 'C'. Thousands of years ago, a huge volcano called Mt. Strongyle stood in the middle of a larger island called Kalliste—the beautiful island. It erupted thirty-seven hundred years ago, destroying most of the island. Plato heard about the catastrophe and called it Atlantis."

This was sounding familiar. "Another Atlantis story? Someone said Atlantis was in Spain."

"The eruption was so enormous," he gestured in the air with his fork and knife, "Plato figured it had to be beyond the Pillars of Hercules which is what the Greeks called the Straits of Gibraltar. After the eruption all that remained was a crescent island surrounding a sea-filled caldera."

"Thus the C-shaped island."

He continued eating. "Thera means the ugly one, probably a name left over from that time period. The island is beautiful now. Still, it's different. For example, it has vineyards because the fungus that infected grapes in California and France never affected it. Oh, and you would be interested to know that swallows are never seen there."

Deborah took a sharp breath. "You said this island is called Thera?"

"Yes. It was renamed Santorini by the Italians. Do you know the island?"

Santorini. A chill started in her neck and crept down her back. Why would Santorini be involved in this? Of all places. Oh, my god. CITIFITBAC. The coincidence is too impossible for it to be a coincidence. *Everything is connected. This will mean one more stop before going home. At the one place in the world that's destroying my reputation.*

"Let's skip the other places and go straight to Santorini."

CHAPTER 19

Deborah's Notes for *Luscinia megarhynchos* Study
A test was conducted on the *L. megarhynchos* species
on the Greek island of Samos in the Eastern Aegean Sea
in collaboration with Dr. Alexander Vassiolades of
Athens University. Sampling was performed on June 8
on *L. megarhynchos,* four adult males, unhealthy for
unidentified reasons. The test determined that a human
tune has been inserted into their song, statistically
matching ($P = 0.015$) a tune entitled *Los Bilbilicos*. A
signal of unidentified origin was recorded along with
samples. It is unknown at this time if the equipment is
malfunctioning or if the signal is being generated by an
undetermined source.

THE AFTERNOON SUN SPARKLED off the water as the small jet
flew toward Santorini. Deborah monitored the interference signal. It
was increasing in strength. Deborah felt like something was pulling her
to the island. She nodded to Giorgio.

From the air, Deborah could clearly see how Santorini's shape
revealed its history. She could envision how much larger the original
island had been before the eruption by extending an imaginary
coastline around the nearby smaller islands. In the center of this
imaginary larger island were two small masses of black and brown rock
breaking through the water's surface.

"Take a few readings," Giorgio shouted. "We'll triangulate the
signal."

Deborah nodded and flipped switches on the RAX-1000 for a
directional readout. Looking out the window, she saw splotches of

Page 216

white that looked like glacier ice clinging to the topside of Santorini. As they flew closer, Deborah could see these were bright white buildings.

Giorgio pointed to the cliffs. "Hardened ancient ash."

Deborah followed his finger. There were layers of rock, each one a different color, but one layer was much larger than the others.

"Thirty meters thick in some places," he shouted. "They used it to build the Suez Canal."

They crossed toward the smaller island. "Therasia." He pointed. "Santorini and Therasia are the edges of the caldera. The original volcano covered all this." He motioned to everything before them and then pointed to the two masses inside the caldera. "New volcanoes. That one is called Palea Kameni," Giorgio gestured. "And that one is Nea Kameni. It's still active."

She shouted back. "People live next to an active volcano?"

"Yep, crazy, but you'll see why. Take another reading here." He banked around Therasia and faced the jet's nose toward Santorini.

The whole reversed C-shaped island was now in front of them. They flew along the south side and Deborah took the third reading. A mountain dominated a flat alluvial plain, stopping at the water's edge.

From the airport, they took a taxi to Hotel Atlantis in the island's capital of Fira. In her room, Deborah opened the window sash and unclasped the wooden covers to see the entire caldera basin before her. She sucked in her breath, stunned by the intersection of blue sky, aqua water, and layered cliffs. The air enveloped her like a baby's arms. How do people live in such beauty and not cry all day, she wondered. Giorgio was right. Living next to a volcano was a small price to pay.

"It's gone." Deborah stood, staring at the RAX-1000 set up on her patio.

Giorgio entered, wearing a white shirt, blue jeans, and a dark grey sweater tied around his neck. "What?"

"I can't find the interference signal." Deborah readjusted the potentiometers.

Giorgio looked at the instrument. "But we tracked it all the way. I thought you triangulated it to here."

"Right, to those rocks out there."

They both looked at the volcanic cones peeking out of the sea.

"How could it stop just as we land? That would be a weird coincidence."

"This whole project has been weird coincidences." CITIFITBAC flashed through her mind.

His voice rose a pitch. "Does your machine wor—do you have confidence in your instrument?"

Deborah could hear what he didn't say. "What am I supposed to say? It's a prototype—it's very complicated. I used it in one other study where I tested European starlings for evidence of mimicry."

He walked toward the machine. "And it worked?"

"Yes, it worked. At least, I thought it worked. That whole study is suspect at this point."

Giorgio paced. "I should have taken the readings from my ADF."

"ADF?"

"The automatic direction finder. I could have aligned the plane with it and read measurements off the indicator."

"I'm no signal-processing expert but, if that signal was transmitting on that frequency, we wouldn't have had accurate readings on the flight instruments."

He stopped pacing and looked out the window. "So now what? I mean, we could go back up. Maybe it's coming from Africa."

"We could, but what's the point?" She rubbed her temples. "It's not the real reason I came here."

"What?" He looked at her.

"I don't care about the signal." She took a deep breath and sat down next to the RAX-1000. "Remember in Sevilla when you asked if I was presenting at the conference? I was supposed to but they kicked me off the program because of a paper I wrote about Santorini. I didn't want to come here, but I had to in order to clear my name."

"Is it tied to the machine?" He sounded wary.

"The RAX-1000 part of the paper isn't the problem. What was questionable was that I included some data about Santorini swallows."

"Swallows on Santorini? I thought there weren't any."

"That's the problem. It was my understanding there were. I mean, all the islands have swallows." She stood up and paced. "I need to find a reliable scientist here to talk to—a biologist or ornithologist, anybody who knows the ecology of the island. I'm hoping to go to a university or something."

"There's no university here."

"Oh." She sat down. Her shoulders slumped.

"There are a few museums, mostly archeological."

She closed her eyes.

"But I know a scientist connected with the conference center."

Her face brightened. "Where's that?"

"Not far."

The Petros M. Nomikos Conference Center, situated on the edge of the caldera, was built on the site of a house destroyed by an earthquake in 1956. The view from its expansive patios was stunning.

Giorgio went into the office to talk with the secretary while Deborah looked around. The red buildings had white cornices and white framed doors and windows. She entered a building where she found herself in a wide tunnel with alcoves. Along the white walls were posters from conferences going back to 1998—political ones, music ones, ones on humans in space, medicine, computer science, and the law. She was looking at a poster on professional misconduct when Giorgio entered.

"My friend's not here."

Deborah's heart sunk.

"But," he pulled out his phone, "he's at his home resting from back surgery in Oia."

Her eyes lit up. "Let me guess. Next town over?"

Giorgio laughed. "It's a small island, I grant you. We'll need some wheels to get there. I'll rent us a motorbike."

Giorgio revved the Piaggio Liberty onto the two lane road out of town. Deborah sat behind Giorgio. After experiencing their flyby, she had a sense of the whole island as a narrow rock where life clung like a fragile butterfly. To their left, she could see the volcanic cones of Nea Kameni and Palea Kameni. In front of her was Giorgio, her arms around his taut body, the feel of his shirt against her skin.

The tiny village of Oia sat at the most northwest point of Santorini at the top front of the reverse C. Labyrinthine streets were wide enough for two donkey carts to pass. Small tourist shops bustled with Greek vases, music, colorful textiles and T-shirts. People's houses, nestled into the cliff side, stood beyond the commercial area.

Giorgio parked the motorbike. They walked past the stores and then down along sets of intertwining whitewashed stairs. Low white walls separated the houses with their open air patios. Giorgio held Deborah's arm, his strong hands steadying her. She couldn't imagine how people could live like this. But then, people lived in Manolates high on top of Samos.

Nearing one of the houses, Giorgio greeted a couple sitting on their patio. The woman stood up.

"*Kalispera*, Giorgio," Chrysoula Papadelos opened the gate, "so glad you called." Dr. Antonio Papadelos smiled but remained seated.

Giorgio hugged Chrysoula and extended his hand to his smiling friend. "You finally took care of your back." He reached down to turn the handshake into a hug.

"Careful." Antonio laughed, taking the greeting. "I had no choice."

Giorgio made the introductions. "Deborah is an ornithologist from the University of Berkeley and is in Europe for the scientists' conference."

"I've been trying to follow that. How is it going?"

Deborah didn't know where to start.

Chrysoula brought out a bottle of wine and four glasses. "The evening's ritual is about to start."

Antonio opened the bottle. "I want details. My wife is referring to the sunset over the caldera."

He toasted. "*Stin ygia sas.* To your health. *Kali týchi.*"

Around them, families and guests gathered on the surrounding white-washed patios as if they were at a sporting event. A big black dog curled up on one of the paths. Deborah could see a windmill to the right of her. A church stood below it with three small bells, a larger one, and a cross above that. Deborah glanced at the blackness of Nea Kameni. The sun was very close to setting.

"Excellent wine," Giorgio said.

"A local wine from the Santo Winery. We have superb grapevines on this island, and tomatoes too." Antonio nodded to Deborah. "You'll try some of our delicacies. We can bring out some mussels."

Deborah gestured. "No, no, thank you. What did the second part of the toast mean?"

"*Kali tychi* means 'good luck'. *Kali* means 'good.' *Kalera* is 'better.' *Kalliste* is 'best'."

The sky turned orange and pink as the sun started to set, spreading a warm glow on everyone's faces. It reminded Deborah of Rachel and Shelley's wedding ceremony, only two weeks ago. Deborah swirled the wine in her glass, picking her words. "You asked about the scientific conference. There was a lot to learn from the data integration. They used a state-of-the-art multi-dimensional display."

"Yes, displaying data is always a challenge." Antonio took a sip.

"I walked through your conference center. Impressive. I saw all those symposia that have been held here through the years, especially the scientific ones."

"People like coming here." He gestured. "What's not to like?"

A butterfly landed on the table. Deborah thought of the moth in Attar's book, the one that flew too close to the fire. "Aren't we like a moth?" She glanced at Giorgio.

He nodded. "Yes, if we sat here as the volcano exploded, we would see something incredible."

She finished the thought, "And only we would see it. We would die but we would have learned a lesson."

"To quote Attar." Giorgio stared at Deborah. "Well-learned but the wrong valley."

She looked at him quizzically.

"Unity is next."

Antonio laughed. "The volcano won't erupt. It hasn't for thousands of years. It won't now." The color blazed through the clouds and sky. Antonio continued, "Giorgio says you've been traveling to various places."

Deborah explained about the swallow and the nightingale research.

Antonio said it reminded him of an ancient myth about two sisters who become birds.

Deborah looked at him. "You know that myth about the woman with no voice?" *Two women ran. They looked frantic and scared, their breathing hard with each step. Their feet became very light, lighter than air. They were floating. Suddenly they were transformed into two birds—a swallow and a nightingale.*

Antonio nodded. "It's quite gruesome. The younger sister has her tongue cut out."

Deborah was surprised. "That's how she loses her voice?"

"Yes. And she weaves the story of what happened into a cloak which she sends to her sister. The older sister is horrified and they plot revenge on the evil husband by killing his son. They turn into birds when the husband chases them."

"Why was her tongue cut out?"

"It's only a myth. Who can believe those anyway, like all the stories of Zeus and Apollo. I'd lend you my copy but it is in Greek."

"*Efxaristo.*" Deborah laughed. "Did I say 'thank you' correctly?"

"Excellent. *Para kala.*"

Deborah tried to be casual. "Is it true swallows don't come to Santorini?"

"Yes, it is true."

"Do you know why?"

Antonio cocked his head. "That's a question I should be asking you."

She carefully put her glass of wine down on the table.

The people on the hillside applauded as the sun dropped below the horizon. Deborah cleared her throat, thinking end credits should roll across the sky. The colors increased into darker pinks and oranges.

Chrysoula returned to the patio. "You see, this is our nightly entertainment. Who needs television?" She carried a wooden tray of little Greek appetizers. "Try the *spanakopita.* I made it myself."

Picking up a small plate, Deborah took one of the spinach-filled filo triangles and bit into it. "It's excellent, much better than any I've tasted in the States."

"We keep the best of the olive oil for ourselves," Chrysoula said.

Antonio smiled. "And the feta. We live in heaven here. Try the tomato dish, *tomatokeftedes.* There is none *kalitero.*"

Deborah stared at him. "It is a beautiful life, the setting, the food, the people. But back to your comment. Soil and insects sampling have proved to be ideal for swallows. There are many similar species here."

Antonio nodded. "I have talked to biologists who come here. No one has been able to explain it."

She took some of the tomato meatballs with a toothpick and ate slowly. The sky deepened to a purple tint. "I wrote a paper about European starlings and in it, I talked about the swallow population in Santorini."

"Strange." Antonio looked at her.

"It was a hard time in my life. But that's no excuse. I—" She fell silent.

"Where did you get the data?"

"I rack my brain trying to understand what happened. It isn't like me to not thoroughly check things." She was silent again, deciding to skip around the family dynamics. "I mean, I do remember needing to get the paper done." She took a deep breath. "It started because I wanted to beat out someone for a grant. We were in a tight race. I remember sitting at my screen having found a dataset—from where, I don't remember. But it seemed plausible. I remember wondering where it came from." She blinked hard. "So I used it because it supported my argument. Not able to cite any sources, I made it look like my own. I was stressed out, which is no excuse. Then I forgot it happened and it wound up in subsequent papers. People started questioning my thesis and when I couldn't explain where I got the data..." *Or why Rachel became a lesbian and Stephen had an affair.*

Antonio was gentle. "Competition—always a great motivator."

"I've been put on administrative leave from Berkeley because of the misconduct, which makes this project suspect as well."

Antonio squinted. "That's absurd. Sure, you competed, that's what everyone does. Two scientists vie for recognition for a particular accomplishment. What's misconduct? You are searching out the truth."

"Don't make this easy on me. I didn't fabricate data *per se*, but I didn't check things out. I used unproven data. I deserve the punishment. And I need to make amends." A *t'shuvah*, she thought. Repentance. She took another bite of *spanakopita*.

"But, you see, there have been swallows on Santorini."

Deborah eyes widened. "What?"

He reached for the plates on the tray and set them aside. "Look at this."

She stared. The tray had the word χελιδόνι above a painting of a bird. "A swallow! Where did it come from?"

Chrysoula said, "This old tray was a sign from a pension. When they were remodeling, I took it and turned it into this tray. I love it."

"Why? What does it say?" Deborah asked.

"It's the word *chelidona*," Antonio said.

"Petrochelidon," Deborah gasped. "The genus of cliff swallows."

"Exactly. It means 'swallow' in Greek."

"Why would the pension have a painting of a swallow?"

Antonio said, "The picture is from the frescoes found at Akrotiri."

"Akrotiri?" Deborah squinted. "What's that?"

Giorgio gestured toward the caldera. "When the volcano erupted thirty-seven hundred years ago, it destroyed the villages that dotted the island. One was uncovered in the Sixties."

Antonio continued, "Archeologists found many buildings and artifacts, including pottery and frescoes. And there's a room with frescoes of swallows and lilies."

Deborah turned to Giorgio. "Can we go there?"

Deborah's Notes for *Luscinia megarhynchos* Study
After numerous attempts to detect it, the signal of undetermined source has been lost. It is unknown whether the signal has stopped or if the RAX-1000 is malfunctioning.

WORLD NEWS – JUNE 9
Shipping Introduces Invasive Species
Exhaust and Sewage From Ships Cause Pollution
Shipping Adds to CO2 in Atmosphere

Giorgio and Deborah drove south on the motorbike. The brisk morning air felt good against her skin. They passed fields of yellow flowers, clothes hanging on lines, and farms. A Mexican restaurant with orange stucco walls seemed oddly out of place. Deborah could see the Santo Winery—its terraced grapes formed into small basket-like clusters protected from the wind. The little clusters of plants looked sad and isolated.

Santorini must have been even more beautiful at one time. She could see beaches to the south and rounded hills. Ancient layers of red and white lava and ash built the bluffs which gently sloped up and down along the horizon.

They reached the ancient village of Akrotiri. Giorgio helped her off the motorbike. Above them, Deborah could see the thick layer of ancient white ash.

He looked up. "That's it. It hardened into pozzolana rock."

They walked down an incline toward the sea to where workers were excavating the ruins.

The complex was covered by a roof. Skylights gave the ruins a yellow tinge. After paying admission, they walked in and saw a convoluted arrangement of streets and houses, reminding Deborah of modern day Fira and Oia with their labyrinthine streets and paths.

Walking down the first street, they gazed into the houses and buildings. They stopped in front of a display of reddish-white vases— some tall, others wide and flat. A few had brown lines encircling the necks and bases. Some had flowers that looked like myrtle, and dolphins could also be seen on the really large round ones. "Doesn't this feel a little creepy to you?" Deborah asked Giorgio, looking inside the pottery.

"What do you mean? My life is about collecting ancient artifacts. You're not going to find anything inside the pots. The archeologists would have emptied them all."

She kept peering in the different vases. "What if in three thousand years people walked through your house and looked at your coffee cups and refrigerator? And from that, they make judgments on your whole culture. They could decide you worshipped coffee and small square cubes."

Giorgio laughed. "You're right. Archeologists make assumptions. Besides, I do worship coffee. Doesn't everyone?"

Deborah stood back up, staring at his incredible smile. "Did they find remains of the Akrotiri inhabitants?"

"No one knows what happened to the people. There are no clues to anything. An earthquake obviously damaged the village." He showed her a broken staircase. "Footprints in the ash prove some returned and lived here after the earthquake."

"Did the people know the volcano was going to erupt?"

Giorgio shook his head. "No bodies have been found, not on the island or under the sea. So they probably escaped, making it to nearby Crete or some other island."

Deborah and Giorgio reached the large square area in front of the complex called the Delta building. A group of tourists came by with an English-speaking guide who described what it meant to be covered by thirty meters of ash. He pointed to the lintel above the door and explained that during the excavation of the ash, the archeologists would find empty holes. By pouring cement into the holes, they could recreate the wooden furniture and lintels of doorways. He also explained how the people worshipped bulls. He said the large animals were a symbol of male strength.

Giorgio whispered, "Actually, it's thought to be a symbol from the matrilineal societies that existed earlier than the patriarchy."

Deborah whispered back, "Here? A God-was-a-woman society?"

He nodded.

She whispered, "I bet you could give this tour better than he can."

"At least I would be more accurate. I've read the research literature. I used to do archeological digs myself."

They walked into the Delta complex. As the guide had mentioned, the walls of the rooms were shorter than modern room height. It gave the appearance that the ancient people were short. But the wall height was due to the pressure of being buried under thirty meters of ash-turning-into-rock for thousands of years.

She stopped in front of the room labeled Delta 2. The three walls of the room were covered with frescoes—all of them with swallows. Deborah's heart started beating quicker. The birds were graceful, like the one on Chrysoula's wooden tray. Judging by their deeply forked tails, red faces and black and white body coloring, she guessed them to be barn swallows.

Tears moistening her eyes, Deborah carefully studied the frescoes. There was something so tender about the pictures. "Look, blue and red rocks." Curving lilies grew out from crags in a multi-color rocky landscape. The rocks undulated under the flowers. She realized this was the island before the eruption. Plentiful fields of lilies growing in the highlands and lowlands. Above them flew the swallows. Who painted these frescoes? Did the artist know his or her life was going to be turned upside down?

On the back fresco, two swallows had their beaks close to each other. The one on the left was male because its tail was longer than the female's on the right. Deborah tried to figure out whether they were competing or cooperating.

She dropped to the ground and looked up at the swallows now flying above her. The lilies caught her eye. Such beautiful flowers. She reached out and touched the lilies. The flowers! She touched her dandelion pendant from the Earth Day fair. What had that woman said? *What am I? Such a profound question.* She started sensing an image.

Ash is falling from the sky. An enormous weight descends, crunching the walls. The buildings lie for eons, the ash slowly hardens into pozzolana rock.

But then there is activity. Big machines come for the pozzolana. Their huge scoopers fill up trucks which cart the rock away to build a canal from the Mediterranean Sea to the Red Sea. Pozzolanic cement makes a strong lining. Ships from Asia and the Middle East can easily get to Europe now. The people are ecstatically happy with their new lives.

Thousands of ships traverse the canal. Oil is spilled, garbage jettisoned, and pollutants seep into the canal and into the groundwater. The canal fills with thousands of tons of pesticides, fertilizer, industrial waste, chemicals, and hormones. Plants and animals from the Red Sea travel the canal, changing the ecological balance of the Mediterranean.

Nearby the people use big machines to build a dam. Behind it fills a reservoir with trillions of cubic meters of water. The dam stops the flooding on the Nile River. The people are ecstatically happy with their new lives.

But annual flooding had brought nutrients to the river delta. Now the delta has lost its fertility, and the number of fish in the Mediterranean has decreased. Algae chokes the Nile. Salt concentrates in the soil. Standing water turns into breeding ground for parasites and disease. Silt deposits increase in the reservoir. Death follows wherever the big machines go: belly-up fish, putrid carcasses of animals, diseased humans wasting away.

Deborah flashed back to when she stood in front of the multi-dimensional display at the Sevilla conference. She grabbed her pendant. *A dandelion. What am I, a flower or a weed? That's what the woman meant.*

There's one resource, but two controllers. Nature and humans.

Nature is about change. The planet is alive, growing and evolving, with no teleological reason other than to be. Stephen talked of nature's baseball games that go on ad infinitum. Balanced between cooperation and competition, the old gets torn down, making way for the new.

Patriarchal man is competing with the laws of nature for his own needs, greed, and pleasure. He cares not about the interrelationships, the cycles, the balances. He wants stability. Kill anything in his way. Give it pejorative names like weed, vermin, disease and blight. Build and maintain the constancy of shelter, infrastructure, energy sources, and food production at all costs. Destroy the pests, bugs, predators, the other. Flame prejudices to cause dissension and separation.

THE SWALLOW AND THE NIGHTINGALE

He's like a child in a kitchen trying to make pancakes. He mixes milk and whole eggs because he doesn't understand why we don't eat eggshells. Then pours the mixture on the counter because he doesn't understand the concept of a stove. Then turns on the gas burner, starting a fire that destroys the kitchen.

Deborah clutched her pendant, staring at the frescoes. Our human species is playing with a fire we cannot grasp. Not only don't we look seven generations into the future when we do things, we're doing things we shouldn't be doing. We don't think of the complexity of the system when we take an action. *We're inside it, we can't see it. Why was I drawn here? For drawn on a path I was. The birds are sending me a message. Is this payback time for our species? Was that interference signal part of it?*

Why did the swallows never return to Santorini? I have to keep my eyes open, follow the path in front of me. It's what Attar said to do. My eyes have been opened.

Deborah stared at the image of the birds. Their wings were spread—their forked tails extending behind them in long wire-thin streamers. But the swallows' positions seemed odd. One looked up at the other. Why would two swallows touch beaks in mid-flight? Were they kissing? The male was lower than the female, looking up from a position of subservience. With a shock, Deborah realized that this was the behavior predicted by the dataset she had used in her papers. It's not the type of behavior seen in contemporary swallows. *My dataset is 3600 years old, documenting subservient male behavior. No wonder I've been so condemned by males. Where did the data come from?*

Why was I brought here? Who is doing this?

She felt a rumble. Giorgio grabbed her and they rushed out. A bit unsteady, Deborah held on to Giorgio feeling disconnected like a time traveler. It was the same as when she went to Dallas and saw where President John F. Kennedy had been shot. The images were so vivid in her cultural memory, it was as if she had been there before.

They walked up onto a red bluff. She could see a red beach and bathers in the afternoon sun. One could see everything on the sea coming toward them.

"They must have used this to protect themselves from enemies." Giorgio looked out over the sea.

"Maybe they protected themselves from enemies, but they couldn't protect themselves from the volcano behind them. Do you think they knew they were living on an active volcano?"

"That's the question."

Chapter 20
The Flight of the Swallow
Part I

"Ars longa, vita brevis."

HER NAME WAS EVEENARA. She was the medicine woman for the Kallisten, a clan that lived on a beautiful island north of Caphtor. The green lushness of the island was graced by Mount Strongyle looming large in the center. A light column of smoke rose from the top of the mountain. Shimmering whitish green olive trees, red lilies, and crocuses surrounded the mountain like a jeweled necklace. The air felt sea-fresh and brilliant, touched by the light smell of sulfur.

Eveenara was tall like the majestic evergreens that dotted the island. Her long black hair curled down on one side of her head. It was cut short on the other side. She wore a flowing yellow dress. Blue and red ties cinched in her waist from which hung a small potion bag. Large hoop earrings hung from her earlobes. A gold pendant set with a crystal stone hung around her long, olive-tinted neck.

She collected myrtle leaves growing on the red bluff looking south over the rolling sea. Her thoughts were interrupted by the voices of Reifte and her crippled daughter Mudia.

The priestess Reifte admonished Mudia. "You have to learn the ways of the Temple. Drawing birds is not service to Kalliste."

"But, Mother, I love drawing swallows. They are graceful as they fly and they are my friends. Can't Kalliste see that?" Mudia drew on a clay tablet in her lap. Her black hair was cut at medium length and she wore a short coarse blue tunic.

Eveenara came out of the grove of olive trees from behind a myrtle bush. As the medicine woman, Eveenara was held in esteem by members of the clan. Yet she owed Reifte respect, the same that was owed to all of the Great Goddess's living creatures. "Reifte, what is wrong with a child trying her hand at drawing? Mudia has had her burden to carry."

Reifte looked at Eveenara. "She has to learn the Ways. Others are destined for artistry. As my daughter, Mudia will follow me into the study of learning and knowledge."

"Yet, what is the harm, an afternoon of drawing? Will it affect her whole life? You know the Ways of Kalliste. Though she is young, she deserves our respect."

Reifte had no choice but to accept. She turned and headed back to organize the scrolls and prepare for afternoon prayers.

Eveenara sat down next to Mudia to watch her draw. "What did you mean, the swallows are your friends?"

Mudia was surprised by the medicine woman's question. "If you hide in the bushes, you will see what I mean."

Curious, Eveenara walked back into the bushes.

A flock of swallows came winging by, powerful and graceful. They began to flutter about Mudia, all chattering together in the light breeze. Eveenara could see that they were tired after the long flight over the calm blue waters.

One of the swallows called out to the young girl. "Why do you sit out here and draw birds?" It landed on the ground.

Mudia looked up. "You came back!" the girl said. "I was hoping you would. The other children don't like playing with me. I cannot keep up with their games."

The bird took a few hops closer to her. "But you have a great skill."

"I want to be an artist when I grow up," Mudia said, her charcoal steady in her hand. The white clay tablet was made from the special rock of their island.

"What will you draw?" the bird asked.

"Swallows like you, so graceful and pretty. Not like me." She looked down at her crippled leg.

The Earth shook lightly. In her hiding place, Eveenara grabbed a tree trunk to steady herself. The bird flew up into the air. "What's that?"

"That's Kalliste, Mother Earth," Mudia said. "She speaks to us now. She warns us of danger. But don't worry, little bird. Don't fly away again. Let me keep drawing you."

"I'll be back tomorrow," the swallow said.

"Little bird! What's your name?" Mudia called out.

The swallow answered, "Chelidona." She flew off with the other birds toward the other side of the island.

Eveenara came out of the grove and sat down beside Mudia. "That is a great friend you have there. The swallow is a sacred bird. You are lucky to be honored by her interest in you and destined to be remembered for a long, long time."

Mudia turned. "I want to serve the Goddess however she wants me. I like drawing Chelidona."

Eveenara looked at the drawing. "You will be a great artist."

"How can I be? Reifte says I'm destined for other things."

Eveenara smiled. "You will be initiated soon and become a woman." She paused for a moment. "I would like if you could come to my house this afternoon and do something for me. But first, if it pleases you, meet me at the Initiation Shrine."

Mudia was excited about being invited to Eveenara's house. Should she tell Reifte? Never having stood up to Reifte before, Mudia knew she could trust in the Ways. At least, that is what they all said. What act would lead to harmony? What was the right Way?

The Initiation Shrine was situated in front of the Square of Canos. Eveenara and Mudia stood inside the gathering room where Eveenara had opened the first set of doors to the altar. The smell of incense was strong. It was unthinkable to open all the doors without a ceremony in progress and impossible when uninitiated were present. Mudia would not be initiated until the next full moon so she still had never seen the whole painting above the altar.

The part of the painting in front of them showed the gift giver bringing a necklace to the divine altar. Her colorful dress was textured with crocuses and lilies, her hair long and her flounced skirt reached her feet. In the painting, the girl's pearl necklace seemed to float in rhythm to her brisk steps. Her eyes glowed with excitement.

"This is one of my favorite temple paintings," Eveenara said.

Mudia held Eveenara's hand. "Because it is so beautiful?"

"Not only that. My mother's consort painted it. See how he used color? See how simple his brush lines are and yet they convey the intensity of the moment?"

"Whenever I am here in the Initiation Shrine, I study this painting. I will analyze more now that I know it is your favorite." Mudia wanted to see the rest of the painting on the hidden walls. It was a very exciting time for her, although scary, because not everyone survived the ritual. One had to be well-prepared to pass the initiation.

"My mother told me he was using me as his model. How he envisioned I would look after I was initiated. Now, if it pleases you, come with me to my house."

Eveenara's house was deep inside the tunnels that connected the mud-brick buildings along the main street of the village. Large wooden timbers outlined the doors and supported the ceilings in the three small rooms. A table stood in the middle of the preparation room topped with finely crafted bronze utensils and pots. The tall pots, covered by painted pictures of birds and spirals, were filled with her medicinal potions. Wicker baskets, each filled with drying leaves and plants, rested along one wall and on a high shelf. A small door accessed the communal rooms. Clan members took their meals in the communal kitchens and dining rooms in the housing block.

The plastered walls of Eveenara's house were brightly decorated with natural scenes. Rocks and hillocks painted with red pigments undulated along the bottom. Above the hillocks grew red lilies with long yellow stems. "I think some beautiful swallows flying above the lilies would be nice, don't you, Mudia?" Eveenara asked.

Mudia looked at the medicine woman. "You want me to paint them? How can I do that? Reifte said I am not to be an artist. Besides, I have difficulty walking. How can I stand and paint a wall?"

"Mudia, I have faith in you. In the Initiation Shrine, you saw the kind of artistic line I like. If Kalliste gave you such a talent, you are destined. The sacred swallows have spoken to you. What can Reifte do to you, or to me, if Kalliste has spoken?" Eveenara went into the storeroom and came back with paint brushes and alabaster bowls. "Here are some pigments to paint with. Be very careful with the blue— it is very hard to get."

While Eveenara dampened the lime plaster on the walls, Mudia studied the colors. The black was from carbon, the red from a blood red stone, and yellow from the earth pigment ochre. The blue was a mineral imported from the clans to the south along the river Iteru. It was mixed with lime water and powdered pigments.

To Mudia, the room was quite tall. She carefully stood on a stool and reached up to the empty area in the mural. With a few sure and quick brushstrokes, Mudia painted in the swallows. From watching them so much, she knew exactly how they related to each other.

Reifte looked for Mudia. Remembering she had last seen her daughter with Eveenara, she went to the medicine woman's house and exclaimed, "Mudia, what are you doing?" Her sudden outburst scared Mudia so much that she spilled the blue paint on one of the hillocks. Reifte was visibly upset. "Now look at the mess you made, Mudia."

"Reifte, I have a right to bargain with whomever I choose. Even your daughter."

"You could have consulted with me. And look at what comes of it."

Mudia looked as though she would start crying.

"But nothing has happened," Eveenara surveyed the accident, "or at least, nothing bad. I think the landscape was too ordinary anyway. Let's paint the rocks and hills as multi-colored as possible."

"You mean..." Mudia asked.

"Yes. Red and blue!"

"That would be fun." Mudia regained her excitement.

"Here, let me help." Eveenara moved to get another brush and more pigments. Together, they painted wide swathes of color across the hillocks, creating an exotic design with blue and red pigments.

Reifte shook her head, gave up and exited.

When they were done, Eveenara and Mudia surveyed their work.

"It looks lovely." Eveenara gave Mudia a hug. She gathered the brushes and bowls.

"Yes, yes. It does. Thank you...."

They heard a sudden commotion from outside. "What's that?" Eveenara ran outside followed by the hobbling girl. Ever since Kalliste's shaking months earlier, members of the clan ran outdoors quickly at the least little quake.

People gathered in the square which formed where many streets came together. It was one of the village's meeting places. On ritual days, incense burned in its many corners.

Chelidona flew along the open street through the elaborate labyrinth of mud-brick masonry tunnels, shrieking, "Attackers! Attackers! Come quickly!"

Mudia cried out to the swallow, "Chelidona! What's wrong?"

The bird landed on her outstretched hand. "There are strangers with weapons sneaking along the western shore!"

Eveenara stared at the bird. "What did they look like?"

"Beards, black beards," the bird squealed out. "Long swords and bags of arrows."

Yidini cried out, "That's the Achaeans!" He started to run.

"Where are they?" Eveenara gasped.

"Near Red Beach, below the bluff." The bird fluttered into the air.

"We must warn the others." Eveenara motioned. "Let us all gather!"

Mudia, trying to run, yelled to the bird. But her feet got tangled up and she fell. "Quick, Chelidona, tell everyone. I cannot run as fast as you can fly."

The swallow flew through the narrow streets, spreading the alarm into the windows. Some women and men scrambled into their houses for their bows and arrows. People began running toward the coast.

Eveenara ran after them. "Don't fight!! Do not take weapons! Kalliste will protect us!"

Yidini ran past her, strapping a short knife to his muscular waist. "We must defend ourselves. It is the only way. There isn't much of a choice anymore. You know what happens."

"No, it's not the only way," Eveenara pleaded. "We are Kallistens! It is their way, not ours. Yidini!! Kitane!! Stop! Where is the harmony in fighting? Come to the Festival Temple instead!"

"Each must do what she must do." Kitane ran with her bow and arrows. "You of all people should know that." Her long robe flowed behind her as she ran.

"Come, Mudia, let us go to Festival Temple," Eveenara called. "We'll be all right there." They hurried to the Temple. Some of the others followed. Reifte and the novitiates were preparing the afternoon meal. A large hearth stood to one side, a glowing brazier was filled with incense. The women wore large gold and silver earrings and long tan robes pinned to one shoulder. The men had on short kilts and thick belts.

"The Achaeans are on the island," Eveenara announced.

"Let us go upstairs to the gathering room." Reifte turned. "We can see what is happening." She motioned to the others as they walked up two half stairways. Reifte sat down on one of the benches by the large front window. "Where were they seen?"

"By Red Beach." Eveenara sat down.

"Who saw them?" Reifte asked.

Mudia spoke up. "My friend, the swallow. She was flying to the island. Yidini and others went off to fight them!"

"Some Kallisten are taking up their fighting ways." The priestess shook her head.

"I knew when we began arming ourselves it would come to this." Eveenara felt helpless. This was not the first attack. But, with the recent shaking, many in the clan had chosen to leave the island. Only a handful remained to live at the base of the sacred mountain. They were more vulnerable than ever before.

Eveenara stood up and motioned toward the altar room. "Come, let us ask Kalliste for protection and guidance. She will help us." The group entered the smaller room. On the walls were images of young men holding bundles of fish as the sacrificial offering for the fishing fleet. Thirteen wall recesses held offering burners, one for each of the thirteen months of the year. The offering table stood at the far corner of the room. The group formed a circle. As the priestesses took up their drums, they began to beat a low slow cadence.

Reifte cried out, "Oh Kalliste, Mother! Hear our voices lift in your praise." Her right hand touched her forehead. Her left hand was held by her side. The people joined in. "You are the One, Blessed Mother. Protect us and guide us. Amen."

The Earth shook violently. A cry of fear rose from their lips.

"Mother Earth!" Eveenara shouted. "Kalliste is with us! She will protect us."

The Kallisten were the chosen ones—the ones allowed to live with Mother Kalliste. But being chosen had its price. They had to build sturdy walls to withstand the power of their Goddess. The small rooms and houses were connected by elaborate labyrinths that supported the weight of the buildings and made the walls less susceptible to collapse. When the Earth had shaken violently three months ago, there was damage and fear. The stairway by the Festival Temple had collapsed, a few walls crumbled. Hundreds of large storage vessels had fallen over, spilling beans and olives. Most of the clan members abandoned the island. But those that stayed saw that their houses and Temples had remained.

As the shaking continued, everyone in the altar room turned toward the corner and made the sign of the Goddess, shaping their arms into a circle above their heads and their hands into a triangle. They intoned, "We are your servants, Kalliste, do with us what Thou wilt." And then they all brought their right hands back to their foreheads and their left hands down to chest level and touched their hearts.

Mudia joined into the chanting. Kalliste's shaking was scary but they believed that Kalliste would not harm them. Sometimes She talked by sending messages through Her light in the sky with loud booms. Eveenara had told Mudia the quaking Earth was a warning. Mother Kalliste was trying to tell them something.

The shaking stopped. Eveenara sat quietly. "The Achaeans are leaving, I can feel it."

A small boy ran out to find out. On returning, he announced, "The strangers are gone."

The group walked outside to meet the returning archers.

Kitane, her breath quick with excitement, told what happened. "The swallow flew ahead, showing us the way. From our vantage point on Beshken Bluff, we could see the Achaean soldiers hidden below. We positioned ourselves so that the attackers were boxed in between our arrows and the sea. We let fly a tremendous volley of lethal arrows and the men below dispersed."

"Was anyone hurt?" Reifte asked.

"No. Only a swallow, hit by an arrow."

Mudia cried out in horror.

Kitane continued, "I saw the swallow get hit. As the swallow fell to the Earth, I was able to fight off strange little monkeys and pick her up."

Mudia yelled, "Is it Chelidona? Is she alive?" Kitane held up the tiny bloody body. "Chelidona!!" Mudia squealed.

Reifte raised her voice in anger. "This is a sacrilege! A swallow is sacred!"

Eveenara carefully took the tiny body and examined her. "She's not dead." She took out some salve and rubbed it into the bird's wing.

"Please, save her!!" Mudia said. "I don't want her to die."

Reifte reached to comfort her daughter. "Chelidona is honoring the great Goddess by helping us. Kalliste will take her back to Her bosom when She is ready."

"Mudia," Eveenara spoke up, "your friend will recover. Those monsters do not respect the sacredness of the Goddess' servants. Here, your hands can heal as well as mine can. Rub these herbs into the wound."

Mudia took Chelidona and sat in the corner.

"This is what happens when we take up their ways," Eveenara said.

"But they are trying to kill us," Yidini argued. His eyes sparkled blue-green like the sea. "They have attacked us before." He stared at Eveenara. "They will attack us again if we don't show strength."

Eveenara said, "There are others who are even worse than the Achaeans. They are destroying villages in the north. And they are forcing believers to pray to a new Goddess, a male Goddess."

"How can a Goddess be male?" Yidini was unable to comprehend such a notion. "Life comes from the female."

"It makes no sense to me either." Reifte shook her head.

Eveenara was impatient. "Kalliste will protect us. She has always protected us. What happens is Her will. She will not let them overthrow us. We are Kallisten!"

Yidini looked at Eveenara. "We cannot hold out forever."

Eveenara looked around at the concerned faces. "Let us have a great council. We'll ask the Goddess to decide our fate. Call all Kallisten together."

Reifte agreed. "We will do this at the coming initiation rites. Kalliste will tell us what to do."

Chapter 21

"...and the bull which they caught they led up to the pillar and cut its throat over the top of it so that the blood fell upon the sacred inscription."

-- *Plato's Critias*

ON THE NIGHT OF THE FULL MOON, clan members gathered along the main street between the Initiation Shrine and the Festival Temple for the sacrifice of a sacred bull.

In the Temple, initiates waited in Preparation Hall while the novitiates helped Reifte dress in a flowing skirt and tunic. Her hair was piled high into curls. They topped it with a regal hat.

Eveenara and Reifte entered the repository room. Papyrus flowers from the river Iteru covered the walls. Preparatory offerings were made using a shell in the shape of a small bull. The medicine woman and priestess each took a sip and made a blessing. Hidden in the floor below them was the sacred repository for seeds that would be used in the Regeneration Festival in the spring.

After the offerings, the two women went out to the square and led a prayer for a successful sacrifice.

The bull was let loose and the hunt began. Adults were armed with clubs or a noose. The bull careened down the street. The hunters chased it, sometimes becoming the chased ones themselves. Others tried to distract the bull. Athletic boys dared the bull by trying to jump over it but Yidini proved to be the best. The frenzied run continued with yells and screams. With the help of strong women and men, Kitane caught the bull.

Eveenara and Reifte led the clan members toward the Initiation Shrine. Yidini, Kitane, and others carried the trussed bull on a large board. A fire danced in the pit in the center of the gathering room. Behind the screen doors, flames rose in the altar. Incense mixing with the smell of smoke thickened the air. The hiss of two large snakes could be heard from inside painted snake tubes.

The adults formed a large circle. Younger children and the uninitiated grouped upstairs where they could not see the altar. As an initiate, Mudia stood to the right of the screen doors, holding a crocus in one hand and the swallow Chelidona in a sling around her shoulder.

Eveenara opened the doors part way to the altar. The painting showing the gift giver was visible to everyone. The rest of the images remained hidden and would only be visible to those descending the stairs to the altar. The bull was brought down the stairs. Eveenara and Reifte descended as well. A soft beat started as the women in the gathering room picked up their drums. Made from the intestinal linings of sacred bulls, the drums vibrated deep into the night air. The swift tempo resonated within the shrine walls. Reifte chanted an invocation from behind the screen.

"As it was in the beginning and it will always be,
Kalliste, our Mother came forth and spoke to the first woman—

"Gather blossoms on the cliff sides
One in spirit with the Earth
Listen gently with the key
The source of every life form's worth"

Glistening men began a frenzied dance. The fire played across their entranced faces. The rhythm of their steps and swirling arms sped up and slowed down as each drummer responded to another. No one was in charge, no one was directing the ritual. It unfolded with its own energy. They chanted:

"The swallows grace us with their winging
Their soulful choir spreads o'er the sea
They teach us caring is our duty
As stewards of the rock and tree"

Reifte came out from the altar and motioned to the initiates. Carefully stepping down into the short stairwell with the others, Mudia had to hold onto the wall so that she didn't trip. She had prepared for this moment for a year. There were mysteries to life that someday she would understand, she was told. The clan had a repository of knowledge passed down from priestess to priestess, from medicine woman to medicine woman. At her ceremony, she would be initiated. Only the most sacred rites were written down on the papyrus rolls.

Turning the corner, Mudia saw the mystery on the murals unfold. An image of a young girl sitting with a bleeding foot stood before her. Quickly, Reifte pricked Mudia's right foot with one of the snakes. She screamed out in pain. A light flashed and Mudia stared at the image of a pillar painted on the wall. Blooming lilies covered its sides while drops of sacred blood trickled from the horns at the top.

Mudia felt herself losing consciousness. She felt an overpowering sense of compassion and tranquility. Her mind expanded into an awakening. She was flying across the island with the swallows, experiencing every blade of grass, every droplet of water. She felt each sad murmur of their wings and heard the exquisite choir of the birds' songs. Roaming in the power of their flight, she experienced a love deeper than she had ever known. Each tree and rock below her wriggled with life like worms on the first day of spring. She flew higher than the swallows and lower than the sea fish. Every animal and plant smiled at her, and she reached out touching each one, not with her hands but her heart. She merged with each drop of water in the sea, each speck of dust on the ground, everything brimming with life. Oneness surrounded her and she was part of it.

Mudia was interrupted from the profound experience but struggled to stay in it. Reifte held her head, making her drink from a golden cup that frothed with a thick, salty-tasting liquid. Mudia coughed and found herself restored back to the Initiation Shrine.

In front of the pillar image was an actual pillar made of white marble and inscribed with Kalliste's Creed. Eveenara stood by the pillar. The bull's throat had been cut and its blood—the blood of Kalliste—flowed over the inscription. Eveenara held a golden chalice with a charging bull hammered delicately into the metal. It was filled with wine and blood.

The screen doors opened and one by one, each adult filed by, filling their drinking vessel. Each cup flashed a brilliant golden radiance from the hot fire.

Eveenara raised the chalice high in front of her, turned toward the mountain. "Great Mother! Kalliste, Mother Spirit! You are the Creator and Giver of Life!"

They all chanted in unison, raising their cups to Kalliste. "Oh, Great Spirit! May You bring bountiful life to us. Hold us in Your love. Help us to honor your gifts!"

Four pipe players began the music. Eveenara took out her Sacred Disc and brought it before Reifte. The two women stood before the altar and held the disc between them. Eveenara had her right hand against it while Reifte had her left. Reifte sang:

> *"My life is love, my life is spirit*
> *I am alive, a song to sing*
> *Respect the water, the land and air*
> *You are the power in every live thing"*

Eveenara harmonized while she sang:

> *"The Earth is round, the Earth is holy*
> *I am the Earth, love fills the need*
> *I am the listener, this is Her song*
> *She has the power, the Lady loves me"*

Their voices and pipes blended into a beautiful harmony. As they sang, the Sacred Disc began to spin. Slowly at first but then faster as it lifted out of their hands and became suspended in the air. A strong white light emanated from the Sacred Disc filling the shrine. An air of expectancy shimmered as if something else was supposed to happen. But nothing did, and the light subsided.

With tears in her eyes, Eveenara replaced the Disc in its pouch. She motioned to a scribe to take out a blank scroll. Taking a laurel leaf from a small round pot and putting it into her chalice, she drank deeply from the red liquid. Reifte took the emptied cup. On her cue, two priests reached into the long snake tubes and pulled out two live snakes. They walked over to Eveenara and handed them to her.

The snakes hissed as they wrapped themselves each about one arm. Without fear, Eveenara let them bite her, putting her into a trance. The potion had immunized her from their deadly venom, letting her fall instead into an altered state of consciousness. As she stood facing the altar, the wall before her came alive with images.

The Achaeans in their gray tunics and other yet unnamed men in darker tunics freely roamed the island, killing everyone they saw. In a low voice, she intoned the nature of the evils:

THE SWALLOW AND THE NIGHTINGALE

"When Evil's fury lashes outward
Causing trembles far and near
Darkness rules by death and slaughter
And multitudes cry out in fear"

She described frightful images—endless numbers of boats filling the seas around the island, missiles being thrown at the shore. The cruelty in the warriors' twisted smiles nauseated her. Men did uncontrolled and unimaginable acts of violence to women, to the land, and to each other. She described seeing men on top of strange beasts, wielding unimaginable weapons. The men killed and conquered more lands. She described how they forced the vanquished into slavery, dirtied the rivers with blood and waste, and built huge fortresses. She watched as they burned down great forests and cleared vast tracts of land, never considering what any other living creature needed. Or what the future held.

But above the ugly scene, high on Mount Strongyle was a bright shining light. Eveenara turned her face toward the light and felt its warmth. Even from within the trance, her voice filled with joy as she felt peace emanating from the light.

She knew this light could save them. How, she didn't know. A powerful unknown menace faced them—faced all the people who followed the Ways.

They had a choice. They had always lived by the good—the Way the Goddess had taught them to live. Why wasn't Kalliste responding? This evil was in direct opposition to all that Eveenara knew and believed. She intoned a prayer,

"Will the winds of evil blow around us?
Or can true goodness thus prevail?
By letting silence reign in wonder
We can hope to never fail"

Eveenara knew with all her being that this light—the Light of Kalliste—would save her and her people. She didn't know how or when. And the Goddess wasn't telling her.

CHAPTER 22
THE SWALLOW'S ANSWER
PART VII

"And will the breezes blow the petals from your hand?
And will some loving ease your pain?
And will this silence drive confusion from your soul?
And will the swallows come again?"
- Richard Fariña

WORLD NEWS – JUNE 10
Only Part of Cruise Ship Pollution Regulated
Mining Causes Erosion and Pollution

DEBORAH FELT shaky after her vision in the Delta 2 room at Akrotiri. She had sensed images before, but this was much stronger.

Giorgio guided the motorbike past the modern village of Akrotiri and along the caldera. Deborah barely noticed the stunning view. Someone had wanted her to come to Santorini—the singing swallow in Capistrano, the placement of the data into her possession, even the ruining of her reputation in order to force her to come. *Who's doing this? And why? Is this Attar's fifth valley of unity?*

Suddenly, the road starting shaking and the motorbike swerved. Deborah yelled, "Earthquake."

Giorgio killed the engine and stopped on the side of the road by two old windmills. The quake stopped. "Are you okay?" he asked.

Her heart beat hard. "I'm fine. That was pretty big."

He helped her off the bike. "We're okay. I don't see any damage."

A short path led down to the water's edge. Deborah could see a Eurasian sparrowhawk and yellow-legged gulls flying above the caldera. The islands of Therasia and Aspronisi stood to the left. The water slapped hard against the rocks. "These earthquakes are happening everywhere now. This is not the greatest place to be during one."

Giorgio looked at the volcanoes. "I don't see any molten lava."

Looking out over the water, Deborah didn't feel like laughing. Nea Kameni and Palea Kameni were in front of them. Anchored in the caldera were four large cruise ships. She squinted to make out some of the names, the *Golden Prince*, the *Dawn Princess*. They reminded her of the ships in her vision, so self-assured in their dominion over the seas. She felt like the ships had won. *I should go home.*

"We should get going." Giorgio stood.

She let out a sigh. "I'm going to take another reading of the signal. Just for completeness."

"That makes sense. We are on the south side of the island."

She set up the RAX-1000. Still no interference signal.

Giorgio leaned over to help her. "Maybe it really stopped." Framed against the blue sea and stunning island contrasts, he looked like a Greek god. Staring at his olive-toned skin and full head of black hair, Deborah felt flustered.

The Earth began to tremble. "Another earthquake!" She grabbed him as they both fell to the ground. Static electrified the air around the machine. Everything momentarily sizzled. Then the trembling stopped. "What happened?"

They stared at each other lying close. He said, "Besides another quake? I don't know." She pulled away, trying to hide her flushed face. "Are you all right?" He helped her up.

Deborah quickly reached for the RAX-1000. "I'm fine. But the machine." She tested the switches and memory banks. "Doesn't look like anything got fried. That's a relief." Turning to put the instrument on the motorbike, she took a step and almost fell into a hole. She grabbed Giorgio to keep from falling. "What the—"

"*¿Qué pasó?*" Giorgio was getting on to the bike and stopped his leg in mid-air.

Deborah sank back onto the ground. "It's a hole. The energy surge must have caused some rocks to shift."

Giorgio peered down it. "It's a cave."

"A cave?" Deborah took a sharp breath.

He dug around the hole with his hands. "We should find out what's here."

"Shouldn't we call someone, like Antonio? He would know an archaeologist. Or tell them at Akrotiri?"

Giorgio was excited. "Don't be silly. I'm a museum curator. I've done archeological digs. I know how to be careful." He walked over to the motorbike. "I've got some tools in my kit, including a flashlight."

Using a long screwdriver, he dug at the sides of the hole while Deborah cradled her hands to catch the clumps of dirt. The space seemed to slant down.

They made the opening larger and Giorgio crawled in. He looked back to help Deborah.

"I can't," she said. "I get claustrophobic." She wished she could clean her hands.

He looked around. "It's pretty large and I've got a flashlight. You can do it."

She took a deep breath and let him help her into the space. The room was about five feet high and extended back for about twenty feet. It had a musty odor, not having been exposed to air for a long time. Giorgio's flashlight played over rows and rows of pots.

"¡Dios mio!" Giorgio shouted. "Look at what we've discovered!"

Vases were covered with all kinds of drawings on them—birds, snakes, and geometric patterns.

"This is amazing." Deborah peered in as far as she could see, trying to breathe steadily.

"No one knows this exists." Giorgio's eyes tried to take it all in.

It seemed untouched by modern humans. There were broken pieces of pottery scattered on the ground. Shards on the ground were covered with all kinds of drawings.

"It's like Akrotiri," Giorgio exclaimed. "Archaeologists have said that they've only exposed about two percent of the ancient village. This must be the other end of it." He excitedly walked toward the back.

They began looking in the vases to get a sense of what was there. If they hoped for a Dead Sea Scrolls type of discovery, this wasn't one.

Deborah stayed near the hole. She called out, "Giorgio, look at this." She stared at a small vase covered with swallows like the ones on the fresco. "It's so beautiful."

"Too bad we only have the motorbike," he said. "Otherwise, we could carry that out."

"Take it?"

He looked at her and smiled. "Just kidding. Of course we'll have to inform the archeologists about this."

THE SWALLOW AND THE NIGHTINGALE

Deborah looked in the vase and saw something. She reached in and pulled out an unusual shard. It didn't look like a broken piece of anything and it had various symbols that looked more like writing.

Giorgio said, "I've never seen anything like it before."

They crawled back out. Glad to be in the sunlight, Deborah took a deep breath, cleaned off her slacks, and looked at the shard. There were two birds on it. One looked like a swallow with its deeply-forked tail. The other wasn't as clear. There were other symbols—a half-moon, an irregular shape, a vertical line with a circle next to it, spirals, hash marks, shapes that looked like figures. Some markings looked like letters of an ancient language.

Giorgio couldn't make out the symbols. "We'll need to show it to a linguist. I know one at my university."

Deborah remembered the linguist from the Paris airport. Dr. Alexandria Fisher. She looked out into the caldera. The *Dawn Princess* was anchored halfway between the docks and Nea Kameni. "There's a linguist on that ship out there." She pointed to the cruise ship.

"You're kidding," Giorgio exclaimed.

"I am not." She limped toward the motorbike.

"Let's cover up this hole before we go," he called after her. He filled it and marked it with three rocks.

The road to the port of Athinois clung to a precipice. They drove along the hairpin turns down to the water through layers and layers of rock and ash. Deborah felt they were descending through time into another world. When they arrived at the port, Giorgio negotiated with the captain of a small fishing boat to take them to the cruise ship.

The small boat rocked its way into the caldera. The sun peeked out of the clouds. Captain Iannos was quite lively in his conversation. In front of them looming larger were the four ships—*Wind Spirit, Aegean Odyssey, Golden Prince,* and *Dawn Princess.*

Once at the side of the ship, they asked the purser about Dr. Alexandria Fisher. He said she and her family were on a sailboat by the island of Therasia. Captain Iannos motored out to the sailboat anchored off the island. Some people were swimming and others were eating lunch on the boat or picnicking on the island.

Deborah spotted Dr. Fisher sitting on the sailboat. The linguist was more than a little surprised to see Deborah. After Deborah introduced Giorgio, the three went to the bow. Deborah explained what happened and showed her the shard.

Alexandria examined it carefully. From her purse, she took out a brush and cleaned it. "This seems like a map," she said. "There are markings, indications of the location."

"What language is it?"

The linguist ventured, "It looks like Linear A, the ancient pre-Myceanen language. The irregular circle looks like a cave." She pointed to the half-moon. "That's a boat. The hatching marks must be a port." She could identify some words, like *Amnissos.* "This is the ancient name for the port near Knossos. These other symbols—the stick, the circle, the spirals, the figures—are harder. It could be many places."

Deborah asked, "Like what?"

"Where did you find it?"

Deborah explained the little cave opening.

Giorgio interjected, "It's hard to say exactly where it is."

"It would help to know." Alexandria looked at him.

He gestured. "Near Akrotiri."

Deborah looked at Giorgio and then back to Alexandria. "By some windmills."

"All right, the south side of the island. It could be a map for a cave on Thera but it could also be the Eileithyia Cave above the Amnissos port." She stopped as if that explained everything.

"Where's that?" Deborah asked.

"On Crete."

🕊 🕊

The mountains of Crete loomed before them as the Diamond Katana jet turned south over the island. Giorgio pointed out the major peaks—Mt. Jouctas, Dikti Oros, and Idi Oros. Roads cut through the hills. The technology made an ugly scar over the beautiful greenery.

As they approached the capital of Heraklion on the north shore, Giorgio shouted, "It's hard to land an airplane here. The winds are all north and south on the island. There is always the danger of a sirocco."

"A sirocco?"

THE SWALLOW AND THE NIGHTINGALE

"The hot winds from Morocco." Giorgio began his runway approach.

Deborah looked down and could imagine ancient ships fighting the winds trying to enter the port. Human lives were tiny compared to the large sea and sky. To Deborah, islands seemed so safe, affording protection from invaders and beasts. And yet, islands can be made of volcanoes.

After they landed, Deborah went into the small terminal and bought a tourist map and guidebook. The airport store was filled with images of various artifacts—bulls' heads, double-axes, and a disc with some writing on it. Giorgio went to rent a small Eurocar.

They drove toward the cave. Deborah studied the map for the old port of Amnissos. After driving about two kilometers, they spotted a sign to the Eileithyia Cave. Deborah could feel her anxiety rising in her chest at the thought of entering the cave.

The entrance was locked. A tree stood in front. Thick chains held a metal gate securely shut. She opened the guidebook. "It says we need permission from the museum to be let in."

"I can handle this. What's the number?"

Sighing a bit of relief, Deborah searched through the book. Giorgio called and asked if they could visit the cave. They were told Spiros would come let them in.

Deborah looked around. Below them were the ruins of the ancient port city of Amnissos. Beyond that, the Aegean Sea. To the south was a large valley filled with olive trees. The smell of rosemary was pronounced. In front of Mt. Jouctas were two hills. She wondered if she was imagining it, but she suddenly sensed in the landscape a giant woman lying on her back—Mt. Jouctas being her nose stuck up in the air, the two hills being her breasts. And where they were standing in front of the cave, Deborah felt they were about to descend into her womb. She took a deep breath.

Spiros arrived from the museum and pulled out a set of keys to unlock the chains. "All the time, American tourists want to see the mother and child cave."

Deborah thanked him. "Do a lot of people come here?"

"Women's groups from California come." Spiros pulled out a butane lighter and lit three gasoline-soaked torches. "They want to pray, but I don't allow."

Giorgio and Spiros entered the cave. Her breath getting shallower, Deborah followed them.

Spiros gave them each a torch. "Watch your step and be careful of the formations. There are many." Deborah gripped her torch tightly, feeling like she was descending into a mine that held potential riches and a living hell. *If miners can do this, so can I.*

Inside the entrance was a large round rock looking much like the rounded stomach of a pregnant woman. Trying not to hyperventilate, Deborah whispered to Giorgio, "This is one of the markings on the shard!"

He nodded his head. "I'll keep Spiros distracted."

Deborah cleared her throat. "I'm not sure how far I want to go into the cave." The two men continued on.

Deborah watched the flickering light from their retreating forms. Grateful for the flames from her torch, she could feel the total silence. Taking a deep breath, she stepped closer to the entrance. She pulled the shard map from her pocket and aligned it with the formation before her. The shard showed a low, long rectangle by the rounded rock. She looked up. There was a stone wall in front of her. Next to the stone wall were two stalagmites which looked exactly like a mother with a child. Again, it fit in with figures on the shard. The shard also had spirals nearby. She looked around but couldn't make a correlation to that. On the cave floor, she saw stones and potsherds. Are these originals, or copies, she wondered.

Monitoring her breath, she looked closer and was stunned. Seashells—spiraling sea shells. Lots of them. She stared at them, remembering Jeff's fossilized brachiopod. Her breathing became more even, thinking about his ritual memorial on the mountaintop.

She looked around and realized that rituals must have been performed in this cave. Was she seeing writing on the cave walls? Or was it thousands of years of water dripping, chemicals leeching, and shadows from the torch?

She studied the shard. It showed a stick with a small circle in front of it near the low stone wall. In the small circle was some spiral writing. What was it referring to? She put the shard down on top of the guidebook and, very hesitantly, took a few steps. Not seeing anything, she looked closer at the mother and daughter stalagmites. With the torch held out in front of her, she walked around behind it. A stone pillar stood there, just as the shard indicated. She shone the light of the torch onto the pillar.

A round hole about fifteen centimeters in diameter lay in front of it. Looking inside, she saw it was empty. The shard seemed to show that something with spiral writing was supposed to fit into the hole. What, like a key?

She took another deep breath and looked around. This is silly, she thought, *I'm way out of my area of expertise. I was drawn to Santorini to save my reputation and in a state of being open, I came to this cave. I should turn all this over to an archeologist. There must be someone on the island, at the museum perhaps. Abi-atoon said to wait for answers, not search for them.*

Glad to be getting out of the cave, she reached down to pick up the shard. As she did, she saw the guidebook below it. There was a photo of a disc with spiraling writing on the cover. Grabbing the book, she looked closer at the name below the picture. *The Phaistos Disc.* The one Alexandria Fisher had talked about.

Spiros and Giorgio returned. She tried to get Giorgio's attention. "Well, this was an interesting cave." She stared at him and motioned with her head. "Don't we have to go now, dear?"

He looked at her quizzically. "Yes, dear. It is getting late."

Spiros asked, "Do you want to see more? Or have you finished looking around?"

Deborah smiled politely at him. "Such a fascinating cave. Look at the time. We really should be going." Spiros extinguished their torches. Reemerging into sunlight, he reclosed the cave gate and locked the chains.

After Giorgio paid him, Spiros left. "What's going on?"

Deborah showed him the guidebook with the picture of the Phaistos Disc. "It's like the image on the shard. I found a hole exactly the same size in the ground."

"What? What's so important about that?"

"The spiral writing in a circle. Do you remember what Attar said about watchfulness?" She pulled out the shard and showed it to him.

He pointed to the post. "You mean this location?"

Deborah nodded her head. She explained how she followed the wall and found the post and the hole. "Where's this disc? We need it."

"It's in the Heraklion Museum."

"Where's that?" She looked at him. "I know, not far."

He laughed. "It's a small country. And we're on an island."

☙ ☙

Deborah and Giorgio entered the Heraklion Museum and walked through the different rooms until they found the Phaistos Disc. Nearby were statues of praying figures, each one with their right hand up and their left hand on their stomach or at their side. One figure with a large headdress had snakes curled around her arms. Cases along the walls held small seals, vases, and tablets with Linear A writing.

Deborah stared at the disc as Giorgio described it to her. Made of clay, the disc was about fifteen centimeters in diameter. It was discovered buried with other artifacts in a Cretan temple in Phaistos. Dating from around 1700 BC, it was the only one ever found.

The clay disc looked somewhat like a saucer for a southwestern style dinner set. By being suspended in a large glass case, people could walk around and see both sides. She read that the disc had 242 distinct symbols imprinted on both sides in a spiral pattern. She looked at the writing. "It's so different than everything else here," Deborah said.

Giorgio said, "It's never been deciphered."

"The symbols look similar to Egyptian hieroglyphs." There were images of women, birds, flowers, helmets, trees, even sarcophagi. The pictures were side by side and converged in the center. A spiraling line made it easier to follow the symbols—much like lined paper.

"See those?" Giorgio pointed to the marks that were after every fourth or fifth character. "Those could be breaking the string into words. With only one instance of this writing, it's impossible to really know what it's saying."

They walked around to the other side of the glass case. The disc's backside had the same type of spiraling. But the pictures were in a different order. There was also a flower in the center.

A strong tremor shook the floor. "Whoa." Deborah grabbed Giorgio.

"Hold on." He held her close to him.

The guards called out something but Deborah couldn't understand. The earthquake felt worse than the others. When the tremor stopped, she realized she was still holding onto his arms, and she let go, a little slower than before. "If there was some way we could perhaps borrow it for a couple of hours..."

Giorgio laughed.

Deborah whispered, "We'll have to steal it then."

He looked at her. "We can't do that. We would go to jail. I would lose my career as a museum curator."

"I'm kidding! Like you joke. I can't believe you believed me."

He laughed her off. "Maybe we could find a copy of it and use that. Museums usually sell replicas of artifacts to tourists."

"Good idea."

The museum bookstore only had pictures of it. They walked over to El Greco Square and went through the tourist shops until they found a replica of the Phaistos Disc. The boy in the store was very proud of the fact that he had such a good copy. He even had a picture of it in a book to show Deborah its exactness.

Deborah's Notes for *Luscinia megarhynchos* Study
It has been determined a clay disc from Phaistos might be useful in gaining more information about the interference signal possibly as a communications device. Dr. Alexandria Fisher from Stanford University indicates it is an undeciphered document from the 17th century BCE (personal communication). A replica of the original, currently in the Heraklion Museum, has been obtained.

Giorgio was very smooth on the phone to Spiros. "I've lost my keys somewhere in the cave."

Spiros bought the story. When he arrived and opened the gate once again, Giorgio took Spiros deep back into the cave while Deborah tried the disc. The boy was right. It fit exactly into the hole by the pillar.

But nothing happened. Deborah wasn't sure what should happen, but obviously a plaster copy wouldn't work.

When Giorgio and Spiros came back, Deborah shook her head slightly. They exited the cave. Spiros relocked it and left.

Deborah leaned against a tree. "I guess that's it then. We did what we could."

"It's too bad it didn't work."

"It makes sense," she said. "A copy is not the real thing. You can make a copy of a key to unlock a door but you can't email a picture of one and expect it to work."

"Or email a smell?"

"Exactly. Well, we tried. It was fun. We'll turn over what we found to some archeology department. We'll tell them about the chamber we found on Santorini. They'll have the resources to study this shard."

Giorgio started picking leaves from the tree. "Wait, let's just think for a second. What would Attar do in this situation?"

"Okay, let's see." She started pacing.

"Careful." He reached out in case she fell.

"I'm fine." She backed up. "He could advise us to keep on detaching. It's worked. But he also talks about the Valley of Unity."

"Right." He smiled and stared at her. "The King gives the beggar everything. And the beggar says, 'I am the shadow lost in the sun.'"

She focused on the plaster disc. "It's a deeper level of experiencing. It's about duality disappearing." She flipped the disc over. "The two sides of this disc becoming one." She looked at the small images spiraling from the outside rim to the center. "There are birds in these pictographs. Two different birds."

Giorgio moved closer to her to see what she was pointing to. He said, "If we tell some academics about this, they won't do anything for years. Things are happening right now—that signal, the quake that caused us to find this. Are those coincidences? We have to do something."

Deborah was surprised. There's that thought again. Is it too impossible to be a coincidence? *CITIFITBAC.* "You think so? Not leave it up to the experts?"

His eyes glinted the way they did when they had stood by the river in Sevilla. "I think so."

She looked back at Mt. Jouctas and the two hills. "That signal led us here. I feel like we're being directed toward something, as if the birds are sending me a message. Why haven't the swallows returned to

Santorini in all these years? There's no physical reason. I agree with you, we have to act now."

"What are you saying?"

"We need the real thing."

"We can't get the real thing." Giorgio started along the path through the brush toward the Eurocar, glancing behind him.

She caught up with him. "There's got to be a way. Where's that bank robber Giorgio?"

He almost exploded and yelled, "That was a joke. And you accuse me of not knowing a joke?"

"I'm sorry. I'm just teasing you. Let's just think for a second."

"We can't steal it. Careful where you step." He kept walking.

"I didn't say steal."

Giorgio stopped and was silent. "What are you saying then? What about that morality issue of yours? Don't the Ten Commandments say thou shall not steal?"

She bristled. "I'm not conforming my life to a 2500-year old document because someone says I should. Morality is about respect."

"And stealing from the museum is respecting it? Just asking because it's my career on the line here." He started walking again and reached the Eurocar. "And atonement in jail is no picnic."

She followed him. "You're right. Let's turn everything over to someone."

There was another tremor and they both grabbed onto the car.

Giorgio shot a look at her and then stared at the sky. "Maybe there's another way to think about it."

Deborah gazed out on the ancient port below them. "On the other hand, if the world is collapsing—you said it yourself, one day the Berlin Wall fell."

"A museum exchange."

"What if the world is ending today instead of a billion years from now? If it's true, what's so important about an ancient piece of burnt clay?"

He repeated, "A museum exchange."

"It's going to get broken into shards along with everything else— what? What do you mean?"

"I can arrange a museum exchange. Artifacts in my museum for it."

Deborah's eyes lit up. "Will that work?"

"It'll work for a while. Then all hell will break loose."

"What?"

Giorgio broke out into his big smile. "Just kidding. Don't worry, we'll return it when we're done. We aren't doing anything wrong. I do this all the time."

🕊 🕊

As clouds began gathering in the sky, they checked into the Irini Hotel in Heraklion. Giorgio logged onto the guests' computer in an alcove off the lobby. Deborah watched over his shoulder as he typed out a letter to the curator requesting an exchange. His museum will provide the Heraklion Museum with their whole collection of Cycladic sistrums in a temporary exchange for the Phaistos Disc for an important exhibit while the scientists are compiling data at the International Conference. He hit send.

Giorgio called the Heraklion curator, pretending he was still in Spain working with the conference organizers. The curator sounded reluctant but Giorgio was very persuasive, throwing in more artifacts. Giorgio assured him. "Of course, of course, for one month. That is the understanding. My assistant will be by tomorrow to pick it up." He closed his eyes waiting for the answer. Giorgio nodded and hung up the phone. "All set."

"Assistant? Me? I can't do this. You do it."

"I can't. I'm in Spain hosting the scientists."

"But I don't know Spanish."

"You've got a good ear for languages. I'll teach you what you need to say. Now let's create a fake museum ID for you."

🕊 🕊

Deborah lay in her hotel room trying to update her journal. Was it only four days ago she was agreeing with Abi-atoon that she should return to California? She had detached and look at how much more she had learned.

Her phone rang. It was Rachel. "Mom, I'm hearing all these things coming out of the conference. I haven't been able to contact you."

Deborah leaned on her elbow. "Rachel, are you okay? I keep worrying about you."

THE SWALLOW AND THE NIGHTINGALE

"Never mind me, are you okay? Where are you?" Rachel persisted.

Deborah laughed. "I can't explain what's going on. I'm fine. I'm in Greece and I'm going to do something very rash."

"You're laughing! It can't be that rash. I know you."

Deborah sat up. "But this is the new me." She realized how excited she was. "Rachel, I've been doing a lot of soul-searching. I need to apologize to you." She explained her awarenesses at the plaza in Sevilla, how she got in touch with her anger at her own father and his religion. "I didn't mean to direct that anger toward you."

Rachel was quiet. "I love you, Mom." Deborah could hear the tears in Rachel's voice.

"I love you so much, Rachel. And I love Shelley—your wife." She chuckled saying the word aloud, then got serious. "Has the Rabbi kicked you out of the synagogue? Robert said you stepped back from something."

Rachel blew her nose. "You know, Mom, you don't have to be Orthodox to go to an Orthodox synagogue. Some people even drive on the Shabbat. We ignore people who give us *the look* and we model knowing that what really matters is our own personal commitment to Torah and Mitzvot."

Deborah ached to hug her. "And safety. Please, stay safe. I'll be home soon."

"You too. Stay safe, come home in one piece. Don't get too rash."

Deborah put down her phone and remembered the hotel's computer. *It is time.* She walked to the alcove off the lobby and sat down. Taking a deep breath, she logged on and started a note to the journal editors who published her paper, cc'ing the Dean and grants agency.

Dear Sirs:

In Judaism, there is a concept called *t'shuvah*. The Hebrew word means 'turning.' Jewish repentance or turning from sins is more than apologizing and more than regretting what one has done. In publications and a grant proposal, I used a dataset that shows male subservience in barn swallows. By representing the dataset as my own, I made a mistake. I apologize to everyone I have hurt and regret what I did.

But to truly achieve *t'shuvah*, I look inside to understand my faults. When I want something, I become bull-headed in order to

Page 256

get it. This trait has helped me as a woman in a society that honors competition, struggle, and battle. But science goes forward through mutual trust of its practitioners. When one fails as I have, it puts facts into question.

But *t'shuvah* also means 'answer.' In searching for answers, I went to Santorini, examined frescoes at Akrotiri and discovered that barn swallows were once on Santorini. No one knows why they haven't returned. The questionable dataset claimed male subservience as a behavioral trait. The representation of swallows in the fresco corroborate this behavior and shows that the painters of the fresco recognized male subservience.

What I did was wrong. But it gives me great peace to have come to Santorini and experience a new insight: that ancient behaviors, whether avian or human, can be role models for us.

Dr. Deborah Wright

She looked over her letter. Something her father used to say echoed in her head: there is nothing more important than being good. She had always looked at the statement as a way to not feel good enough in his eyes. Now she realized it meant what it said—there is nothing more important. And even if we are frail humans who mess up, we can commit to being good by doing good acts. She hit send.

She went back to her room and the RAX-1000 caught her eye. Remembering that she hadn't listened to the recording from Manolates , she pulled the instrument out and set it up on the bed.

Putting on the headphones, she turned it on and flipped some switches. The steady pulse of the recorded signal started playing. She remembered thinking the dying birds might be detecting this. But that made no sense. What is it and where has it gone? She changed modes from PLAY to ANALYZE. Bringing in the semantic processor, she began adjusting the speed of playback.

The audio signal became slower and elongated. But it had no content. Listening carefully and looking at the small screen, she realized the signal was a carrier. There were other signals modulating on top of the carrier. Quickly, she canceled the carrier signal using the demodulator and listened again.

THE SWALLOW AND THE NIGHTINGALE

The resulting signal was cacophonous. She pulled off the headphones and turned the volume down as thousands of noises clashed against each other. Adjusting the speed, she slowed it down more. She scanned over the controls, not sure how much processing power to bring to bear. With thousands of filters, she had numerous options, more than she could actually understand.

She started with the controls she was familiar with. Order began in little snippets. "What the—". It was beginning to sound like bird calls. The sharp piercing alarm calls that signal danger. There were so many of them, repeated over and over. Not just one species of bird, but many. The call of the swallow was clear.

That's weird, she thought. Good thing the signal stopped. Someone must have been playing a joke on someone to have constructed such a signal. Well, at least it brought her to Santorini. Deborah shook her head and started resetting the controls. Then she thought better of that and decided to leave the settings just in case.

She didn't realize she was leaving the controls in an unknown state.

That evening it rained. Giorgio took Deborah up into the hills below Mt. Jouctas to a small village called Archanes. Near the village were more ruins from ancient civilizations.

The quiet taverna was filled with faint images painted onto the stucco walls. Deborah looked around while Giorgio went off to make another phone call. Woven into the wall hangings were images of athletes and mountain scenes. She stared at the athletes as they jumped over bulls. *Why would anyone do that? It seems so dangerous. But then, what isn't dangerous these days?* She thought about the conference display at Sevilla and her vision at Akrotiri. *How could I have been so naïve? What's happening in the world is deadly serious and yet we act as if nothing's wrong. There's even danger in just eating dinner. One can't tell what poisonous chemicals are in the food one's about to eat. Food is supposed to bring life, but it can as likely cause sickness and death.*

Deborah was stunned by this realization. *Whatever's happening is beyond anyone's comprehension.* The bird alarm joke had thrown her for a loop. *What if it's not a joke?* She wished she could talk to Stephen about it. She was surprised to realize she hadn't thought about him in the last few days.

Giorgio returned and sat down with a smile. In the Greek tradition, they ordered a variety of appetizers for dinner—dolmades grape leaves, Greek salad, *tzatziki, kefides*, Cypriot sausages, and *spanakopita*. It reminded Deborah of the Spanish *tapas*. She stared at the feast before them, knowing she had no control over it. Glancing at the bull jumpers on the walls, she started to eat. Giorgio taught her some words and phrases in Greek and Spanish to say to the museum curator.

After dinner, they drove to a spot along the road that looked out over the plains toward Heraklion. The storm had abated and a full moon shown above Mt. Jouctas. They got out of the car. A large dark valley spread out before them, rolling hills and the Aegean Sea beyond that.

"Do you have a girlfriend?" Deborah asked.

He looked down at the ground. "It's hard to maintain a relationship because I travel so much."

"The story of my life," she said.

"It must be hard to maintain a marriage with two careers." He looked at her, but she was silent. "Tell me about Stephen."

Deborah wasn't sure where to begin. "What I like most about Stephen is that he's a good listener which is rare in men. You're like that also."

"There is a distance between the two of you."

Deborah frowned. "I wanted Stephen around and present. But he isn't. He's so involved with his work. Maybe the longer two people are married, they finally beat love out of each other."

"Do you love him?"

Deborah looked out over the black valley. "Stephen betrayed me with a graduate student last year."

He leaned on the hood of the car. "If Stephen told you about it, then he was being honest. Isn't honesty worth anything? Isn't it the foundation of all relationships? Governments without honesty usually fail, as do relationships between people."

"But he wasn't honest while it was happening."

Giorgio looked down at his hands. "Maybe Stephen had some deep need he had to explore."

She turned around and stared at Mt. Jouctas. The moon made it stand out against the black sky. "Maybe. The girl was African-

American. I've worried that I couldn't be what he needed because I'm the wrong race. I can't change my race."

Giorgio was gentle. "Neither can Stephen. Doesn't he get to have needs?"

Deborah looked at the invisible sea. "He does. But why did he have to sleep with another woman?"

"What is so terrible about that? Is a heart so small it cannot inclusively love?" He straightened and walked closer to her. "When people live in fear, they fear love. What are you afraid of?"

Deborah was quiet. She looked out over the valley again, imagining ancient campfires dotting it with clans and families. "I'm afraid of losing Stephen."

"It is your fear that is driving him away."

Deborah didn't know how to answer that. She leaned her back against the car door. "I want him to apologize to me for what he did."

"What did Abi-atoon say about human life being a journey? How long will you carry this pain?"

"I don't know. Abi-atoon also talked about confessing our weaknesses and faults to ourselves. Stephen and I have been drifting further and further apart. Like the winds across the waters."

Giorgio leaned against the car next to her. "It is easy to find someone to blame instead of accepting what happens. I'm certain he is sorry for what he did to you, although not sorry for what he needs. Maybe he needs something from you, like forgiveness for being human or gratitude for what he has been able to give you."

Tears came to Deborah's eyes. She looked away toward the moon. "That's too hard to think about at the moment."

"It sounds like you and Stephen have raised a beautiful daughter in Rachel."

Deborah rummaged through her bag for a packet of tissues. Taking it out, she said, "She did something two years ago, and it changed the dynamics of our family. It upset me very much." She wiped her eyes. "Maybe I did push him away."

"Perhaps if you accepted, you would both blossom instead of fight. Things happen," his eyes were wide open and soft, "for whatever reason. Life is a journey, it's about going forward, but you have to want to go forward."

They drove back to the hotel, in silence. The night was warm and crystal clear. At Deborah's door, Giorgio said goodnight. But then he reached out and touched her cheek.

Deborah turned her head but didn't pull back. "I don't do this."

"This is not forever. This is for confusion. You are lonely, sad. You need to be held." It was a statement of fact, not a question.

Deborah said, "You don't even know."

He gently pulled her chin until her head faced his. "Then show me." He leaned over and kissed her.

She was so tired. His arms felt so comfortable. This wouldn't cause anything to make more sense but she knew she couldn't fight her feelings. She opened the door to her room and let him in.

Chapter 23
What The Nightingale Said
Part VI

"In the Valley of Astonishment one is overcome
By pain and dejection. Sighs are like swords
And each breath is a bitter lament."
                    -- Attar, The Conference of the Birds

I TURN AND STARE AT the King and then at the beggar. The King
needs the beggar in order to be King. The beggar needs the King. They
can easily exchange places—it is only a matter of birth. The King is no
wiser or richer by anything he has done. The beggar knows his place
and accepts it and is complete with the King. They share a unity. He is
lost in the King's shadow, lost in his brilliance.

I have been thinking of a shadow as distinct, but it is the sun that
makes the shadow and therefore, the shadow is lost in the sun. It is
what the nightingale said. And now I finally understand. No matter
who I am, I am a shadow lost in the sun. God is the sun, and I am lost
in the brilliance of God.

Excitedly, I go back to my ship quarters, and work on completing
my poem. I feel I have finally found the answers—my search is over.
There is no reason to continue traveling. I can stop sifting through the
dirt. I have found the golden bracelet. My birds and I have made a
tremendous journey, through many dark valleys of ignorance. Now we
have emerged and discovered the Truth. I can return home with the
merchant and go see my father. I won't need to find ibn 'Arabī.

I write the ending to my masterpiece. The hoopoe tells the birds
that they must struggle with themselves in order to find the King. After
all, if one will not digest a single grain, how can one share in the
feasting with the King? Most importantly, all the different types of

birds are the shadows of the King himself as he manifests himself—
thus casting thousands of shadows.

I write and write, unaware that the ship has set sail for Al-Andalus
as it fights the hot winds coming from the coast. I scribble furiously
into the night using every spare candle I can find, unable to put down
my quill in my excitement. Finally, as morning light touches the bow of
the ship, I fall asleep, exhausted.

In my dream, a beautiful princess abducts me. She takes me to her
palace, covers my body with fine silks and luxurious oils. Her body
coils around mine, enflaming my every pore. I have never known such
sensations. Her fragrant perfume makes my head dance in its
honeysweet nectar. Her fingers gently massage the oil into every crevice
of my body. My skin takes on a new dimension and I feel youthful and
alive in a way I have never felt before. We spend night after night
making love, lost in ecstatic sensations.

When I awake, I can still smell her perfume, and feel her soft silky
skin on my palms and chest. Even though it was nothing but a dream, I
cry out, "I heard everything, but there is nothing to hear. While seeing
nothing, I saw everything." I am at the brink of tears. "I am in love, but
I don't know who is the object of my love. I have everything and
nothing. My heart is both full and empty."

I look down at the pages of my masterpiece in scorn. "What have I
experienced? I have learned, but what is it?" I say to no one. "It is all
like a dream—it only seems real. It seems I have learned something in
my travels. But it is an illusion. My dream is more real than my life. It
all happened to me, but in another body. Can I know what Allah
knows? What can I learn compared to Him?"

I am amazed by my brashness in believing I knew something. And
I am astonished to realize how little I know. The shadow is lost in the
sun. Yes, it is true. And the nightingale talked to me. What of that?
Soon enough, I will die as everyone will. Everything is an illusion. What
is this poem I have written but empty paper?

I quickly gather all my pages and run to the deck. Staring out over
the dark waters, I am ready to throw away my poem. But its existence
and its destruction are the same illusion. There is no action that will
make a difference one way or another. And even though it doesn't
matter, I begin to cry, bitterly defeated.

CHAPTER 24
THE SWALLOW'S ANSWER
PART VIII

"Come more quickly dove, more quickly come with me;
More quickly come, beloved, run and save me."
- Sephardic folksong

SCIENTISTS FLYING TO SANTORINI
HeraldTribune.com - June 11
A powerful high-frequency signal of unknown origins has been
detected by researchers at the Paris National Academy of
Sciences. The signal seems to be emanating from Santorini, a
small island in the Aegean Sea about 80 kilometers north of
Crete. Scientists from the International Conference on
Anomalous Events (ICAE) flew today to Santorini to
investigate. Before getting on the plane, Dr. Stephen Wright,
US Geological Survey said, "An unknown signal this large is
monumental. It is necessary that we evaluate this."

DAYLIGHT BROUGHT THE rain again. Shaking it off, Deborah
walked through the long portico into the curator's office at the
Heraklion Museum. The balding man in his crumpled suit reminded
her of Milhouse.

In her carefully rehearsed Spanish, she said she was from the Sevilla
Museum.

The curator stood up and said first in Greek and then in Spanish,
"Your ID."

Giorgio had trained her well. She pulled it out. The curator looked
it over carefully, sizing her up. Deborah held her breath.

Satisfied, he had her sign several papers. She knew if she breathed,
she would begin to hyperventilate. Instead, she silently counted to ten

and back down again. She wrote the signature that she and Giorgio had practiced dozens of times the day before.

The curator said in Spanish, "Come with me." They walked past room after room of the museum. Deborah didn't know whether he was leading her to the Phaistos Disc or to a waiting police car at the rear of the museum. The walk seemed endless. She started silently reciting the different species of the Passerine birds.

Finally, the curator stopped at the room with the Phaistos Disc. Deborah turned and looked in. There it was in its special glass case in the center of the room. He said something in Greek.

Next to the glass case was an open packing box. The curator reached into his pocket and took out a set of keys. Selecting one, he opened the glass case. Putting on a special pair of gloves, he carefully picked up the disc and put it into the box. There was extensive packing material around it. Making sure all was safe, he closed the box and locked it with the same key. Looking Deborah over, he presented her with the key. He said something else in Greek, to which she only had a blank stare. He repeated it in Spanish and she nodded her head, pretending she understood. Was he saying this was the Phaistos Disc key? How appropriate she thought, since the Phaistos Disc itself was a key. She took the key from him, said thank you in Spanish and put it in her pocket. And then he handed her the packing case. Together they walked back to the front of the museum, toward the door.

As she was walking out, he said, in English, "I am looking forward to getting the sistrums."

Without thinking, she automatically responded, "Of course."

Then she was out the door, back in the rain. She jumped into the car where Giorgio was on his phone, trying to hide his head. He said something in Spanish into the phone, threw it down, and sped away toward the Eileithyia Cave. This time they had wire cutters.

"Incredible." Deborah laughed, the town quickly receding behind them.

"We've got it, I don't believe it," Giorgio yelled and drummed on the steering wheel in double-time to the windshield wipers.

"Of course we do. You said museum exchanges are no big deal." The excitement of what she had just done intermingled with memories of the night before. She watched the wet medieval narrow streets give way to a more open road along the coast. Her body still tingled as she remembered the gentleness of his hands all over her. Through the light rain, she could see large ships were coming into the port. She looked at Giorgio. "Last night..." She stopped not knowing what to say.

He glanced at her and smiled. "It was beautiful. People reach out in need, or for whatever reason."

Was it just curiosity, she wondered. She squeezed her thighs, her senses more awake than in a long, long time.

He reached out and took her hand. "One doesn't always have to be strong on one's own."

She caressed the white skin on the back of his hand. "Stephen and I can't seem to break out of who we are." Her eyes moistened, hoping she hadn't lost Stephen. She looked to her right at the sea where small waves were lapping at the shore. A pair of ruddy shelducks flapped hard above them, their rust-colored plumage standing out against the downpour. She could hear their calls. *Rrowl. Rrowl.* "You know I don't do things like this."

He smiled. "I don't steal famous artifacts every day either."

"I'm talking about sleeping with men other than my husband." She pulled her hand away.

He stammered in confusion. "Oh, of course. I knew that. I didn't mean—"

"Why do you keep using the word steal? We're going to return it as soon as we figure out what it is." She cocked her head, looking at him.

"Yeah, well. I'm not going to return it."

Deborah couldn't believe what she just heard. "Are you serious? What are you saying?"

The wipers swished louder. "I'm stealing it."

"You're stealing it?" She repeated it in order to make his words dissipate. But he wasn't laughing this time. "That will destroy everything I've uncovered. No one will believe the birds' singing songs or what we're going to find in this cave if we go to prison. Why?"

"Don't worry, I know how to do this." He looked to the side to make sure there were no cars to the left.

She sat up and turned in her seat. "You've done this before?"

"Okay, sometimes I deal in illegal antiquities." Giorgio shrugged. "I'm not proud of it. It's the way of the world. How do you think I can afford our little flying carpet? Not on a curator's salary."

The slick road started climbing as the flat landscape gave way to rounded hills. "I trusted you. I thought you a serious scholar. Is that what this whole trip was about?"

His face looked sincere. "I wanted to help you, but what we found on Santorini—that unexplored cave—it's worth a fortune. More than a fortune."

She was incredulous. "So it's all about money?"

"No, no, there was so much more to this trip." He almost swerved the car.

Her palms started to sweat. She rubbed them on her slacks. "Right, was it just about getting into my bed?"

"No," he tried to catch her eye, "your research is fascinating even if I had doubts about it."

His words pounded in her ears. The car felt like a prison in the increasingly driving rain. "So much for unity. Attar said astonishment is the next valley. Is this my astonishment? Giorgio, please, don't do this. Maybe you'll get away with it, but you'll absolutely ruin me." She stared at the road as it sped by, the gravel edges crumbling into the wild grasses being pressed into gathering puddles.

"How was I to know what would happen? It looked like your machine wasn't working, that we were on some crazy duck chase when we lost the signal." He glanced in the rear-view mirror again. "Besides, it's too late, my friends are digging at the Santorini find."

"What? It's not yours for the taking. I can't believe it. These are your friends?"

"Colleagues, whatever. I just talked to one of them. He's meeting us at the cave to take the disc." Giorgio grasped the steering wheel tighter and raised his voice. "There's nothing extraordinary that's going to happen at the cave. We'll put the disc in the ground and sit there for what? At least, this way, we'll be rich. How's that sound?"

Deborah heard a loud *zeeee*. It was the unmistakable call of a kingfisher. Having never seen one, she looked up to see the flash of pale turquoise-blue wings speeding by. "I heard something yesterday in the signal."

Looking over his shoulder again, Giorgio sped up to pass a car. "The interference signal? That stopped. It meant nothing. You said so yourself."

She turned toward him. "I reviewed it yesterday, the recording from Samos. There are bird calls being transmitted on that signal. It's real."

He swerved back into their lane and looked at her. "Bird calls? But that signal is huge. I thought it was part of a space program or something really big. Something governmental."

Deborah leaned toward him. "Right. And I thought it was some sort of a joke, but think about it. Who would do that? Bird calls are alarms. These were cries of danger. Someone put them onto that carrier signal. Giorgio, please, we have to finish this path we're on. There's something in this cave. We both know it. I don't know what's going to happen, but we've got to find out."

Giorgio stared at the wet road. The wipers beat loudly in the silence. With the rain increasing, he cranked up their speed.

Her voice raised a notch. "Everything we've been doing. Hearing the nightingales singing the song, the interference signal, Akrotiri and the shard. It's all pointing toward something. Someone is doing this. You just said how big it is. Please, Giorgio."

He passed another car and again looked out the rear-view mirror. Water splashed high as their car sped through a large puddle.

Deborah sat back and stared out her window. The kingfisher was gone. "Is Abi-atoon in on this as well?"

He looked at her. "You heard his opinion of people on a hedonistic path. He was talking about me." Giorgio looked back and pulled off to the side of the road onto wet grass. The cave was not far. "Okay. Listen. I'll tell my colleague I'll bring the disc to Santorini. That will hold him off until we know for sure."

Deborah let out a deep breath. "Thank you, Giorgio."

"Deborah—"

"What?"

"Stay hidden in the car until he's gone. I don't want anything to happen to you." He looked in the back seat. "Just in case anything gets out of control, let's swap the discs. Give me the key." He held out his hand.

She looked at his hand. Was it really the same hand that she had just been caressing? She took the key out of her pocket and handed it to him.

He reached in the back, opened the packing case and pulled out the real Phaistos Disc. Deborah took the replica out of her travel bag and gave it to him. He put it into the packing case.

To protect it from the rain, she put the real one into the drawer in the RAX-1000 and hoped it was as waterproof as Dan had promised.

He stared at the rear-view mirror again. "If he comes toward the car, don't do anything stupid. Just give him the packing case. He won't know the fake from the real thing."

"Giorgio—"

He looked at her.

"Be careful."

Abi-atoon had said to wait for the answers. There were different ways to wait, Deborah had learned. The wait for Giorgio's colleague to leave had been interminable. Angry words in Greek were exchanged, but no one came shooting bullets through the car window while she had huddled on the floor in the front seat. The man had agreed to wait for the disc and Deborah was grateful they didn't have to risk giving him the replica.

The cave's coolness was alive with expectancy. The only sound was a slight drip of water from back in the cave. The torchlight played over its surface making it look alive. The Phaistos Disc sat in the circular space under the pillar. Deborah had the RAX-1000 next to her. Giorgio smiled but looked impatient.

Deborah could remember that moment she first heard the song in the cliff swallow recording. And then just three days ago listening to the nightingales on Samos. It had all lead to this moment. Was her next stop jail?

Very faintly, they began to hear an ethereal voice as a shimmery light played on the cave walls. It slowly increased in volume and colors. An image of a woman came into focus with long black hair curling down one side of her head. Glimmering on the glistening walls like at a carnival, it looked like an illusion. But then, they heard her speak.

"I am Eveenara, medicine servant of the most honored and revered Kalliste, the Goddess of the Earth. The clan of the Kalliste were a beautiful and gentle people who cherished Kalliste and her Ways of goodness. But a great ugliness covered the lands, bringing evil and fighting to more and more clans. We chose to protect ourselves and our sacred objects from being ravished by such evilness. If you are

hearing this message, you have found a Sacred Disc—the key which allows us to communicate with Kalliste. Other Discs may still exist, but if evil people found them, they were destroyed. The swallows and the nightingales have been helping to preserve the sacred tunes. The birds are exhausted trying to get humans' attention. Humans have stopped listening to nature—instead, they use nature. The birds that still try, die. But they all call out in agony. Your new machine allows humans to listen to the birds. I have been trying to get your attention with the earthquakes and the signal. My crone keepers have monitored you.

"If you are ready for the Good, you must try to talk to Kalliste. She is tired of the ugliness and is going to destroy the human race if nothing changes. With your machine's ability to interpret the signal, you now have proof that the path humans are on is wrong. Take this Sacred Disc to the center of Mt. Strongyle and convince the Goddess that nations will respond to the conclusions from the scientific conference. Hurry, there is very little time. But I warn you, it is dangerous. Only take it there if you have pure love in your heart. Otherwise, you too will be destroyed. Prove to Her there is still Good in the land."

Then there was silence. And darkness. The torch went out.

Suddenly, a noise filled the cave. The RAX-1000 had spontaneously activated. Deborah pulled open the cover. The machine lit up with pulsing LED lights. Voices, both faint and loud, thousands of them, were speaking. Deborah reached for the volume and turned it up.

Giorgio was stunned. *"¿Qué es eso?"*

Words—phrases repeated one on top of each other. She elongated the signal. It became understandable.

"Shema Israel, adonai elohainu, adonai echad. I confess I am in bondage and cannot free myself. For the sake of your Son, Jesus Christ, have mercy on me. La illaha illa Allah Muhammad uv Rasool Allah."

These were prayers in different languages. It wasn't a joke. Deborah stared at the machine, astonished. With the settings in an unknown state, the meaning of the calls was being interpreted.

🜨 🜨

They flew back to Santorini. Giorgio struggled to control the small plane in the driving rain. "The instruments are all off. I'm going to have to fly by radio and line of sight." He flipped switches on the control panel and yelled into the radio in Greek. The control tower crackled back.

Deborah shouted, "Can you see anything?"

"Barely."

The noise from the storm and the engines was too much. She quickly scribbled some notes and then looked out the window, searching for land.

Deborah's Notes for *Luscinia megarhynchos* Study
The semantic processor worked. We experienced a miracle.

The scientist in me says what we experienced is impossible. There's no logical explanation. Did the machine actually interpret the signal? Maybe it's all a shared hallucination with more in store. Who is Eveenara? What is this disc? A key, yes. The instructions were clear—take it to the center of the volcano only if you have love in your heart. If you don't, you will be destroyed.

Deborah hugged the RAX-1000 with the Phaistos Disc in its drawer. She felt like she was holding a bomb that was about to explode.

Giorgio landed the jet and taxied to a stop. Turning around, he reached for the packing case. "Deborah, what that voice said—"

"We can do this, Giorgio." Her heart beat quickly. "Go rent a car. I'll be right behind you."

"I didn't believe any of this in the beginning. But this is real…" his voice trailed off as he grappled with his feelings. "You've found something. It's different than anything I've experienced."

She turned toward him. "Giorgio, you're part of this, every step of the way. You made it happen."

His eyes were wide and bright. He looked like he wanted to say something else. He kissed her hard on the lips. "Meet me at the car rental booth." Then he was out the door with the case.

She reached to pick up her travel bag and heard angry voices. Looking out the window, she ducked down. Two men approached Giorgio, yelling at him.

Giorgio shouted and kept walking away from the plane. They followed him, sliding on the wet tarmac, loudly yelling. Giorgio held up the packing case and gestured for them to follow. They did, still yelling. Giorgio stopped and made a threatening gesture. The shorter one pulled out a knife. Giorgio started walking again and then the taller one punched Giorgio. He dropped the case and fought back. The taller man fell to the ground in a splash. Giorgio picked up the case again and ran. The shorter man chased after him.

He caught up with Giorgio and tackled him. They fought. Giorgio managed to pull himself up and pummel the man with quick jabs. He grabbed the hand with the knife and tried to slam it against the tarmac. But the man wouldn't let go. Giorgio tried punching him again. They wrestled into a standing position. Giorgio ducked away as the man lunged at him. But the man landed a hard jab at Giorgio's jaw and then lunged again. Giorgio fell to the ground, the knife sticking out of his chest.

Deborah looked on in horror. She stifled a scream.

The man grabbed the case and ran to his car. He got in and sped away, spraying puddles into the air. The taller man struggled to his feet.

She wanted to see if Giorgio was all right, but he wasn't moving. Dark red blood was pooling beneath him. Rain was filling his open mouth.

She tried to think through her tears. She wanted to run to Giorgio but that could get her killed or detained. Eveenara's words were echoing in her head. *If you are ready for the Good, you must try to talk to Kalliste. Hurry, there is very little time.* Who did she know on the island? Antonio and Chrysoula Papadelos. They could help her and help Giorgio if he was still alive. She got out of the plane, the RAX-1000 around her shoulder, and ran toward the rental cars.

Turning a corner, she bumped into a man. She did a double take as she fell. "Stephen! What are you doing here?"

"Deborah!" Stephen's face burst into happiness. "I came to find you! They said at the hotel you'd be arriving at the airport." He knelt down next to her.

She sobbed uncontrollably. "I love you so much. Everything got so crazy..."

"I'm sorry. I'm sorry. I want to be with you. Whether the world is ending or not, I want to be with you."

She reached for him and they kissed, tears streaming down their cheeks. "Stephen....I...love you. I forgive you. I really do. I understand now why you did it, but Stephen...."

He didn't let her finish. "I love you so much. I'm so sorry for what I did, the pain I caused you.

"I know. I know. But we've got to get away from here right now."

He helped her up. "It was never my intent to hurt you."

"Stephen! Do you have a car?"

"Yes, right here. What's wrong?"

"Everything's happening at once. We need help."

"It's why I'm here. Do you know about the signal?"

She tried to shake and nod her head at the same time. "It's too complicated. We have to go immediately. I know people who can help us."

"What about your pilot friend?" He held her arm.

Giorgio! She started crying again. *Convince the Goddess. Hurry, there is very little time.* What should she do? She wanted to help him. *If he's still alive.* She sucked in her breath. *Giorgio knew the chances he was taking, dealing with criminals. The airport people will find him on the tarmac. They must have seen the whole thing.* "We can't wait for him."

Stephen guided her to his rental car. "Deborah, whatever you think is happening...the signal—"

"The signal! Do you know what's in it?"

"The Earth's magnetic field is shifting."

Stunned by what he said, she fell into the car seat. "What? We lost the signal when we arrived here."

"This is ground zero," Stephen said. "You can't detect it here. We're inside some sort of bubble. Even cell phones don't work on the island."

There's no time to think. I need a plan. It started to dawn on her what was happening. *It's not a hallucination.* What they experienced on Crete in the cave, why she and Giorgio had to come back to Santorini. She closed her eyes thinking of him, tears streaming down her cheeks. What did Eveenara say? *Take the Disc to the volcano if you have pure love in your heart. Otherwise, you too will be destroyed. Prove to her there still is Good in the land.*

Iannos.

Stephen got into the driver's seat. "Where to?"

"The docks."

Under Captain Iannos' steady hands, the boat ploughed along Santorini's south shore in the driving rain. Deborah could barely see the red beach where she and Giorgio had stood two days earlier. To the right were cliffs with a formation that looked like a Native American face. There was a barely visible lighthouse. Above it was an ancient lava formation that looked like three horses galloping across the cliffs. A communications antenna whipped wildly. As the small boat bounced in the rough water, Deborah tried not to think about Giorgio. Stephen watched the tears streaming down her checks.

At the island's rock edge, they turned north around the bottom of Santorini's reversed letter C shape. Iannos shouted from the helm, "We go into the caldera."

Stephen looked at her.

Everything looked different from her previous boat ride into the caldera. She said, "There's no time to explain. You'll have to trust me."

"He's the museum curator, isn't he?" Stephen asked and she nodded.

Iannos liked to talk, oblivious to the danger. "I was the first scuba diver to descend when the water had been clear. Now spear guns and electric systems are used to find the fish. I tell the farmers, what do you do? Only collect, collect. We must to protect where the fish are born, so that when you go there, you'll have fish."

Deborah could see the small island of Aspronisi to their left. The white pozzolana rock was thick above brown layers of older ash. To the right was Santorini. Deborah could see its layers towering down into the water, sinking into the sea. Therasia looked like two rounded breasts. Even in the rain, one could match the layers on the three islands.

"I can't explain everything," she said to Stephen. "Whether we survive this or not, believe that I love you."

"What are you saying? Is this all part of the bubble we're in?"

In the center of the caldera Palea Kameni loomed large, as black as the Theran walls. Fighting against the rain, smoke rose from the crater at the top of Nea Kameni. It looked like a moonscape of badlands in layers of dusty colors.

Tongues of old lava covered Nea Kameni. Deborah pointed to the top of it. "Stephen, we're going there." She lightly shook the RAX-1000. "This holds the key that'll unlock the answer to what's happening in the world."

"How do you know? At the conference, the multi-dimensional display…"

THEA IBERALL

Deborah looked at him, tears streaming down her cheeks. Even in spite of the crying, the scientist in her felt calm. They were about to stare a volcano in the face. She fingered the pendant around her neck and answered him. "Exactly. I saw it, too. Are you ready for the Good?"

On Nea Kameni, red and black rock piled high like a garbage dump. The smell of sulfur hit Deborah as they neared. Rust swirled along the bottom of the rocks where they touched the rough waters.

Captain Iannos yelled out, "We can't land at the dock. Can you swim?"

They nodded their heads.

"I will take you through another route that only I know about. There are snorkeling masks below."

Stephen got the gear. He pointed to the RAX-1000. "What about that?"

Deborah shouted, "It's water-tight. We need to bring it with us."

Iannos guided the small boat into an inlet that looked like a lake in the old lava.

Fully dressed, with masks and snorkels on their faces, they jumped into the water.

Iannos yelled, "I'll be back for you."

They swam past black rocks covered with slimy red iron bacteria that bubbled to the touch. The lake was green with orange seaweed floating along the water's edge. Stephen helped Deborah out of the water and then over a wall of rock onto the solid ground of Nea Kameni.

The footing was slippery in the rain. They scrambled along the oldest black lava flows, trampling wet beach grasses. When Deborah stumbled, Stephen grabbed her and continued. They managed to find a path and picked their way down a slope onto a more recent lava flow, this one consisting of brown rock. They came to the crater consisting of rough black and brown flows with brand new tufts of grasses. Hobbling to the top where the rocks were yellow and red, Deborah could see Santorini across the caldera. In front of them, clouds of steam escaped from a vent.

The force of the storm abated. A man-made cement column marked the 1946 flow. An old woman sat next to the column. She wore a long black dress. Her long gray hair was pulled back. Seemingly calm to the rain, she sat on a bench that was built into the old lava. Her hands were folded in her lap.

She started speaking in English. "There was a land where a people once talked to the Lady. The Lady lives. You've made her mad. For a coin, I'll tell you the rest."

Deborah searched to find a coin in her wet jacket pocket and put it in the old woman's hand. When she did, there was a spark. Deborah quickly pulled her hand away. "Ow! That tingled." The woman looked vaguely familiar.

The rain stopped. The woman spoke, "Evilness is destroying the world and the Lady is tired of it. See the smoke," she said. "The Lady is mad."

With Stephen standing next to her, Deborah opened the RAX-1000 and pulled the Phaistos Disc out from the drawer. She held it high above her head and above the vent. She wasn't sure what to expect—Eveenara's voice in the cave wasn't specific. Nothing happened.

The old woman spoke again. "You have the Disc." She didn't seem surprised. "It is said that two people whose hearts are filled with pure love can stand side by side with the Disc between them. If the hands that try to activate it are not pure, the two will die and destroy the Disc."

I was right. I am holding a bomb. Deborah looked at Stephen, remembering what she had first thought when Eveenara had talked about true love. She nodded to her husband. "Stephen, I love you and have always loved you."

He looked at the disc and then at Deborah. "What are we about to do?"

"You'll have to trust me."

He took a deep breath and stepped forward, kissing her with all the force he could muster. She returned the kiss as hard. "I love you."

They held the disc between their hands above the volcano vent. Stephen had his right hand against one side while Deborah used her left hand against the other.

"We could die right now," Deborah said to Stephen. She thought back to everything that had happened to bring her to this moment. From the first moment she heard the cliff swallow sing at Capistrano to connecting to the *Swallow Song. There had been so much to understand— the birds, Rachel, Jeff. Myself. Detaching from my pain. Walking into the Valley of the Nightingales and going to Akrotiri. Then the miracle in the Cretan cave. It's been a path, a journey.* She loved her family fiercely and could see how her own doubts and fears had pushed Stephen away. She looked into his brown eyes, seeing all the love and courage she could ever want from him.

Stephen nodded. He understood about being ready to die. As a geologist, he knew the illusion of solid ground—that heat can turn rock into liquid and pressure builds between continents so that they crash into each other. At any moment, the ground could crumble, tsunamis could rise. He stared at her. "You're different. You're at peace. I feel it, too. So, if we're going to die, then so be it."

"I love you."

The old woman said, "Now, sing."

Deborah looked at her.

The old woman said, "Sing the Song of Love and the Song of the Earth. You know the songs."

Deborah didn't understand. Then her eyes brightened. The two songs. She motioned to Stephen to follow her as she sang *The Swallow Song.* The song of the Earth. As soon as he got the hang of it, Deborah switched over to *Los Bilbilicos,* the Ladino song of the nightingales. The song of Love.

At first, nothing happened. A worried frown crossed her face and her words faltered. But then, a light filled the vent and the disc started spinning in their hands. An ethereal sound of hundreds of voices began singing along in an ancient language. Some voices sang the swallow song, others the nightingale song. The songs intertwined, weaving the tunes and words in some unimaginable way.

Deborah and Stephen were transfixed. The old woman had a slight smile on her face. They continued singing but then, in some incomprehensible way, they themselves sang in the ancient language. The words were repetitive and very beautiful. They flowed from their lips as naturally as if they had been singing them their whole lives.

The voices then began an ethereal chant.

"The Goddess awakens and rises
to embrace this star-sprinkled void
Divine Mother crowned with the blazing green light

of a billion trees reaching for the sun,
bathed by the moon, penetrating the Earth,
feasting on the soil, and breathing the soft and endless
sapphire sky in and out and in again.
Say it again Wise Women; Sing it again!
Affirm it in unison with your daughters and sisters,
mothers and grandmothers and great-grandmothers
back even before the mists of time condensed
before the rains fell and the worlds formed.
Holy is the Earth and all within her
Holy is the star-filled void in which She spins
Holy is the light in whom we live
Holy is the Earth and all within Her."

In the silence that followed, Deborah held her breath.

And then, another voice began speaking, unlike anything they had ever heard. Ancient and powerful, certain and peaceful, it came from a mighty depth, resonating with everything around them. *"Call me Gaia, Themis, Rhea, Selene, Hera, Kalliste. I am known by many names and many attributes. All are facets of the omnipotent Gaia, the harmonious bonds of nature.*

"There was a time when humans had keys that freely connected them to the Good when two pure souls in love harmonized the Songs of the Love of the Earth. But with the birth of your Bronze Age, you turned my gifts into misery and evil. Instead of respect and compassion, you began to live by greed, selfishness, and jealousy. And the keys were forgotten.

"I thought that you would wake up to see the evil of your ways and grow out of them. That, as a group, you would gain empathy and compassion with maturity. Become principled by respect and service. But you only continue. Instead of bringing peace on Earth, your religions bring perpetual war. Thousands of years of wars caused by the imbalance that has taken you over.

"And now you have the power to kill all my children and this beautiful world. If you want to kill off each other that is one thing, but you are killing off my whales in the seas, my gorillas on the land, my eagles in the air. Your imbalance is ruining everything. You know the harm you are doing and yet you persist. You do not act with the future in mind. You work against nature trying to control and manipulate. You compete with me instead of cooperate. You are disrupting the life cycles of my children, and destroying plants and water with inept experiments because you do not understand me fully. And you seem determined to kill every living thing on this

planet as you perpetuate your greater greed. You don't care what you do as long as you gain profit from it.

"I am the One. Echo it to the top of the hills, deep into the water, I am the One. What are you? You are all part of this One Earth, I can rid myself of you whenever I wish. And if you continue, I will. Turn away from this evil imbalance. Prepare yourselves for the Good. Each of you as individuals. All of you as collective groups and nations. Ask yourselves over and over until you can answer yes: Are you ready for the Good?

"I have warned you. If you maintain your current imbalanced ways, I will destroy you all."

The voice stopped speaking. The enormity of the silence left Deborah's limbs tingling. She could still feel the presence of the power as she grasped for the message Eveenara had told her to say. *How do you speak to a god—if that's what this is?* She tried to formulate words about the proof her machine provided. Without faith that governments would act responsibly for the life of the planet, she felt defeated.

But she had to say something.

Deborah stepped forward. "I, too, am a mother, and although I have only one child, my child is good and I want her to live. She is kind and loving. There are many, many mothers and fathers, good people with good children who are respectful and who work for the good. And I will soon have a grandchild, which gives me infinite joy. How can we save our innocent children?"

At first nothing happened. But then, the voice said, *"Release me to release me."*

The light disappeared and it was all over.

The silence was almost deafening in its suddenness. No one moved.

But then there was a noise. The RAX-1000 had activated, spitting out a printout. It was interpreting the meaning of the bird calls. Thousands of bird voices began echoing:

"Shema Israel, adonai elohainu, adonai echad. I confess I am in bondage and cannot free myself. For the sake of your Son, Jesus Christ, have mercy on me. La illaha illa Allah Muhammad uv Rasool Allah. Shema Israel, adonai elohainu, adonai echad. I confess I am in bondage and cannot free myself. For the sake of your Son, Jesus Christ, have mercy on me. La illaha illa Allah Muhammad uv Rasool Allah."

Deborah whirled around in disbelief, her eyes shooting toward the machine. *These are the prayers said when you know you are going to die. Nature is crying out as we kill it.*

We have to release her. Remembering what she saw on the multidimensional display in Sevilla, Deborah realized this was the only hope for humankind. *The weight of the civilized foot on the world is too much. Those ready for the Good are going to survive. I am good, Stephen is good—we just proved it. When Stephen and I are back in California, we will be able to release Her.*

And Rachel is good. Deborah's eyes brightened with her love for Rachel. She was willing to do anything to help prove the goodness of her daughter. *How could I have been so stupid thinking there was something wrong with Rachel just because she loves someone?* Her heart bursting, she remembered the stunning beauty of Rachel and Shelley together on Doheny Beach. *Ultimately, isn't that what we wish for others—that they find love?* Deborah floated in bliss, experiencing what Stephen's and her powerful love had created—first Rachel and now bringing forth this voice. *Can Rachel's and Shelley's love do the same? Of course it can. But who would risk everything when Stephen and I already proved we can do it?*

Deborah knew what she had to do.

Steam burst from the volcanic vent. Hot billows of smoke belched higher and higher.

Stephen yelled, "We're going to die!"

Then there was another noise. A helicopter came hovering over the ridge.

Captain Iannos was a man of many resources. He shouted to them, "Let's get you out of here."

Stephen grabbed the Phaistos Disc and RAX, and he ran toward the helicopter. He looked back and saw that Deborah was not moving. He cried out to her, "Deborah! We have to get out of here."

But she was transfixed, her blank eyes staring into the volcano.

CHAPTER 25

SANTORINI ERUPTS!
NewYorkTimes.com - June 12

A major volcanic eruption occurred on the island of Santorini late yesterday afternoon. Plumes were seen rising to the height of 10 miles. Damage has been extensive. There are no reports of any survivors.

Experts at the Geological Survey of Greece report that a signal which has been emanating from Santorini has now spread in frequencies. Locating its new source has proved impossible.

THE BIG ONE HITS LOS ANGELES!
NewYorkTimes.com - June 12

A major earthquake was reported in the Pacific Ocean just south of Los Angeles this morning at 2:48 AM local time. Its severity was 8.2 on the Richter scale. Extensive damage was reported. Losses are in the billions of dollars. Los Angeles International Airport has closed, and people are encouraged not to travel in the area. Scientists returning from the International Conference on Anomalous Events (ICAE) say the Southern California quake may be related to the unexplained Santorini Energy Surge (SES) and to the recent volcanic activity observed on Santorini itself.

MAGNETIC POLES SHIFT!
NewYorkTimes.com - June 12

In stunning news, a worldwide state of emergency has been declared as the Earth's geomagnetic poles shift. What was the geomagnetic north is now centered near the island of Santorini. For safety, air flight has been immediately suspended. The interference signal is now stopping all cell phones, radios, and television transmission.

Chapter 26
What The Nightingale Said
Finale

"Finally comes the Valley of Nothingness,
A place where one forgets. Struck dumb,
One cannot hear or think. Multitudes of shadows
Disappear in the sun."
          -- Attar

I MOVE FORWARD BECAUSE I am on a ship, but I no longer care where I am or go. A person by his own volition moves forward and by his own volition can stop. By binding ourselves to other means of conveyances, we move forward whether we care to or not. I sit on a stack of ropes on the deck, watching the sea but not really seeing anything. Not even with my heart.

I feel alone. I am crossing the *Baḥr al-Rūm* to Al-Andalus, although what does it matter anymore. Is there a reason to see Ibn 'Arabī? Will the famous poet even see me? And if I do see him, what could come of it? What have I accomplished in my own poem? A few stories, some birds worrying about the proper way to live. What do I know about life? I have grown old. I will never see my father again. All that I know in my village is probably gone. I now understand the message of the nightingale. What of that? My quest has put me on a path. My passion has opened my eyes. I have been watchful to lessons in front of me. I have detached from expectations in order to let lessons in. I am a man lost in the shadow of every other man. I am left bewildered.

The *Ivory Merchant* reaches Tangiers on the northernmost tip of Morocco.

I sit by a fire with a group of other men, some from the ship, others are land-bound travelers on their own journey. The ship is docked for the night. I am told it is quite dangerous to be so visible sitting by the fire in the open. I don't know about the others, but I don't care. I have nothing more to learn.

A moth flies near the flames. Then it flies away. A man with a black-streaked gray beard says, "That moth didn't learn much about the fire."

Without caring about the man's response, I ask, "What do you mean? It flew up to the fire and away from it. Wasn't that the smart thing to do?"

The man replies, "But what if the reason that a moth flies toward flames is from a desire to unite with the fire? Then flying near the flame is to gather information about it."

"But it has learned to not fly too near."

The man gestures. "What will happen if he flies so close to the flame that his wings are singed?" The man's hand is up close to my face. I can smell ashes and animal sweat.

"He will learn that the heat is too great to be that close," I answer as I pull my face away.

The man presses further. "And what if he flies right into the fire embracing it and, in effect, uniting with it?" Again, his hand comes in close to me.

This time, I grab the man's wrist. "Then he will die."

"Exactly!" The man drops his hand and stares into the fire. I follow his gaze as the moth starts circling closer and closer to the hot fire. The man continues. "But, in the process, the moth will become one with the flame. And he will learn what he wishes to know..."

I finish the thought. "...but only he will understand what that is."

"Yes, he will achieve nothingness."

"Nothingness," I echo. "He will achieve nothingness." I reach my hand out toward the flame. I hold it open, slightly cupped. There is heat but I do not move. My skin becomes red and then redder. Feeling intense pain, I hold steady. Sweat beads over by body. Still, I do not move. I remark, "When you realize what you are the shadow of, you no longer care about life or death." The realization stuns me. I suddenly see that it is fear holding me back. Fear of losing things. Fear of loving. To truly love, one must forget oneself. Achieve nothingness. But a nothingness beyond disillusionment and despair. If one's desires do not match one's spirit, sacrifice the desires. This is how one reaches the end of the journey.

If robbers descend upon our group at the fire, I will feel nothing. In my state, I have no desire to live or die—to possess things or not. If they want all I have, that is fine. If they don't, that is fine, too. He who leaves the world to follow the way finds death. He who finds death finds immortality. Either way, I know I will win. No matter how much evil there is in the world.

I now know the reason to see ibn 'Arabī.

Chapter 27

"Should a single pure drop fall into this ocean,
it will lose its individuality, it will become part
of this ocean's waves and tides, and cease an
isolated existence, it will henceforth be beautiful."

-- *Attar, The Conference of the Birds*

I REACH THE PORT town of Sanlúcar in Al-Andalus. I find a small boat going up the river to Ishbiliya, the great western center for learning. Along the Great Al-Wādi al-Kabīr River are larger and larger villages. Ishbiliya itself is bustling and busy. The bazaar is noisy, with people jostling each other, trying to find the right purchase. Surrounding it is a labyrinth of stucco houses.

I go to the mosque in search of ibn 'Arabī. The magnificent brick and plaster structure has recently been constructed. Next to it, they are building a great minaret. The mosque is filled with men praying and talking. I am directed to a small tent at the edge of the market. The wise man ibn 'Arabī lives there. He is called *al-Shaikh al-Akbar*, the great master.

I put my manuscript down in front of him. "Shaikh al-Akbar, I have taken a great journey."

"Please just call me by my name," the shaikh tells me.

"Ibn 'Arabī, I began life as a perfumer. All I lived for were the beautiful smells of the flowers and the scented oils. Then, one day, a nightingale sang to me and challenged me to question my life. Until that moment, I did not know my eyes were shut. The great shaikh Bukn-ud-din told me to take a journey, to seek the door. When I did, I couldn't stop looking. I expected to be gone six months and to return to my village in Persia to see my father alive. Instead, I have had many experiences and learned many unexpected lessons. I have written a great epic, but I do not know how it ends. I do not know its purpose."

Ibn 'Arabī sits on thin pillows in simple robes. He is thoughtful as if he is reading me. "Tell me your story."

I begin to sing. I sing of the hoopoe, the crowned bird who is so vain. Birds assemble before the hoopoe who desires to guide them to the King of the Birds. But they have excuses and they have to struggle with themselves.

People begin gathering outside the tent. They come from the bazaar, they come out of their houses. There are Arabs, Persians, Berbers, Christians, and Jews. My voice is pure. It fills the streets, the valleys between the mountains. Adults and children come running from all over, in order to hear my recitation. My audience wants to know more. Someone calls out, "What did their journey entail?"

I sing out how the birds finally agreed to take the journey to the King and set out with the hoopoe as their leader. They grow apprehensive facing a journey through seven great valleys. The first is the Valley of the Quest. You'll meet hundreds of painful challenges but you must find the door, I sing out. You will have to be willing to give up all that is precious. Next is the Valley of Love. To dive into the fire, we ourselves must be on fire. To love is to give up one's ordinary life. Then, the Valley of Understanding. No one will know all there is to know and understanding is enduring, I sing. There is the Valley of Detachment. Nothing is new or old. No matter what you do, there will always be more. There is the Valley of Unity. When duality disappears, unity is found. I am his shadow, lost in the sun of his face. Then, the Valley of Astonishment. I am in love, but with whom, I do not know. Finally, there is the Valley of Nothingness—of deafness and forgetfulness. A drop of water becomes part of the ocean, and stays there in peace forever."

I stop. Everyone is overwhelmed by the beauty of the poem. Who can speak after such a recitation? Finally, a young Jewish girl near the front asks, "What happened after the birds travelled through all the valleys?"

I look at her. "I do not know." I turn to ibn 'Arabī. "I have come to you for help. That is as far as I am able to write."

The shaikh stands and bows his head. "Attar, you are the greatest poet who has ever lived. Surely Allah has honored us with your presence. Your poem will live forever. It will teach humanity the spirit and subtle reflection of life."

"But, ibn 'Arabī, how do I end my poem? There are so few birds left. They will reach the King and then what? They have gone through all these trials and reached the end. I am at the edge of the world. Is that all there is to spiritual understanding? Is that all I have achieved? In the end, nothingness? I can burn my poem up in your fire and it would be the same as not writing it at all. In the end, I have achieved the same."

"Yes. But Attar, don't you see?" ibn 'Arabī asks me. "How can the moth save itself from the flame when it wishes to be one with the flame? The birds are like the moth. Even though the aim is impossible because the moth's heart is given to the flame forever, nothing else matters. The end is the same. The birds are the birds and they will be with the King. When they are, they are a mirror of each other."

I bow my head. "I do not understand."

Ibn 'Arabī continues, "As a poet, you understand words. Words can enlighten but they can also hide, even lock in secrets. When something is easy to obtain, it has little worth. Look at the work you have done to reach this point. And look at all the languages spoken around you, here and through all your travels. How will the wisdom of your thoughts be transmitted? How will your poem be translated into those and future languages? You need to create a key with your words, one that locks in its meaning so that the core of the meaning stays no matter what. You yourself are wise and can manipulate words so that the meaning of your poem is never twisted."

I am silent. When the language at the end is aligned, the whole poem will be aligned. How can I make sure people will know it is aligned? The word in Persian for king of the birds is *Simurgh*. The words for thirty birds in Persian is *si murgh*. Thirty birds meeting the King of the birds. This is unity. This is complete.

Will anyone understand? Does it matter? They will have to work for the meaning. And that, in the end, is the point.

I pick up my manuscript and thank ibn 'Arabī. "Now I am ready to return home." With that, I turn and walk back into the dying light.

The young Jewish girl has sat waiting, long after everyone else left. Her name is Ruth. She is fifteen years old. "Wise one, oh Great one, if

I may ask," her voice is barely above a whisper, "may I hear the end of the poem?"

I look down and smile. "For you, I will end the poem." I take a breath and then continue my story. "The remaining thirty birds enter the kingdom and are amazed by its vastness. They walk through a huge hall and stand before the great Simurgh, the King of the Birds. He is like no bird they have ever seen, with the claws of a lion, the plumes of a great peacock, tails like snakes, and the head of a griffin. Beckoning them to sit in front of him, he explains that He is only a mirror, reflecting the thirty birds onto themselves. The shadow is lost in the sun, he says. So long as you are identified with the things of the world, you will not set out on the Path. But when the world no longer binds you, you enter into a dream. And when you are in that state, he says, keep silent." My poem finally complete, I bow to her.

My audience of one young girl bursts into applause. "Oh, Great One," she responds, not knowing how to address me, "teach me to sing with such beauty."

"You may call me Attar. I don't need such an important title."

"But that is the name for a simple perfumer."

"We are all simple. And it is what I am," I reply.

"A perfumer with great words and thoughts." Ruth bows her head.

I look down at her kneeling frame, so frail and timid. "To sing a great song, the song must come from one's soul. But you cannot sing if you are afraid."

"But you are so great, oh Great One...Attar. You have traveled the world and have seen so much."

"You, too, are great, little one. You can sing as beautifully as I can."

"Do you believe I can?" Ruth asks, her eyes shining.

"Come, try." I lean down and smile. "Now, begin."

Ruth's voice is halting. Even though the flow between our cultures is easy and respectful, I see the Persian words are uncomfortable for her. She stops. "I cannot."

"But you can," I insist.

She falters. But she tries again, this time in her own *espagnol* language. Her voice rises as clear as the wind, the gentle melody springing to life like a rose petal being touched by dewdrops. The words flow from the depth of her soul. She sings of the hoopoe, of the parrot. "I like the part about the nightingale the best."

THEA IBERALL

I sit down next to Ruth. "That's where it all started, you know. So many years ago. It was a real nightingale that told me the song."

"The whole story?"

"In a way. She began me on my path and told me many things. It took me years to understand what she told me."

"Then I, too, will work at understanding the nightingale."

"The important thing is the journey and what you learn on the way."

Ruth nods. "I will remember. But Attar, when one takes the journey, does one have to go through all seven valleys? What happens if you don't do them all?"

I look at her. She is full of insights for such a young person. "A seeker on such a journey is one who must make great efforts to obtain true knowledge and understanding. But unless you have examined yourself thoroughly and confessed that you really understand nothing, then all that has been acquired will be ephemeral."

"Ephemeral?"

"Yes, like wind in the hand."

"I will remember this advice. And your poem."

I stand up. I have a long journey in front of me. "Don't ever forget the song."

"I won't." Ruth gleams. She stands up.

I dig into my sack to find a small pouch of perfume.

Ruth pulls back. "You have already given me so much."

"No," I reply, "it is you who gives me gifts today. It is you who will carry my song—as our cultures continue to grow in peace."

"You are the world traveler, not I."

I shake my head. "But you will sing to your children. And they will sing to their children. Are you arguing with this old, wise Attar?"

In gratitude, Ruth takes the gift. Then she runs off, clutching the pouch, eager to sing to the young daughter she will have some day.

I head back to my ship, ready to make the long journey home.

Chapter 28
The Flight of the Swallow
Finale

"They despised everything but virtue, thinking lightly of the possession of gold and other property, and saw clearly that all these goods are increased by virtue and friendship with one another, whereas by too great regard and respect for them, they are lost and morality with them."
-- *Plato's Critias*

WHEN THE CEREMONY was over, the Kallistens sat around a fire, its flames dancing on the walls. Smells from incense drifted around them. With Eveenara and her mother on each side, Mudia felt exhausted from her ordeal. She had seen things she never knew possible.

"They will kill us, like they have killed the tribes to the north," Yidini said. He hunched forward close to the fire.

"They will make slaves of us if we don't kill them first! Where is the respect in that?" Kitane stood up. Her black eyes flashed. "They will deface our sacred tablets, burn our sacred text. We cannot practice the Ways as their slaves."

Many voices called out in anger. "We are free people! We are Kallisten! They do not understand our customs. They do not respect the Ways."

"We must kill them first," Yidini bellowed. His face was red.

Eveenara was upset. "Where is the compassion in that? How is that practicing the Ways?"

A rumbling came from inside the Earth, shaking the stone building. Bronze plates rang out as they clanged against the walls. People grabbed each other and tried to stand up. Kitane tumbled to the ground. But it was over as quickly as it started.

Eveenara took a deep breath. "There is another option."

Kitane righted herself. "How can there be another way?"

"Our choices are simple," Eveenara said. "We can fight or submit. Fighting is not our custom. If we submit, we will lose the Ways along with our customs, our sacred heritage, and probably our lives."

"That's what the others have done, the ones who took off for the north," Reifte said.

"Yes, they think they will be able to fight or survive on the mainland," Eveenara said. "But I fear, without being close to Kalliste here at Mount Strongyle, we will never survive."

"What is our choice? The Achaeans will continue attacking. You say there will be worse tribes coming. Daily our island shakes. What is Kalliste telling us?" Kitane asked.

"We can join with the Caphtorites to the south," Yidini suggested. "They have the Great Funerary Temples at Knossou and Phaistou."

Eveenara shook her head. "They, too, are on an island, one that can be surrounded and strangled."

"But a strong one," countered Kitane. "It's many times larger than ours."

"But the shaking affects them, too," Reifte pointed out.

"We have only one choice," Eveenara argued. "We must ask Kalliste."

"We have tried," Reifte looked at her. "You and I tried with the Sacred Disc. But Kalliste won't provide an answer. We have yet to know Her wishes."

"You have seen the air at the top of Mount Strongyle." Eveenara pointed toward the mountain. "Smoke has emerged ever since the strong shaking of the Goddess began."

They all remembered the damage and how most of the clan had left. "What is She saying?" Kitane asked.

"She is telling us of the danger," Eveenara said. "Perhaps this visit from the Achaeans is part of a sign.

"You're suggesting we find a way up to Mount Strongyle?" Reifte said.

"Exactly! In my visions, I've seen the answer is there."

"You gather herbs on the path."

"I could read the signs. I know the path part way. But to go higher, I need a guide."

Mudia spoke up. "Chelidona knows the way. She flies over Mount Strongyle every day. But she is still recuperating."

Eveenara turned to the swallow resting in the sling. "Little bird, is it true? Do you know the way to the top of the mountain?"

"Yes, I have flown there. I can guide you."

Eveenara raised her cup. "Then let it be so." They drank to affirm the decision.

When the swallow could fly again, she and Eveenara set out to the top of the mountain. Chelidona soared high above her while Eveenara's progress was slower. The medicine woman followed trails she had created in order to gather crocuses for women's cramps. Flocks of thousands of other birds joined them, all calling out, but they flew off. On the higher slopes, Eveenara looked up and saw the graceful power of Chelidona showing the way through the bushes and stout pine trees. Below, rivers in the distance snaked through rich forests. The air chilled, filling with pine incense. Breathing became difficult. Eveenara smelled sulfur and saw smoke. Her olive skin glistened with sweat.

By afternoon, Eveenara stood on a ridge below the crater vent. Smoke emerged from the top of Mount Strongyle. The swallow circled above. The air felt incredibly hot. Eveenara struggled to breathe. There seemed to be a writhing mass bubbling in the caldron above her.

She called to the bird, "Chelidona, what do you see?"

The swallow swooped down to Eveenara. "There is great smoke coming from inside the mountain. The red goes on for a great distance. It flows like an ocean. It boils like water on a fire. What is it?"

Eveenara was silent. "I do not know. Kalliste has never spoken like this before." She closed her eyes and with her two hands made the sign of the Goddess. Then she sat down to meditate.

A great belch from the center of the caldera singed Eveenara's face and the swallow's wings. Chelidona flew up and out of the heat. "We must get away! She is going to kill us!"

Eveenara didn't move. She believed in Kalliste and was not afraid of Her power. The strong heat of the Goddess felt comforting. "She will not hurt us. She is our Mother. I must understand what She wants us to do."

The bird flew down and perched by Eveenara. It was hard for Chelidona to remain stationary as she watched the medicine woman passively sitting. After some time and although it wasn't her usual song, Eveenara began singing the Love Song to Kalliste.

"My life is love, my life is spirit
I am alive, a song to sing
Respect the water, the land and air
You are the power in every live thing"

Chelidona began singing with her.

"The Earth is round, the Earth is holy
I am the Earth, love fills the need
I am the listener, this is Her song
She has the power, the Lady loves me"

The voices, woman and bird, rose in harmony. The writhing mass lessened in intensity, as if the mountain were listening.

When their singing finished echoing through the forest, Eveenara asked, "And how do you know the Earth Song of Kalliste, little bird?"

"I wasn't always a bird. My sister Philomela and I were initiated into the Ways. When I was younger, we used to share the Sacred Disc."

"Who are you? What happened?"

Chelidona told Eveenara about her royal family, the evil that occurred, and how she killed her son. "I do not know how I became a swallow or why. I don't know how I did what I did. Killing is wrong. I was crazed. Somewhere, I must find peace so that I can once more live by the Ways."

Eveenara looked at the small bird and then to the belching smoke. She remembered the first time the large foreign ships landed on their docks. Her mother's consort had been open and friendly to the landing party. But as soon as the ship began emptying, the purpose of the visit became obvious. The battle that ensued was etched in her memory. "There are all kinds of ugliness."

The bird agreed. "You must think me as cruel as the rest of them."

Eveenara was quiet. "You sent your son back to Kalliste for a better life."

"But I killed him. I killed another human being," the swallow cried.

"Killing is not unknown to us. When I was a young girl, I watched my mother's consort die at the hands of the Achaeans. They landed their ships and we were surrounded. My mother's consort was a priest of Kalliste and would never hurt a living soul. He lived by the Ways. But he knew we would all be dead if he did nothing. He made a decision of his own free will. He killed the first one with his own bare hands and then grabbed the Acheaen's heavy bronze sword. He wielded the weapon as if he had lived by the sword all his life. By the time they killed him, he downed half the raiding party and rallied the others to push back the enemy. He died saving us."

Chelidona listened.

Eveenara continued, "I wanted to kill them. But the way we live is a choice. We can live in anger or we can live in respect and empathy. I chose to live by the Ways—to not become evil, no matter what. I don't have the words to describe their method of living. You know the Ways. Life comes from Mother Kalliste who lives in every living creature, plant and rock. When we die, we rejoin Kalliste in the Earth. Death is not a bad thing. We sacrifice a bull every year to remind ourselves of that. What is bad is not being respectful to that which is Kalliste's."

Eveenara smiled at the swallow. "Your consort Tereus had no respect for life. Because you have used the Sacred Disc, you know what it means. If a person is not pure in her or his heart when one stands to face the Disc, that person will die instantly. So I know you believe in the respect of life, you believe in the Good. You deserve that respect from all others living. Including me."

"Everywhere I have flown, it is the same—wars and fighting. Only on your island did I find people practicing the Ways. It's why I choose to stay. Everywhere else has been overrun by the evil. And now, we've had this horrible attack." Chelidona shuddered.

Eveenara was thoughtful. "I am sorry you had to go through that. It was very brave what you did for us. You saved our lives with your quick thinking." She reached out and lifted the bird. "Kalliste has brought us together for some reason."

With the information given to her by Chelidona, Eveenara realized things were much worse than she had thought. The lands around them had changed. It was as if the Ways were being funneled into a smaller and smaller place—to just one island. Her home island.

She stared at the rising smoke realizing they had only one option.

"It is very hot in the heart of the Goddess," Eveenara reported. They were in the gathering room at the Festival Temple. What was left of the clan grouped around her, even the children. Chelidona sat on Mudia's shoulder. "The air above Mount Strongyle is very hot. The center of the mountain is filled with red blood which is boiling like water over heat."

"The blood of the Goddess. Mother Kalliste's blood!" Reifte nodded. "The blood of life!"

Yidini cried out. "You said it was bubbling like boiling water on the fire. The blood in the mountain's center will explode and cover us all. We have to leave the island like the others did."

"Kalliste won't harm us. She loves us," Eveenara responded.

Yidini argued, "But the blood of life doesn't boil and burn. You know that. You are a woman!"

"We cannot leave the Goddess," Reifte stated. "But we must protect the ancient knowledge and the sacred mysteries."

Kitane spoke up. "Eveenara, what can we do?"

"We have simple choices," Eveenara said. "We can fight and die, we can submit and become slaves, or we can join Kalliste and protect what we have and know. If we choose the latter, it would be our own decision. In that way, history will never say the Kallistens submitted to some male Goddess."

"You mean...."

"Yes, what other choices do we have? The vision is clear. Chelidona confirms it. The evil is everywhere, in all the lands. We will be surrounded soon enough and then what? Kalliste is telling us what to do. Our only hope is to live in Kalliste's Light."

They all looked at each other in silence. Eveenara said, "Who will take a stand here?"

The adults stared at their children. And they thought about their communal possessions and lives.

"We have nothing more important than the Goddess," Eveenara said. "Without respect, there is no goodness. Without goodness, there is no life. Even this little bird knows that." She gestured to the swallow who sat on Mudia's shoulder.

THE SWALLOW AND THE NIGHTINGALE

Yidini looked from Reifte to Eveenara. He wanted to argue for life, but he knew that without respect for life, without respect for the Great Mother Spirit in all things—there is no life. Not for women, not for men. Not for anything. He bowed his head in agreement. "We cannot let the Ways of the Goddess be desecrated. We must live and die as Kallistens. Encompassing the good. There is no other way."

"Take us to Thine bosom, oh Kalliste, Great Mother!" Eveenara made the sign of the Goddess and brought her right hand to her forehead. The others followed suit. They raised their arms and made a circle.

The Earth shook violently. No one moved. They were not afraid.

Chapter 29

"There occurred violent earthquakes and floods;
and in a single day and night of misfortune all your
warlike men in a body sank into the earth, and the island
of Atlantis in like manner disappeared in the depths of the sea."
-- Plato's Timaeus

THEY STOOD ON the edge of the crater, high above the rolling sea. The air was thick with smoke. They carried small statues of Kalliste, the sacred vision texts, and tablets with their prayers and stories. Reifte held the golden chalice. Eveenara carried the sacred snake tubes.

Eveenara looked down to the port below where foreigners' ships were landing. She spoke from an inner peace to the clan. "Today, we gather to become one with Kalliste instead of letting the Achaeans defile Her. We will truly understand all mysteries. Kalliste will prevail, always. She is the Mother Spirit, the Giver of all life!!"

The Earth trembled. A low chanting began. It was taken up by the adults and then by the young girls and boys. Ceremonial drums played under the voices.

"The Earth is round, the Earth is holy.
I am the Earth, love fills the need.
I am the listener, this is Her song.
She has the power, the Lady loves me."

The chanting grew louder. Powerful male voices called on Kalliste for courage. But then they gave way to the gentle women's voices floating high above like crystals. The two ebbed and flowed, back and forth, without either dominating and controlling.

THE SWALLOW AND THE NIGHTINGALE

Eeveenara surveyed the calm scene. She had sat on this very spot with Chelidona, the brave swallow. And now, everyone was here—the Kallistens had decided their own fate.

But she had done something that she kept as her own secret. It had been only a short trip to the island of Caphtor.

She did it as a precaution. There was no problem if the Achaeans or any other impure person found a Disc. If they tried to use it, they would be instantly killed and it destroyed. But if all Sacred Discs were destroyed, there would never again be a way for people to communicate with Mother Kalliste. Eeveenara feared that attackers and ground shakings would break things and therefore nothing made of clay could be protected. So, with the help of strong rowers and favorable winds, she had quickly traveled to Caphtor where she knew of a secure place to hide her Disc. Deep in the Temple at Phaistou.

But there was one other problem. What if her Sacred Disc was discovered one hundred or two hundred years into the future and the Good people no longer knew how to use it? Eeveenara stopped at the Mother and Child Cave while on Caphtor. Eeveenara was a powerful medicine woman. When she returned to Kalliste, she had even stored away a shard map in a safe storeroom.

The heat from the crater chafed their skin. Mudia drew nearer to Eeveenara. "Eeveenara, I don't want to die."

She knelt down, picked some white lily petals, and put them into Mudia's hand. "My little one, what is life if it is not good? It is not living. Flowers return to life, like these petals. You have been initiated. You already know what the other side looks like. It will be more alive than here. Look, down below." Eeveenara pointed to the men getting out of the ships below them. They uncaged small furry monkeys and prepared weapons for fighting. Mudia clung closer to Eeveenara.

"Will anyone remember us, Eeveenara?" Mudia asked. The ground beneath them trembled, making standing difficult.

Eeveenara smiled and looked at the young girl. She felt a bit of her own sadness. "A dark period is descending upon the Earth. But good people of the future will find our remains and see the beauty in which we lived. There will be the Good again." She looked up and saw Reifte nearby. "Now, go to your mother. And don't let the breeze blow the petals from your hand."

Mudia gave Eveenara a loving hug and ran to Reifte. The priestess knelt down to fiercely grab onto her daughter. Mudia showed her the petals in her hand.

Above the gathered clan, a flock of swallows circled trying to stay in an updraft of the light wind, their powerful wings flapping. Reifte stood up and pointed to the sky. "The swallows will remember us. And the people of the future will find your painting, Mudia. They will know what a beautiful artist you became."

Mudia smiled. "Chelidona wants to rejoin the Goddess with us." She pulled the bird out of her carrying pouch.

Eveenara came near. "Chelidona, you must fly free with the other swallows. You have saved us from slavery. We need you to do even greater deeds."

"Anything! Anything at all!" The swallow flew to Eveenara's hand.

"You must save the tune of the Earth Song! And your nightingale sister the Love Song! You must let everyone know that Good people once existed on this Earth before the Evil took hold. And help people prepare for the Good again! Remind the world there is a better way to live, without killing, greed, and hatred! Tell them!"

Chelidona responded to Eveenara's plea. "I will teach good people the Song of the Earth. We swallows will keep the message alive."

"You truly are a symbol of the Earth. But be careful, Chelidona, about speaking to humans. The longer you do, the harder it will become. If it takes too long for them to hear, the birds spreading the word will begin to perish. Choose wisely who to tell. Find the Good people. I'll do whatever I can to help. Now fly away and don't look back. Don't return here, ever, not until the world is filled with Good people living in respect."

The Earth trembled again, harder than before. Reifte drew Mudia to her and walked with Eveenara and the others. In the abandoned village, clay vases smashed into pieces. The armed men reached the town. Their small animals helped in their deadly search for victims. But the Kallisten were walking toward the heat of their Goddess, in silence, with certainty, beyond evil's reach.

The birds flew toward freedom not looking back. As Chelidona left the island ready for her voyage across the great seas, her heart was heavy. But she was singing the Song of the Earth, the song of Kalliste, the song of her youth.

CHAPTER 30
THE SWALLOW'S ANSWER
PART IX

"My life is love, my life is spirit
I am alive, a song to sing
Respect the water, the land and air
You are the power in every live thing"
- ancient Kallisten song

WORLD NEWS – JUNE 25
Air Pollution Near Roads Increase Risk of Diseases

THE ALTA BATES HOSPITAL room seemed muted by its pale charcoal-colored walls. "I don't know what happened," Stephen repeated, almost as if he, too, were in a state of shock. His dark face was drawn. Low-level beeps came from the machines and a slight gasping escaped from the respirator. He sat on the window sill, half watching people down below emerging from the parking garage.

"Nothing?" Thomas sat in a chair next to the hospital bed.

Stephen shook his head. "The doctor says I have selective amnesia. I just can't remember. But Deborah saw it, too. And whatever she saw put her into this coma."

The two of them stared at Deborah's body. Tubes snaked into her arm. Her head was turned slightly to the left as if she were sleeping. Stephen had brought her back from Europe to Berkeley. Communications were extremely difficult with the interference signal broadcasting on most frequencies. Commercial flights were out of the question. Thomas's wife Susan had managed to get them onto a ship leaving Europe for New York. Being a Senator, she was able to get them diplomatic immunity since Stephen had been representing the United States at the conference. In the chaos, it saved him hassles around the equipment and it being searched. Since Stephen's UCI sabbatical was finished and because of the earthquake in Los Angeles, Susan got them onto a military transport to Northern California.

Stephen stood up and moved closer to the hospital bed. "Maybe Deborah was exhausted, that's why it hit her so badly. You know how intense she gets." He adjusted the pendant around her neck. He didn't know what it was but knew it meant something to her.

Thomas shifted in his seat. "The real miracle is that she got over her anger at you. She did, right?"

He smiled at Deborah's unconscious face. "She said she forgives me and loves me. You should have seen it—how we literally bumped into each other at the airport. I definitely remember that. I went to Santorini not knowing if she would speak to me but I had to try."

Thomas leaned forward. "How did she get over it? Because the last time we talked, she was speaking of divorce."

"I don't know. We didn't have time to talk about it."

"She was so adamant about going to Seville and determined to participate in what was happening."

Stephen sat back on the window sill and looked out to see if he could spot Rachel. "The conference, right. It seems so long ago." No one was coming out of the parking garage.

"Only two weeks ago." Fretting, Thomas stood up and walked toward the machines attached to Deborah. Turning, he said, "Stephen, it's my fault. I pushed her into getting involved."

Stephen looked at him. "Thomas, what are you talking about? She pleaded with me to help her. I was too angry to do it. Look, I was following the planet's energetics from before the New Jersey earthquake and she still managed to stay one step ahead of everyone. Considering all the systems being affected, it's amazing. She wanted to talk about the birds. Her rejection by the scientific community made her all the more determined to be heard."

Thomas started pacing, tossing his dreadlocks as he shook his head. "It was Harvey that was stopping her. You knew about his jealousy, didn't you? Someday her instrument will do what she envisioned, be a semantic processor. Without his algorithms."

"That's if she comes out of this coma."

Thomas stopped and looked at her still body. "She will, she has to."

A nurse came in to check up on Deborah. He shot a puzzled glance at the two black men in the hospital room of a white woman. Thomas moved out of the way. A large man, the nurse leaned over to check her blood pressure and oxygen rate. As he turned to leave, he came face-to-face with Thomas and stared at him. Then he left.

Stephen said, "The stares we get when the four of us are together. God knows what people are thinking."

Thomas smirked. "You and I know as well as God. Two black boys with white women."

"Or who's that nobody with the hall-of-famer, the U.S. senator and her beautiful friend?"

Thomas laughed. "You aren't exactly a nobody. Major speech at a very prestigious conference. I read it. Batter up, really." He sat back down again. "So what were the results of the conference? There was a lot of hoopla and now silence."

"Publishing takes time." Stephen fidgeted.

Thomas stared at him. "Bull. Calling a TV station doesn't. What's going on?"

Stephen started pacing. He walked toward the window, looked down at the parking garage, and then paced some more.

"Well?" Thomas asked. "Or is this more selective amnesia?"

"I wish it was. You're an anthropologist, you study ancient cultures affected by climate change. What's happening isn't news to you."

Thomas sat back. "It's that bad?"

"When you look at the integrated data, it's worse than anyone thought."

Thomas whistled. The machine softly beeped in the background. He looked at Deborah's inert form. "Is that what sent her into a coma?"

Stephen stared at him. "But she didn't know."

"Didn't she though? One can only imagine what she picked up with that instrument of hers."

Stephen's mind was racing as he looked out the window. Down below, he could see Shelley's unmistakable red hair, even under her scarf. Rachel was next to her. "They're here."

Rachel entered the room, followed by Shelley. "We left *Nonna* Anna and Robert at your house. They're still recuperating from the trip up here yesterday." She greeted Thomas. "You weren't here yesterday when we arrived. I'm so glad to see you, Uncle Thomas."

He smiled at them, knowing a hug was inappropriate. "What's it like in Southern California? The pictures on the news…"

"The tsunami was unbelievable." Rachel adjusted her scarf. "It's like a war zone. So much of the coast affected, the beaches, all those fancy houses and hotels. The marinas destroyed. Debris and pollution everywhere—"

"My God! It's toxic. All the oil refineries there."

"We packed up what we could and left. The gridlock of cars on Interstate 5. Couldn't use cell phones, couldn't get information on radio or TV. Luckily we had gas. It was easier to travel once we got north of Los Angeles. What have you heard?"

The doctor came in and looked at the readouts. He had dark Indian features and black hair. Under his white lab coat he wore a green scrub shirt. He examined Deborah's eyes and pinched her nails. "We don't understand why she's in coma. She was traumatized by something. What was she doing?"

Stephen frowned. "I can't remember exactly what happened."

Rachel turned to the doctor. "When will she come out of this coma?"

He shook his head. "She's at about an 8 on the coma scale where 15 is fully awake. That's not great. Honestly, I can't tell you one way or the other." He left.

Rachel walked over to the bed. "Mom, we need you to wake up."

They all stared at Deborah's lifeless form. She looked like an oracle—enigmatic and full of answers, but not saying a word. Her face was relaxed and her chest moved up and down with each slow breath. Mechanical beeps echoed through the room.

Shelley said, "The news reports have commented on how nothing is being affected here. The destruction is strangely selective."

Rachel touched her mother's hair. "It's like wherever Mom is, things are okay."

Thomas added, "Except for the volcano erupting." It sounded almost funny but no one was laughing.

Stephen took a deep breath. "Which we survived, against all odds if you think about it."

Rachel started crying. "Mom's gotta be all right. I know she will be."

Stephen came close to her. "I have a vague memory of being on the volcano, like it's real and unreal at the same time."

Shelley stood up. "Mystical experiences are very powerful. One feels like one's eyes are opened. What happened?"

"I can't remember much. I can't...I can't explain. I ran for the helicopter. But then I realized Deborah wasn't moving. So I threw the equipment into the cockpit, went back, and grabbed her. She started yelling something about a moth and prayers. She said Rachel's name and then she went limp, her eyes in that blank stare."

"My name?" Rachel leaned over her mother's body and stroked her check. "She heard or saw something that put her into this state." She raised her voice. "What is it you saw, Mom?"

Deborah lay in the bed not moving. She took a long breath and let it out. They waited but she didn't take another one. The beeps stopped. The silence in the room became deafening. Then an alarm sounded.

Stephen took a step forward. "Call the doctor!"

Rachel cried, "No, no." She looked over her father's shoulder.

The male nurse came running in, followed by the doctor and others. They pushed everyone out of the room as they went into a code blue.

In the hallway, Stephen comforted Rachel. "We don't know what's happening."

Shelley stepped toward Rachel. Stephen began pacing, trying to listen to what was happening in the room. Thomas looked down the hall and back at Stephen.

The time passed in agony. Then two nurses filed out, then the rest. They all had grim looks on their faces.

The doctor came out. He shook his head.

"Mother!" Rachel collapsed into Stephen's arms, tears streaming down her face.

Shelley hugged them both, their sobs pulsating with convulsions. Thomas joined them, all trying to comprehend what had happened. They huddled as a family, swaying in grief, swaying beyond grief.

Preparing himself, Stephen entered the room first, followed by the others. The silence was palpable. The nurse had removed the tubes from Deborah's arm and disconnected the monitors. After two days of listening to the beeps, a pallor hung over everything. Deborah's face looked serene. The years of stress that strained lines into her forehead and cheeks were lifted as though she was now permanently staring at the vision she had seen on the volcano, a peaceful past and the potential future.

The hospital made the arrangements and told them someone from the funeral home would be coming. After the social worker left, Stephen stood by the door not knowing what to do next. Shelley comforted Rachel.

Rachel walked over to her father and said through her tears, "Dad, I prayed for your reconciliation."

"So did I, honey. Your mom was the most remarkable person I've ever known." He smiled with wet eyes, despite feeling numb. "I guess we just wait. Or do we leave?"

Rachel looked at Deborah's body. "I'd rather wait. We don't want to leave her here."

Shelley agreed. "In Judaism, it is a sign of respect not to leave the body alone. We are the *shomrim*, the guards. I won't ask the hospital staff if we can light candles. Deborah wasn't a practicing Jew, but it would be a nice way to honor and respect our mother." The word caught in her throat.

Stephen took the pendant off Deborah and put it around Rachel's neck. "I'm sure she wants you to have it." Rachel clasped it and felt her tears start again.

They encircled Deborah's body. Shelley intoned, "*Barukh ata Adonai Eloheinu melekh ha'olam, dayan ha-emet*. Blessed are you, Lord our God, Ruler of the universe, the true Judge. Deborah, thank you for waiting for us to arrive before you left. You were an inspiration and a guiding light for us all. We were enriched by your presence in our lives. We will miss you." She turned toward Thomas.

He had tears glistening in his eyes. "Deborah, you were my friend for longer than I can remember, the first person I met at Berkeley who didn't care I had been a football player." Everyone laughed lightly. "It's true," he said, looking around and then back at Deborah's body. "I loved every conversation we ever had, I loved your curiosity, your willingness to search and to put yourself on the line for your beliefs."

THE SWALLOW AND THE NIGHTINGALE

Rachel was next. She wiped the tears from her eyes but they wouldn't stop. "Mom," she said, choking on the word. Taking a deep breath, she tried again. "Mom, it's true we didn't see eye to eye all the time, but you gave me so much. When it came down to it, you were there for me even when it was hard for you. You were my beacon. You taught me to never back down and I am grateful for all you did for me and everyone else." The tears streamed down her face and she tried to wipe them away again.

Stephen was last. He struggled to speak. "My love," he began. "You and I know what we had. Every moment of our lives together, from when we met at that dance in graduate school onwards, I will hold in my heart. You are what everyone has said you are. In my mind and heart, you will always be alive."

They stood, not knowing what else to do but to stare at her, trying to hold onto every last wisp of her hair, each finger, the bend of her elbows, the smoothness of her face.

Stephen's phone rang. The number wasn't familiar. "Stephen Wright." The caller said he was from Interpol. He explained that something was missing from the Heraklion Museum on Crete. It was tracked to an international art theft ring involving a curator. "A Giorgio Fuentes? Excuse me, but my wife just passed away," Stephen said and hung up his phone. He looked at everyone. "Something's been stolen and they think Deborah was involved."

Chapter 31
The Origins

HER NAME WAS PHILOMELA. She was the youngest daughter of Queen Zeuxippe and King consort Pandion. Her skin was soft, textured like milk, and her jet-black hair curled down her back in long luxurious locks. For sixteen years, Philomela had lived under the protection of her mother, learning the feminine skills of spiritual leadership, medicine, and governing. The masculine skills of cooking, cleaning, and labor were taught to the boys. Both genders learned child-rearing, and both were taught to live in harmony with everything on the Earth.

So when a strange tribe appeared from the east with opposing beliefs, they had been ill-prepared for such a fight. As a result, a stranglehold had been placed on their city-state. Thrust into this strange situation, Queen Zeuxippe had reached out for help. It took intervention from Tereus, the new king consort from Thrace, to obtain their freedom.

In her gratitude, Queen Zeuxippe had accepted the great warrior as consort in marriage for her eldest daughter Chelidona. After the royal wedding, Chelidona went to Thrace to rule as Queen.

When Tereus came to the palace of Queen Zeuxippe with the message that Chelidona missed her little sister, Philomela was ecstatic. Tereus vowed by the Great Goddess for the virgin princess' safe passage. He spoke earnestly of his respect for all women and the Goddess, a trait trained into all males from childhood. Queen Zeuxippe, confident in this man, entrusted her youngest daughter into Tereus' care.

Philomela stood on the deck of the trireme, the cool breeze tingling across her skin. She held her favorite white flower, a lily, in her hand. She had been separated from her older sister Chelidona for seven years, almost half her lifetime. Philomela had never even met her nephew Itys, who was five years old now. Philomela remembered when she was that age. Chelidona had received the Sacred Disc for her twelfth birthday. They would stand side by side, holding the Disc between them,

THE SWALLOW AND THE NIGHTINGALE

Philomela's left hand facing Chelidona's right, each singing their given song. Their voices would swirl in a magic harmony too beautiful to even comprehend, and the Disc would spin as the Goddess Supreme emerged. It was a wondrous moment to be in the Presence and to receive Her Blessing.

As children, Philomela and Chelidona pretended to be scribes, using writing tools to track temple inventories. The two girls invented a secret code, something they thought grownups too stupid to follow. Philomela wondered if someday her own children would think the same of her.

Tereus came up behind her. He had initially taken the trip without enthusiasm, but the sight of Philomela's beauty had enflamed his loins and he had waited for this moment. Tereus grabbed her by the waist.

Philomela pushed him away. "Consort Tereus, what are you doing?"

Tereus sneered. "You think you are so much better than me. Your fine manners compared to my warring life. I'll show you who is better."

Philomela stared at him. She had never been spoken to in this way. "What are you talking about? You are my sister's consort."

Tereus tore at her clothing. She tried to fight him off, horrified by his sudden change in behavior. "Stop this at once!!"

He laughed, enjoying her struggles and helplessness in his hands. "Your anger makes you even more a beauty!"

"You can't do this. I'm a woman and princess of the Great Goddess!" Her hands pushed at his thick neck and bulging face. His strength was too much.

"Quiet, princess of the 'great nobody'! The title 'King' has new meaning in these lands. You shall see." His contorted smile was close to her face. "No one will help you. I can do anything, and I desire to have you." He threw her down on the deck and pushed himself on her.

Her eyes were large. "Stop, Tereus! Your vow to my mother!"

"What do I care for you or 'the Ways'? Who is your mother compared to me? Or even your father, a weakling who bows to the Goddess. There are stronger forces. See, this! No Goddess can stop this!"

With that, Tereus ravished her, thrusting his hard member into her without regard to her pleas. Philomela screamed in pain. He laughed. "Your bellowing makes it all the more exciting." He attacked her again ignoring her flailing arms and the pool of blood forming under her body.

He stood up and adjusted his short tunic. He had never had such a beauty before. She curled on the deck, whimpering, torn lily petals turning red. He laughed. "Now I am done with you. So much for the *fakery of a Goddess! As if She could protect you from me. She doesn't exist. Women no longer lead." His laughter ricocheted off the islands.*

Philomela pulled herself up and looked at him in horror. "You have defiled a woman against her will. It is unheard of." She spat at him. "The Goddess will see this crime. I shall proclaim the shameful truth across the land and your name will be despised forever."

Tereus spit back. "Don't you ever forget this, priestess. There are no consequences to what I do." He grabbed her, twisting her arms behind her back. "You want to live?" He ripped off a piece of cloth and tied her wrists. "Go live in the seas. But you'll never speak about this." He drew his bronze sword and seized her tongue. Pulling at it, he hacked it off as she screamed. He dragged her to her feet and threw her overboard. His laughter echoed as the rowers carried the royal boat away.

More a rag than a human and bleeding profusely, Philomela freed her arms and swam toward land. Fishermen found her more dead than alive. Two men carried her to a small stone house where Lettle and her consort Manos lived. Lettle cauterized her wounds, bandaged her, and gave her a warm tea drink of mint leaves. With the help of the other women, she cleaned her. Philomela slept.

In the days and months, Philomela's body restored to health. Lettle fed her fish, olives, cheese and artichokes, washed down with a light wine. She learned to gesture to the kind couple. She had few requirements, because killing Tereus was the only thing on her mind. In the nights, she cried out in angry blood-curdling screams. Lettle and Manos huddled afraid to even imagine what events had occurred.

Each day, Philomela awoke with the same thought of revenge. A cloak, she thought. I'll weave a cloak, with a secret message woven into it that only Chelidona will be able to read. No one will suspect anything!

Lettle helped construct a loom. Lettle and Manos were glad that their charge began to do something that lessened the ghoulish screams. The loom was set up overlooking a garden filled with chamomile, sugar violets, and marigolds. Philomela would sit, sew, and hum the only song she knew, its beauty echoing off the hills. The soft linen cloak was long and white. Along one side, Philomela wove graceful flying birds with bright feathers and pointed beaks. She added red roses with tiny leaves and thorns. Hidden among the idyllic scenes using their secret code, she described the horrible events that had transpired.

THE SWALLOW AND THE NIGHTINGALE

When the cloak was finally done, Philomela handed it to Manos and gestured. "Please take this to Queen Chelidona. When she receives it, you will be rewarded."

Manos didn't know what to believe. The girl was obviously of high class birth, but how would she know the Queen? What if the Queen didn't like the gift? Would she make trouble for him and his family? In his pity, Manos agreed. He left in his small boat with the cloak and some fish. Arriving at the great royal capital of Thrace, he told the guardsmen at the palace gate he had fine fish for the Queen.

A servant was summoned. "I'll take your fish to the Queen."

"No," argued Manos. "I want to show her my appreciation. And," he tapped his bag, "give the noble Queen a small gift from my wife and the women of my village."

The servant peered into the bag at the brightly decorated cloak and let him pass into the palace. Soon, he was summoned by the Queen.

Manos bowed and laid the basket of fish before her feet. Chelidona motioned to a servant to take the fish to the kitchen.

"Your Majesty, as a token of gratitude, I'd like to give you this cloak."

Chelidona glanced at it. She thought the work was quite refined for a fisherman's wife. She was about to tell the servants to fold it away, but something caught her eye. The symbols reminded her of something, something she had once known. Chelidona looked very carefully. It was the secret code she and Philomela had devised as children! But Tereus had told her that her sister had died on the journey. Chelidona studied the cloak and suddenly, she saw the story unfold before her eyes—the way Tereus was openly received by Queen Zeuxippe, the trip back, the attack, the horrible mutilation. "Fisherman! Where is the person who sewed this cloak?"

"Why, in my village." Manos was amazed.

"I must go there at once!" Chelidona paid Manos generously and summoned subjects she knew to be loyal.

Philomela waved with excitement watching the royal barge approach. As the trireme was landing at the crude dock, Chelidona jumped off, ignoring the King's soldiers watching her from the shore.

"Oh, my sister!! You are alive!" Chelidona grabbed Philomela with a fierce love. "We are together again."

Philomela was filled with joy and hugged her and cried.

"You cannot speak!" Chelidona pulled away and stared. "To think of what he did to you, I cannot bear it."

Philomela hugged her sister again, grateful her torment was over.

Chelidona reached to raise Philomela's head. "Let us go to the palace together and we will decide what to do." Philomela cowered, but Chelidona continued, "Do not worry. You will be safe from him." Chelidona could not even say his name anymore.

On board the royal ship, they settled into Chelidona's silk-covered state room. A small fireplace kept them warm as rowers carried them back to Daulis. Chelidona could not stop talking. "Mother did not know what a horribly cruel man he is. He may have political ability but he does not know decency, the order of things." Her eyes clouded over, remembering the process of having a son by him. It was her duty but not her desire. Luckily, on her first birthing, a son was born.

At five years old, Itys was already becoming his father. He taunted other children unaware they had feelings. The first time Chelidona had watched Itys skin a yellow, long-haired cat alive, she had tried to stop him. He laughed at her. When she asked him why he had done it, he had said he liked the color of the fur and couldn't understand her when she said it was wrong. She told him just because you have the ability to do something, it doesn't mean you should. He ran to his father who showed him how to pull out the animal's eyes and eat them.

To communicate, Philomela took a piece of coal and wrote in a fury. "I want to kill him. With my bare hands."

Chelidona was stunned. "But we are not like him. We were born of the Ways. Brought up to believe in respect. Believe in the Goddess."

Philomela almost snarled at her sister's innocence. She wrote back. "What use are the Ways when this evil is taking over the lands? Can the Ways defend against it? Where was the Goddess when he did this?"

Chelidona was in deep moral conflict. She knew first-hand about this evil. It was spreading, engulfing men's minds. Men no longer acted in respect to women and children. There was warring everywhere. Tribes cut down vast tracks of forests to make more warships. Armies went on rampages, hacking up people with their new bronze swords and throwing the body parts into the seas—keeping only the armor for their own use. It was a new world, filled with cruelty. Her consort husband didn't even recognize the title of consort. Chelidona and Philomela were brought up to live in peace. To respect all living creatures. To respect the Earth. But looking at Philomela, Chelidona could feel her grief also turn toward anger. She stood up and paced back and forth to stop trembling. "Tereus must suffer," she said, "the way he makes you suffer, the way he makes me suffer."

THE SWALLOW AND THE NIGHTINGALE

Philomela stated in big bold letters. "We must take revenge."

"But how?" Chelidona asked.

"Killing him is not good enough. What is most precious to him? We must take it away from him."

Chelidona continued to pace, her mind racing through this new territory of ideas. "He cherishes his bronze sword. He took it from the King consort of Boetia after he killed him."

"Something even worse. We must stop at nothing, since he's willing to stop at nothing. Set his rooms on fire. Cut his own tongue out? Or his eyes? Or maybe his manhood!"

Chelidona jumped in. "And then keep on cutting until nothing is left of him. Whatever we do, its horror should be a reminder to men forever, to warn them of women's strength."

Her face in a rage, Philomela wrote out, "There must be something he deeply, deeply cares for. A mistress?" She looked up at her sister and gestured, "We must take away from him something he loves."

Chelidona stared at Philomela. "There is only one person he cares about. His son Itys." Suddenly, she saw the whole picture in front of her, how this son would one day grow up to become a beast like his father. Her life would continue on, with her own son as tormenter.

Philomela motioned. "Then that is where we must attack him."

Slowly, Chelidona nodded her head. They, too, were now forever changed by the new vision taking hold of the world.

In the palace, news spread quickly that the Queen had been joined by her sister Philomela who had no tongue. Tereus didn't care. Women were useful for only one thing. Besides, Philomela could not tell anyone what had transpired. And if she did, so what? He was the King! He had full control of everyone in his Kingdom. These were modern times, not like the old ways when women and men strove for compromise. He had his own concerns. Scythian tribes were attacking his eastern borders. His ten-thousand man army was to be divided into brigades that would tear into the enemy from six directions. As practice to keep them in fighting form, he had the groups battling against each other to the death.

The two sisters waited for their chance. It came when the Dionysus' Festival began, a week-long party with celebrations filled with music makers and drunken revelers. Chelidona invited Tereus to a special dinner. She explained it was an ancient custom of her people, a sacred feast for husbands only. He was surprised by her offer. "I honor my

Page 312

THEA IBERALL

heritage," she said, head demurely bowed in respect. "You are my husband."

"Then I will." Tereus enjoyed her submissiveness, so much so that he failed to realize she didn't say 'consort husband.'

Chelidona found her son Itys in the west courtyard. He was taunting his favorite pet dog with a knife trying to cut off his tail. The dog was already bleeding. Chelidona grabbed the boy, disarmed him, and dragged him to the small kitchen in the servants' quarters where no one could hear. Her heart was so hardened—she didn't think about what she was doing. She drew a butcher's knife from the rack. Ignoring the terrified boy's pleas, she struck him in the chest with the knife and his little body went limp. Philomela joined her and together, they butchered him up into steaks. Then they threw portions into stewpots and skewered others on the spits in the grill, creating their banquet of retribution.

Chelidona dressed in her Dionysus' costume, resplendent with vines and a deerskin. Carrying the large platter of meat into the banquet hall, she placed it before Tereus at the grand table. Servants brought in the large stewpot. As the plates were put before him, Tereus grinned at how his wife bowed. He gorged himself on each fine morsel, not knowing the magnificent meal was the tasty young flesh of his own flesh.

When finished, he bellowed out to his wife, "Now bring me my son."

Chelidona came out and sneered. "What you seek you already have."

"Where?" Tereus looked around.

"Within you."

Tereus stared at her, unable to understand. At that moment, Philomela burst into the hall, her hair wild, her eyes gleaming with revenge. In her hand, she held his son's head. As a final mocking gesture, she threw it at Tereus.

The blood drained from his face as Tereus screamed in rage. He began vomiting and violently weeping. In utter despair, he grabbed his sword and chased the two women.

Chelidona grabbed Philomela by the hand. The two sisters ran as fast as they could, with Tereus close behind them. In their rage for revenge, they hadn't thought through how they would escape.

Down a long corridor they ran. He was catching up quickly. They jumped over a short wall into a large courtyard. Heather and Queen Anne's lace clung to their heels. They looked frantic and scared, their breathing hard with each step. They looked over their shoulders, terrified they wouldn't get away. He was about to grab them, when

🦋 Page 313

THE SWALLOW AND THE NIGHTINGALE

suddenly, their feet became light. Lighter, even lighter than air. They were floating, as if they could take flight, as if winged. And then, the two women began to transform!

They became two soaring birds, spiraling upwards, upwards into the clouds. Chelidona, a graceful and powerful swallow with long tail streamers, quick wings, and a dark-colored throat. And Philomela, a nimble and sure nightingale, with red-brown wings stroking powerfully through the air.

They circled each other in joyous grace. Two flying birds, no longer rooted in the Earth. Tereus stood on the ground, stamping his feet, wildly thrusting with his sword. "Stop! Stop, come back! At once!"

But they were gone, flying away. Away, leaving him far below.

They flew more as lovers than sisters. Free, high above the land, they sang their beautiful song in exquisite harmony with crystal clear voices. Slowly flapping their wings, their graceful bodies soared through the clouds. They circled each other in joy over goat herds and burnt fields. Below them, rounded gray outcroppings peeked out from under the dark green forests.

Philomela, the nightingale, happy to have regained her voice, called to her sister, "Let us fly across the sea to the mountains of the North."

"I became one of them!" Chelidona, the swallow, replied, guilt twisting her heart. "I must go away. I must fly over the seas."

"And I must stay near," Philomela sang, looking over the countryside. She did not want to think of their heinous immorality. "We cannot fight this evil. Someday, we'll be together again. When the evil is gone."

"But it won't go away! It will grow upon itself destroying all that is good!" The swift powerful swallow flew out toward the sea, searching for a way to find peace and forgiveness from the Goddess.

Philomela sang out. "Then fight it we must! If we do survive, we'll know each other by our songs." And the graceful gentle nightingale turned to the northeast. Finally able to speak once again, she vowed to never stop singing as melodious and sweet a song as was ever possible. She would find someone to tell her story to so all she knew would not be lost. There had to be a way to stop the great evil so that balance would once again fill the Earth—and she could reunite with Chelidona, her sister, the beautiful swallow.

Chapter 32
The Swallow's Answer
Finale

"Will the winds of evil blow around us
Or can true goodness thus prevail
By letting silence reign in wonder
We can hope to never fail"
- ancient Kallisten song

STEPHEN SAT NEXT TO Rachel on the loveseat looking out over the low deck where Deborah's bird feeders were alive with afternoon avian visitors. The noise of people talking and eating masked the low-level interference signal.

The doorbell rang. Stephen stood up to greet Susan.

"Mourners aren't supposed to stand when sitting *shiva*." She walked over to him, grabbing his hands and hugging him, her blonde hair getting mussed. "It was a very tasteful funeral."

"Thank you for everything you did, Susan. There was no way I could have gotten her home otherwise." His eyes were tired.

"What are U.S. Senators for?" She reached to hug Rachel. "I'm so sorry, honey. Your mom was one in a million."

Rachel looked haggard. "Aunt Susan, thank you for speaking at the funeral. If we were really sitting *shiva*, we'd be sitting on the floor." As per Jewish tradition, her blouse had a slight rip on the left side of her chest. "It must have been hard to get back to California from Washington."

Susan caressed Rachel's chiffon scarf. "Mint green, your mom's favorite color." She paused. "Sit, sit. We got out before the ban."

Thomas came up and stood next to his wife. "Leaving the FAA to sort out the problems."

Susan gave Thomas a quick peck on the cheek.

THE SWALLOW AND THE NIGHTINGALE

Dr. Alexandria Fisher came over to them. "Dr. Wright, I'm so sorry for your loss."

She was shorter than Stephen anticipated. He shook her hand. "Please call me Stephen. Thank you for coming to this little gathering. This is our family friend Susan and her husband Thomas."

Alexandria did a double take as they shook hands.

Rachel struggled to try to stand again. "Dr. Fisher, I wasn't sure how you met my mother, but when I found your card, I figured you met her somewhere on her European trip. Please." She motioned to the couch.

They both sat down. "Please call me Alexandria. We met in the Paris airport when we were traveling to Greece. We were lucky to get out alive. Our ship was arriving at Pireus when the volcano blew."

Rachel sucked in her breath and stared at the fireplace.

Stephen explained to Susan in a heavy voice. "We've invited people who were connected with Deborah's work. Something happened out there and we want to know what put Deborah into that coma and me into this selective amnesia."

Susan quickly turned to him. "Is it all right I'm here?"

Stephen nodded. "It's fine. You're family."

Rachel looked to Alexandria. "So, is your family all right?"

"Yes. Europe had been untouched until that moment. Now, of course, people are stranded all over. We had the ship."

Susan leaned toward Thomas. "Wouldn't it be better to just leave well enough alone?"

"What's that mean?" He glanced to see if Stephen had heard her.

Shelley was monitoring Rachel's state. She came over behind the loveseat. Her blouse had the same rip and she also wore a head scarf. "Can I bring anyone some coffee? It's Deborah's favorite. Jamaican Blue Mountain."

Rachel looked up. "Thank you, my love."

A young man walked over to Stephen. "My name's Michael Bridgeman. I was a student of Dr. Wright's. We helped her leave for Europe."

Stephen shook his hand and tried to smile. "That's what we heard when we asked around the department."

Alexandria turned to Shelley. "I'd love a cup of her coffee." Everyone agreed.

Shelley walked to the kitchen as Robert rolled his wheelchair next to the loveseat.

Their grandmother Anna brought a tray of hard boiled eggs and bagels. "Can I serve anyone something to eat?"

Stephen took the tray. "Please sit, *Nonna* Anna. Thank you." He put it on the RAX-1000 which was on the coffee table. "You can help us figure out what Deborah was doing." He shot a glance at Susan. "It's the least we can do for someone we all loved so much."

"I don't have to prove how much I cared for Deborah." Susan shrugged. "I'm just saying it's not worth putting it all together. Leave well enough alone."

Thomas squirmed. "You don't know what you're talking about." Susan walked away from him.

Anna sat down next to Rachel. "Dr. Wright definitely was on a journey to find something."

Michael sat down on the other loveseat. "This is the machine." Moving the tray of food to the side, he opened the RAX-1000.

Rachel stared at it. "It's so complicated looking."

Susan continued, "Stephen, I didn't mean to say anything negative. I just think her research got off-track. Look what it lead to."

Michael sat up. "Dr. Wright showed us how to use the machine." He pointed to the switches. "Those control it for the analysis and recording states."

Robert leaned forward in his wheelchair. "What's in the drawer?"

"Not much. It holds memory sticks and tools and things." Rachel and Robert huddled around Michael as he explained how the machine worked, not listening to the ongoing conversation.

Thomas moved closer to Susan. "Is that what you're spreading around Washington? You don't know the whole story."

She crossed her arms. "Oh, really, what's the full story?"

Thomas backed off. "This isn't the time or place to get into this." He looked at Stephen who nodded. "All right. Harvey Milhouse was jealous of her because she didn't use his algorithms. Half of her problems were caused by him. We'll find the real reasons underlying the misconduct charge. I don't believe them. She was a great scientist."

Susan stared at him. "Oh, so you don't know about the letter?"

Thomas blinked.

"Exactly. She admitted to the whole thing. Misconduct."

"What?" Thomas spun around to look at Stephen. "Is this true?"

Stephen's head reeled back. His eyes went wide and he looked helpless. "She never said any of this to me."

"And she never really proved this so-called semantic processing capability. I went out of my way to get her funding and it never worked." Susan shook her head.

Michael leaned over to open the drawer in the RAX-1000, but changed his mind and took a hardboiled egg instead.

Thomas bound over. "What about her journal?" It was next to RAX-1000. "She always maintained it. There's got to be clues to what really happened." He shot a look at Susan.

Rachel rubbed its stippled cover. "There's no context to understand what she writes. And it abruptly ends."

Shelley returned with a tray of coffee cups.

Stephen took a deep breath. "Okay, okay, we've gathered the right people to understand what happened. Collectively, we can piece it together. Coffee's good, it'll help us. Here," he handed a cup to Anna.

Michael looked at Stephen. "I know the research. I was there as she was designing experiments."

Thomas took a proffered coffee cup. "I know her mindset. We had conversations about what she was trying to accomplish."

"I know the science. And I was at the volcano." Stephen said.

Taking a sip, Alexandria said, "I saw the shard map. This is great coffee."

Their heads snapped toward her. "What?" Stephen asked. "Oh, my God. Something did occur. Let's do this logically and start at the beginning."

Leaving her cup on the coffee table, Shelley went to bring the dining room chairs into the living room. Thomas helped her.

Michael offered, "Dr. Wright found a swallow singing Fariña's *The Swallow Song*. It must have come from an ancient song."

Robert raised his hand. "That would be the Ladino song *Los Bilbilicos* about nightingales that Shelley and I taught her."

Thomas returned with two chairs. "Deborah went to Europe to determine if nightingales were singing one of these songs. Plus to give a talk about the need for scientists to address the morality of their work." He offered a chair to Susan.

As she sat down, she balanced her cup and muttered under her breath. "That's a funny one." Thomas stared at her.

Alexandria spoke up. "I met her when she landed in Europe. We were on our way to Greece."

Shelley brought a third chair and sat down. Rachel handed her her coffee.

Robert asked, "Did she find out if nightingales were singing it?"

"Yes," Rachel continued the story, "but not in Spain. For some reason, she went to Greece where she found evidence of the nightingales singing the nightingale song. But then what happened?"

Alexandria sat forward. "Deborah showed me a shard map in Santorini when she and the Spaniard motored up on a boat. I was able to decode the map and tell her about the Eileithyia cave on Crete."

Stephen looked more drawn than before. "The Spaniard?"

Alexandria was oblivious. "Some younger man with an Italian first name. He seemed to be traveling with her."

Stephen persisted. "Do you know what happened to him?"

Alexandria shook her head and looked up at him. "I don't know. That's the last I saw of them." She took a sip of coffee.

Stunned, Rachel grabbed the journal and tried to read between the lines. "It says there was a professor from Athens. But it's a Greek name. She mentions him when she first recorded the interference signal on Samos."

"That's a reason I went to Santorini," Stephen was evasive.

"What a coincidence you met up with Mom on Santorini. It was, wasn't it?"

He sat down on the other loveseat next to Michael and slowly took a swig of coffee. His eyes were bright with memories. "When I realized she wasn't at the conference anymore, I went to the biology department. Mercedes Asturias told me they had gone into the field to perform some experiments, and then Deborah went to Samos to record nightingales. When the Paris Academy told us about the interference signal, I knew if she was doing recordings, the RAX-1000 would pick it up. And whether she wanted to or not, she would head straight for Santorini. Once I got to the island, I asked around at the main hotels in Fira until I found a manager who said Deborah had checked in three days earlier with Fuentes."

Thomas looked at him. "Fuentes? So, you knew about this Spaniard?"

Stephen stared out the sliding glass door at the birds. "He's the museum curator at the Seville museum. I watched them have drinks at the reception. His staff told me he has a private jet, that's how she flew to Greece. The hotel manager in Fira said to watch the airport for his jet and I'd find her."

Rachel's hand went to her mouth.

The low-level hum could be heard below the buzz of the hummingbirds. Shelley asked, "Would anyone like more coffee?"

Rachel remembered her mother's voice on that phone call—how excited she was. "So, what happened to this man?"

Stephen shook his head and rubbed his temples. "I don't know. When I finally found Deborah at the airport, she was in such a state. It was pouring rain and hard to see anything. We rushed to the volcano." He stopped for a moment, remembering.

Rachel devoured the last entries in the journal. "Did she do any writing from the time you found her until she went into the coma?"

Stephen was lost in memories. "No, there was no time. We were in a boat. Then—and then, we were snorkeling and then running. On the volcano."

"Her journal says something about a clay disc."

Stephen rubbed his forehead. "There was a..."

"Disc?" Anna asked. "Like a plate?"

"Or a Frisbee?" Robert added.

Rachel scanned for the entry. "She had realized a disc from Phaistos was some sort of communications device. Maybe to control the signal."

Stephen sat upright. "There was...a disc."

"The Phaistos Disc?" Alexandria tilted her head up.

"She says she bought a copy of it. What is it? Her notes say you told her about it."

Alexandria said, "It's an ancient object with symbols stamped into the clay, you know, like the mechanism of a typewriter."

"Typewriter? I thought you said it was really old," Michael said.

Alexandria shook her head. "It is very old, but I meant like a typewriter stamps letters on a page. That way it's rather easy to make a mass-produced document. It's a mystery to archeologists."

Stephen looked stunned. "My God. It's coming back."

Rachel stared at the last entry in the journal, realizing they had had the RAX-1000 on the volcano. She turned to Michael. "How do you activate this machine?"

"This is the power on button. It might come up in any one of numerous states. I don't know what all the controls are." Both he and Rachel reached to turn it on. As their hands collided, the pendant around her neck accidentally hit the controls. "Oh, no!"

An ethereal sound filled the room—voices singing in multiple harmonies. Stephen exclaimed, "Oh, my God! That's from the volcano. The whole thing was recorded."

Michael did a double-take. "Voices on the volcano? That's cool. That didn't get into the news."

Rachel's hand cupped her mouth. "That's you, Dad. And Mom." Her eyes filled with tears. Shelley rushed over, crying.

Stephen rose, staring at the machine. He raised his hand. "I held the disc up while Deborah pressed from the other side—and it spun. The old woman said only two people whose hearts are filled with pure love can do it. Otherwise, they'll die."

The ethereal chanting began. Then the ancient voice resonated through the room. Stephen fell back into his chair. "*Call me Gaia, Themis, Rhea, Selene, Hera, Kalliste. I am known by many names and many attributes...*" The voice went on talking about how humans were killing everything with their imbalance.

When she said she could rid herself of humans whenever she wished, Thomas stood up. "I knew it."

"*I will if you continue. Turn away from this evil imbalance. Prepare yourselves for the Good. Each of you as individuals and all of you as collective nations. Ask yourselves over and over until you can answer yes: Are you ready for the Good? I have warned you. If you maintain your current imbalanced ways, I will destroy you all.*"

There was a stunned silence. Rachel nodded to Michael to turn off the machine. Before he could, they heard Deborah's plea for her daughter and grandchild and for all innocent children. They heard the voice say, "*Release me to release me.*" Michael turned off the machine.

Rachel sobbed. "Mom did that?" She ran to Stephen.

"A voice?" Shelley stared at the machine.

Hugging her father, Rachel said, "I never knew how important family was to her."

His eyes glistened. "When were you going to tell me about your plans to give me a grandchild?"

"When you and Mom got back together again." She blew her nose.

Alexandria regained her senses. "Stephen, do you still have this disc?"

Thomas paced like a wild tiger. "Forget the disc. Did you hear what that voice said?"

"And is it real?" Shelley's mouth was agape.

"I put it back where Deborah kept it." Stephen reached inside the drawer of the RAX-1000 and pulled out the Phaistos Disc. He handed it to Alexandria.

"Is it real?" Robert asked.

Alexandria smiled at the disc. "Rachel said it's a copy. It's easy to buy replicas of museum objects."

Stephen's eyes went wide. "Museum? What do you mean?"

"The real priceless one is in the Heraklion Museum on Crete."

"It's from a museum?" Stephen ran his hand over his hair.

Anna leaned over to look. "What does all the writing on it mean?"

"Forget the disc," Thomas iterated louder, "this is serious."

Shelley said, "*Nonna*, didn't you hear that voice? It's…supernatural."

Anna wasn't fazed. "*Mija*, there's obviously much that religions don't know."

Rachel closed her eyes, trying to connect this to hers and Shelley's research. "It's starting to make sense."

Alexandria stared intensely at the disc. "They've been trying to decipher it for at least a hundred years. Someone thought it was a calendar, others think it contains a message." She turned it over and over in her hands. The feel of it, the texture of the clay, the telltale signs of something very, very old. Alexandria cleared her throat. "This isn't a replica. This is the real Phaistos Disc."

Stephen whirled around. "Oh, no!"

Alexandria reached for a napkin. "How did Deborah get it?"

They all watched her carefully cradle it, stunned at the idea that it was sitting there before them.

The sound of Stephen's phone made him jump. He answered it and blinked hard. "The missing object you're looking for is a priceless disc? Have I seen it?" He looked around the room.

"Hold them off," Alexandria whispered. "This is an archeologist's dream."

"What? No, I haven't seen it. Yes, yes. I will look through her suitcases and wait for your call in an hour." He hung up. "Interpol saw her on surveillance cameras stealing it from the museum."

Rachel was incredulous. "She stole it?"

Michael asked, "Are they going to arrest us?"

Stephen pressed against the fireplace. "How could they? They know Deborah was involved by some bizarre twist of events. We didn't know she had it until just now. When they call back, I'll tell them I found it."

Susan nodded. "We'll definitely explain everything to them."

Robert said, "Maybe the Spaniard made her do it. Interpol will find him."

Rachel shook her head. "But then he could implicate her when he finds out she's dead. She'll get the blame. Why would Mom steal this, especially when they already had a copy?"

"Deborah somehow learned that this disc is a way to communicate with—that voice." Stephen stared at his hand and tears welled up in his eyes. "You heard the whole thing. I mean, it was hot against my hand and then it was spinning in the sky. I felt it! I saw it." He took the disc back and molded it between his big hands, trying to recreate the sensation he had experienced.

Alexandria watched him. "That's why it's a stamped document."

Thomas started pacing again, throwing his hands in the air. "Okay, we're not going to get arrested. Let's focus on what that voice said. She said she wants to kill us all off for what we're doing to the planet."

"Maybe it's just a metaphor," Shelley said. "Whatever that voice is, she can't really mean it."

"That can't be real," Alexandria agreed.

Thomas stopped in front of Stephen. "Stephen, what were the conclusions of the conference?"

"Are you sure?"

Thomas nodded. "This is it, my friend. You heard that voice speaking of humankind being unbalanced, right?" Stephen looked at him. Thomas stared back at him. "Well?"

Stephen handed the disc back to Alexandria, drew in his breath and pulled a carefully folded paper out of his pocket. He held it for a minute with his head down. "At the conference, when we reached a consensus, we didn't know what to do because publishing it could cause wide-spread panic." He cleared his throat and read aloud.

CONCLUSION OF THE INTERNATIONAL CONFERENCE ON ANOMALOUS EVENTS

The damage to the hydrosphere and atmosphere caused by unsustainable practices in energy generation, agriculture, ranching, fishing, transportation, communications, manufacturing, waste management, weather modification and war is having irreversible effects on the biosphere and planet. Damage done by rising carbon dioxide due to the burning of fossil fuels will continue for centuries even if greenhouse gases are stabilized: average world and ocean temperatures are rising, oceans are acidifying, sea levels are rising, weather systems are more extreme, and tropical diseases are spreading. Earth systems are responding by amplifying the situation. Instead of stopping their practices, human attempts to solve it with bad technology is making the situation worse. The tipping point has occurred, and we are headed to a degraded state, one that may not sustain human life. With careful management, this degradation phase can be a gradual slope.

The pulsing hum of the low interference signal could be heard almost as if it was speaking to them. Rachel finally said, "Dad, is this saying what I think it is saying?"

Stephen's shoulders slumped. "People are doing things they shouldn't be doing because we're invested into a way of life. Look how angry we get when we lose power or when our cell phones don't work. Meanwhile, pollution poisons our common resources and our addiction to fossil fuels has destabilized the environment. We just don't think of the complexity behind any of our actions."

They let his words sink in and passed the paper around as if seeing it in black and white would help get the information into their brains.

Stephen turned to Susan. "You knew what was going on."

Susan looked at him, quizzically. "Me as an invested private citizen or me as part of the government?"

"The government should be doing something."

"We read the reports along with everyone else." Susan snickered. "We've tried. What's the government going to do? As long as people care more for their entertainment than their futures, there's nothing we can do. Frankly, sometimes it's like trying to push a helium balloon from the inside. Running the government is not about leadership, it's about compromise."

Thomas added, "And lots of competition."

"What's wrong with competition?" Susan shot back. "It's the way of the world."

Michael stood up. "Dr. Wright talked about competition. As long as competition and cooperation aren't balanced, it's hard to get ahead. Too much competition kills, too much cooperation suffocates."

"Dad," Rachel interrupted, "how can you be so calm about this?"

Stephen squinted and shook his head. "When we put it all together, it was a wakeup call. No one left that conference unchanged." He started pacing. "As the oceans rise, shorelines will be lost. People are already buying their own generators because the grid has become unpredictable. And some of our solutions are making it worse."

Robert asked, "What do you mean?"

"Our food is being compromised by toxins and genetic modification. The grid itself is causing illness with these smart meters in people's homes. Attempts at weather control are causing who knows what. It's like our eyes are closed."

Michael shook his head. "Corporations are trying to bleed every last ounce of gas and oil out of shale, creating more greenhouse gases and damaging water aquifers. I've been studying this since my best friend died from drinking contaminated water. Dr. Wright, what does it mean, a tipping point?"

"The planet is being pushed into a new state. If that state isn't hospitable to human life, that's it for us. It could mean no more fresh water or our running to higher land. It could mean half the human population wiped out. It could mean anarchy and war. Who knows? From our perspective, it will all be a change, catastrophic or otherwise." He swallowed hard.

THE SWALLOW AND THE NIGHTINGALE

Susan laughed. "Don't get so melodramatic and scare people."

Stephen turned to look at her. "Susan, this is reality. The water in the aquifers is thousands to millions of years old. When it's gone, it's gone. There's no time for pretending anymore. You heard that voice."

Shelley said, "It's saying we're all being immoral."

"My God," Stephen slapped the side of his head, "it wasn't a coincidence Deborah was drawn to Santorini. Someone wanted her on that volcano with her machine."

Michael jumped up. "To record it!"

Susan was incredulous. "You're now trying to say there was no misconduct by Deborah? That there was some woo-woo instead?"

Thomas gritted his teeth. "She was your friend, Susan. Stephen is our friend. Didn't you hear that voice? It's telling us to wake up. You know my research. The ancient Pueblans couldn't survive at their population density after they compromised their environment. We're facing exactly the same thing but on a grander scale."

"I went out on a limb to get her funding. And the semantic processor never worked. So big deal, it can record audio signals. So can my cell phone."

Rachel's eyes flashed as she stood up. "Aunt Susan, you're wrong. The last entry in Mom's journal said that the semantic processor was working. And from what Dad said, it happened before they went to the volcano."

"Do you have proof it worked?"

Rachel racked her brain reconstructing what Deborah knew from the journal entries. She lowered her head and shook it no.

Thomas exploded, "I don't care about a damn letter. I don't care how much it took to build that machine. Look at what happened on the volcano."

Stephen breathed hard. "And if she came clean about what happened, she wasn't trying to deceive."

Thomas agreed. "Right. Deborah was on to something."

Susan walked toward the dining room. "But where's the proof?"

Robert waved his arms like a signalman. "Excuse me. We can argue about this all day, but isn't the only thing that matters what that voice said? It said it can get rid of us unless…"

They all looked at him.

Michael finished the sentence. "…unless we prepare ourselves for the Good. He's right." He stared at the RAX-1000. " 'Are you ready for the Good?' What does that mean?"

Alexandria said, "It's the type of statement an oracle would say."

Shelley stood up and spoke loudly so that Susan could hear. "Not just teaching the golden rule but living it. We started a non-profit to teach ethical behavior to children. Deborah helped us by finding a guide for our curriculum. The Sufi mystic Attar and his seven valleys."

Stephen grabbed the paper with the conference conclusions. "The voice said an evilness has descended on the world. This is what she is talking about. We're part of it. We have to wean ourselves off all this."

Rachel sat up. "Its effects are everywhere. I see the results in my patients who come for hypnotherapy. Abuse, rape, post-traumatic stress disorders, addictions to everything from drugs and alcohol to food, gambling, television and the Internet."

Robert turned his wheelchair toward Stephen. "Sometimes I think about revenge against the company that killed our parents, but that too would be evil."

Susan came back into the living room with her coffee cup refilled.

Thomas stared at her. "Fracking, toxic waste…"

Shelley looked at her. "Commerce without morality, politics without principles, wealth without work."

Michael continued, "The world's been at war since I was born."

Susan stared back at Thomas. "What, don't blame me for all these things."

Shelley broke the standoff and looked agitated. "It's not government per se. It's the imbalanced institutions stemming from patriarchal values that disrespect female energy in religions, governing, and societies."

Michael stood up. "Dr. Wright said we can't see the big picture and," he got confused for a second, "the other Dr. Wright said," he pointed to Stephen, "we can't see the complexity. She taught us—we're inside it, we can't see it."

Shelley said, "It's the constant fight for control of everything— women, nature, land, resources, other nations. People not taking personal responsibility, letting corporations lead with their focus on money. We're letting it all happen."

Alexandria said, "There have been cultures where a balance is maintained, but they get conquered by the imbalanced ones."

Rachel sighed deeply and brushed strands of hair back under her scarf. "How do we become ready for the Good? There's so much evil, everywhere we turn. We can't fight it."

Michael asked, "Yes, how can one compete with evil and still remain good?"

Susan took a sip of coffee. "You can't."

Stephen inhaled hard. "Good people for years have tried to stand up to evil. They get shot down like Martin Luther King, like John Kennedy. What are we going to do, go tell everyone to wise up and be nice? I'd lose my tenure and be put in the loony bin."

Rachel looked defeated. "Those seem to be our only choices. We can fight evil with violence and become evil ourselves. Or we can ignore evil as so many people have done—let it take us over, enslave us, and eventually kill us."

Stephen said, "Gandhi's approach was nonviolence."

Shelley shook her head. "At this juncture, that's the same as submitting and letting oneself be enslaved or killed. A nonviolent response assumes the evilness will wake up to the horrors of its ways, tire of the killing and eventually stop. But that's less likely to happen going forward. With more and more technology being used, the evil is impersonalized by machines and hidden in corporate bottom lines."

Alexandria nodded. "There are examples historically of people taking a third option. In the Great Jewish Revolts at the start of the first millennium, the rebels were surrounded by the Roman legions on the top of Masada in Judah. Instead of succumbing and becoming slaves, they committed mass suicide. Left their food stores filled to show the Romans that they didn't starve to death but willingly preferred to die than be enslaved."

Rachel slumped into her seat. "That makes our options even more stark. As the world degrades, we can become killers to protect ourselves, be killed by or become slaves to these patriarchal forces, or commit mass suicide."

Anna asked, "What are we going to do?"

Thomas stood up. "Let's publicize Stephen's experience. With his position and my fame, this can go wide."

Rachel sat up, excited.

Susan stepped forward and gestured. "Hold on, that's crazy."

"And we've got proof," Shelley said. "This recording. We'll play it for everyone—it'll change everyone's behavior. It will be hard to remain apathetic after listening to this."

"Who's going to believe you?" Susan sneered. "Hearing voices and discs spinning—don't you hear yourselves? It sounds a bit far-fetched."

Stephen's voice raised up enthusiastically. "I'll risk my whole reputation on it. I'll disseminate it." He started looking through his phone's contact list.

Susan laughed. "Audio recordings like this can be doctored."

"This will work. This will work."

Rachel closed her eyes. "She's right. The only reason we believe it is because we believe our living eyewitness. But not everyone will."

Stephen stopped and put his phone down. "That's true." His shoulders sagged. "Deborah's shaky reputation will be doubly dragged through the mud. Mine too will be questioned."

Susan nodded. "Especially if you start talking about a stolen museum object." She walked toward the fireplace and put her cup on the mantel.

Robert sat up in his chair. "Then let's restage it and video it."

"What?" Stephen spun around to look at him, stunned by the idea.

Shelley said, "It could work. Why not?"

Stephen started pacing. "What do you mean, why not? It wouldn't be like making a documentary."

"If you believe that voice," Susan said, "then activating that disc would risk the lives of everybody on the planet."

"Including our own. And our children." Rachel looked at Shelley who walked over to her.

Shelley's mind was going in all directions. "The voice said, 'Release me to release me.'"

Alexandria said, "It's another oracular statement. It could mean something good or bad. The double wording means that we have to be prepared for the consequences, whatever they are."

Stephen nodded. "It would be a fourth choice. And the video would give us irrefutable proof. Those who survive will be those ready for the Good. They will be the ones who try to build a new planet—hopefully taking into account complexity, striving for respect and balance."

Michael added, "And think of the future the way the Iroquois Nation does. Planning for seven generations." He felt in his pocket and pulled out Jeff's fossil.

"Sorry, I don't buy it," Susan said. "It's got to be some sort of trick." She picked up her purse. "I can't participate in international theft or in some sort of mass hypnosis. I don't believe in God or the judgment day being upon us. And what Deborah did was plain wrong." She turned to Stephen. "Thank you, Stephen, I'm truly sorry for your loss, our loss, but I can't be part of this." She walked out, slamming the front door.

Thomas rubbed his forehead, embarrassed. "Susan's under a lot of pressure right now. Stephen, I'm sorry for what she said."

"Thomas, forget it. We don't have much time and we have to make a huge decision here."

Rachel turned to Alexandria. "What about your family? They aren't here to decide with us."

"I believe they are good men with a capital G. And I believe all good people will survive no matter what it is we'll be releasing."

They all looked at each other and nodded their heads in agreement.

"Now," Alexandria said, "how do we get this thing activated?"

Stephen was excited. "On the volcano, the old woman said it was activated by two good people, pure and in love, one on each side, singing the two songs." He thought of Deborah, remembering standing by her.

Michael said, "We'll have to find two people quickly before Interpol shows up and takes the disc away."

Everyone racked their brains, listening to the hum of the low-level signal. Small chickadees called out.

Stephen looked at Shelley and Rachel. "The two of you. Your love is pure. You can do it."

Rachel stood up. "What are you saying? That we activate the disc?"

Thomas nodded. "Exactly. You can do it."

Shelley stepped backwards. "Communicate with that voice?"

"But this is huge," Rachel said.

Thomas nodded. "Put your love to the test."

Rachel whirled around. "This isn't some football game."

Stephen smiled gently. "Do you believe in your love or not?"

Rachel's eyes welled up with tears as she remembered her mother marching into the synagogue to argue with the Rabbi.

"This is no time for doubt. You've got to put it all on the line."

Stephen agreed with Thomas and walked over to them. "As I recall, there's only one question. 'Are you ready for the Good?' "

Shelley swallowed. "You're right." She turned toward Rachel. "I am."

Rachel took a deep breath. "Love doesn't make you immoral."

"I'll write out the songs," Michael said.

Stephen stood at the end of the loveseat with a video recorder set up on a tripod. Rachel and Shelley stood in the middle of the living room. Alexandria and Michael were behind Stephen.

Stephen asked, "Are you ready to do this?"

Rachel closed her eyes. "We're like two sides to a puzzle. We committed to work together to heal the world. *Ki aza kamoves ahavah.*"

Shelley smiled. " 'For strong till the death is my love.' "

Stephen nodded his head.

Rachel picked up the disc and extended it out to Shelley. Stephen adjusted it so that it they held it the same way he and Deborah had. Using the words Michael wrote out, Rachel sang *The Swallow Song* and Shelley sang *Los Bilbilicos*. Their voices blended beautifully, soaring like two birds in flight. They smiled while they sang to each other with utter love in their eyes. Everyone in the room was taken by the sound.

But nothing happened.

Rachel started crying. "There's something wrong with us." She dropped the Phaistos Disc back onto the loveseat as Alexandria ran to grab it. "Is it true what people have said about gay love?"

Shelley closed her eyes. "No, I won't believe that." She turned to Rachel. "After all we've been through, we can't give in to our own homophobia."

Michael tried to lighten the mood. "The world didn't end. That's a good thing."

Alexandria was pragmatic. "There are many reasons why it didn't working. The songs are being sung in translated tongues. That could be significant."

The phone rang. Everyone looked at Stephen. He answered it. "Yes, I looked through her suitcases. No, I didn't find any disc. Yes, I'm sure." He hung up and rubbed his forehead in agitation. "They're on their way. We probably have an hour or so before they arrive."

"We can figure this out." Robert said, his voice rising.

Shelley excitedly sat down next to Alexandria. "Maybe there's a secret hidden in the original language that didn't cross over the translation barrier."

Alexandria's eyes lit up. "And if some part of the secret is missing, then the whole secret key is not being said."

Stephen's voice crackled. "But these were the two songs we were singing on the volcano."

Rachel breathed rapidly. "What's different then? Think back, Dad."

"An old woman sang along with us. Maybe she added the missing words."

Alexandria leaned forward. "What were you singing? Were these the words exactly?"

Stephen frantically tried to remember. "I was singing *The Swallow Song*. Deborah was teaching it to me as we started. Once I got it, she switched to singing...the other song." He rubbed his forehead. "But then...I started singing...something else...I don't know what it was. I don't even know what language it was."

"An ancient language," Alexandria stood up. "Maybe the whole message was in the ancient version of the song. If Shelley or Rachel sang those words, perhaps the key would work then."

"The words are on the recording." Michael ran over to the coffee table. "Let's relisten to the RAX-1000 and get the ancient words." He touched PLAY.

With Shelley's help, Alexandria copied down the strange words. "I can't be sure these words are correct. It's hard to hear them on the recording with so much going on."

Stephen grabbed the paper out of her hands. "They'll do."

Michael restarted the recording. Holding the ancient words in one hand and the Phaistos Disc between them, Rachel and Shelley sang along with Stephen and Deborah. The words sounded awkward. Fear began closing Rachel's throat. She could hear Rabbi Stern's admonishments. Images flashed before her eyes—meeting Shelley at the synagogue, the Havdallah services, walks on the beach. The surprise of attraction. Her breathing got more and more irregular as she worried her love wasn't good enough.

But again nothing happened.

"Maybe we're not moral." Rachel sounded horrified and couldn't look at her father or Shelley. "We're proving something is wrong with gay people," she yelled over the recording.

"Stop it," Shelley lurched but didn't sound convincing.

Rachael cried out, "If only Deborah had lived. We wouldn't be going through this."

Then the voice began again. "*Call me Gaia, Themis, Rhea, Selene, Hera, Kalliste…*" Its power stopped everyone cold. And after having heard the conference conclusions, the words took on an even more profound meaning.

Thomas whispered, "We have to find a way to activate this disk."

They were frozen in place listening to Deborah's plea for them. And then they heard more.

"*Shema Israel, adonai elohainu, adonai echad. I confess I am in bondage and cannot free myself. For the sake of your Son, Jesus Christ, have mercy on me. La illaha illa Allah Muhammad uv Rasool Allah.*"

The voices had a desperate quality that went beyond anything anyone had ever heard.

Rachel drew in a sharp breath. "What's that?"

Shelley's eyes widened. "I don't know. It almost sounds like…"

Stephen nodded his head. "I remember now. That began playing on the volcano. Deborah was staring at the machine. She must have known what it is."

"Mom did know something else! But she didn't have time to write it down."

The cacophonic voices somehow mixed hopelessness with hope as they repeated the same words over and over.

Shelley spoke in a whisper. "It sounds like prayers in different languages. I can hear the Hebrew prayer."

Alexandria cocked her head. "I hear Arabic."

Stephen said, "And I hear a Christian one. What does it mean?"

No one knew.

"Let's not get discouraged," Alexandria said. "There are so many variables. We have no real idea what we're doing. It's as if we're suddenly asked to defuse a nuclear bomb."

Stephen hit his fist in his hand. "We must be overlooking something."

Shelley shook her head. "Let's go through it again. Quickly."

Rachel started listing everything. "The swallows are singing a human song. The nightingales are singing the same song. Richard Fariña stole the tune and wrote new lyrics to the old Ladino song. We have the translation of the ancient words. The magnetic poles have shifted and now one is over Santorini…"

Michael interrupted. "But the songs aren't exactly the same. It was the first thing we noticed in our study group."

Rachel turned to look at him. "What?"

"One of the tunes goes up where the other one goes down."

They all started trying to remember the songs.

Michael was the first to get it. "The song's not stolen, they're parallel songs! They're two separate songs."

They looked at him not understanding.

"Dr. Wright kept trying to figure out the connection between the songs. Fariña didn't steal anything from the Ladino song. He heard it from a primary source. There are two parallel tracks through time, the swallow track, the nightingale track. They each have their own meaning."

Rachel looked confused. "So what?"

Shelley got excited. "To find the right words, we have to find something that has ancient words on it with two parallel tracks."

Stunned, they looked at each other and then at the coffee table. "The Phaistos Disc!" Shelley whispered. "The two songs must be on the two sides of the disc!"

Rachel said, "The original words to the swallow song and the nightingale song."

"But how can we decode them?" Stephen asked.

"I can do it." Alexandria nodded.

They looked at her. Shelley asked, "Without a key or similar documents?"

"The writing on the disc could be an alphabet, syllabry or rebus," Alexandria said. "All were in existence at that time in the second millennium BC."

"Can you figure it out?" Rachel asked.

Alexandria was holding the paper with the words. "Armed with this, I can. No one else has had this. I'll have to figure out what kind of language it was, whether it was Indo-European or Semitic. It's unclear who the early settlers on the island were. They could have been from Anatolia, mainland Greece, or even Africa."

"How long will it take you?" Stephen asked.

"Hard to say." Alexandria stared at the disc. "I'll go to my office at Stanford where I have ancient dictionaries and decoding tools."

Stephen shook his head. "There's no time. Interpol is coming."

Rachel stared at Deborah's journal. "It's not the language."

"What?"

"In her journal, she says that a Persian scholar Abi-atoon told her the language doesn't matter. The secret transcends it. The true meaning is held in whatever language you sing in."

Robert said, "So even the English lyrics should activate the disc."

"But they're not doing it." Rachel slumped down, feeling for the pendant around her neck. She felt hopeless. "Deborah's sacrifice was for naught. The evilness of the patriarchy has won."

Stephen stared out at the birdfeeders, watching the small flying visitors come and go. There is a mystery to life—shifts can happen without awareness. He felt like his eyes had suddenly opened. "There's one more variable," he said.

Shelley asked, "What's that?"

"The location. Perhaps it only works at places like Santorini. Geologically, Santorini is very powerful. I mean, the magnetic pole has shifted there."

Alexandria said, "Clans that worshipped the goddess were pushed onto those islands in the Mediterranean as the rest of the lands were taken over by warring patriarchal tribes. The last groups were on islands like Crete and Santorini before they all disappeared. No one knows what happened to them. Killed by invaders or assimilated as slaves."

"So, that means…" Rachel looked at her.

Shelley sat up, opening her eyes wide. "Santorini is sacred." She turned to Stephen. "You said that the RAX-1000 started spontaneously printing something at the volcano?"

Stephen nodded.

"And there must be other sacred places."

Alexandria said, "There are many in the world. They get reused as one tribe replaces another and a new religion takes hold. Like a marketing ploy by invaders to gain converts from the native people. But the meaning associated with the place gets lost. Dig into an old Christian church and you'll find a pagan temple or sacred landscape."

Rachel asked, "Are there any here in the States? Nearby?"

"We would have to do a search to find them," Alexandria said.

Michael asked, "Dr. Wright, where did the machine print out?"

"I don't know. I've got the printouts in the other room." He ran to get them and then rushed back, spreading the papers out on the coffee table.

Rachel said, "Mom marked the two where she got results—the Mission of San Juan Capistrano and the island of Samos. Here's a printout from the Eileithyia cave on Crete." Her voice broke. "She didn't mark the fourth one from Santorini."

Stephen stared at the printouts. "I've looked at lots of seismograph recordings, and these all have the same signature. She may have been recording bird songs, but there were no birds in the cave or on the volcano."

Shelley stared at the printouts. "These sites are places sacred to various religions. Samos was Hera's birthplace."

Alexandria nodded. "Crete shows evidence of a goddess civilization at many sites, especially caves."

Rachel touched the pendant. "I wonder if that's where the pendant is from."

Shelley completed the list. "San Juan Capistrano is a Christian mission and was a sacred place to the Acjachemen tribe before that."

Stephen laughed. "This machine is sensing sacred places. We just have to find another one in the next twenty minutes that's not in Greece or southern California."

Playing with Jeff's fossil, Michael said, "I know where there's one nearby."

CHAPTER 33

STANDING LOOKING WEST below the summit of Mt. Tamalpais, Stephen could hear the crash of the ocean waves. Live oak trees scented the already moist air. Under it, the smell of a distant forest fire burned. Above him sounded the *keeer-r-r-r* of a hawk soaring on a thermal in the sky. He looked up, his eyes burning at the feeling that Deborah was speaking to him. California poppies and purple lupine protruded below the rock outcropping. The recorder sat on a tripod.

Robert faced him looking east. Anna stood next to him. Thomas looked south. Michael stood looking north, Alexandria standing next to him. They created a circle around Shelley and Rachel.

Susan arrived out of breath.

"Susan!" Thomas broke into a big grin. "You came back."

She kissed him hard on the mouth. "It was fear. I was afraid of being hurt politically. Of a potential scandal." She shook her head and looked at Stephen. "But now's not the time for fear, it's the time for change—and Deborah was right to point it out."

Stephen nodded. "Thank you, Susan. I knew you'd see the light. Thomas, can you start us off?"

Thomas kicked up a piece of black dirt contemplating what to say. "Deborah began this journey with a scientific question and a personal question from her daughter. Both questions opened a whole new world to her. We may never understand everything she experienced on that journey but we do know morality underlay both questions. Secular and religious ethical systems have suggested codes of conduct based on a sense of duty, consequences, or character. We have an economic system based on the bottom line of revenue and profit margins. In a world of the Good, the new economic system has to have a new bottom line, not just profits, but one that includes a sense of sacrifice for others and an ethic that preserves the integrity of living systems. An economic system not based on getting, but on giving, out of a sense of duty, consequences, or character. I pledge to develop a system of exchange based on morality." He looked across from him.

Michael could smell the distant forest fire. It reminded him of Jeff. He pulled the fossilized seashell out of his pocket. "My friends all think I'm just a surfer, only into pleasure and fun. Because of her passion for teaching, Dr. Wright changed my life when she taught us the impossibility of seeing the big picture of how everything is connected to everything else. Sure I like fun, but fun with a conscience. I can see the difference between right and wrong. Not all competition is bad, not all cooperation is good. Dr. Wright taught us how both are needed. In the world of the Good, there will be a balance between competition and cooperation. And when my best friend Jeff died, I learned about the Great Law of the Iroquois which is to work for the benefit of seven generations into the future. This, too, is in the world of the Good. Everything is connected to everything else, in time and in space." Michael looked over to Stephen who nodded. He smiled, shrugged, and looked next to him to Alexandria.

She looked down for a second to collect her thoughts. "I've spent my academic life studying ancient languages. It has made me educated but not necessarily wise. It's not enough to just have knowledge. Wisdom involves examining one's self. It involves character. The word character comes from the ancient Greek *charaktêr* which refers to a mark impressed into a coin. When I met Deborah, she was in the process of trying to understand something. She had character and taught us all. Just because you know how to do something, it doesn't mean you should do it. In the world of the Good, knowledge will be tempered by this wonderful mantra of Deborah's that this boy, Michael, has shared. We're inside it, we can't see it." Alexandria turned to her right and nodded to Stephen.

Stephen knelt down and picked a white petal from a jewelflower sticking out of a crack in the rocks. As he stood up, his face glowed in the setting sun. "Science organizes knowledge in testable predictions and explanations. The scientist does this detached from consequences and distractions, being open to exploration for the truth as Deborah did pursuing her questions. We scientists are even encouraged to write in the passive voice, as if the experiments have no human intervention. But this approach takes the humanity out of the work. Science evolved devoid of ethics. In the world of the Good, science will help make wise decisions with selfless values attached." Stephen's tears ran down his cheeks as he looked over to Anna across the circle.

Her back to the setting sun, Anna spoke next. "I was poor most of my life, my immigrant parents struggling to raise my three sisters and me. Joseph and I were blessed with a beautiful daughter Sarah. I learned about the depths of grief when Sarah and her husband died due to the immorality of an unnecessary accident. Now I am blessed with two—excuse me, three—exceptional grandchildren," she smiled at Rachel, "thank you to the two Dr. Wrights. And with a great deal of monetary wealth. But wealth without work is nothing. That money is being used to teach others to not work for wealth, but to work for humanity and for everything on the planet. In the world of the Good, there is no 'other,' only all of us helping each other in a unified way." Anna finished and nodded to Susan.

Susan closed her eyes for a moment. "I've always thought that politics is about power. It's how I got ahead in Washington." She opened her eyes. "Deborah taught me an important lesson which, frankly, I am astonished by. When I left you all in anger, I swore I was justified in my stance. Halfway home, I began thinking over what Deborah had experienced up on that volcano. Politicians, like scientists, have a great deal of responsibility. As young Mr. Michael has pointed out, we can't see the big picture. However, politicians have to make decisions based on incomplete information. And those decisions affect people's lives down to the core of their being. So we politicians need principles. Deborah stood up to that voice—whatever it was—on that volcano and pleaded for her daughter's life. If she can do that, I can make a pledge that in the world of the Good—if I survive this situation here—I will stand for all your lives out of a sense of sacrifice and moral obligation to help make your lives better and to be a better steward for the common resources." Susan hung her head down when she was finished and then turned to Robert on her right.

Robert adjusted the red blanket across his legs. "I'm the man everyone has to lean down to speak with, the man with a joke. Shelley's younger brother. My life changed when I was eight years old and I experienced nothingness. Instead of becoming a Rabbi, I became a singer. The word 'worship' comes from an Old English word meaning to give worth to something. True worship involves translating prayer into action—such is the Jewish concept of *tikkun olam*—to heal the

THE SWALLOW AND THE NIGHTINGALE

world. I believe Deborah was doing that on that volcano. In the world of the Good, churches and temples will not stand in judgment but in service. They will open their doors, and religious people will sacrifice by performing selfless service for all creatures and for nature." Robert looked at Shelley in the middle of the circle.

Shelley searched out everyone's eyes. She had a bright smile on her face. In her hand, she held Deborah's toy compass. "There's a myth about two sisters who are transformed into a swallow and a nightingale. My life also was transformed by an immoral act. As a result, I have strove to find a way to counterbalance the patriarchy and the evil it brings with its imbalanced, cloudy thinking. But we cannot resist evil. World peace begins at the personal level of connection. Deborah led me to the Sufi poet Attar whose spiritual awakening involved seven valleys on a path toward peace, connection, and enlightenment. I led her to Gandhi's seven social sins. In the Jewish Kaballah, seven symbolizes perfection achieved through natural means. When enlightened people avoid these social sins, they create an enlightened society. And what Michael reminds us today—making decisions to benefit seven generations according to the Great Law of the Iroquois—creates a path toward a peaceful future. That is the world of the Good." She smiled at everyone. "And you all embody it." She turned toward Rachel.

Rachel squeezed her hand and let go. "My mother was on a path we only vaguely understand. While on it, she showed me what's real in a very deep sense. This relationship between mother and child is probably the most important relationship anyone ever has. It's permanent and non-voluntary. It's not between equals so it imbues responsibility for teaching another human being. Let us build a world of the Good that's not based on contracts but on relationships. Let us build a world that has rights—the rights of life, liberty, and the pursuit of happiness. But let us honor those rights with a twist: we need these rights because without them, we cannot raise our children." She was silent for a moment. "When we lost Deborah, we lost so much. We've reconstructed some of what she learned, but there must be more. Like this pendant." She touched it. "Where did Deborah get it, what does it mean. We don't know. What the recorded prayers are, we don't know." She pointed to the compass in Shelley's hand. "We found this toy among her things. What it meant to her, we don't know. But I think we

Page 340

can all agree, in the world of the Good, the only thing that matters is the love of the Earth and everything in it. The world we rebuild will be right-side up, not upside-down."

In the distance, a siren sounded.

Shelley handed the Phaistos Disc to Rachel who began *The Swallow Song* as she held the disc up in her right hand. Shelley put her left hand on the other side and began *Los Bilbilicos*. Their voices blended in beautiful harmony. They mixed the old and new words, their sound soaring as if gathering the mysteries of the ages. The others joined in.

They had no idea if it was going to work. The love between the two people had to be pure. If the hands that try to activate it are not pure, the two will die and destroy the disc.

Rachel thought about what the spirit voice said: *Are you ready for the Good?* Am I, she wondered. She felt safe wearing Deborah's pendant.

The disc started to feel warm. Rachel felt it begin to spin against her hand. The light changed, filling the sky with a bright expanding aura. The low-level hum of the interference signal stopped.

An ethereal sound of hundreds of voices arose. The songs intertwined tunes and words in some unimaginable way. A chorus of other voices began weaving in 'Holy is the Earth and all within her, Holy is the star-filled void in which She spins, Holy is the light in whom we live, Holy is the Earth and all within Her.'

Rachel felt lifted by the realization that this was proof for Rabbi Stern's challenge. They were proving the morality of their love. By surviving the activation of this disc, they were ready for the Good. She placed her left hand above her womb and felt new life kicking.

Stephen looked at the recorder—it was capturing everything. In the distance, alarms started as driverless cars crashed and fires began. People not ready for the Good were disappearing all over the world. Some machines carried on without operators, others ground to a halt. The siren stopped.

Circling above Mt. Tamalpais two birds flew, more as lovers than sisters, singing two beautiful songs in crystal clear voices, their harmony exquisite. With graceful bodies and slow-flapping wings, they soared through the clouds, Chelidona the swallow singing the Song of the Earth, and her sister Philomela the nightingale singing the Song of Love.

This time, it wasn't a warning. This time, it was for real.

Are you ready for the Good?

THE END

GLOSSARY

acupuncture – an ancient Chinese medical approach based on a theory that bodily functions are regulated by energy.

Al-Andalus (Arabic) – medieval Islamic state that at one point included the entire Iberian peninsula. By the 12th century, during the Almohad Dynasty, it only covered the southern portion.

Alaudidae – the family of passerine birds containing larks.

Aleinu l'shabeach la'Adon hakol. (Hebrew) – "It is our duty to praise God"

al-Jazā'er (Arabic) - Algiers

allopathic –Western medical approach using pharmacological agents to treat or suppress symptoms

altruism – the principle or practice of concern for the welfare of others.

Al-Wādi al-Kabīr (Arabic, "great valley") – Arabic name for the Guadalquivir River in Spain

anthropology – the study of humankind, past and present.

anti-Semitism – prejudice against Jews for reasons connected to their heritage.

Ars longa, vita brevis (Latin) – "art is long, life is short."

Ashkenazi – Jews of France, Germany, and Eastern Europe, and their descendants.

avian – of or relating to birds.

Baḥr al-Rūm (Arabic) – Mediterranean Sea

Bat mitzvah (Hebrew) – Jewish coming of age ritual for girls at age 12. (A boy's *bar mitzvah* occurs when he is 13).

basari (Hebrew for "meat") – Jewish law prohibits the mixing of meat and milk based on a verse in the Book of Exodus.

bikur cholim (Hebrew) – refers to the mitzvah to visit and extend aid to the sick.

bimah (Hebrew "elevated place") – platform in the synagogue on which stands the desk from which the Torah is read.

bioaccumulation – accumulation by absorption of substances such as pesticides or other organic chemicals in the tissues of an organism.

biomagnifications – process whereby certain substances such as pesticides or heavy metals move up the food chain and are eaten by fish which in turn are eaten by large birds, animals or humans (from Wikipedia).

boureka – a pastry stuffed with cheese, potato, spinach or mushrooms.

brachiopods -- marine animals that have hard shells. In ancient China, these stone fossils were thought to be swallows.

casada (Spanish) – "married"

Centigrade or Celsius – a scale and unit of measurement for temperature. Used by scientists and most of the world.

cholent (Yiddish) or *hamin* (Hebrew) – a traditional Jewish stew, simmered overnight and eaten for lunch on the Sabbath when Jewish law prohibits certain activities such as cooking.

davening (Yiddish) – to pray

Dhu'l-Hijja (Arabic) – 12th month of Islamic calendar, marking the end of the year.

Dios mio (Spanish) – "my God"

d'var Torah (Hebrew) – a talk related to the Torah portion given by the Rabbi.

espagnol (also called Ladino or Judeo-Spanish) – a language derived from Old Spanish enriched by Semitic vocabulary, such as Hebrew, Arabic and Ottoman Turkish.

efxarasto (Greek) – "thank you"

etes-vous bien (French) – "are you okay?"

Fourier analysis – the study of the way general functions may be approximated.

fracking – (short for hydraulic fracturing) – a process whereby rock is fractured by a pressurized liquid in order to extract underground gas and petroleum.

fractal processing – algorithms for synthesizing, analyzing, and processing various classes of signals.

gay – term for male homosexual.

greenwashing – deceptive marketing to create the perception that an organization is environmentally friendly.

Haftarah (Hebrew "parting") – selection read from the books of the Prophets that is thematically linked to the Torah portion.

hajj (Arabic) – pilgrimage to Mecca that takes place in the last month of the year; all Muslims are expected to make at least once during their lifetime.

Halakhah (Hebrew) – Jewish Law; increases spirituality in a person's life, turns the most trivial, mundane acts into acts of religious significance. (from jewfac.org)

hamin (Hebrew) – *see* cholent.

haqiqat (Arabic "truth") – a higher level of consciousness, one of 4 stages in Sufism.

harei at mekudeshet li (Hebrew) – "You are hereby betrothed to me."

THE SWALLOW AND THE NIGHTINGALE

Hatzi Kaddish (Hebrew "Half Kaddish") – the Kaddish is a hymn of praises to God. The *Hatzi Kaddish* separates sections of the service.

Havdallah (Hebrew) – a Jewish religious ceremony marking the symbolic end of Shabbat to usher in the new week.

hazzan (Hebrew) – a Jewish cantor who leads the congregation in singing prayers.

heterosexuality – romantic attraction to a person of the opposite gender.

High Holidays – Jewish New Year and Day of Atonement, and the days between.

Hirundinidae – a family of the Passeriformes order containing the swallows.

holistic – concerned with wholes or with complete systems rather than with the analysis of, treatment of, or dissection into parts. (Free Dictionary)

Holocaust – systematic mass murder of approximately six million Jews by Nazi Germany between 1940-1945.

homophobia – an aversion to homosexuals.

homosexuality – romantic attraction to a person of the same gender.

huevos rancheros (Spanish "rancher's eggs") – Mexican egg dish consisting of fried eggs served on corn tortillas topped with chili sauce.

Id al-Fitr (Arabic) – religious holiday celebrated by Muslims marking the end of Ramadan.

infradian – repeated cycles that are larger than 24 hours.

Ishbiliya (Arabic) – Arabic name for Sevilla.

Ladino – *see* espagnol.

lesbian – term for female homosexual.

Kabbalah (Hebrew) – Jewish mysticism; the Tree of Life is the central mystical symbol.

kali týchi (Greek) – "good luck."

kalispera (Greek) – "good evening"

ketz kol basar (Hebrew) – "the end of all flesh" from Genesis 6:13.

Ki aza kamoves ahavah —— (Hebrew) "For strong till the death is my love" – Song of Songs 8:6.

ki male'ah ha'erets chamas mippeneihem; v'hinni mashchitam et ha'aretz (Hebrew) – "For the Earth is filled with violence through them; and, behold, I will destroy them with the Earth." Genesis 6:12-13.

kiddushin (Hebrew "sanctification") – first part of two-part Jewish marriage; creates the legal relationship without the mutual obligations.

klutz (from the *Yiddish*) – a clumsy person.

mathnawi (Persian) – a characteristic form of Persian poetry that combines narrative and didactical elements (Lewisohn 1999, page 365).

Mazandaran Sea – the Caspian Sea (also known as the *Bahr-e Qazvin*).

mazel tov (Hebrew "good luck") – expresses congratulations.

mehitzah (Hebrew "partition") – divider used to separate men and women. From an old Jewish practice during the times of the temple in Jerusalem.

mezuzah (Hebrew "doorpost" plural *mezuzot*) – parchment with prayer from Torah placed on doorways.

mija (Spanish slang for "*mi hija*") – "my daughter."

mijo (Spanish slang for "*mi hijo*") – "my son."

minyan (Hebrew "count") – quorum of ten Jewish male adults needed for certain religious obligations.

Mishnah (Hebrew "repetition") –oral law that clarifies and systemizes the commandments of the Torah.

mitzvot (Hebrew; singular is *mitzvah*) – commandments God gave to the Jewish people.

necropsy – an autopsy performed on an animal.

ornithology – branch of zoology concerning the study of birds.

oscines – singing birds, subgroup of Passerine.

pardonne moi, s'il vous plait (French) – "excuse me, please."

passerine – perching birds (in the order Passeriformes).

para kalo (Greek) – "you're welcome."

patriarchy – a social system in which the male is the primary authority figure, central to social organization and the central roles of political leadership, moral authority, and control of property, and where fathers hold authority over women and children (from Wikipedia).

Petrochelidon pyrrhonota – scientific name for American cliff swallow.

plinian – eruptions marked by columns of gas and volcanic ash extending high into the stratosphere.

PMS – emotional symptoms related to women's menstrual cycle.

pozzolana – a siliceous material from volcanic ash now used as an additive to Portland cement (see Wikipedia).

Qamar-al-deen (Arabic) – classic Ramadan drink.

que lástima (Spanish) – "that's too bad."

THE SWALLOW AND THE NIGHTINGALE

¿qué pasó? (Spanish) – "what happened?"

Quran (Arabic "the recitation") – central religious text of Islam.

Rabbi (Hebrew "my master") – a teacher of the Torah.

racism – views reflecting the belief that humanity is divided into distinct biological groups called races and that members of a certain race share certain attributes which make that group as a whole inferior or superior. There is little scholarly agreement about the meaning of the concept "race". (from Wikipedia)

Ramadan (Arabic) – ninth month of Islamic calendar, observed by fasting.

sabbatical – a period of paid leave granted to a college teacher for study or travel.

seismograph – instrument used to detect and record earthquakes.

semantics – the study of meaning.

Sephardic – descendants of Jews from Spain, Portugal, North Africa and Middle East.

seven-pointed candelabra – in Hebrew, *menorah* – a symbol of Judaism.

sexism – discrimination based on a person's sex.

shaakshuka (Arabic "mixture") – eggs poached in tomatoes, chili peppers, onions.

shabbat shalom (Hebrew "Sabbath peace") – "may your day of no work be peaceful."

Shacharit (Hebrew) – morning prayers.

shavuah tov (Hebrew) – "good week."

shomrim (Hebrew "watchers") – Jewish ritual of watching over the deceased person from the time of death until burial.

shiva (Hebrew "seven") – Jewish week-long mourning period for parents or children.

shul (Yiddish) – synagogue.

sinistrophobia – fear of left-handed people or left-handedness.

sociobiology – field of science based on the assumption that social behavior has resulted from evolution (from Wikipedia).

spanakopita (Greek "spinach pie") –pastry stuffed with spinach and feta mixture.

stin ygia sas (Greek) – "to your health."

Sufism – the inner, mystical dimension of Islam. (Wikipedia)

synergy – the interaction of multiple elements in a system to produce an effect greater than the sum of their individual effects.

taifa (Arabic) – an independent Muslim-ruled principality in the Iberian peninsula.

tallis (Ashkenazi Hebrew; *tallit* in Sephardic Hebrew; plural *tallism*) – ritual shawl worn during certain Jewish religious services and ceremonies. (from Wikipedia)

Talmud – Rabbinical discussions and commentaries on the Oral law.

Tanach – the Jewish Bible.

teleological – with an end purpose.

Ten Commandments – set of biblical principles found in the Hebrew Bible in Exodus 34:28, Deuteronomy 4:13 and 10:4.

tenure – a permanent post, for example as a teacher or professor.

Thraupidae –the family of passerine birds containing tanagers.

tikkun olam (Hebrew "world repair") – pursuit of social action and social justice.

Torah – Jewish Written Law, consists of the first 5 books of the Hebrew Bible.

t'shuva – (Hebrew "return") -- the concept of repentance in Judaism. (see Wolpe 1995, p 24).

tsunami – waves caused by the displacement of a large volume of a body of water.

UCC -- the United Church of Christ.

ultradian – repeated cycles that are smaller than 24 hours.

USGS – United States Geological Survey.

yarmulke (Hebrew) -- a hemispherical cap worn by Jewish men to cover their heads.

Za'atar is a spice mixture popular through the Middle Eat prepared using spices such as dried thyme, oregano, marjoram, toasted sesame seeds, salt, and sumac.

Zohar (Hebrew "splendor") – the foundational work of the Kabbalah.

zooplankton – organisms drifting in oceans, seas, and bodies of fresh water.

ENDNOTES

All characters are fictional, as is the RAX-1000. Real people are listed here. Places are real except for Synagogue Sepharad, Iron Horse Bookstore, Green Parrot Café, the Carmel music store, Berkeley United Church of Christ, and the interior of the *Rectorado* building. All world events are real except for the conference. The dates for some have been changed. In reality, the swallows at San Juan Capistrano are not dying and do not sing human songs; they just aren't returning.

Page 3 WORLD NEWS: New Jersey had a 5.3-magnitude earthquake November 29, 1783. A 7.2-magnitude quake hit 110 miles from Tijuana, Mexico on April 4, 2010. A 7.0 Earthquake hit Guadalajara, Mexico on December 4, 2012.

Page 9 The Milhouse Effect is fictional.

Page 11 St. Patrick –5th century Christian missionary

Page 12 "a billion birds die" — when tangling with humans, birds die due to collisions, pesticides, loss of habitat, and cats. See Migratory Bird Mortality

THE SWALLOW AND THE NIGHTINGALE

(2002). Stutchbury (2007) calls birds "nature's blue-collar workers, helping to sustain the environment." Yearly counts show that songbirds are on the decline.

Page 12 Operating since 1968, the San Onofre Nuclear power plant in Southern California closed in 2013.

Page 17 The swallows spend the winter in Goya, Argentina.

Page 17 "The Sephardic…" Over 1,000 years ago, Jews separated into Ashkenazi and Sephardim (see glossary). The Ashkenazi developed different denominations, but the Sephardim did not: Sephardim are Orthodox. In the Ashkenazi tradition, there are Orthodox, Conservatives, Reform, Reconstructionist, and Secular Humanism movements.

Page 20 "…asked Rabbi Stern to marry us." As of 2014, neither Sephardic nor the Orthodox Ashkenazi allow same-sex marriage. The Ashkenazi Reform and Reconstructionists allow same-sex marriage; the Conservative movement established guidelines for same-sex marriages (see the Committee on Jewish Law and Standards at www.rabbinicalassembly.org).

Page 20 The Talmud says there are 613 commandments or *mitzvot* in the Torah that must be followed.

Page 21 California same-sex marriage was permanently legalized in 2013 (although it was legal for some months in 2008).

Page 22 "won't shake your hand"—as part of *Halakhah* (Jewish law), Orthodox men and women do not touch in public as a sign of respect.

Page 25 "Orthodox rulings have changed…"—see Greenberg (2004, p. 16)

Page 28 Farid ud-Din Hamid Muhammad bin Ibrahim (1142-1220), known as Attar, was a Sufi master. He wrote *Mantiq al-tayr (The Conference of the Birds)*, a type of poem called a *mathnawi* (see glossary). Attar did travel but not to Spain. During his lifetime, the Almohads ruled Moorish Iberia, the southern part of Spain where Seville is located. My fictional story combines aspects of Attar's life (e.g., Shah (1999, pgs 104-14)) with narrative and didactical elements from his poem.

Page 29 "…the nightingale sings out…"—the language of birds has been postulated in myth as a magical language to communicate with the initiated (see Wikipedia/Language of the birds)

Page 35 WORLD NEWS: Hawaii's Mauna Loa volcano erupted in March 1984. Alaska has over 100 volcanoes. Beached whales—see Podesta et al (2006).

Page 36 Earth Day is April 22. Created in 1970 after the massive 1969 oil spill in Santa Barbara, California, it led to the creation of the US Environmental Protection Agency and the passage of the Clean Air, Clean Water, and Endangered Species Acts (from earthday.org). Earth Day Awareness Fair on the Berkeley campus is fictional.

Page 37 Sir James Galway (b. 1939) – virtuoso flute player from Northern Ireland.

Page 37 The Enigma Code was used by the Germans in WWII for enciphering military communications.

Page 38 "Space and time scales..."—see page 167.

Page 38 Competition and cooperation exist through nature—see (Arbib 1989) and see Rolston essay in (Callicott 1987, p. 246-274).

Page 39 "People as cells and collectives..."—see A. Iberall (2014), Soodak and Iberall (1978).

Page 39 Isaac Newton (1642-1727) – English physicist and mathematician. Formulated law of universal gravitation which states how masses in the universe attract each other (Wikipedia).

Page 39 The prefrontal cortex of the human brain is involved in planning complex cognitive behavior, personality expression, decision making, and moderating social behavior. The vestibular system contributes to balance and spatial orientation in mammals (Wikipedia). For more on the brain, see Kandel, Schwartz and Jessell (2000)

Page 40 "dynamic balance"—energy is being expended to guarantee the balanced condition.

Page 40 Johnny Carson (1925-2005)—host of The Tonight Show, a talk show on late-night television; occasionally did skits involving a character Carnac who could psychically divine answers to unknown questions.

Page 41 Helium balloons float because they are filled with a gas lighter than air.

Page 41 "...the global global problem"—James Lovelock's Gaia Hypothesis suggests that the biosphere (living organisms) is a self-regulating entity with the capacity to keep the planet healthy by controlling the environment (Lovelock 1995, p. xv); this in effect would be the 'global' global problem.

Page 44 WORLD NEWS: Volatile Organic Compounds (VOC) —see www.epa.gov/iaq/voc.html; Herbicide—see (Shehata, 2012), (Samsel and Seneff, 2013); Engineered corn as pesticide—see (Lemaux, 2008)

Page 46 "...genetically engineer food" – see pages 44, 50

Page 50 WORLD NEWS: Smart grid—see lessEMF.com. Cell phone transmitter stations—see Wolf and Wolf (2004). Toxic waste dumping – see Troubled Waters, 2012, p. 1). Nuclear spent fuel—see necir-bu.org/investigations/the-canary-in-the-nuclear-plant-the-spent-fuel-crisis/main-story/. Plastic in Pacific—see Gold et al (2013); Greenhouse gases—see IPCC (2007, p. 2);

Page 50 Mozart and pet starling—Rothenberg (2005, p. 188).

Page 52 "Genetically-engineered corn and soybeans are linked to cancer." From Séralini et al (2012), Séralini et al (2013).

THE SWALLOW AND THE NIGHTINGALE

Page 53 "What you resist persists" was said by Carl Jung (1875-1961)—Swiss psychiatrist.

Page 53 "...laws about interracial couples marrying"—in the United States, anti-miscegenation laws were declared unconstitutional in 1967.

Page 54 Magnetic poles are locations on the planet's surface where the planet's magnetic field lines are vertical; during the 20th century, the North Magnetic Pole has moved 1100 kilometers (Wikipedia).

Page 54 Japan's Tohoku 9.0 earthquake in 2011 caused a tsunami up to 133 feet high and 10,000 aftershocks.

Page 54-55 "genetically-engineered perfectly safe to eat." —see www.monsanto.com.

Page 55 "...adverse health effects of electromagnetic waves..." —see page 50. "a smart energy grid..."—see energy.gov/oe/technology-development/smart-grid.

Page 55 "Coal-fired power plants..."—see www.epa.gov/cleanenergy/energy-and-you/affect/coal.html

Page 56 "...toxic waste being dumped in a city in Africa." -- on August 19, 2006, a ship offloaded 500 tons of toxic waste at Port of Abidjan, Côte d'Ivoire; the waste caused burns, vomiting, diarrhea, and loss of consciousness; 17 people died and 30,000 were injured; the company Trafigura agreed to pay claimants while still denying any wrong doing. (Wikipedia).

Page 56 Dumping mine waste—see page 50.

Page 57 "Mercury turns toxic in water..."—see Mercury Alert (2011, page 4). "birds eat the fish." This is an example of biomagnifications (see glossary).

Page 57 "Carbon accumulating in our atmosphere..." —see IPCC (2007).

Page 57 "ancient Pueblo Indians in New Mexico..." (Diamond 2005, pp 136--156)

Page 58 "51,000 tons of spent nuclear fuel"—see page 50.

Page 58 "10,000 year old picnic is over'—see McKibben (2010), Orr (2009).

Page 59 "climate change..." —see IPCC (2007). "...in 1896..." In 1896, Nobel laureate Svante August Arrhenius (1859-1927) calculated how changes in atmospheric carbon dioxide could raise the surface temperature of the planet (Wikipedia). A 3.6 degree Fahrenheit rise is equal to a two degree Centigrade rise—see IPCC (2007).

Page 59 Plastic in ocean—see page 50. For why we don't act in response to climate change, see Gifford (2011).

Page 59 "...transform ethane into plastics...hydrocarbon fuels...net-zero energy...CO2 capture technology"—these are activities being done by a variety of companies such as Dow (www.dow.com/sustainability), GE (www.gecitizenship.com/focus-areas/economy/sustainable-systems),

Schlumberger (www.slb.com) and www.co2captureproject.org/. For "solar shingles" – see www.dowpowerhouse.com

Page 60 "…large-scale reengineering of the weather"—there is much disagreement about whether this is occurring. See Wikipedia/climate engineering or www.geoengineeringwatch.org. See House 1996. See Wikipedia/Cloud_seeding.

Page 61 The black suits are fictional.

Page 61 William H. Masters (1915-2001) and Virginia E. Johnson (1925-2013) pioneered research on human sexual response. Alfred Kinsey (1894-1956) – American biologist, did research on human sexuality.

Page 62 Bonobo chimpanzees use sexual activity for many social functions. (Wikipedia).

Page 62 "And God said unto Noah, the end of all flesh is come before me; I will destroy them with the Earth"—from Genesis 6:13. "Homosexuality is an abomination"—Leviticus 18:22. "Homosexuals will not inherit the kingdom of God"—1 Corinthians 6:9.

Page 64 Castro Street. The Castro District of San Francisco is one of the first gay neighborhoods in the United States (Wikipedia).

Page 65 WORLD NEWS: Oil pipeline bursts – e.g., Exxon's Pegasus pipeline bursting in Mayflower, Arkansas in 2013 and spilling about 6,000 barrels of bitumen (with hydrocarbon diluents) (Wikipedia) ; Cancer alley—see Billings (2005); Tropical diseases spreading—see Irfan (2012)

Page 68 WORLD NEWS: Massive Gulf oil spill – e.g., the Deepwater Horizon oil rig explosion in 2010 which killed 11 people and discharged about 4.9 million barrels; 1.9 million gallons of Corexit dispersants were used to disperse the oil (see Wikipedia; also see Atlas and Hazen (2011)). Deformed shrimp –see (Sewall, 2012). Sink holes—see Wikipedia/Bayou_Corne_sinkhole. Fire season—see (Pittalwala, 2013).

Page 69 Bob Dylan (b. 1941), Phil Ochs (1940-1976), and Joan Baez (b. 1941) are American folksingers.

Page 71 "Religions based on a book follow morals" Deontology is the ethical position that judges the morality of an action based on the action's adherence to a rule or rules; some Rabbis say this is the underlying nature of Jewish ethics; others say it is secular and that Jewish ethics is about creating a holy person imitating God; in contrast, utilitarianism emphasizes the consequences of one's actions. Virtue ethics emphasizes moral character. See more at p. 341. Judaism's central teaching is that each human being is created in the image of God (Wolpe 1995, p 6).

Page 72 Immanuel Kant (1724-1804) – German philosopher. John Stuart Mills (1806-1873) – British philosopher. St. Augustine (354-430) – early Christian theologian.

Page 72 Hammurabi Code – Babylonian law code from 1772 BC.

THE SWALLOW AND THE NIGHTINGALE

Page 72 "Someday we'll be legally responsible for the consequences of others' actions" —see Iberall (1971, p. 305).

Page 72 "The Twilight Zone" – TV anthology series with science fiction stories (1959-1964)

Page 72 Socrates (469-399 BC) – Greek philosopher.

Page 73 "If sexuality was for only that…"—see Shlain (2003, p. 16).

Page 74 "women used to be priests"—see Torjesen (1995).

Page 74-75 "our hierarchical view of the world…it's all about competition…white privilege…"—Shiva (2005, p 62) points out that competition hasn't always been the driving force in human societies. For white privilege and unacknowledged male privilege, see (McIntosh 1988).

Page 75 Richard Fariña (1937-1966) and his wife Mimi Baez Fariña (1945-2001) were American singer-songwriters. He wrote *The Swallow Song*. You can hear it on youtube.com

Page 77 The Farinas performed at the 1965 Newport Folk Festival (Hajdu, 2001, p. 254) and at Carnegie Hall (Hajdu, 2001, p. 267).

Page 79 WORLD NEWS: Deforestation—see (Parry et al 2007, p 38). Birds moving north—see (Zuckerberg 2009). Treelines—see (Woodall et al 2009)

Page 80 The Juaneño Band of Mission Indians, Acjachemen Nation—original inhabitants of the lands that ultimately became Orange County, see juaneno.com.

Page 80 Honeyguide behavior – see (Attenborough 1998, p. 162)

Page 81 "…respond to…others' flee alarms" —see (Magrath et al 2007). Alarm calls of black-capped chickadee—see (Templeton et al 2005).

Page 81 "lyrebird in the 1930s" — see (Rothenberg 2005, p. 55). Range of birds moving north—see page 79.

Page 83 WORLD NEWS: Antibiotics—see (Frieden 2010). Coal-burning power plants—see (Mercury Alert 2011, p. 3). Mercury in lakes—see (Mercury Alert 2011, p. 4), (UNEP 2013).

Page 84 "Oneida"—see www.oneidaindiannation.com

Page 85 WORLD NEWS: CO_2 at 400 ppm level—see 400.350.org. Sea level rising – see (IPCC 2007, page 2). Drought and flooding—see Mimura et al (2007, p 695). Alaskan villages—see Bronen and Chapin (2013)

Page 87 "scenarios to predict" – I am only guessing at this, but see, for example, the US Army's "Internment and Resettlement Operations" report on preparations for societal failure (at various Internet sources).

Page 87 "my Staley Prize lecture, about the ancient Puebloans" – see page 59. The J.I. Staley Prize—see sarweb.org.

Page 87 "garden of Eden" — Genesis 2-3;

Page 88 "technology will fix things" – this is an example of what Gifford calls a dragon of inaction, see Gifford (2011).

Page 88 "CO2 capture at coal-burning plants" – see page 59.

Page 88 "geoengineering..."—see page 60.

Page 88 "We'll all be okay…what can be done anyway" – this is another dragon of inaction, see Gifford (2011).

Page 88 "Oka River in Russia" – Dzerzhinsk on the Oka River is listed by Guinness Book of World Records as the most chemically polluted place on Earth. http://www.guinnessworldrecords.com/records-3000/most-chemically-polluted-town-life-expectancy/

Page 88 "Marshall Islands" – one of the four low-lying coral atoll nations in the Pacific Ocean under threat of having to move http://www.nytimes.com/2013/09/25/opinion/climate-change-has-reached-our-shores.html?_r=0

Page 90 "wanted to cover her own white skin" – In Poe (2011, p 7), William C. Gay argues for the need for cultural diversity in the quest for global peace and justice. Sexism, racism, heterosexism, etc are labeled as pervasive and pernicious forms of violence.

Page 99 WORLD NEWS: Fracking contaminates water—see (Colborn et al 2011, p. 1053). Injection wells and earthquakes—see stateimpact.npr.org/texas/tag/earthquake/. Fracking adding to GHG -- see (Howarth et al 2011). 'Scientists alarmed' -- the conference is fictional

Page 100 St. Francis of Assisi (1182-1226) – Italian Catholic friar (Wikipedia).

Page 101 "500 earthquakes a week"—although I am pretending something strange is occurring, in reality, my numbers are similar to data from earthquake.usgs.gov/earthquakes/eqarchives/epic; for example, the year 2007 averaged 570 earthquakes a week, 3.8 major ones (magnitude 6 or higher) a week, and 44 of magnitude 5 or higher.

Page 102 "…generate…magnitude fours."—the USGS says this is not possible. See earthquake.usgs.gov/learn/topics/megaqk_facts_fantasy.php.

Page 103 "millions of gallons of fluid…chemicals" —see Colborn et al (2011).

Page 103 Benzene..."—these four chemicals (called BTEX) are volatile organic compounds that, besides being in petroleum products, are in common household products. See toxics.usgs.gov/definitions/ btex.html.

Page 104. "…conference to discuss anomalous events" is fictional. In reality, the International Panel on Climate Change, formed in 1989 to advise the UN, brings hundreds of scientists together to study climate change. (IPCC 2012)

Page 106 WORLD NEWS: War pollution – see costsofwar.org/article/ environmental-costs and prorev.com/du.htm.

Page 106 "…dress had a high neckline…"—Orthodox Judaism requires both men and women to substantially cover their bodies. See Wikipedia/Tzniut.

Page 108 The Torah is divided into 54 portions (corresponding to Hebrew calendar). One portion is read each Sabbath morning.

Page 108 Mahatma Gandhi (1869-1948)–leader of Indian nationalism. He first outlined his seven social sins in the *Young India* newspaper on October 22, 1925. For more, see http://www.jpcarter.com/Spirituality/PDF/ SevenDeadlySinsExplained.pdf.

Page 108 Rabbi Akiba ben Joseph (50-135)—great Jewish scholar.

Page 113 "Marriage as sociosexual institution.." – this is the interpersonal aspects of sexuality. See www.britannica.com/EBchecked/topic/537102/human-sexual-behaviour/29349/Sociosexual-behaviour.

Page 115-6 "…hotels with a big atrium."—e.g., the Hyatt Regency walkway collapse in 1981 in Kansas City, Kansas.

Page 118 Joseph Priestley (1733-1804)—English theologian and scientist discovered oxygen. See Johnson (2008)

Page 118 "synergies"—See glossary and Corning (2005)

Page 119 WORLD NEWS: Raising livestock and pollution—see www.nrdc.org/ water/pollution/nspills.asp, Steinfeld et al (2006). Meat leads to resource depletion -- see Steinfeld et al (2006).

Page 121 Sephardic history—see Gerber (1992), Johnson (1987).

Page 121 "Anti-Semitism, racism, sexism, homophobia" – see p 90.

Page 124 *Tzur mishelo*—this liturgical text was put to the melody of *Los Bilbilicos* by a process called *hat'ama* (adaptation). See www.jewishfolksongs.com/en/jewish-folklore

Page 126 *Los Bilbilicos* – Ladino song developed from an oral tradition. Available on youtube.

Page 129 WORLD NEWS: Disease-causing microorganisms -- see Adegboye et al (2012). Toxins released into air—see www.worldometers.info/view/toxchem/ and www.epa.gov/air/airpollutants.html

Page 133 Count Lev Nikolayevich Tolstoy (1828-1910) –Russian writer; Tolstoy and Gandhi corresponded from 1908-1910.

Page 134 "common resources…a few are exploiting"—In *Earth Democracy*, Vandana Shiva shows how the exploitation of common lands has extended to the privatization of water and patents on life forms. See Shiva (2005).

Page 135 WORLD NEWS: Wildfires—see Parry et al (2007). Health risks near wells—see Colborn et al (2011), McKenzie et al (2012) and www.epa.gov/airquality/oilandgas/. Forests less hardy—see Kim et al (2012).

Page 135 The Miwok Indians lived for thousands of years in Northern and Central California. (www.ionemiwok.org).

Page 136 "great law of the Iroquois." See wikipedia/Seven_generation_sustainability

Page 137 Matrilineal societies—see Goettner-Abendroth (2009). Goettner-Abendroth (2004) argues for the use of the word 'matriarchy' which is not in contrast to patriarchy ('rule of the fathers'). Matriarchy can be translated as 'the mothers from the beginning.'

Page 137 "...women's rights movement started in upstate New York..." —see Wagner (2001).

Page 138 brown-needled branches. See www.climatecentral.org on bark beetles

Page 139 WORLD NEWS: Compact Fluorescent light bulbs—see Havas (2008).

Page 140 "United Church of Christ" The "Christian Church" is the name shared by several branches of an early 19th-century movement for Christian unity on the American frontier. The oldest of these branches united in 1931 with the Congregational Churches to form the Congregational Christian Churches—now a part of the United Church of Christ. See www.ucc.org.

Page 141 "Are religions weighing in..." see Bron Taylor essay in (*Moral Ground* 2010, p. 378-386).

Page 141 "...depletion of common resources"-- the commons we share are the atmosphere, oceans, rivers, fish stock, lands, aquifers, etc. (Shiva 2005) shows examples. "land ethic.." Aldo Leopold defined a land ethic in 1949 in a landmark book which focuses on respect and the biotic rights of species. See (Callicott 1987, p. 196).

Page 142 "Condones slavery" – e.g., Deuteronomy 20:10-11, Leviticus 25:44-46.

Page 142 "God is not imprisoned in the Bible..." See www.ucc.org/beliefs/theology/john-thomas.html.

Page 142 "Like incest... biologically, close proximity in early years turns off sexual attraction." See Wikipedia/Westermarck effect

Page 143 "...Wouldn't having non-burdened adults be useful..."—Leonard Shlain expands on an earlier argument from 1978 saying, "E.O. Wilson proposed that the emergence of human homosexuality increased the likelihood that ancestral children would survive." (Shlain 2003, p. 242)

Page 145 WORLD NEWS: Urban runoff—see Ahn et al (2005). Sea temperature rising -- see IPCC 2007.

THE SWALLOW AND THE NIGHTINGALE

Page 146-148 Ceremony adapted from work by Rabbi Steven Greenberg. Personal communication.

Page 151 "Black people don't surf…"—this idea stems from racism. See whitewashmovie.com, or buy the documentary "White Wash" (Trespass Productions, 2011). "Sundown towns" –towns that didn't allow people of color to remain in after dark.

Page 152 In the Siege of Baghdad of 1157, the caliph Muqtafi defended his city against the Seljuk sultan Muhammad II (Wiet 1971, page 131). Attar was most likely not there at the time.

Page 158 WORLD NEWS: Air travel causes GHG emissions—see www.foe.co.uk/resource/reports/aviation_climate_change.pdf. Airport pollution—see www.onearth.org/articles/2013/08/aiplanes-flying-on-leaded-gasoline-are-still-poisoning-us. Benzopyrene in jet fuel—see aviationjustice.org/impact/aviation-and-air-pollution/

Page 161 The Phaistos Disk was found on the island of Crete and it is undecipherable because it is the only example of this form of pictographic writing. See (Fischer, 1997, Robinson 2007).

Page 161 WORLD NEWS: Polar caps melting—see IPCC 2007. Methane release—see IPCC 2007. Oceans more acidic—see IPCC 2007. Agriculture and aquifers—see IPCC 2007. Storms, see page 51.

Page 162 "Arabs who used to dominate Andalusia"—see Lewis (1982)

Page 163 For more on nightingale singing — see Sprau et al (2013).

Page 165 The Rectorado is a building on the campus of the University of Seville. I have fictionalized the interior.

Page 166 Geology lecture: On April 11, 2012, two massive earthquakes in the Indian Ocean were part of the process of the Indo-Australian tectonic plate breaking in half (Shen 2013). From December 6, 1811 to February 12, 1812, earthquakes along the New Madrid Fault and Reelfoot Rift in Missouri and Tennessee caused the Mississippi River to flow backwards and jump its banks (Wikipedia). Earthquakes of magnitude 3 or greater have averaged 21 events/year in the mid-Continental U.S. until 2005 when they began increasing, coinciding with the rapid increase in shale gas wells and deep waste-water injection. See Ellsworth (2013). In Oklahoma, studies show one to three magnitude 3.0 earthquakes or larger occurred yearly from 1975 to 2008, while the average grew to around 40 earthquakes per year from 2009 to mid-2013. See http://www.usgs.gov/newsroom/article.asp?ID=3710. In 2010, there actually were about 1100 earthquakes of magnitude 5 or higher. See page 103 for explanation.

Page 166-172 Systems lecture: "our planet is a living thing"—see Lovelock (1995) for the Gaia Hypothesis. Stephen's lecture is based on Arthur Iberall's theory of complex systems, a branch of physics called homeokinetics (Soodak and Iberall 1978). For the baseball analogy, see A. Iberall (2014, p. 19-25). Complex systems have atomistic-like units bound in interactive ensembles to form systems, level by level in a nested hierarchy of systems. The players at any level in the atomistic hierarchy are engaged in a statistical mechanics-thermodynamics game with the same physics specialized for each of their games. Chart data compiled from numerous sources. Project Stormfury used planes to seed tropical storms with silver iodide in order to weaken them from 1962-1983. (see Wikipedia).

Page 175 "the Goddess was worshipped"—see Eisler (1987), Gimbutas (1991), Stone (1978). For argument against a One Goddess theory—see Frymer-Kensky (1992, p. vii), Goodison and Morris (1998). For matrilineal society—see page 137.

Page 180 WORLD NEWS: Endocrine disruptors—see Bergman et al (2012); Herbicide, see Shehata (2012); Engineered corn as pesticide, see Lemaux (2008); Human population—is expected to peak at 9-10 billion in 2050-2100 and then stabilize after that. See www.economist.com/node/14743589. Whether the population flattens below the carrying capacity for food, water, energy, and other necessary resources is a question. See Theis and Tomkin (2012).

Page 180-183 Endocrine disruptor lecture: Bergman et al (2012), Smolen & Colborn (1997), Univ Berkeley (2009), Colborn et al (1993), Nicolopoulou-Stamati et al (2007, p 7); 85,000 chemicals—see Schettler (2002), www.cdc.gov. "doesn't take much" –see Vandenberg et al (2012)

Page 183-184 GMO lecture sources: Friends of the Earth Europe (2013), Martín-Orúe et al (2002), Shehata (2012), Lemaux (2008). "Red list"—see IUCN (2013)

Page 190 WORLD NEWS: Pharmaceuticals in water—see Brodin et al (2013)

Page 191 – "Many claim that as a poet, Attar was better than Rumi, another Sufi poet…"—see Lewisohn (1999, p. 361)

Page 192 "…life's journey toward…Divine Reality." -- Nūrbahš (1986, p. 3) says, "In Sufi terminology, 'seeking' connotes the pain and attraction which cause the novice wayfarer to set out in quest of the Divine Reality (*haqiqat*)."

Page 192-3 "…Sufi masters put secrets into their poems and stories in such a way to survive translations…like Aesop's fables." —see Shah (1964, p. 11-13)

Page 199 "…they thought Jews killed Christian children."— this is called blood libel, see http://en.wikipedia.org/wiki/Blood_libel. In 1171 in Blois, France, Jews were burned at the stake for refusing to renounce their faith and they went to their deaths singing this Aleinu prayer (Wikipedia).

Page 204 Ibn ʿArabī (1165 – 1240)—Sufi mystic and philosopher

Page 206 WORLD NEWS: overfishing—see Census of Marine Life www.coml.org Mediterranean pollution—see Ferrante et al (2013). Sonar activity—see Podesta et al 2006

Page 208 WORLD NEWS: coral reef bleaching—see. www.noaa.gov. Toxins in Mediterranean shellfish— see Ferrante et al (2013)

THE SWALLOW AND THE NIGHTINGALE

Page 224 WORLD NEWS: Shipping invasive species—see Hooff (2009). Shipping pollution and CO2—see www.onearth.org/article/meet-the-change-makers-maersk-gets-shipshape and Wikipedia/ship_pollution.

Page 226 Bull worship as symbol-- see Gimbutas (1982, p. 91); "matrilineal societies" see page 137. "God-was-a-woman" see page 175.

Page 228 "…documenting subservient male behavior." This is fiction.

Page 229 This is a fictional story based on theories that the Minoan civilization was a matrilineal society and that there was a Goddess (e.g., Eisler (1987), Gimbutas (1991), Stone (1978)). The Theran eruption that tore the island apart and possibly destroyed the Minoan civilization has been dated to 1628 B.C. (Pelligrino 1991). Plato heard about the eruption hundreds of years later and thought it was so huge, he placed it beyond the Straits of Gibraltar in the Atlantic Ocean in *Timeaus* (Jowett 2013). The ruins at Akrotiri on Santorini are remnants of the island's civilization. The Akrotiri frescoes, including the Spring Fresco, have been moved to the National Archeological Museum of Athens. Caphtor is the biblical name for the Greek island of Crete.

Page 235 For drums in ritual, see Redmond (1997).

Page 238 The bull hunt is described in *Critias* by Plato. Gimbutas (1982, p 91-93) discusses the symbolism.

Page 243 WORLD NEWS: Cruise ship pollution—see Klein (2009). Mining causes erosion, see Wikipedia.

Page 248 "in the landscape, a woman" – see Streep (1994, p. 143)

Page 252 "statues of praying figures…" – this posture for praying is seen on clay figures found at the Gournia palace complex and at Tylissos on Crete. See http://www.latsis-foundation.org/megazine/publish/ebook.php?book=27&preloader=1

Page 277-78 *"The Goddess awakens and rises…"* – poem by Rod Boyer

Page 281 These three headlines are all fictional, although see p. 302.

Page 300 WORLD NEWS: L.A. earthquakes have caused swells in the ocean (e.g., 1755). Earthquakes in other parts of the world have also caused tsunamis to hit L.A. (e.g., 1868, 1960, 1964, 1975, 2009, 2011). Ross et al (2013) shows a tsunami simulation performed by the USGS. "Air pollution near roads" —see European Lung Foundation (2013), Lue et al (2013)

Page 303 "her scarf" - Jewish law requires married women to cover their hair (Wikipedia)

Page 307. In this story, I combine two Greek myths and place them into a matriarchal world being taken over by a patriarchal mindset. The first myth about the two sisters Philomela and Procne was collected from earlier myths into Ovid's *Metamorphoses* (see Slavitt 1994). The myth has been referred to in plays, poems, and paintings. Robert Graves (1955, p. 167) suggests the myth is an example of iconotropy where a story is made up by misinterpreting an earlier culture's image. In this case, an image of a priestess was ingesting laurel leaves (misinterpreted to be her tongue) while using divining sticks (misinterpreted as stitches). She was a member of a bird cult and wearing feathers (misinterpreted as her becoming a bird). The second myth about two sisters Aedon and Chelidona is very similar and was collected in Antoninus Liberalis' *Metamorphoses* (see www.bracchiumforte.com/PDFs/celoria.pdf, p. 62).

Page 315 "blouse had a slight rip…" – Jewish custom to express grief as a symbol of a broken heart

Page 320 "typewriter." The symbols on the Phaistos Disc were stamped into the clay (Fischer, 1997)

Page 324 Conference conclusions: these are my own compilation from many sources and personal communications to summarize our overconsumption of natural resources, our poisoning of the commons, and our development of bad technology.

Page 324 "People are doing things…pollution poisons our common resources" —see page 136. "…destabilizing the environment."—see McKibben (2010).

Page 336 "Sacred places are used and reused…" – see p. 250. However, when a place is reused by others, the connection to its sacredness is lost.

Page 337 "codes of conduct" – In their book *Moral Ground: Ethical Action for a Planet in Peril* (2010), Moore and Nelson have collected the moral arguments for acting to avert future harm grouped by duty, consequences, or character. "…ethic that preserves the integrity…" – See page 71.

Page 340 "The relationship between mother and child…"— theory of noncontractual society by Virginia Held. See (Tong 1993, p. 52)

References

Adegboye, M.F., O.O. Babalola, and D. A. Akinpelu. Issues of resistance of pathogens to antimicrobial agents. *Scientific Research and Essays* Vol. 7(41), pp. 3468-3478, 27 October, 2012 . www.academicjournals.org/SRE

Ahn, Jong Ho, Stanley B. Grant, Cristiane Q Surbeck, Paul M. Digiacomo, Nikolay P. Nezlin, and Sunny Jiang. Coastal Water Quality Impact of Stormwater Runoff from an Urban Watershed in Southern California. *Environ. Sci. Technol.* 2005, 39, 5940-5953,

Arbib, Michael. *The Metaphorical Brain 2: Neural Networks and Beyond.* New York: John Wiley, 1989. Print.

Attenborough, David. *The Life of Birds.* Princeton, NJ: Princeton UP, 1998. Print.

THE SWALLOW AND THE NIGHTINGALE

Atlas, Ronald and Terry C. Hazen. Oil Biodegradation and Bioremdiation: A Tale of the Two Worst Spills in U.S. History. *Environmental Science and Technology*, 2011, 45, 6709–6715

'Aṭṭār, Farīd Ad-Dīn. *The Conference of the Birds = Mantiq Ut-tair : A Philosophical Religious Poem in Prose.* Trans. C. S. Nott. Boston: Shambhala, 1993. Print.

Bergman, Åke, Jerrold J. Heindel, Susan Jobling, Karen A. Kidd, and R. Thomas Zoeller, eds. *State of the Science of Endocrine Disrupting Chemical 2012: Summary for Decision-Makers.* United Nations Environment Programme and the World Health Org, 2012

Billings, Frederic. T. Cancer Corridors and Toxic Terrors—is it Safe to Eat and Drink? *Trans Am Clin Climatol Assoc.* 2005; 116: 115–125

Boswell, John. *Same-Sex Unions in Premodern Europe.* New York: Villard, 1994. Print.

Brodin, T., J. Fick, M. Jonsson and J. Klaminder. Dilute Concentrations of a Psychiatric Drug Alter Behavior of Fish from Natural Populations. *Science* 15 February 2013: Vol. 339 no. 6121 pp. 814-815

Bronen, Robin and F. Stuart Chapin III. Adaptive governance and institutional strategies for climate-induced community relocations in Alaska. *Proc National Academy of Sciences.* vol. 110 no. 23, 9320–9325 , (2013)

Callicott, J. Baird. "The Conceptual Foundations of the Land Ethic." *Companion to A Sand County Almanac: Interpretive & Critical Essays.* Ed. J. Baird Callicott. Madison, WI: University of Wisconsin, 1987. 186-217. Print.

Callicott, J. Baird (Ed.) *Companion to A Sand County Almanac: Interpretive & Critical Essays.* Madison, WI: University of Wisconsin, 1987. Print.

Colborn, Theo, Frederick S. vom Saal, and Ana M. Soto. "Developmental Effects of Endocrine-Disrupting Chemicals in Wilfdlife and Humans." *Environmental Health Perspectives* 101, 5 (1993): 378-384.

Colborn, Theo, Carol Kwiatkowski, Kim Schultz, and Mary Bachran, Natural Gas Operations from a Public Health Perspective, *Human and Ecological Risk Assessment,* 17: 1039-1056, 2011.

Corning, Peter A. *Holistic Darwinism: Synergy, Cybernetics, and the Bioeconomics of Evolution.* Chicago: University of Chicago, 2005. Print.

Derryberry, Elizabeth. Duke University (2009, May 21). Bird Songs Change With The Landscape. *ScienceDaily.* Retrieved September 13, 2013, from http://www.sciencedaily.com/releases/2009/05/090520114710.htm

Diamond, Jared. *Collapse: How Societies Choose to Fall or Succeed.* NY: Viking, 2005.

Eisler, Riane Tennenhaus. *The Chalice and the Blade: Our History, Our Future.* Cambridge [Mass.: Harper & Row, 1987. Print.

Page 360

Ellsworth, William L. Injection-Induced Earthquakes, *Science,* 12 July 2013: Vol. 341 no. 6142, *DOI:* 10.1126/science.1225942

European Lung Foundation (2013, March 21). Road traffic pollution as serious as passive smoke in the development of childhood asthma. *ScienceDaily*. Retrieved September 10, 2013, from http://www.sciencedaily.com-/releases/2013/03/130321205530.htm

Fariña, Richard. *Been Down So Long It Looks Like Up To Me.* New York: Random House, 1966.

Fariña, Richard. *Long Time Coming and a Long Time Gone.* New York: Random House, 1969.

Ferrante, Margherita, Salvatore Sciacca, Roberto Fallico, Maria Fiore, Gea Oliveri Conti and Caterina Ledda. Harmful Algal Blooms in the Mediterranean Sea: Effects on Human Health. *Journal of Aquaculture Research and Development*, 2.1 (2013): 1-5. dx.doi.org/10.4172/scientificreports.587

Fischer, Steven R. *Glyphbreaker.* New York: Copernicus, 1997. Print.

Frieden, Thomas R. *Antibiotic Resistance and the Threat to Public Health*, U.S. Department of Health & Human Services. April 2010, http://www.hhs.gov/asl/testify/2010/04/t20100428b.html

Friends of the Earth Europe. *Introducing Glyphosate, the world's biggest selling herbicide*, 2013. www.foeeurope.org

Frymer-Kensky, Tikva Simone. *In the Wake of the Goddesses: Women, Culture, and the Biblical Transformation of Pagan Myth.* New York: Free, 1992. Print.

Gerber, Jane S. *The Jews of Spain: A History of the Sephardic Experience.* New York: Free, 1992. Print.

Gifford, Robert. "The Dragons of Inaction: Psychological Barriers That Limit Climate Change Mitigation and Adaptation." *American Psychologist* 66.4 (2011): 290-302. Print.

Gimbutas, Marija. *The Civilization of the Goddess.* San Francisco, CA: HarperSanFrancisco, 1991. Print.

Gimbutas, Marija. *The Goddesses and Gods of Old Europe: Myths and Cult Images.* Berkeley, CA: University of California Press, 1982. Print.

Goettner-Abendroth, Heide, ed. *Societies of Peace: Matriarchies Past, Present and Future : Selected Papers : First World Congress on Matriarchal Studies, 2003, Second World Congress on Matriarchal Studies, 2005.* Toronto, Ont: Inanna Publications, 2009. Print.

Goettner-Abendroth, Heide, "Matriarchal Society: Definition and Theory." In (Genevieve Vaughan, ed), *The Gift, A Feminist Analysis*, Athanor book, Meltemi editore, Roma 2004. Published in English by Meltemi Press. http://www.gift-economy.com/athanor/athanor.pdf

Gold, Mark, Katie Mika, Cara Horowitz, Megan Hezog, and Lara Leitner. "Stemming the Tide of Plastic Marine Litter: A Global Action Agenda." *Publication Number Pritzker Policy Brief No. 5,* Emmet Center on Climate Change and the Environment, Oct 2013. www.law.ucla.edu/emmet

Goodison, Lucy, and Christine Morris, eds. *Ancient Goddesses: The Myths and the Evidence.* Madison, WI: University of Wisconsin, 1998. Print.

Graves, Robert. *The Greek Myths.* Baltimore: Penguin, 1955. Print.

Greenberg, Steven. *Wrestling with God and Men: Homosexuality in the Jewish Tradition.* Madison: The University of Wisconsin Press, 2004. Print.

Hajdu, David. *Positively 4th Street: The Lives and times of Joan Baez, Bob Dylan, Mimi Baez Fariña, and Richard Fariña.* New York: Farrar, Straus and Giroux, 2001. Print.

Havas, Magda. *Health Concerns associated with Energy Efficient Lighting and their Electromagnetic Emissions.* Research paper to SCENIHR, Peterborough, Canada, 2008 weepinitiative.org

Hooff, Rian. *Managing Aquatic Invasive Species Risks from Shipping Transport Pathways,* A report prepared by The Oregon Task Force on the Shipping Transport of Aquatic Invasive Species for the 2009 Oregon State Legislature, 2009.

House, Tamzy J., James B. Near, Jr., William B. Shields, Ronald J. Celentano, David M. Husband, Ann E. Mercer, James E. Pugh. *Weather as Force Multiplier: Owning the Weather 2025,* 1996.

Howarth, Robert W., Renee Santoro, and Anthony Ingaffea, Methane and the greenhouse-gas footprint of natural gas from shale formations, *Climatic Change,* DOI 10.1007/s10584-011-0061-5

McKenzie, Lisa M., Roxana Z. Witter, Lee S. Newman, John L. Adgate. *Human Health Risk Assessment of Air Emissions from Development of Unconventional Natural Gas Resources,* Sci Total Environ (2012), doi:10.1016/j.scitotenv.2012.02.018

Moore, Kathleen Dean and Michael P. Nelson (Ed.) *Moral Ground: Ethical Action for a Planet in Peril.* San Antonio, TX: Trinity UP, 2010. Print.

Iberall, Arthur S. *Homeokinetics: The Basics,* 2014. Print.

Iberall, Arthur S. *Toward a General Science of Viable Systems.* New York: McGraw-Hill, 1971. Print.

IPCC, 2007: *Climate Change 2007: Synthesis Report. Contribution of Working Groups I, II and III to the Fourth Assessment Report of the Intergovernmental Panel on Climate Change* [Core Writing Team, Pachauri, R.K and Reisinger, A. (eds.)]. IPCC, Geneva, Switzerland, 104 pp.

IUCN 2013. IUCN Red List of Threatened Species. Version 2013.1. <www.iucnredlist.org>. Downloaded on 27 August 2013.

Irfan, Umair. Exotic diseases from warmer climates gain foothold in the U.S. ClimateWire: Monday, June 4, 2012, E&E Publishing, http://www.eenews.net/stories/1059965253

Johnson, Paul. *A History of the Jews*. New York: Harper & Row, 1987. Print.

Johnson, Steven. *The Invention of Air: A Story of Science, Faith, Revolution, and the Birth of America*. New York: Riverhead, 2008. Print.

Jowett, Benjamin, trans. *Critias by Plato. The Internet Classics Archive*. MIT, n.d. Web. 10 Aug. 2013.

Jowett, Benjamin, trans. *Timaeus by Plato. The Internet Classics Archive*. MIT, n.d. Web. 10 Aug. 2013.

Kandel, Eric R., James H. Schwartz, and Thomas M. Jessell. *Principles of Neural Science*. New York: McGraw-Hill, Health Professions Division, 2000. Print.

Kim, Soo-Hyung, Uran Chung, Joshua J. Lawler, and Royce E. Anderson. Assessing the Impacts of Climate Change on Urban Forests in the Puget Sound region: Climate Suitability Analysis for Tree Species, forterra.org, Sept. 2012

Klein, Ross A. *Getting a Grip on Cruise Ship Pollution*. Friends of the Earth, 2009.

Lemaux, Peggy G. Genetically Engineered Plants and Foods: A Scientist's Analysis of the Issues (Part I). *Annual Review of Plant Biology*. Vol. 59: 771-812 (June 2008)

Lewis, Bernard. *The Muslim Discovery of Europe*. New York: W.W. Norton, 1982. Print.

Lewisohn, Leonard, ed. *The Heritage of Sufism. Volume 1*. Oxford: Oneworld, 1999. Print.

Lovelock, James. *The Ages of Gaia: A Biography of our Living Earth*. New York: W.W. Norton & Co., 1995. Print.

Lue, S.-H., G. A. Wellenius, E. H. Wilker, E. Mostofsky, M. A. Mittleman. Residential proximity to major roadways and renal function. *Journal of Epidemiology & Community Health*, 2013; DOI: 10.1136/jech-2012-202307

Luther, David A. and Elizabeth P. Derryberry. Birdsongs keep pace with city life: changes in song over time in an urban songbird affects communication. *Animal Behaviour*, 2012; 83 (4): 1059

Magrath, Robert D., Benjamin J. Pitcher and, Janet L. Gardner. A mutual understanding? Interspecific responses by birds to each other's aerial alarm calls. *Behavioral Ecology* (2007) 18 (5): 944-951. First published online: July 17, 2007

Markale, Jean. *The Great Goddess: Reverence of the Divine Feminine from the Paleolithic to the Present*. Rochester, VT: Inner Traditions, 1999. Print.

Martín-Orúe, Susana M., Anthony G. O'Donnell, Joaquin Ariño, Trudy Netherwood, Harry J. Gilbert and John C. Mathers. Degradation of transgenic DNA from genetically modified soya and maize in human intestinal simulations. *British Journal of Nutrition* (2002), 87, 533–542.

McIntosh, Peggy. *White Privilege and Male Privilege: A Personal Account of Coming To See Correspondences through Work in Women's Studies*. Wellesley, MA: Wellesley College Center for Research on Women, 1988. Print.

McKeon, Richard. *The Basic Works of Aristotle*. New York: Modern Library, 2001. Print.

McKibben, Bill. *Eaarth: Making a Life on a Tough New Planet*. New York: Time, 2010. Print.

Mercury Alert: Cleaning up Coal Plants for Healthier Lives, Environmental Defense Fund, March 2011.

Migratory Bird Mortality, U.S. Fish and Wildlife Service, January 2002

Mimura, N., L. Nurse, R.F. McLean, J. Agard, L. Briguglio, P. Lefale, R. Payet and G. Sem, 2007: Small islands. *Climate Change 2007: Impacts, Adaptation and Vulnerability. Contribution of Working Group II to the Fourth Assessment Report of the Intergovernmental Panel on Climate Change*, M.L. Parry, O.F. Canziani, J.P. Palutikof, P.J. van der Linden and C.E. Hanson, Eds., Cambridge University Press, Cambridge, UK, 687-716.

Morris, Desmond. *The Naked Ape*. New York: Dell Pub., 1984. Print.

Nicolopoulou-Stamati, P., Luc Hens, and C. Vyvyan Howard, eds. *Congenital Diseases and the Environment*. New York: Springer, 2007. Print.

Nurbahsʾ, Gawād. *Sufi Symbolism*. London [u.a.: Khaniqahi-Nimatullahi Publ., 1986. Print.

Orr, David W. *Down to the Wire: Confronting Climate Collapse*. Oxford: Oxford UP, 2009. Print.

Parry, M.L., O.F. Canziani, J.P. Palutikof, P.J. van der Linden and C.E. Hanson (eds). Contribution of Working Group II to the Fourth Assessment Report of the Intergovernmental Panel on Climate Change, 2007, Cambridge University Press, Cambridge, United Kingdom and New York, NY, USA.

Pellegrino, Charles R. *Unearthing Atlantis: An Archaeological Odyssey*. New York: Random House, 1991. Print.

Pittalwala, Iqbal. Prediction for Southern California's 2013 Fire Season. UCR Today, July 2013. http://ucrtoday.ucr.edu/16285

Podesta, Michela, Angela D'Amico, Gianni Pavan, Aimilia Drougas, Anastasia Komnenou, and Nicola Portunato. A review of Cuvier's beaked whale strandings in the Mediterranean Sea. *Journal Cetacean Res. Manage.* 7(3):251–261,2006. Print.

Poe, Danielle (ed). *Communities of Peace: Confronting Injustice and Creating Justice*. Amsterdam: Rodopi, 2011. Print.

Redmond, Layne. *When the Drummers Were Women: A Spiritual History of Rhythm*. New York: Three Rivers, 1997. Print.

Robinson, Andrew. *The Story of Writing: Alphabets, Hieroglyphs & Pictograms*. London: Thames & Hudson, 2007. Print.

Ross, S.L., Jones, L.M., Miller, Kevin, P., K.A., Wein, A., Wilson, Ri.I., Bahng, B., Barberopoulou, A., Borrero, J.C., Brosnan, D.M., Bwarie, J.T., Geist, E.L., Johnson, L.A., Kirby, S.H., Knight, W.R., Long, K., Lynett, P., Mortensen, C.E., Nicolsky, D.J., Perry, S.C., Plumlee, G.S., Real, C.R., Ryan, K., Suleimani, E., Thio, H., Titov, V.V., Whitmore, P.M. and Wood, N.J., 2013, SAFRR (Science Application for Risk Reduction) Tsunami Scenario—Executive Summary and Introduction: U.S. Geological Survey Open-File Report 2013–1170–A, *in* Ross, S.L., and Jones, L.M., eds., The SAFRR (Science Application for Risk Reduction) Tsunami Scenario: U.S. Geological Survey Open-File Report 2013–1170, 17 p., http://pubs.usgs.gov/of/2013/1170/a/.

Rothenberg, David. *Why Birds Sing: A Journey through the Mystery of Bird Song*. New York: Basic, 2005. Print.

Samsel, Anthony, and Seneff, Stephanie. Glyphosate's Suppression of Cytochrome P450 Enzymes and Amino Acid Biosynthesis by the Gut Microbiome: Pathways to Modern Diseases. *Entropy* (2013): 15, 1416-63.

Schettler, Ted. A Challenge to Health-Care Providers—Changing Patterns of Disease: Human Health and the Environment. *San Francisco Medicine*, 75.9 (Nov- Dec 2002).

Séralini, Gilles-Eric, Emilie Clair, Robin Mesnage, Steeve Gress, Nicolas Defarge, Manuela Malatesta, Didier Hennequin, Joël Spiroux de Vendômois, Long term toxicity of a Roundup herbicide and a Roundup-tolerant genetically modified maize. *Food and Chemical Toxicology* 50 (2012) 4221–4231

Séralini, Gilles-Eric, Robin Mesnage, Nicolas Defarge, Steeve Gress, Didier Hennequin, Emilie Clair, Manuela Malatesta, Joël Spiroux de Vendômois. Answers to critics: Why there is a long term toxicity due to a Roundup-tolerant genetically modified maize and to a Roundup herbicide. *Food and Chemical Toxicology* 53 (2013) 476-483

Sewall, Anne. Gulf of Mexico coast closed to shrimping. *Digital Journal*. May 2, 2012. http://digitaljournal.com/article/324071

Shah, Idries. *The Sufis*. London: Octagon, 1964. Print.

Shehata, A. A., W. Schrodl, et al. The effect of glyphosate on potential pathogens and beneficial members of poultry microbiota in vitro *Curr Microbiol*. Publ online 9 December. (2012). www.ncbi.nlm.nih.gov/ pubmed/23224412

Shen, Helen. Unusual Indian Ocean earthquakes hint at tectonic breakup. (2012). schools.shorelineschools.org

Shiva, Vandana. *Earth Democracy: Justice, Sustainability, and Peace*. Cambridge, MA: South End, 2005. Print.

Shlain, Leonard. *Sex, Time, and Power: How Women's Sexuality Shaped Human Evolution*. New York: Viking, 2003. Print.

Slavitt, David R., trans. *The Metamorphoses of Ovid*. Baltimore, MD: Johns Hopkins UP, 1994. Print.

Smolen, Michael and Theo Colborn. Endocrine Disruption: Hidden Threats to Wildlife, Endangered Species Update. (1997). 14:9-10, 6-10. http://www.umich.edu/~esupdate/library/97.09-10/smolen.html

Soodak, H., and A. Iberall. "Homeokinetics: A Physical Science for Complex Systems." *Science* 201.4356 (1978): 579-82. Print.

Sprau, Philipp, Tobias Roth, Valentin Amrhein, Marc Naguib. The predictive value of trill performance in a large repertoire songbird, the nightingale Luscinia megarhynchos. *Journal of Avian Biology*, 2013; DOI:10.1111/j.1600-048X.2013.00113.x

Steinfeld, Henning, Pierre Gerber, Tom Wassenaar, Vincent Castel, Mauricio Rosales, and Cees de Haan. *Livestock's Long Shadow: Environmental Issues and Options*. United Nations Food and Agriculture Organization, Rome, 2006.

Stone, Merlin. *When God Was a Woman*. New York: Harcourt Brace Jovanovich, 1978. Print.

Streep, Peg. *Sanctuaries of the Goddess: The Sacred Landscapes and Objects*. Boston: Little, Brown, 1994. Print.

Stutchbury, Bridget. *Silence of the Songbirds*, NY: Walker Publishing Co, 2007.

Theis, Tom and Jonathan Tomkin, eds. *Sustainability: A Comprehensive Foundation* . University of Illinois Open Source Textbook Initiative, 2012. cnx.org/content/col11325/1.40

Templeton, Christopher. N., Greene, Erick., & Davis, Kate. (2005). "Allometry of alarm calls: black-capped chickadees encode information about predator size." *Science* 308 (5730): 1934–7

Tong, Rosemarie. *Feminine and Feminist Ethics*. Belmont, CA: Wadsworth Pub., 1993. Print.

Torjesen, Karen Jo. *When Women Were Priests: Women's Leadership in the Early Church and the Scandal of Their Subordination in the Rise of Christianity*. San Francisco: HarperSanFrancisco, 1995. Print.

Troubled Waters: How mine waste dumping is poisoning our oceans, rivers, and lakes. Earthworks and MiningWatch Canada, February 2012.

UNEP, 2013. *Global Mercury Assessment 2013: Sources, Emissions, Releases and Environmental Transport,* UNEP Chemicals Branch, Geneva, Switzerland. www.unep.org/newscentre/Default.aspx?DocumentID=2702&ArticleID=9366

University of California - Berkeley (2009, May 9). Unprecedented Use Of DDT Concerns Experts. *ScienceDaily.* Retrieved September 10, 2013, from http://www.sciencedaily.com/releases/2009/05/090504122058.htm

Vandenberg, Laura N., Theo Colborn, Tyrone B. Hayes, et al. "Hormones and Endocrine-Disrupting Chemicals: Low-Dose Effects and Nonmonotonic Dose Responses." *Endocrine Reviews* 33.3 (2012): 378-455. Print.

Wada, Haruka. "The Development of Birdsong." *Nature Education Knowledge* 3.10 (2012): 86. Web.

Wagner, Sally Roesch. *Sisters in Spirit: Iroquois Influence on Early Feminists.* Summertown, TN: Native Voices, 2001.

Wiet, Gaston. *Baghdad; Metropolis of the Abbasid Caliphate.* Trans. Seymour Feiler. Norman: University of Oklahoma, 1971. Print.

Wolf, Ronni and Danny Wolf. Increased Incidence of Cancer near a Cell-phone Transmitter Station, *International Journal of Cancer Prevention.* (2004) 1:2, 123-128.

Wolpe, David J. *Why Be Jewish?* New York: H. Holt and, 1995. Print.

Woodall, C.W., C.M. Oswalt, J.A. Westfall, C.H. Perry, M.D. Nelson, and A. O. Finley. An indicator of tree migration in forests of the eastern United States. *Forest Ecology and Management,* 257(5), 28 Feb. 2009, Pages 1434–1444

Zuckerberg, Benjamin, Anne M. Woods, and William F. Porter. Poleward shifts in breeding bird distributions in New York State. *Global Change Biology.* Volume 15, Issue 8, pages 1866–1883, August 2009

THE SWALLOW AND THE NIGHTINGALE

DISCUSSION TOPICS

1. In Deborah's lecture, she says 'we're inside it, we can't see it.' What is she referring to? Do you see examples of this concept in your world?

2. In Attar's book *The Conference of the Birds*, he describes seven valleys toward spiritual enlightenment. Do you think Deborah follows them? How do the valleys lead toward enlightenment?

3. Gandhi defined seven social sins. What are they and what do you think social interactions would be like if society put them into practice? Where else does the number 7 appear?

4. Many Native American tribes have practiced making collective decisions based on the benefit of seven generations in the future. What does this mean to you and how does it relate to the way our leaders make decisions today? Think back 140 years.

5. Both mainstream religion and mysticism are discussed. What is the difference and how do they relate? What do you think about the way of life that is Orthodox Judaism? Islam? Christianity? What is the purpose of these ways of life?

6. In her essay "*White Privilege*," Peggy McIntosh says, "I was taught to see racism only in individual acts of meanness, not in invisible systems conferring dominance to my group." How is conferred dominance and unearned privilege shown in the book? What do you think it means to be morally normative and ideal?

7. Homosexuality has been condemned by religions throughout history as being immoral. When Deborah speaks to the minister, she offers a scientific explanation for it. Which do you agree with? What are other aspects of human behavior that are not mainstream but are inherent?

8. What is the significance of the pendant? Why did the author include it? What other material items does Deborah connect to and why?

9. Robert Gifford from the University of Victoria argues that seven psychological barriers or "dragons of inaction" stop us from acting on climate change. These are manifested in such things as our ancient brains, uncertainties, denials, optimism biases, financial investments, political ideologies, and belief in techno-salvation. Where in the book do these occur? What are you doing about climate change?

10. There is discussion about the dirtying of our commons, the overuse of Earth's resources, and the development of bad technology. Where and how are these discussed? Do you think they are real or fiction?

11. What do you think of the conclusions from the International conference? Do you think that is the world we have today or is it the world of fiction?

If you liked *The Swallow and the Nightingale*, you'll love the forthcoming novel *The Mind and the Star*

Rachel Wright and Shelley Abenacar have started a non-profit for teaching ethics to children but some cannot be reached. As a hypnotherapist, Rachel discovers how some people are controlled by authoritative voices. Racing to help free people before the authority of corporations destroys our food supply and seasons, Rachel and Shelley find themselves on a parallel path to Dr. Deborah Wright. The novel weaves together four stories that explore the birth of agriculture, the birth of consciousness and religions, and how the ancient volcanic eruption at Thera affected western civilization.

If you liked *The Swallow and the Nightingale,* you'll love the forthcoming novel *The Rock and the Seashell*

Berkeley undergraduate student Jeff Hodgdon, a Native American from the Oneida Nation, visits Pennsylvania during spring break to meet his girlfriend's family. Fighting prejudice and doubts, he uncovers the dangers of fracking. The novel weaves together four stories that explore the Iroquois Confederacy and matrilineal societies, Christian values, and the birth of the Marsala shale.

Made in the USA
Charleston, SC
24 March 2014